ANN CLEEVES

RED BONES

PAN BOOKS

First published 2009 by Macmillan

First published in paperback 2010 by Pan Books
an imprint of Pan Macmillan, a division of Macmillan Publishers Limited
Pan Macmillan, 20 New Wharf Road, London N1 9RR
Basingstoke and Oxford
Associated companies throughout the world
www.panmacmillan.com

ISBN 978-1-4472-9370-5

1 3 5 7 9 8 6 4 2

A CIP catalogue record for this book is available from
the British Library.

Typeset by Intype Libra Ltd
Printed and bound by CPI Group (UK) Ltd, Croydon, CR0 4YY

Praise for the Shetland series

RED BONES

'Ann Cleeves' fellow crime fiction practitioners (from Colin Dexter to Peter Robinson) have been lining up to sing her praises, and it's unlikely that there will be any blip in that chorus of praise on the evidence of *Red Bones*, which is quite as assured and entertaining as its predecessors'

Barry Forshaw

'On an island shrouded in mist, amid a community with secrets, a visiting archaeologist uncovers mysterious human remains . . . This award-winning writer weaves an intriguing, chilling web'

Best Magazine

WHITE NIGHTS

'Decades-old amorous betrayals resurface in a plot that makes much of the tension between incomers and islanders. Ann Cleeves' intriguing mystery is tangentially energized by the "simmer dim"'

Financial Times

'Cleeves deftly paints in the personalities and their relationships, as the police inquiries disrupt the close-knit community. It's a good, character-led mystery, which displays the art of storytelling without recourse to slash and grab'

Sunday Telegraph

'This is wonderful . . . Part of the wonder of this book is the domestic detail that becomes iconic within the novel . . . This is a very good author. This is an author that bears criticism'
Radio Four's 'Front Row'

RAVEN BLACK

'*Raven Black* breaks the conventional mould of British crime-writing, while retaining the traditional virtues of strong narrative and careful plotting'
Independent

'Beautifully constructed . . . a lively and surprising addition to a genre that once seemed moribund'
Times Literary Supplement

'*Raven Black* shows what a fine writer Cleeves is . . . an accomplished and thoughtful book'
Sunday Telegraph

'Ann's characterization is worthy of the best writers in the field . . . Rarely has a sense of place been so evocatively conveyed in a crime novel'
Daily Express

'A fine and sinister psychological novel in the Barbara Vine style. Cleeves is part of a new generation of superior British writers who put refreshing new spins and twist on the old forms'
Globe and Mail

RED BONES

Ann Cleeves is the author behind ITV's VERA and BBC One's SHETLAND. She has written over twenty-five novels, and is the creator of detectives Vera Stanhope and Jimmy Perez – characters loved both on screen and in print. Her books have now sold over 1 million copies worldwide.

Ann worked as a probation officer, bird observatory cook and auxiliary coastguard before she started writing. She is a member of 'Murder Squad', working with other northern writers to promote crime fiction. In 2006 Ann was awarded the Duncan Lawrie Dagger (CWA Gold Dagger) for Best Crime Novel, for *Raven Black*, the first book in her Shetland series. In 2012 she was inducted into the CWA Crime Thriller Awards Hall of Fame. Ann lives in North Tyneside.

www.anncleeves.com
@anncleeves
facebook.com/anncleeves

By Ann Cleeves

A Bird in the Hand   Come Death and High Water

Murder in Paradise   A Prey to Murder

A Lesson in Dying   Murder in My Back Yard

A Day in the Death of Dorothea Cassidy

Another Man's Poison   Killjoy

The Mill on the Shore   Sea Fever

The Healers   High Island Blues

The Baby-Snatcher   The Sleeping and the Dead

Burial of Ghosts

The Vera Stanhope series

The Crow Trap   Telling Tales   Hidden Depths

Silent Voices   The Glass Room   Harbour Street

The Shetland series

Raven Black   White Nights   Red Bones

Blue Lightning   Dead Water

Acknowledgements

Whalsay is a real island and one of the friendliest places I know. It doesn't have a community called Lindby and all the people and places described there – including the camping bod where the students live – are fictitious. Symbister exists – it's where the ferry arrives – but it doesn't have a Pier House Hotel.

Lots of people helped with the writing of this book, but despite the collective expertise there are probably mistakes; they're all mine. I'm grateful to Anna Williams and Helen Savage for their advice on archaeology, and to Cathy Batt and her colleagues at the University of Bradford for talking me through the Shetland excavations and showing me real red bones. Val Turner helped by reading the manuscript, putting me right on details of procedure and allowing me to use her name.

David Howarth's excellent book *The Shetland Bus* provided information on the Norwegian resistance operation based in Lunna during the Second World War. While he describes the building of small boats for use in Norwegian inland waters, I can only guess that this might have taken place in Whalsay.

Once again Helen Pepper advised on crime-scene management. Sarah Clarke provided information on the possible complications of a difficult birth. Bob Gunn told me about rabbits and shotguns. Ingirid Eunson, Ann Prior and Sue Beardshall shared conversation and wine and ideas about the islands.

Thanks to our friends on Whalsay – to Angela and John Lowrie Irvine for their hospitality and sharing with me the photo of the knitting women, and to Paula and Jon Dunn for finding us a fantastic place to stay. I'm especially grateful to the Whalsay Reading Group for their honesty, their warmth and one of the most fascinating evenings of my writing career.

The Visit Shetland team and Shetland Arts officers have again provided support and assistance, and it's always a delight to work with everyone at Shetland libraries.

Finally a huge thank you to Sara Menguc, Moses Cardona and Julie Crisp for their contribution to the book. Julie is every writer's dream editor.

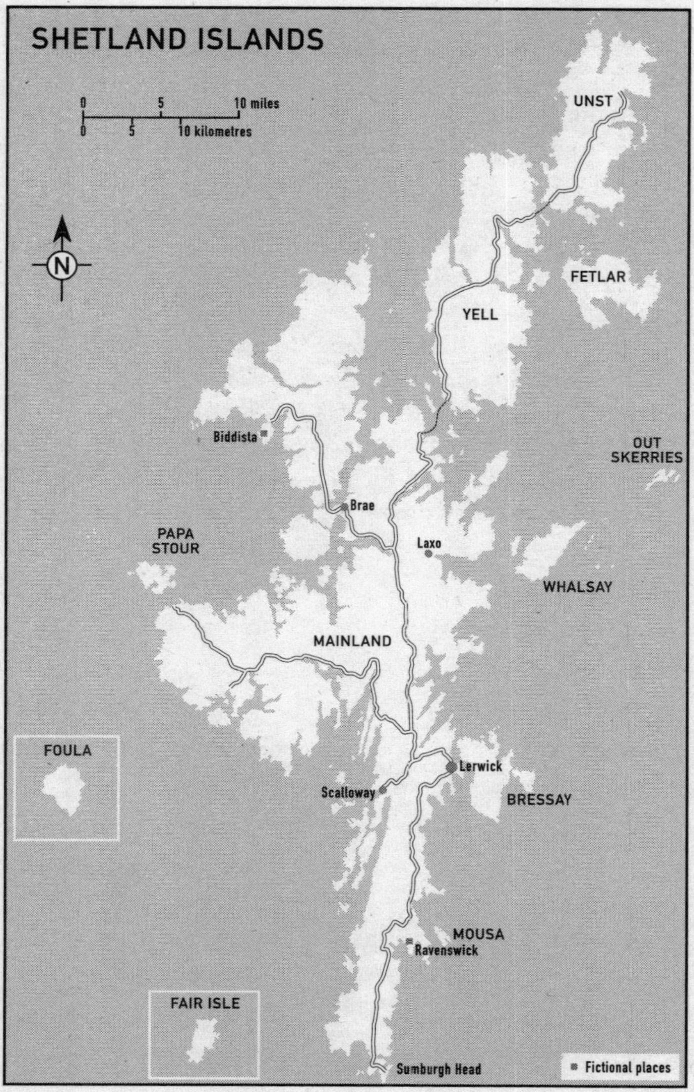

SHETLAND ISLANDS
0
5
10 miles
0
5
10 kilometres
N
UNST
FETLAR
YELL
Biddista
OUT
SKERRIES
Brae
PAPA
STOUR
Laxo
WHALSAY
MAINLAND
FOULA
Lerwick
Scalloway
BRESSAY
MOUSA
Ravenswick
FAIR ISLE
Sumburgh Head
Fictional places

Chapter One

Anna opened her eyes and saw a pair of hands, streaked and shiny with blood. No face. In her ears a piercing squeal. At first she thought she was at Utra and Ronald was helping Joseph to kill another pig. That would explain the blood, the red hands and the terrible high-pitched sound. Then she realized the noise was her own voice screaming.

Someone rested a dry hand on her forehead and murmured words she didn't understand. She spat out an obscenity at him.

More pain.

This is what it is to die.

The drug must be wearing off because she had a sudden burst of clarity as she opened her eyes again to bright, artificial light.

No, this is what it is to give birth.

'Where's my baby?' She could hear the words slightly blurred by the pethidine.

'He was having problems breathing on his own. We've just given him some oxygen. He's fine.' A woman's voice. A Shetlander, slightly patronizing, but convincing, and that mattered most.

Further away a man with blood to his elbow grinned awkwardly.

'Sorry,' he said. 'Retained placenta. Better to get it out here than take you to theatre. I thought you wouldn't want that after a forceps delivery, but it can't have been very comfortable.'

She thought of Joseph again, the hill ewes lambing, the ravens flying off with placenta in their beaks and on their claws. This hadn't been what she'd been expecting. She hadn't thought childbirth would be so violent or so raw. She turned and saw Ronald; he was still holding her hand.

'I'm sorry I swore at you,' Anna said.

She saw he'd been weeping. 'I was so scared,' he said. 'I thought you were dying.'

Chapter Two

'Anna Clouston had her baby last night,' Mima said. 'A difficult birth apparently. She was in labour for twenty hours. They're going to keep her in for a few days to keep an eye on her. It was a boy. Another man to take on the *Cassandra*.' She shot a conspiratorial look at Hattie. It seemed to amuse Mima that Anna had had a difficult labour. Mima liked chaos, disorder, other people's misfortune. It gave her something to gossip about and kept her alive. That was what she said, at least, when she sat in her kitchen cackling into her tea or whisky, filling Hattie in on island events.

Hattie didn't know what to say about Anna Clouston's child – she'd never seen the appeal of babies and didn't understand them. A baby would just be another complication. They were standing at Setter, in the field at the back of the house. A wash of spring sunshine lit the makeshift windbreak of blue plastic, the wheelbarrows, the trenches marked with tape. Seeing it as if for the first time, Hattie thought what a mess they'd made of this end of the croft. Before her team from the university had turned up, Mima had looked out over sloping low meadow to the loch. Now, even at the beginning of the season the place was muddy as a building site and Mima's view was interrupted by the spoil heap. The wheelbarrow run had scored ruts in the grass.

Hattie looked beyond the disturbance to the horizon. It was the most exposed archaeological site she'd ever worked. Shetland was all sky and wind. There were no trees here to provide shelter.

I love this place, she thought suddenly. *I love it more than anywhere else in the world. I want to spend the rest of my life here.*

Mima had been pinning towels on to the washing line, surprisingly supple despite her age. She was so small that she had to stretch to reach the line. Hattie thought she looked like a child, prancing on tiptoes. The laundry basket was empty. 'Come away in and have some breakfast,' Mima said. 'If you don't put on a bit of weight you'll blow away.'

'Pots and kettles,' Hattie said as she followed Mima across the grass to the house. And she thought Mima, trotting ahead of her, did look so frail and insubstantial that she might be swept up in a storm and carried out to sea. She'd still be talking and laughing as she went, as the wind twisted her body like a kite-tail until it disappeared.

In the kitchen a bowl of hyacinths was in bloom on the windowsill and the smell of them filled the room. They were pale blue, streaked with white.

'They're pretty.' Hattie sat at the table, pushing the cat off the chair so she could sit down. 'Spring-like.'

'I can't really see the point of them.' Mima reached up to lift a pan from the shelf. 'They're an ugly kind of flower and they stink. Evelyn gave them to me and expected me to be grateful. But I'll kill them soon. I've never kept a houseplant alive yet.'

Evelyn was Mima's daughter-in-law and the subject of much complaint.

All the crockery and cutlery in Mima's house was slightly dirty, yet Hattie, usually so fastidious, so fickle in her appetite, always ate whatever Mima cooked for her. Today Mima was scrambling eggs. 'The hens are laying well again,' she said. 'You'll have to take some with you back to the Bod.' The eggs were covered in muck and straw, but Mima cracked them straight into a bowl and began whisking them with a fork. Translucent white and deep yellow yolk splashed on to the oilskin tablecloth. Using the same fork she scooped a lump of butter from a wrapped packet and shook it into the pan on the Rayburn. The butter sizzled and she tipped in the eggs. She threw a couple of slices of bread directly on to the hotplate and there was a smell of burning.

'Where's Sophie this morning?' Mima asked when they'd both started eating. Her mouth was full and her false teeth didn't quite fit, so it took Hattie a moment to understand what she was saying.

Sophie was Hattie's assistant on the dig. Usually Hattie did the planning and the preparation. It was her PhD after all, her project. She was obsessive about getting things right. But this morning she'd been eager to get on to the site as soon as possible. It was good to get away from Sophie sometimes, and as much as anything she was glad of a chance to chat to Mima on her own.

Mima liked Sophie. The season before the girls had been invited to a dance at the community hall and Sophie had been the life and soul of the party, so the men had been queuing up to swing her around in the eightsome reel. She'd flirted with them all, even the married ones. Hattie had watched, disapproving and anxious, but jealous too. Mima had come up behind Hattie and yelled in her ear above the noise of the music: 'That lass reminds me of myself at that age. I had the men flocking around me too. It's all just a bit of fun to her. It means nothing. You should lighten up a bit yourself.'

How I've missed Whalsay over the winter! Hattie thought. *How I've missed Mima!*

'Sophie's working in the Bod for a while,' she said. 'Paperwork. You know. She'll be along soon.'

'Well?' Mima demanded, bird-like eyes bright over the rim of the mug. 'Did you find yourself a man while you were out? A good-looking academic maybe? Someone to keep you warm in bed in those long winter nights?'

'Don't tease, Mima.' Hattie cut a corner from the toast, but left it uneaten. She no longer felt hungry.

'Maybe you should find yourself an island man. Sandy's still not found himself a wife. You could do worse. He's got more life about him than his mother, at least.'

'Evelyn's all right,' Hattie said. 'She's been good to us. Not everyone on the island supported the dig and she's always stood up for us.'

But Mima wasn't ready yet to let go of the subject of Hattie's love life. 'You watch yourself, girl. You find yourself the right one. You don't want to get hurt. I know all about that. My Jerry wasn't the saint everyone made him out to be.' Then, lapsing into dialect. 'Dee can live without a man, dee ken. I've lived without a man for nearly sixty years.'

And she winked, making Hattie think that though Mima might not have had a husband for sixty years, she'd probably had men enough in her life. Hattie wondered what else the old woman was trying to say.

Immediately after the plates were washed, Hattie went back on to the site. Mima stayed inside. It was Thursday, the day she entertained Cedric, her gentleman caller. Thoughts of this place had been with Hattie all winter, warming her like a lover. Her obsession with the archaeology, the island and its people had become one in her mind: Whalsay, a single project and a single ambition. For the first time in years she felt a bubbling excitement. *Really*, she thought, *I have no reason to think like this. What is the matter with me?* She found herself grinning. *I'll have to watch myself. People will think I'm mad and lock me away again.* But that only made her smile some more.

When Sophie arrived, Hattie set her to preparing a practice trench. 'If Evelyn wants to be a volunteer we should train her to do it properly. Let's clear an area away from the main excavation.'

'Shit, Hat! Do we really have to have her on site? I mean, she's kind enough but she's a real bore.' Sophie was tall and fit with long tawny hair. She'd been working as a chalet maid in the Alps over the winter, helping out a friend, and her skin was bronzed and glowing. Sophie was easy and relaxed and took everything in her stride. She made Hattie feel like a neurotic drone.

'It's a condition of our work in Shetland that we encourage community involvement,' Hattie said. 'You know that.' *Oh God*, she thought, *now I sound like a middle-aged schoolteacher. So pompous!*

Sophie didn't answer. She shrugged and went on with the work.

Later, Hattie said she'd go to Utra to talk to Evelyn about training to work on the dig. It was an excuse. She hadn't had the chance to revisit her favourite places in Lindby. The sun was still shining and she wanted to make the most of the good weather. As she walked past the house, Cedric was just driving away in his car. Mima was at the kitchen window waving him off. When she saw Hattie she came to the open door.

'Will you come in and have a cup of tea?'

But Hattie thought Mima just wanted to prise more information from her and to give her more advice. 'No,' she said. 'I've no time today. But Sophie's due a break if you want to give her a shout.'

And she walked on down the track with the sun on her face, feeling like a child playing truant from school.

Chapter Three

Anna's baby spent the first night of his life in Intensive Care. The midwives said it was nothing to worry about. He was doing fine, a lovely little boy. But he still needed a bit of help with his breathing and they'd keep him in the resussitaire for a while. Besides, Anna was exhausted and she needed the rest. In the morning they'd bring the baby through to her and help her to feed him. There was no reason why they shouldn't both be home in a couple of days.

She slept fitfully, drifting in and out. The doctor had given her more painkillers and her dreams were very vivid. Once, waking suddenly, she wondered if this was what it would be like to be on drugs. At university she'd never been tempted down that route. It was always important to her to be in control.

She was aware of Ronald beside her. A couple of times she heard him talking on his mobile. She thought the conversations would be with his parents. She started to tell him that he shouldn't be using a phone in the hospital, but lethargy overcame her and the words didn't come out properly.

She woke when it got light and felt much more herself again, a little bruised and battered, but alert. Ronald was fast asleep on the chair in the corner, his head back, his mouth open, snoring loudly. A midwife appeared.

'How's my baby?' Anna found it hard to believe now that there *was* a baby, that she hadn't imagined the whole experience of giving birth. She felt quite disconnected from the evening before.

'I'll bring him through to you. He's doing very well now, breathing normally on his own.'

Ronald stirred in his chair and woke too. He looked like his father with the stubble of beard on his chin, his eyes slightly vacant from sleep.

The baby was lying in a plastic box that reminded Anna of a fish tank. He was lying on his back. His skin had a faint yellow tinge; Anna had read the books and knew that was normal. He had a downy covering of dark hair and there was a pink mark on each side of his head.

'Don't worry about that,' the midwife said. She assumed she could guess what Anna was thinking. 'It's because of the forceps delivery. It'll go in a couple of days.' She scooped the baby up, wrapped him in a blanket and handed him to Anna. Anna looked down at a tiny, perfect ear.

'Shall we have a go at feeding him?'

Ronald was properly awake now. He sat on the bed next to Anna on the opposite side to the midwife. He held out his finger and watched the baby grip it.

The midwife was showing Anna the best way to feed the baby. 'Put a pillow on your lap like this and hold his head with this hand and guide him to your nipple like this . . .' Anna, usually so competent in practical matters, felt clumsy and inadequate. Then the baby latched on to her and began to suck and she could feel the pull of it down through her belly.

'There you are,' the midwife said. 'You're a natural. If everything goes well there's no reason you shouldn't be home tomorrow.'

When the woman had gone they continued to sit on the bed and look at the baby. He fell suddenly fast asleep and Ronald lifted him carefully and put him back in the plastic cot. Anna had been given a room of her own with a view across the grey houses to the sea. They drafted the notice they would place in the *Shetland Times*:

> To Ronald and Anna Clouston on March 20th, a son, James Andrew. First grandchild to Andrew and Jacobina Clouston of Lindby, Whalsay, and James and Catherine Brown of Hereford, England.

The timing of James's birth had been planned, as everything in Anna's life was planned. She thought spring was the perfect time to bring a baby into the world and Whalsay would be a wonderful place to bring up a child. The process had been more painful and messy than she'd imagined, but now that was over and there was no reason why their family life shouldn't run smoothly.

Ronald couldn't keep his eyes off his son. She should have guessed he might be a doting father.

'Why don't you get off home?' she said. 'Get a shower and a change of clothes. Everyone will want to hear the news.'

'I might do that.' She could tell he wasn't comfortable in the hospital. 'But should I come and visit you tonight?'

'No,' she said. 'It's such a long drive, and then the time on the ferry. You'll need to be in first thing in the morning to take us home.' She thought she'd welcome some time alone with her son. She smiled as she imagined Ronald doing the grand tour of the island, full of news about the birth and his son. He'd have to visit all his relatives, repeating the tale of how her waters burst while they were shopping in the Co-op, the difficult labour and the child who was pulled screaming into the world.

Chapter Four

Hattie could have done without having Evelyn here at Setter at all today. They'd only been back in Whalsay for a week and she had other things to think about, anxieties that snagged at the back of her mind along with the moments of joy. Besides, she wanted to get on with the dig. Her dig, which had lain covered up since the autumn. Now the longer days and finer weather had brought her back to Shetland to complete the project. She itched to get back into the main trench, to continue the sieving and dating, to complete her meticulous records. She wanted to prove her thesis and to lose herself in the past. If she could prove that Setter was the site of a medieval merchant's house, she would have an original piece of research for her PhD. More importantly, the discovery of artefacts dating the building and confirming its status would give her grounds to make a funding application to extend the excavation. Then she would have an excuse to stay in Shetland. She couldn't bear the idea that she might be forced to leave the islands. She didn't think she could ever live in a city again.

But Evelyn was a local volunteer and she needed training and Hattie needed to keep her on side. Hattie knew she didn't handle volunteers well. She was impatient and expected too much from them. She used language they had no hope of understanding. Today wouldn't be easy.

They'd woken again to sunshine, but now a mist had come in from the sea, filtering the light. Mima's house was a shadow in the distance and everything looked softer and more organic. It was as if the surveying poles had grown from the ground like willows and the spoil heap was natural, a fold in the land.

The day before, Sophie had marked out a practice trench a little way off from the main site and dug out the turf. She'd exposed roots and a patch of unusually sandy, dry soil and levelled the area with a mattock so the practice dig could begin. The topsoil had been dumped on the existing spoil heap. Everything was ready when Evelyn turned up at ten, just as she'd said she would, wearing corduroy trousers and a thick old sweater. She had the anxious, eager-to-please manner of a pupil sucking up to the teacher. Hattie talked her through the process.

'Shall we make a start then?' Hattie knew Evelyn was enthusiastic, but really the woman should be taking this more seriously, making notes for example. Hattie had gone through the methods of recording a site in some detail, but she wasn't sure Evelyn had taken it all in. 'Do you want to have a go with the trowel, Evelyn? We wouldn't sieve everything in a site like this, though we might work it through the flotation tank, and every find would need to be set in context. You do understand how important that is?'

'Yes, yes.'

'And we work from the known to the unknown so

we always trowel backwards. We don't want to tread on the things we've already uncovered.'

Evelyn looked up at her. 'I might not be working for a PhD,' she said, 'but I'm not daft either. I have been listening.' It was gently said but Hattie felt herself blushing. *I'm no good with people*, she thought. *Only with objects and ideas. I understand how the past works but not how to live with people in the present.*

The older woman squatted in the trench and began to scratch tentatively with the trowel, beginning in one corner, scraping away the upper layer of soil, reaching up to tip it into the bucket.

She frowned like a child concentrating on routine homework. Over the next half hour, whenever Hattie glanced across to her, there was the same expression on her face. Hattie was just about to check on Evelyn's work when the older woman called over to her.

'What's this?'

Hattie stretched and went to see. Something solid was revealed against the lighter colour of the sandy soil and the particles of shell. Hattie was excited despite herself. This was a fragment of pottery perhaps. Imported pottery would give the house the status she hoped for. They'd dug the practice trench away from the excavated dwelling precisely because they didn't want the amateurs to come across any sensitive finds, but perhaps they'd stumbled across a midden, even an extension to the house itself. She crouched beside Evelyn, almost pushing her away, and brushed the soil away from the revealed object. It was not pottery, though it was reddish-brown, the colour of clay. Bone, she saw now. As an undergraduate she'd expected old bone to be white or cream or grey and had been surprised at the richness of the colour. A large piece of bone, round, she thought, though only a fraction had been uncovered.

She was disappointed, but tried not to show it. Beginners were thrilled by their first finds. In the Shetland digs they were always finding shards of bone, sheep mostly; once there was a horse, the skeleton almost entirely preserved.

She began to explain this to Evelyn, to tell her what they could learn about the settlement from the animal remains.

'We can't just dig an object out,' she said. 'We have to keep it in context, to continue to trowel, layer by layer. This'll be good practice. I'll leave you to it and come back later.' She thought how awkward *she* would feel to be digging while someone was staring over her shoulder. Besides, she had her own work to do.

Later they went into the house for a break. Mima made sandwiches for them and then came out herself to see what was happening. When Evelyn went back to work on the practice trench, the older woman stood watching. Mima was wearing black Crimplene trousers and wellingtons that flapped around her knees. She'd thrown a threadbare grey fleece over her shoulders. Hattie thought she looked like a hooded crow, standing there watching her daughter-in-law work. A hooded crow ready to snatch at a fragment of food.

'Well, Evelyn, what do you look like?' Mima said. 'On your hands and knees like some sort of beast. In this light you could be one of Joseph's pigs, grubbing around in the soil there. You be careful or he'll be slitting your throat and eating you as bacon.' She laughed so loud that she coughed and spluttered.

Evelyn said nothing. She knelt up and glared. Hattie felt sorry for her. She'd never known Mima be so cruel. Hattie jumped into the trench beside Evelyn. The bone was protruding from the earth now, largely uncovered. Hattie took her own trowel from her jeans pocket. With intense concentration she stripped away more of the soil, then took a brush. The shape of the bone became more defined: there was a pleasing curve, a sculptured hollow.

'*Pars orbitalis*,' she said. Shock and excitement made her forget her earlier resolve not to show off, to keep her language simple so Evelyn would understand.

Evelyn looked at her.

'The frontal orbit,' Hattie said. 'This is part of a human skull.'

'Oh no,' Mima said. Hattie looked up at her and saw that her face was white. 'That cannot be right. No, no, that cannot be.'

She turned and scurried back to the house.

Chapter Five

Sandy Wilson crossed the field unsteadily. It was a few weeks after Hattie had found the skull, one of those thick black nights that often came in the spring. Not cold, but the island covered by low cloud and a dense, relentless drizzle that hid the moon and stars and even the lit windows of the house behind him. He didn't have a torch, but he didn't need one. He'd grown up here. If you lived on an island six miles long and two and a half miles wide, by the time you were ten you knew every inch of it. And that internal map stayed with you even after you'd left. Sandy lived in town now, in Lerwick, but he reckoned if he was dropped blindfold anywhere on Whalsay he'd be able to tell you where he was after a few minutes, just by the way the land lay under his feet and the touch of the nearest dyke on his hand.

He knew he'd had too much to drink, but congratulated himself on leaving the Pier House Hotel when he did. His mother would be waiting up for him. Another couple of drinks and he'd be steaming. Then he'd get the old lecture about self-restraint and about Michael, his brother, who'd given up the booze altogether. Sandy thought maybe he'd call in to his grandmother's house on the way and she'd make him a cup of strong black coffee so he'd be quite sober when he got home. She'd phoned him earlier in the week and told him to call at Setter next time he was home. Mima never minded seeing him a wee bit worse for wear. She'd given him his first dram, one morning when he was on his way to the big school. It was a chilly sort of day and she'd said the whisky would keep out the cold. He'd spluttered and choked like it was the worst kind of medicine, but he'd developed a taste for it since. He thought Mima had had a taste for it from the cradle, though it never seemed to affect her. He'd never seen her drunk.

The field sloped down towards the track that led to Mima's croft. He heard a gunshot. The noise startled him for a minute, but he took no notice. It would be Ronald, out after rabbits with his big spotlight. He'd talked about going when Sandy had gone to see the new bairn and it was a good night for it. The rabbits, dazzled by the light of the torch, stood like statues, just waiting to be shot. Illegal, but rabbits were such a nuisance in the islands that nobody cared. Ronald was his cousin. A sort of cousin. Sandy began to figure out the exact relationship but his family tree was complicated and he was drunk, so he lost track and gave up. The rest of his walk to Setter was peppered with the occasional noise of a shotgun.

There was a bend in the track and Sandy saw, just as he knew he would, the light in Mima's kitchen window. Her house was tucked into the hill and you came on it very suddenly. Many of the islanders were pleased that it was hidden from view by the land curved around it, because it was a scruffy sort of place, the garden overgrown with weeds, the windowframes bare of paint and rotting. Evelyn, Sandy's mother, was mortified by the state of Mima's croft, nagged his father about it regularly. 'Will you not go and sort the place out for her?' But Mima would have none of it. 'It'll last me out,' she'd say, complacently. 'I like it fine as it is. I don't want the fuss of you around the croft.' Joseph took more notice of his mother than he did of his wife, so Mima was left unbothered.

Setter was the most sheltered croft on the island. The archaeologist who'd arrived last year from a university in the south said people had been living on that land for thousands of years. He'd asked if they might dig a few trenches in a field close to the house. A project for a postgraduate student, he said. One of them had an idea that there had been a grand dwelling on the site. They'd put the land back the way they'd found it. Sandy thought Mima would have let them on anyway. She'd taken to the historian. 'He's a fine-looking man,' she'd said to Sandy, her eyes glittering. Sandy had seen what she must have been like as a girl. Daring. Shameless. No wonder the other island women were wary of her.

There was a noise from the field next to the track. Not gunshot this time but a muttering, ripping and stamping of feet. Sandy turned, saw the silhouette of the cow just a few feet away. Mima was the only person left on Whalsay who milked by hand. The rest had stopped decades ago, put off by the work, and the hygiene regulations, which prevented the milk being sold. There were people though who still liked the unpasteurized milk and fixed Mima's roof or slipped her a bottle of whisky in return for a jug of the yellow liquid every morning. Sandy wasn't sure they'd be so keen if they saw Mima milking. Last time he'd seen her do it, she'd blown her nose on the filthy tea-towel she went on to wipe the udders with. As far as he knew, though, no one had gone down sick as a result. He'd been brought up on the stuff and it had done him no harm. Even his mother scooped the cream off the top of the churn and put it on her porridge for a treat.

He pushed open the door into the kitchen, expecting to see Mima in her chair by the Rayburn, the cat on her knee, an empty glass by her side, watching something violent on the television. She was never one for going to bed early, hardly seemed to sleep much at all, and she loved violence. She was the only one of his family who'd been pleased by his choice of career. 'Fancy,' she said, 'a cop!' She'd had a kind of dreamy look in her eyes and he'd been sure she'd been imagining New York, guns, car chases. She'd only been south once, to Aberdeen for a funeral. Her pictures of the world came from the TV. Policing in Shetland had never been much like that, but she still enjoyed hearing his stories, he exaggerated them, just a touch, to make her happy.

The television was on, the sound horribly loud. Mima was going deaf, though she refused to admit it to the family. But the cat lay on its own in the chair. It was large and black and vicious to everyone but its owner. A witch's cat, his mother called it. Sandy turned down the sound, opened the door to the rest of the house and shouted. 'Mima! It's me!' He knew she wasn't asleep. She'd never leave the light and the telly on, and the cat shared her bed as well as her chair. Mima's husband had died in an accident at sea when she was still a young woman. There were rumours of her being a wild young widow, but since he'd known her she'd lived on her own.

There was no answer. He felt suddenly very sober and walked through to the rest of the house. There was a corridor which ran along the back of the three rooms and led into each one. He couldn't remember ever going into her bedroom before. She'd never been ill. It was a square room taken up with a heavy dark-wood wardrobe and a bed so high that he couldn't see how Mima could scramble on to it without a step. There was the same thick brown lino on the floor as in the kitchen, a sheepskin rug, white once, now grey and rather matted. The curtains, faded and tatty, cream with a design of small roses, weren't drawn. On the windowsill stood a photo of her husband. He had a thick red beard, very blue eyes, was dressed in an oilskin and boots and reminded Sandy of his father. The bed had been made and covered with a quilt of crocheted squares. There was no sign of Mima.

The bathroom was a more recent addition, built on to the back of the house, though it had been there as long as Sandy could remember. The bath and the basin were an improbable blue, though there was still brown lino on the floor, partly covered by a bright blue shaggy rug. A smell of damp and wet towels. An enormous spider crawled around the plughole. Otherwise the room was empty.

Sandy tried to think rationally. He'd dealt with missing-person inquiries and knew that families always panicked unnecessarily. He'd made fun of the anxious parent or partner once he'd put down the phone. 'There was a party at the Haa last night. That's where they'll be.' But now he felt the shock of the unexpected, the unknown. Mima never strayed from her house at night these days, unless there was a family do at his parents' house or a big island event like a wedding, and then someone would have given her a lift and he'd know about it. She had no real friends. Most Whalsay folk were slightly afraid of her. He felt his thoughts spinning out of control, tried to keep calm. What would Jimmy Perez do in this situation?

Mima always shut her hens up at night. Maybe she'd gone out to do that and tripped and fallen. The archaeologists had dug their trenches on some land right away from the house, but she was getting on now and it was possible that the drink was at last clouding her judgement. If she'd wandered down that way it would be easy enough to lose her footing.

Sandy went back to the kitchen and collected a torch from the drawer in the table. It had been there from the time when every house had its own generator, which only ran for a couple of hours in the evening. Outside, he felt the chill of the mist and drizzle, biting after the heat of the Rayburn. It must be nearly midnight. His mother would be wondering where *he* was. He walked round the house. Here was the shed where Mima brought in the cow for milking. Once his eyes adjusted to the dark there was enough light spilling from the house for him to see quite clearly where he was going. He'd left on the bathroom light and the window faced this way. No need yet for the torch. The hens were already shut up. He checked the catch on the wooden henhouse and could hear the rustle of movement inside.

Earlier the day had been fine and Mima must have done her washing. The line stretched away from the house down towards where the archaeologists had set up the dig. There were still towels and a sheet pegged to the nylon rope. They hung lifeless and heavy, like the sails on a becalmed boat. Other island women would have taken down the washing as soon as the weather closed in, but Mima would probably not have bothered if she'd been eating her tea or reading a book. It was this fecklessness that so irritated some of her neighbours. How could she not care what people were thinking of her? How could she keep such an untidy house?

Sandy walked past the washing to where the students had been working. A couple of poles with string stretched between to mark out the search area, or maybe for measuring. A windbreak made of blue plastic strung on to metal stakes. A pile of turfs, neatly stacked, and another of soil. Two trenches cut at right-angles. He flashed the torch into them, but they were empty apart from a couple of puddles of water. It occurred to him that the area looked like a crime scene in one of the programmes his grandmother liked to watch.

'Mima!' he shouted. He thought his voice sounded very thin and high-pitched. He hardly recognized it.

He decided he should go home, switched off the torch and started back to the house. He could phone Utra from there. His mother would know where Mima was, she knew everything that happened on Whalsay. Then he saw that a coat had fallen from the line and lay in a crumpled heap on the grass. He recognized it as one of the students' waterproofs and thought Mima had probably offered to get rid of all the mud for them. He was going to leave it: wouldn't it need to go through the machine again anyway? But he stooped to pick it up and take it inside.

It wasn't just a coat. It was his grandmother, looking very small inside the yellow jacket. He thought she was hardly bigger than a doll, thin, her arms and legs like twigs. He touched her face, which was cold and smooth as wax, felt for a pulse. He supposed he should call for the doctor, but he couldn't move. He was frozen, paralysed by shock and by the need to take in the information that Mima was dead. He looked down at her face, chalk white against the muddy ground. *This isn't Mima,* he thought. *It can't be. There's been some terrible mistake.* But of course it was his grandmother; he looked at the ill-fitting teeth and the wispy white hair and felt sick and very sober at the same time. He didn't trust his judgement though. He was Sandy Wilson, who always got things wrong. Maybe he'd fumbled for the pulse and she was really alive and breathing fine.

He picked her up in his arms to carry her indoors. He couldn't bear to leave her here out in the cold. It was only when he had her in the kitchen that he saw the wounds in her stomach and the blood.

Chapter Six

Inspector Jimmy Perez arrived in Whalsay on the first ferry. He was there at Laxo, the terminal on the west of Shetland mainland, waiting on the pier when the boat arrived from Symbister. There was no one else in the queue; that time of the morning traffic was mostly the other way: folks coming off the smaller island for work in town, teenagers too old for the Whalsay Junior High, still half asleep, on their way to meet the bus for Lerwick. He watched the ferry approaching, waited for the half-dozen cars to leave and the gaggle of sixth-year students for Anderson High to walk off to the waiting bus, then he started his engine. Billy Watt was working the ferry today. The crew were all Whalsay men; that was how it worked with the inter-island ferries. Billy waved Perez's car into position, watched while he drove slowly forward so his bumper was inches off the iron ramp, then gave a genial nod. Whalsay was known as the friendly island; it was famous for the way folk waved when cars passed on the road. When he came to take Perez's money, Billy didn't ask what the detective was doing there. He didn't need to: by now most of the people in Whalsay would have heard about Mima Wilson's accident.

Perez had been in the sixth form with Billy,

remembered him as a pale, quiet boy who'd always come top in French. Perez wondered if he used his flair for languages on the overseas visitors who came to the islands. Not that Whalsay was really on the tourist map. There wasn't anywhere for them to stay apart from the camping bod that attracted students and backpackers, and one hotel. Symbister was a working harbour and seven of the eight pelagic fishing boats in Shetland put in there. For this reason Whalsay folk didn't need to sell cups of tea or hand-knitted mittens to make a living. They kept up the old traditions of hospitality and knitting but money didn't come into it.

Sandy's phone call had woken Perez up. His first reaction had been fear, which had nothing at all to do with his work as a detective. His girlfriend, Fran, had gone south for a couple of weeks over Easter, taking her daughter Cassie with her. 'My parents haven't seen her for months,' Fran had said. 'And I want to catch up with all my friends. It would be so easy to lose touch, living here.' Perez knew it was ridiculous but when he thought of London he thought of danger. So while Fran dreamed of nights out at the theatre with her friends, leaving doting grandparents to make up months' worth of babysitting, he'd been thinking gun crime, stabbings, terrorism.

The anxiety must have been with him even in his sleep, because the noise of the phone triggered an immediate panic. He sat up in bed and grabbed the receiver, his heart was racing and he was wide awake. 'Yes?'

Only to hear Sandy Wilson, mumbling and incoherent as only he could be, with some story about his family, an accidental shooting, his grandmother dead.

Perez listened with half his brain, the other half flooded with relief, so he found himself grinning. Not because an old woman was dead but because nothing terrible had happened to Fran or Cassie. He saw from the clock on the bedside table that it was nearly three o'clock.

'How do you know it was an accident?' Perez had said, interrupting at last.

'My cousin Ronald was out after rabbits and it was such poor visibility, you can see how it might have happened. What else would it be?' A pause. 'Ronald likes his drink.'

'And what does Ronald say?'

'He couldn't see how it could have happened. He's a good shot and he'd not have fired into Mima's land.'

'Had he been drinking?'

'He says not. Not much.'

'What do you say?'

'I don't see what else could have happened.'

On the ferry, Perez left his car and climbed the stairs to the enclosed deck. He bought a cup of coffee from the machine and sat, looking through the grimy glass to watch Whalsay emerge from the dawn and the mist. Everything was muted green and grey. No colours and no hard edges. *Shetland weather*, Perez thought. As they came closer he could make out the shape of the houses on the hill. Large, grand houses. He'd grown up with myths about how rich the Whalsay folk were and he was never sure how much of it was true: Shetland was full of stories of buried treasure and trowie gold. It was said that one year a skipper was worried about the tax he'd have to pay and needed to take some money out of the company accounts. His crew were called to the pier on Christmas morning and each found a brand-new Range-Rover with his name on it. Perez couldn't remember seeing any of the Whalsay men driving a Range-Rover and anyway the boats were co-operatively run, but it was a good story.

Sandy was waiting for him in his own car at the pier. Before the ferry had tied up, Perez saw him get out. He stood, his hands in his pockets, the hood pulled up against the damp, until Perez had driven his car from the boat, then walked up to join him. He climbed into the passenger seat. Perez could tell that he'd had no sleep.

'I'm sorry about your grandmother.'

For a moment there was no reaction, then Sandy smiled grimly. 'It's how she'd have wanted to go,' he said. 'She always liked a bit of drama. She'd not want to slip away in her sleep in some old folks' home.' He paused. 'She'd not want Ronald to get into any bother over this.'

'Unfortunately,' Perez said, 'it's not her decision.'

'I didn't know what to do.' Sandy seldom knew what to do, but didn't usually admit it. 'I mean, should I have arrested him? He must have committed some sort of crime, mustn't he? Even if it was an accident. Reckless use of a shotgun . . .'

Perez thought recklessness was a tricky concept to prove in law. 'I don't think you could have done anything,' he said. 'Besides, you're involved. You found the body and you know everyone. It's not allowed. Certainly, it won't be your decision whether or not to arrest Ronald.' *Nor mine*, he thought. *That'll be down to the Fiscal*. The Fiscal would take formal charge of the case and he didn't know her well enough to guess what her response would be. His windscreen had steamed up. He wiped at it with a cloth. Now there was only mist on the outside. The ferry had already loaded the cars and started to make its way back to Laxo. Perez thought that would be a relaxing sort of job, moving back and forth between the islands. Perhaps that was what had drawn Billy Watt to it. Though he supposed it might get boring after a while.

'You know you should go back to Lerwick,' he said to his colleague. 'Leave the case to me now.' If there was a case, which most likely there wasn't.

Sandy looked wretched, fidgeted in his seat but made no move to leave the car. Perez wondered how he would feel if his own family was caught up in a sudden death. If anything happened to Fran and Cassie. In the past, they'd been too close to one of the cases he'd been working on and he could never have walked away from that and handed responsibility to another officer.

'I don't know Whalsay,' Perez said slowly. 'I suppose it would be helpful to have you around for a while to show me the lie of the land. But you don't interfere. You introduce me to your folks and then you keep quiet. Do you understand?'

Sandy nodded gratefully. His long fair fringe flapped over his forehead.

'We'll leave your car there then, shall we? You're in no state to drive. Let's go to Setter and see where you found your grandmother.'

'I moved her body,' Sandy admitted. 'It was dark and cold and I couldn't see the wound then. I thought she was ill and she might still be alive. I'm sorry.'

There was a moment's pause. 'I would have done exactly the same myself,' Perez said.

Sandy directed Perez to his grandmother's house. Perez could count the number of times he'd been to Whalsay on one hand. There'd been a piece of vandalism – one of the yoals they used for racing had been holed and then tipped into the harbour. No one else had been available and he'd come to deal with it out of interest. Then Sandy had asked him and Fran along to his birthday party – a do organized by his parents in the Lindby community hall. Perez knew that the night before Sandy had been out in Lerwick with his younger friends, but Perez hadn't been invited to that. The party in Whalsay had been an old-fashioned community do – a hot meal of boiled mutton and tatties, a band, dancing. It had reminded Perez of the dances at home in Fair Isle, raucous and good-natured.

His infrequent trips to Whalsay had given him no real idea of the geography of the place or of the relationships there. *People from the outside see Shetland as one community,* he thought, *but it's not like that at all. How many of the people who live in Lerwick have ever been to Fair Isle or Foula? Some of the Biddista folk managed to keep secrets from the rest of us for decades. The visitors are more adventurous than any of us.*

Sandy directed him to take a road to the right from Symbister and soon they were on the southern shore of the island, in the community of Lindby, a scattering of crofts running down to the water, surrounded by the crumbling walls of old abandoned houses. Not a village in the English sense of the word, but half a dozen families, mostly related, separated from the rest of Whalsay by sheep-grazed hill, peat banks and a reed-fringed loch.

Setter took Perez back to the old days at home too,

to a croft run by an old man who found the work too much for him but refused to let anyone help.

Someone had let out the hens and they were scratching around in a patch of weeds by the door, looking damp and bedraggled. Everything was untidy and overgrown. An ancient piece of agricultural machinery – quite unidentifiable now – rusted against the cowshed wall. These days, people wanted a better income than this sort of smallholding could provide. In Fair Isle families from the south had taken over some of the crofts and set up small businesses – IT, furniture-making, boat-building. There were even recent incomers from the United States. He knew he was a soppy romantic, but he quite liked the old ways.

'What happens to this place now?' he asked Sandy. 'Did your grandmother own it, or was she a tenant?'

'It was her own place. It always was hers. She inherited from her grandmother.'

'What about her husband?'

'He died very young. My father was just a bairn.'

'Had she made a will?'

Sandy seemed shocked by the idea. 'It'll just come to my father,' he said. 'She had no other close relatives. I don't know what he'll do with it. Take on the land and sell the house, perhaps.'

'You said there was a cousin, Ronald. He has no claim?'

'Ronald's related to me on my mother's side. He won't get anything as a result of Mima dying.'

They were still standing outside the house. Perez was what the locals called a black Shetlander; his ancestor had been washed up from a sunken Spanish Armada ship. He'd inherited the name, the dark hair and Mediterranean skin. Now he felt the cold seeping into his bones and thought he'd inherited a love of sunshine too. He couldn't wait for the summer.

'We should tape off the garden where the body was found,' Perez said gently. 'Even if the Fiscal puts it down as an accident, at the moment we have to treat it as a potential crime scene.'

Sandy looked up at him, suddenly horrified. Perez realized the suggested piece of routine police work had made Mima's death real again.

Sandy pushed open the door and they arrived in the kitchen. Again Perez was taken back to his childhood. His grandparents, and a couple of elderly aunts, had lived in houses like this. It was the smell as much as the furniture that took him back: the smell of coal-dust and peatsmoke, a particular brand of soap, damp wool. At least in here it was warm. The solid-fuel Rayburn must have been banked up the night before and still gave out plenty of heat. Perez stood in front of it and put his hands on the covered hotplate.

'I don't know what will happen to the cow,' Sandy said suddenly. 'My father milked her this morning, but I know damn well he'll not want to do that twice every day.'

Reluctantly Perez pushed himself away from the range.

'Let's go outside,' he said. 'You can show me where she died.'

'I keep thinking that if I hadn't stayed for that one last drink I might have been here in time to save her,' Sandy said. 'I might have stopped her going outside at all.' He paused. 'But I only came in to give me time to sober up before going back to my parents' house. If I'd gone straight home, I'd have taken the first ferry out this morning and someone else would have found her.' He paused. 'She phoned me earlier in the week and asked when I'd next be home. "Call in and have a dram with me, Sandy. It's a long time since we had a chat." I should have spent the evening with her instead of going down to the Pier House with the boys.'

'What was she doing outside at that time of night?' Perez asked. He tried to imagine what would have taken an elderly woman from the warmth of her fire into a sodden, cold field long after darkness had fallen.

'There was washing on the line. Maybe she'd gone to fetch it in.'

Perez said nothing. Sandy led him round the house. The laundry was still there, so wet now that it dripped on to the grass beneath it. This was rough grazing rather than garden, though a strip of ground running parallel to the washing line had been dug over for planting. Sandy saw Perez looking at it. 'My father did that. She'll have one strip of tatties and another of neeps. He sows a planticrub with cabbage each year for feeding the cow.'

'There's no laundry basket,' Perez said. 'If she'd come outside to fetch in the washing, what would she put the clothes in?'

Sandy shook his head, as if he couldn't see how such detail could matter.

'What's going on down there?' Perez nodded towards the trenches at the end of the field.

'An archaeological dig. A postgraduate student is researching it for her PhD. She'll be here for the next few months, working on it with her assistant. A couple of lasses. They were here for a few weeks last year and they've just arrived back. They're camping out at the Bod just now. This time of year there aren't too many people wanting to stay there. There's a professor who visits every now and again to keep an eye on things. He's here at the minute, staying at the Pier House Hotel. He came in with them.'

'We need to speak to him,' Perez said.

'I thought you might do. I called in to the Pier House while I was waiting for your ferry. He said he'd meet us here.'

Perez was surprised that Sandy had shown so much initiative, wondered if he should congratulate him or if that would just be patronizing. In the office Sandy was always considered a bit of a joke. Perez had shared the low opinion at times. He was still making up his mind how to respond when a big figure appeared out of the mist, as if Sandy had conjured him up by talking about him. He wore a full-length Barbour jacket and big boots. He was a big man, very blond, with cropped hair. He approached them, hand outstretched. 'Hello. I'm Paul Berglund. You wanted to talk to me.'

Despite the foreign name, the accent was northern English. It was a hard voice and suited the man. Perez wasn't sure what he'd been expecting in an academic. Not this large male with his uncompromising speech and the shaved head.

'Sandy will have explained that there was an accident here last night,' Perez said. 'We'd prefer it if your student stays off the site for the day.'

'No problem. Hattie and Sophie will be here to start soon. I'll hang on and tell them what happened. Is it OK if I wait in the house? It's a bit damp out here.'

For a moment Perez hesitated, then he recalled this

was an accident, nothing more. It wouldn't be sensible to get dramatic about it. 'Is that OK, Sandy?'

Sandy didn't hesitate. The Whalsay hospitality again. 'Sure. Why not?'

Berglund turned round and left them alone. Perez felt a little ridiculous because the encounter had been so brief, but just now he had nothing specific to ask the man. If he'd asked about the archaeology he'd have shown his ignorance. Besides, what relevance could the archaeological work have to Mima Wilson's death? Instead, he directed his questions to Sandy.

'Have the students found anything?' Perez was intrigued by the idea of digging for a living. He thought he'd enjoy it. Detailed, meticulous, picking his way through other people's lives. With the right sort of case it was what he liked most about his work.

Sandy shrugged. 'I haven't taken much interest,' he said. 'I don't think there was much. A few bits of pot. Nothing exciting. Though they did find an old skull a couple of weeks ago. Val Turner, the archaeologist from the Amenity Trust, came into the station to report it. She said it wasn't likely to be suspicious and the Fiscal wasn't interested.'

Perez thought he remembered talk of that in the canteen.

'My mother was here when they turned that up.' Sandy's voice had brightened at the mention of the skull, but Perez thought it would take treasure to excite Sandy. Gold bars. Jewels. He was still like a boy.

They stood for a moment looking into the hole in the ground, their shoulders hunched against the damp. Like mourners, Perez thought, at an open grave.

Chapter Seven

Ronald Clouston lived in a new house close to the shore. It seemed even bigger than the places Perez had seen from the ferry, a dormer bungalow with a long single-storey extension on one end. They sat outside it for a while in the car while Sandy filled in some of the background to the family.

'His mother and mine are second cousins,' he said. He frowned in concentration. 'Second cousins. Yes, I think that's right. His father sold him that bit of land. Ronald wanted somewhere to set up house with his new wife. He had the place built a couple of years ago.' He paused. 'They've just had a baby. That's one of the reasons I'm in Whalsay. I wanted to bring them a present, my best wishes. You know.'

'His dad didn't mind losing the land?'

'It was only a bit of rough grazing and he was never a farmer.'

'What does Ronald do for a living?'

'He's got a place on his father's pelagic trawler. The *Cassandra*. She's a beauty. Four years old now, but still state-of-the-art.' It was what Perez had been expecting and fitted in with the image of the hard drinker who went out in the middle of the night shooting. Most of the Whalsay boats were family-owned. Fishing was a tough life and the men let off steam when they came ashore.

'He was the brainy one at school,' Sandy went on. 'Not much good at anything practical, but OK at passing exams. Kind of dreamy, you know. He went off to university, but his father was taken ill and the place came up on the boat. He had to take it. You understand how it works. Maybe he was glad of the excuse to leave and he wouldn't have got his degree anyway. That's what my mother says.'

A bit of jealousy there, Perez thought. Or competition between the two cousins, Sandy's mother and Ronald's mother, comparing their sons. No one would ever have called Sandy brainy.

'Is the wife a Shetlander?'

'No, Anna's English. They had their wedding here, though, a couple of years ago. All her folks came up for it. It was a grand do.' Sandy's eyelids drooped for a minute and he shook himself awake, stared out at the drizzle. Condensation ran down the inside of the windscreen.

Perez thought this was still a huge house for two people and one baby. He wondered where Ronald had met his Anna. There was a history of Shetland men going out to find their wives. During his brief spell at university perhaps. Perez had married an Englishwoman. Sarah, soft and gentle, pretty and fair. But he hadn't had it in him to be the sort of husband she'd wanted. He'd always been too easily caught up in other folks' problems. 'I always come at the bottom of the pile,' she'd said. 'After work and your parents, sorting out the neighbour's delinquent son and the plumber's cat. You're drained when you do find time for me. You've nothing left to give.' At the time he'd thought she was talking that way because she'd just been through a miscarriage. Now he could see there was some truth in her words. He couldn't keep his nose out of other people's business. He told himself it was about being a good detective, but he'd have been curious even if work weren't involved.

Sarah was happier now without him, married to a doctor and living in the Borders with him, her children and her dogs. And Perez had taken up with another Englishwoman, divorcee Fran Hunter. Sarah had always been needy. Fran, he thought, didn't need him at all.

Sandy was shuffling in his seat. Perez's long silences always made him uneasy. 'Shall we go in then?'

'You're not to speak,' Perez reminded him, then told himself that Sandy had just lost his grandmother and smiled to soften the words. 'Just introduce me, then keep your mouth shut.'

Sandy nodded and got out of the car.

Perez guessed that the building plot had been chosen for its view. It was on a low promontory and the sea would be visible on three sides. To the west it would be possible to see Laxo and the mainland. You'd be able to measure your days by the ferry moving backwards and forwards across the water. It was a square bungalow, low like the traditional croft houses, but made of wood so it looked Scandinavian and with windows in the roof. It was painted blue. The long extension at the side had a lower sloped roof. Perez wondered what the extra space was for. They wouldn't keep animals there: it had a row of glazed windows. At the back of the house a small garden led down to the shore. A bed of daffodils was sheltered from the wind by a drystone wall – a patch of colour in the mist. An upturned dinghy had been pulled above the tideline. Sandy opened the front door and shouted. Perez heard a muted reply from further inside the house and followed him in.

The couple were both sitting in the kitchen. It seemed to Perez that they hadn't moved much since returning from Setter, after Sandy had rushed into the house to tell them Mima was dead. The shock had frozen them.

'What did you do that for?' Perez had demanded when Sandy had confessed that he'd left Mima and run to the Clouston house. *For God's sake, the man could be a suspect.*

'The doctor was off the island. Away on holiday. I knew it would take time to get the air ambulance here. I thought someone else would know best what to do. Their house is closest to Setter.' Sandy had looked up, staring at Perez. *I know I'm stupid, but let it go. Just today. Today I can't face a bollocking.* 'And Anna, she's kind of organized. Capable.'

You wanted her to tell you what to do, Perez had thought. *And you've always hated being on your own.*

So here the couple sat, in silence, still dressed in the jeans and jerseys they'd pulled on when Sandy had roused them from their bed. Ronald must be in his late twenties if he was close to Sandy's age and they'd been to school together, but he looked older. Grey somehow. Perez thought realizing you'd killed someone would do that to you. Ronald looked up when the men came into the kitchen, half rose in his chair, then the effort seemed too much for him and he sat down again. The woman had dark hair, twisted into a band at the back of her head, but untidy now, starting to come down. She sat very straight despite her obvious exhaustion, the shadows under her eyes. It seemed to Perez that she was furious, so angry that she didn't trust herself to speak. He couldn't tell if the fury was directed at her husband, at Sandy or at the situation in which they found themselves. Or Perez, for the intrusion into their grief. On one of the workbenches lay half a dozen rabbits ready for skinning and gutting. Baby clothes hung from an airing rack lowered from the ceiling.

'This is my boss,' Sandy said. 'Detective Inspector James Perez.' He followed Perez's instructions to the letter, said nothing more, leaned against the wall in the corner of the kitchen, an attempt to be inconspicuous. Perez took the spare chair and sat at the table, between the man and wife, sensed again the tension in the room.

'Sandy took your gun,' he said. Not a question. He'd checked already. Sandy had got that part of procedure right at least. It was one way to start the discussion, factual, safe.

Ronald looked up again. 'I don't see how it could have happened,' he said, almost on the verge of tears. 'I was shooting between here and Setter, but nowhere near the house or garden.'

He turned towards his wife. She stared stonily ahead of her. Perez saw that this was the conversation that had been going on all night. The man had spent hours trying to convince the woman that the tragedy hadn't been his fault and she had refused to excuse him, to make his guilt any less. Clouston looked like a child desperate to be held.

'It was very dark,' Perez said. 'Dreadful visibility. You must have lost your bearings. It happens.' Despite himself he felt sympathy for the man. This was his curse, what his ex-wife had called 'emotional incontinence'. The ability always to see the world through other folks' eyes.

Anna Clouston remained rigid.

'Tell me in some detail what happened yesterday evening,' Perez said.

And now the woman did speak. 'He was drinking,' she said. Her words were bitter and accusing. 'As he does every night when he's not actually working.'

'A couple of cans.' Ronald looked up at Perez, pleading. Perez resisted the temptation to reassure him. 'Friday night I deserve a couple of cans.'

'Were you working at all yesterday?' Perez asked. Back to the safety of facts.

'No. These days we just do two or three long trips a year with the deep-sea ships. I got back about a month ago.'

'So you were in all day?'

'No. I went into Lerwick. I wanted to go to the library.'

Perez would have liked to ask what books the man had chosen – he was fascinated by the detail of other people's lives, even when it had no direct relevance to his work – but Ronald was continuing: 'Then I stocked up in the supermarket. The shop in Symbister is fine, but sometimes you'd like something a bit different. Since we brought the baby home we've not managed to get into town. I got back about seven thirty.'

'Nearer eight,' Anna said. Not contradicting her husband, but trying to be accurate. Perez thought she was starting to relax a little. At least she was prepared now to participate. He smiled at her. 'But you stayed here?'

'Yes. Perhaps Sandy explained, the baby's only a few weeks old. He certainly hasn't got the hang of sleeping at night yet. I took the opportunity to grab some rest.' And Perez saw now that she was very tired. Without the adrenalin triggered by Mima's death she'd be asleep on her feet.

'Did you work before you had the baby?' It wasn't relevant, but he wanted to know, to understand her better.

'Yes, from home, so I'm hoping to get back to it as soon as I can.'

'What is it you do?'

'Traditional crafts,' she said. 'Spinning, weaving, knitting. I work mostly with Whalsay wool, either the natural colours or I dye it myself. The fish is already disappearing. Sheep prices have gone down. The oil's nearly gone. Eventually we'll have to develop new industries in Shetland. Or go back to the old ones.' Perez thought it was an old argument; she'd had this discussion many times before. He wondered what the wealthy Whalsay fishing families made of it.

'You sell the clothes you make?'

He could tell she was confused by his questions. What could this have to do with an old woman's death? But his interest pleased her too. 'Mostly over the internet. I hope to develop the business, to teach the old skills to other people. That's why we built on at the side of the house. The idea is to run residential fibre workshops. I only started advertising at the end of last year and I've already got some takers. A small group from the US have booked up for the summer. We won't be quite ready to put them up in the house – especially with a young baby – so they'll stay in the hotel and come here for workshops.' For a moment her anger seemed to dissipate and her face lit up. Work mattered to her. 'What will they think when they hear about this? It's the sort of business where you pull in customers by word of mouth. No one will come to the island if they think they're going to get shot!'

'Fibre workshops?' It seemed an odd sort of title. Besides, he was hoping it would calm her to talk about it.

'Any of the crafts based around wool.'

Perez saw now that she must be wearing one of her own creations, a hand-knitted jersey in natural fleece colours, mostly greys and moorit, a rich dark brown. 'You spent most of the evening together?'

'I had dinner ready for Ronald when he got back,' she said. 'Neither of us got much sleep the night before. The baby was restless, colicky. I knew Ronald would be tired. And James slept for most of the afternoon.'

Again Perez would have liked to ask where the couple had met. Even on this short acquaintance they seemed an ill-matched partnership. Perhaps Sandy's description of Ronald had coloured his opinion, but Perez thought the man came across as vague, passive, even allowing for the shock of Mima's death. Although she looked younger than her husband, Anna was forceful and ambitious. But she cared enough for him to have prepared a meal, to understand that like her he'd had a long, tiring week.

'Any visitors?'

'Sorry?' Ronald frowned.

'Did you have any visitors yesterday?'

'Sandy came for lunch to see the baby.'

'And in the evening?'

'Aunt Evelyn called in just as we'd finished eating.'

Perez wondered what sort of a cook Anna was. If she was interested in the old Shetland crafts, was she a traditional cook? He wished there was a lingering smell of the food, some dirty pots by the sink, to give him a clue. Why did it matter? Why was he so fascinated by the minute details of other people's lives? He wanted to recreate in his mind the scene in the kitchen before Ronald had gone out after the rabbits.

'Who's she?' he asked, trying to focus again on the conversation.

'Evelyn Wilson. Sandy's mother.' Ronald shot a quick look at his cousin, almost asleep on his feet, slumped against the workbench.

'Where was your shotgun during this time?'

'Locked in the cupboard in Anna's office. Where it always stays unless I'm using it.'

'And the key?'

'In the drawer in Anna's desk. What is all this about? Nobody else took the gun away. It was there when I decided to go out later.' Ronald wiped his hand across his face. Although it wasn't particularly hot in the room there was sweat on his forehead.

'How long did Mrs Wilson stay?'

'I made her a cup of tea,' Anna said. 'She wanted to talk about the dig. They found the piece of a human skull and it's been sent away for dating. She's a great one for community projects. She chairs the island Community Forum and thought it would be a good idea to put a page about my workshop project on the Whalsay website.'

'She sees you as a natural ally?'

'Yes,' Anna said, considering. 'I suppose she does. Not everyone on the island takes much interest. Ronald's always been passionate about history – it was his subject at university – and I find the Setter dig fascinating too.'

She looked across at her husband. Perez supposed this was something they had in common, but Ronald showed little enthusiasm for the archaeology now. His face was still blank and grey.

'Evelyn was here for about half an hour?' Perez asked.

'Something like that.' Anna stood up, stretched. 'Would you like some coffee? I should have offered before. I don't know what's wrong with me. The shock, I suppose.'

'You were fond of Mima?'

There was a pause. 'I'm not sure she liked me. But of course I'm sorry she's dead.'

Perez thought this was a strangely careful and honest description of the relationship. After a sudden death many people pretended to a closeness that didn't exist.

'Coffee would be brilliant,' Perez said. 'Black for me. You'll know how Sandy takes his. So much sugar it's like treacle.'

They waited in silence while Anna filled the kettle and switched it on. She reached into a high cupboard for mugs. Watching, Perez thought she'd already lost some of the weight around her belly. He imagined she'd be a great one for keeping healthy, a regular visitor to the Whalsay swimming pool, built with the oil money that had come into the islands in the eighties. He could imagine her jogging. He wondered if Ronald had ever taught her to shoot.

'So what time was it that Mrs Wilson left?'

'Nine o'clock perhaps.' Anna spooned sugar into Sandy's mug and handed it to him, then set the second in front of Perez. Sandy had been right: she was the organized one in the relationship, taking the lead and answering his questions. 'The baby woke and needed feeding. She saw herself out.'

'What did you two do then?'

'We had a row,' Anna said, 'about my husband's drinking.' She was still on her feet and the anger suddenly returned. Perez thought she looked rather magnificent standing there, straight-backed, eyes flashing. Perhaps it was the new baby, the hormones. He was glad the fury was directed at Ronald and not at him.

'He seems incapable,' she went on, 'of going a single night without a drink.' From the corner of the room, Sandy caught Perez's eye and looked suddenly sheepish. There would be lots of Shetland men who would find it hard to keep off the booze for a night. 'I suggested that just for once he should try. We eat healthily, take plenty of exercise. Now we've got the baby to think about.'

'A couple of cans,' Ronald said. A repeated mantra. He looked at both men in the room for support.

'But then to take out your gun,' she said. Perez

could tell she was almost losing control. 'Just to spite me because I asked you to stay in. I'd been in all day and I wanted some company. Was that too much to ask? Can't you see what you've done? You'll go to court, maybe to prison. If you weren't working with your family you'd almost certainly lose your job. And you know what it's like here. Wherever we go there'll be people whispering behind our backs. *There's that fool that shot Mima Wilson.* I don't think I can bear it.' She caught her breath at the start of a sob.

Ronald looked wretched. He got up and put his arms around her, tentatively at first. For a brief moment she allowed herself to rest her head on his shoulder.

From another room came the wail of a baby. It was piercing and relentless and Perez had to stop himself covering his ears to shut it out. How could you live with a noise like that? Anna pushed herself away from her husband and left.

There was an awkward silence. Perez could hear a ringed plover calling from the shore. He thought Anna had married Ronald believing she could change him. She treated him more like a son than a lover. And he behaved like a naughty little boy. Obviously embarrassed by his wife's outburst, Ronald returned to his seat.

Perez took a sip of the coffee. Instant but strong and hot. 'What time did you go out last night?'

'Ten o'clock. A bit later maybe. It was eleven-thirty when I got in. Anna had already gone to bed. Look, I don't know what had got into me. The strain of the baby maybe. I should have realized how much difference a child would make, the sudden responsibility.

James seems to have taken over our lives. I should have been more thoughtful, but I wanted to get out and clear my head, to forget about the family, just for a while. I had stuff to think about. Perhaps it was to spite her, to show her I didn't have to put up with her nagging. I don't see how I could have hit Mima. I wasn't shooting near to her house. And how could I have known that she'd be wandering around outside? It's a nightmare. I keep thinking I'll wake up and it'll be over.'

'Were you out on your own?'

'Yes, I was on my own!' He looked directly at Perez. 'Nobody else was out shooting last night. I'd have heard them. I'm not blaming anyone else. I don't know how it happened. Some freak shot maybe. Or like you said I must have lost my bearings in the fog. What will happen now?'

'We'll need a statement,' Perez said. 'You'll probably have to come into Lerwick. Not now. I'll let you know.'

'Will I be charged?'

'Not my decision. That's down to the Fiscal.' Again Perez felt an impulse to reassure the man. One foolish action leading to terrible consequences which would haunt him for ever. *Most likely it'll go down as a dreadful accident. Although shooting in those conditions was crazy, reckless, there was no criminal intent. We can all see that. Everyone hates the rabbits.* But there was nothing kind about making promises he wasn't sure he could keep. He really didn't know what the outcome would be.

Perez stood up. 'Stay here until we get in touch with you. Try to get some sleep.'

'I'll try, but I can't get that picture of Mima out of

my head. Such tiny bones. Like a snipe that's been shot. That frail.'

On the way out of the room, Perez stopped so suddenly that Sandy, shuffling behind, almost bumped into him. He turned back towards Ronald. 'Where did you meet your wife?' In the end he couldn't resist the question, which had been haunting him throughout the conversation.

Ronald answered immediately. 'She came into Shetland on holiday. She's always been interested in the traditional crafts and she came to Whalsay to talk to Evelyn about the island knitting. It has its own unique pattern, apparently, and Evelyn's a kind of expert. We met in the Pier House Hotel one night and kept in touch. She came to visit a few times . . . Maybe she fell in love with the place and not the man.'

Sandy had described Ronald as intelligent. For the first time Perez caught a glimpse of that. The man turned away suddenly and put his head in his hands. Perez and Sandy saw themselves out.

Chapter Eight

Sandy felt shattered. He'd always prided himself on being able to manage without much sleep. At Up Helly Aa he'd keep going for two or three days without getting to his bed, fuelled by the drink, the dancing and the company. He supposed this tiredness was to do with the shock. He'd never much understood the response of bereaved relatives when he'd come across them at work. He'd known he should be sympathetic, but their slow blankness and dull exhausted eyes had irritated him. He'd wanted to shake them. Maybe in the future he'd be less impatient. It had been such a relief when Jimmy Perez had arrived. Sandy had watched the ferry cross from Laxo with a sort of desperation, willing it to put on a bit of speed, knowing it was pathetic to want his boss to take things over, but not being able to help himself.

Now he was grateful that Perez had been so gentle with Ronald. Sandy had always got on well with Ronald, even though they were different. Sandy had never been one for schoolwork. He considered Ronald to be his best friend; when he finally took the plunge and decided to get married, he'd ask Ronald to be his best man. Jackie and Evelyn had never been friends. There'd always been the grit of envy and competition, and while Joseph and Andrew had been more civilized, Sandy had sensed a tension there too. Perhaps he and Ronald had become so close partly because their parents disapproved.

Perez hadn't said anything after they'd left the Clouston house, except that he'd wished he'd thought to bring his wellies because the grass was so wet. He could go half an hour at a time without saying a word, and that really spooked Sandy. He liked chat, even as background noise, always had the radio or the telly on if he was on his own in his flat.

They were back standing by the car. 'Where now?' he asked, thinking if he didn't move them on they could be here all day with Perez staring out towards the shore.

'I don't know about you, but I'm starving. Anywhere we could get a decent breakfast?'

'There are no cafes on the island, but my mother does a good fry-up.' As soon as he'd spoken, Sandy knew this was probably a mistake. Evelyn was an embarrassment. She'd be telling the inspector stories from his childhood, bringing out the photographs of him with the chickenpox, asking how soon Sandy could think about putting in for promotion, telling him about Michael's new job in Edinburgh. She could talk for Shetland, mostly about her sons. But it was too late to take back the offer; Perez had already got into the car and started the engine. The inspector leaned forward and wiped the condensation from the windscreen with a dirty handkerchief.

'Sounds just the thing. Which way are we going?'

They drove down the road past Setter and along the loch where the divers would breed later in the year, then came to the field with the pig arcs and the four russet-coloured pigs. Of all the beasts on the croft Sandy liked the pigs best. His mother must have heard the car coming down the track because she had the door open and was standing there waiting for them. Utra was the biggest croft in Lindby, because it included most of the Setter land now. Sandy's father had extended the house over the years, bullied by Evelyn, who'd wanted separate rooms for her sons, a decent-sized bathroom. Money had been tight in those days. Joseph Wilson hadn't worked on the boats, had never made as much money as the fishermen. Evelyn had never said but Sandy thought it must have been hard for her, watching the other women with their smart clothes bought on the trips to Bergen or Aberdeen.

'Come in,' she said, as soon as they got out of the car. 'You'll need to get warm and you'll be ready for something to eat. The kettle's just boiled. What a terrible thing! I couldn't believe it when Sandy told me. Poor Jackie. I don't know how she'll stand the shame of it.'

Sandy hoped Perez hadn't picked up the unpleasant note of satisfaction in her voice. Sandy knew what Evelyn was thinking. *Her son's fancy education and all that money he's making will be no use to him now.* Standing back to avoid her embrace, he saw that the drizzle had stopped and the sky was lightening a little. Perhaps the weather would clear soon. Then he thought that of course Perez would know just what his mother was thinking. He could pry inside people's heads like a mind reader or a magician.

Inside the house, he saw his mother through

Perez's eyes: little, round, short hair that she trimmed herself if she couldn't get into Lerwick, dressed today in her best hand-knitted sweater because she was expecting guests. Enough energy to power Shetland Hydro. She'd already warmed the pot and made the tea and she was still talking. *But she's not a stupid woman,* Sandy thought, *and Perez will see that too. She got all that money out of the Arts Trust for the community theatre project last year and everyone says she's the best chair the island forum has ever had.*

There was a newborn lamb in a cardboard box next to the Rayburn. 'An orphan,' Evelyn said. 'We're hand-rearing her. No one else would bother, but Joseph's a soft old thing.'

Now that the tea was brewing she turned back into the room. 'What can I get you to eat? We've got some of our own bacon and Mima gave me a dozen eggs yesterday, so I have plenty to spare. Will that do you?'

Sandy found himself remembering the day his father had killed the pig. Because it was for the family's own use there'd been no need to send it out to the abattoir, but it was a horrible job. The pig always made a dreadful noise before the throat was cut. He'd seemed to sense what was about to happen to him. Sandy had been on the island that day, but he'd not been a lot of use. He'd stood watching along with Anna. His father had been the strong one, finishing off the job with Ronald's help, and Evelyn had caught the blood in a bowl.

'It sounds brilliant, Mrs Wilson,' Perez said. He'd made himself at home already. His shoes were left in the porch and he'd taken the chair by the table where Sandy's father usually sat. She beamed, took down a heavy frying pan from the wall, opened the Rayburn hotplate.

'Mrs Wilson, indeed! No one's called me that in this house since that politician from the SNP came canvassing at the last election.'

It was warm in the kitchen and Sandy felt himself nodding off, heard the conversation between Perez and his mother as though from a long distance.

'What time did you last see Mima?' Perez asked.

'About two o'clock. I called round to have a chat about the dig. The two lasses from the university were there. What nice wee girls they are, though I think that Hattie could do with a bit of feeding up. She's a skinny little thing. All eyes and bone.' She paused to take breath.

Sandy knew his mother had hoped he'd take up with one of the 'nice wee girls'. She thought he should settle down and give her grandchildren. Michael, after all, had obliged by marrying an Edinburgh lawyer and producing a daughter who was already attending private nursery. But that wasn't like having a grandchild close at hand to meddle with. Jackie scored now on that too. Sandy had liked the students well enough. Not Hattie so much, who was intense and far too clever for him, but Sophie, who was more laid-back. She liked a few beers and a bit of a laugh, she was kind of flirty. Posh, but friendly all the same. The boys teased him because he always had a different woman on the go, but he was starting to think it was time for him to settle down. It was tiring chasing after the lasses and there were more single men in Shetland than there were women. But would he really want to be like Ronald, married to a woman who nagged and bossed? It would be like living at home again.

'The dig is so exciting!' Evelyn was distracted from Mima's death by her passion of the moment. 'Hattie thinks there's a merchant's house there. It was built at the time when the Hanseatic League was starting to collapse and folk were told they couldn't trade through Bergen any more. I found a skull, you know. Part of a skull. Hattie thinks it might belong to the merchant who built the house. It's been sent away for carbon dating. They've been exploring the same trench and Sophie found more bone. Part of a rib and maybe the pelvis. Imagine what a tourist attraction it would be, if we excavate the site properly. I'd like to build a house, just as it would have been. We could run workshops, family days. We have to look to the future if we're going to provide work for our young people.'

Sandy stifled a yawn, thought again that Evelyn had a lot in common with Anna. He couldn't get worked up about the island's future. He'd left Whalsay for Lerwick as soon as he could escape from his mother and felt more at home in town now. 'That bacon's not burning, is it, Mother?'

Evelyn shook the pan, scowled at Sandy for questioning her ability to fry a couple of rashers.

'When you visited Setter, was Mima in the house, or outside with the women?' Perez asked.

'We were all inside. The weather had just turned nasty and Mima had invited the girls in for a hot drink. When I arrived the three of them were in the kitchen, giggling over some silly joke. You'd have thought Mima was the same age as they were. This project seemed to have given her a new lease of life. That's why this stupid accident is such a tragedy.'

For the first time Sandy thought his mother was genuinely upset. She'd always treated Mima as a bit of a nuisance, a wayward teenager likely to cause the family embarrassment, but now he saw she'd miss her. Which didn't mean she wasn't a little bit pleased Ronald had got himself into bother over it.

His mother was still talking, her words running as a background soundtrack to his thoughts. 'I had some tea with them then the girls went back out. They'd been drenched through and Mima had put their coats and socks near the Rayburn to dry. It was steaming like a laundry in there, condensation running down the windows so you couldn't see out. Mima already had the eggs ready for me and I couldn't waste any more time chatting. I was driving and got wet just running from the house to the car. The students went back to their work though. I could see their bright yellow waterproofs from the car.' Evelyn lifted the bacon from the pan and put it on a plate in the bottom oven to keep warm.

'So you had a little time with Mima on her own?'

'Just a few minutes.' She cracked four eggs into the pan, flipped the bacon fat over them, turned back to the table to slice bread.

'How did she seem?'

'Like I said, on fine form. Mischievous. But then she was always that way.'

'Did she tell you she had any plans for the evening?'

'No, she never went out much at night. She liked her telly too much.'

'Did you notice if her washing was out when you left?' Perez asked.

'I noticed it was there when I arrived, asked her if she'd like me to fetch it in for her. She said it had been there two days already and one more wouldn't hurt. That was Mima for you.'

She set the table and put the food in front of them. Sandy roused himself from his stupor long enough to eat, was vaguely aware of Perez complimenting his mother on the food, a discussion about the problems of rearing pigs, the best treatment for pigs' sunburned nipples.

Sandy watched with admiration as Perez brought the conversation back to Mima's death. He thought he'd never be such a skilful interrogator even if he worked for the rest of his career as a detective.

'Later you went to see the Cloustons?' Perez asked Evelyn, as if it were the most natural conversation in the world.

'After tea, yes. Sandy was back for the weekend but he was away to the bar to catch up with his pals.' She looked disapprovingly at her son; Sandy pretended not to notice. He'd heard it all before. 'He tends to treat this place like a hotel. Joseph had sport on the television. There was nothing to keep me in and I don't like to bother Anna during the day. With a new baby you catch up on your sleep when you can and I know she's always busy. Young mothers these days don't seem to think they need to rest.'

'How did you find them?'

'Well enough. Tired, of course, but that's the way when there's a new baby in the house. Anna's always very pleasant, though she seemed kind of tense. I wondered if I'd walked in on a row.'

'And Ronald?'

'Ronald's always been a moody sort of man. He was the same as a boy.'

Now Sandy felt compelled to speak. 'You can't say that, Mother. It's just not true. Maybe he wanted some time to himself.'

'He was lucky to find that woman and he treats her badly.' Evelyn piled the plates into the sink and switched on the tap, swished the washing-up water with her hand. 'I'll leave these to soak for now, do them later when you've gone.'

'Badly in what way?' Perez asked.

'She's new here. They've only been married a couple of years. He should make more of an effort to help her settle. The trouble with Ronald Clouston is that he's lazy. He'll not put himself out. The *Cassandra* suits him just fine. He's only working for a few months of the year. The rest of the time he sits on his backside reading. He likes the money right enough. The Cloustons all like money. But they're not prepared to contribute anything back to the community.' She took a towel from the rail on the Rayburn, dried her hands, folded it back neatly.

'Fishing's not pleasant work,' Perez said. 'I get seasick going home to Fair Isle on the *Good Shepherd*. I'd not fancy weeks in the Atlantic in winter.'

'Hmm.' Evelyn was dismissive. 'These days on the fancy ships, it's all pushing buttons. Not much different from being in an office.'

Sandy wondered how his mother could know anything about fishing. If Perez weren't there he'd have made some sort of sarcastic comment: *You'll know all about that, will you? When was the last time you were out in a force-eight north-westerly? Could you cope with the sleet and cold, the deck running with ice and the stink of fish?*

'Did Ronald talk about his plans to take the gun out while you were there?'

'He didn't talk about anything much. Anna had some ideas about funding for the dig. She had experience in putting together funding applications in her previous work. Ronald's always claimed to be interested in the history of Whalsay but he won't put himself out to preserve it.'

'What did Anna do before she moved here?'

'She was a kind of social worker, specializing in young offenders. But she's always been interested in traditional crafts; that's what brought her here.'

Sandy caught the inspector giving a little grin and wondered what was going through his mind. Maybe he was thinking Anna treated Ronald like one of her naughty boys.

'Did Ronald have anything to drink while you were there?' Perez asked.

'One can, but I was only there for half an hour.'

'Does Ronald drink too much?'

'All the boys here drink too much,' Evelyn said sharply. Sandy knew she was preparing to sound off on the subject, and was relieved when they were interrupted by a bang on the kitchen door. Before anyone could answer it, the door was pushed open. One of the archaeology students was standing there. She was small and slight and to Sandy she looked about twelve. She had short choppy hair and enormous black eyes and seemed swamped in the cagoule that reached below her knees and met the yellow wellingtons.

'Evelyn,' Hattie said. 'Is it true? I've just heard that Mima's dead.'

Chapter Nine

That morning Hattie had woken early. She was lying curled, foetus-style, inside her down sleeping bag, but she still felt cold. They'd lit a fire in the Bod the evening before to warm up when they got back from the dig, but then they'd gone to the Pier House Hotel and by the time Hattie got back the fire was out. She had gone to the Pier House to be sociable, but soon felt uncomfortable and she'd left Sophie drinking with a couple of the local lads. Sophie could drink as much as the men, stumble back to the Bod in the early hours, fall into a deep sleep and be wide awake and hangover-free ready to start work on the dig the next day. Hattie had never got the knack of either holding her drink or sleeping. Ideas and plans seemed to swirl around in her head. She'd been awake when Sophie came in the night before. She'd lain still on the hard wooden bunk but she saw the swinging beam of torchlight, heard the whispered oaths as Sophie tripped, climbing out of her clothes, then almost immediately afterwards her regular deep breathing. Sophie sounded like a child when she was sleeping, or an animal.

She could hear the same sound now. Sophie's sleeping bag wasn't as good as hers but the cold never woke her. Hattie flicked on her torch. Six o'clock. Still dark outside and still misty. She could hear the regular moan of a foghorn far in the distance. Since they'd returned to the dig at Lindby, it seemed to her that Whalsay had become her entire universe. It was as if the fog cut the island off from the rest of the world. Her mother was a politician, a junior minister, and growing up Hattie had been surrounded by discussion of current affairs. The latest policy on healthcare, education, overseas aid, had governed their daily lives. Here she rarely read a newspaper, only saw television if it was on at Mima's house or in Utra where Evelyn lived. World affairs had no relevance to her here. Digging away the layers of soil from the buried house at Lindby, she found herself engrossed in political concerns – the decline of the Hansa, the emergence of wealthy men in Shetland – but ones that had nothing to do with the present.

Sophie thought Hattie was driven on by ambition, and it was true that at one time the only future she saw for herself was as an academic. That meant a good PhD and a reputation as a solid and intelligent archaeologist. Now another, more personal obsession had taken over. She wanted to stay in Shetland.

The site had been a merchant's house, much grander than she'd first thought. Whalsay had been an important port in the Hanseatic League – the medieval trading community of towns along the Baltic and the North Sea coasts – and she'd assumed that the owner had been a trader. But there were no records, no name for the owner. The university had been working in Shetland for years and Hattie had come first as an undergraduate, working on the dig at Scatness. She'd come across the site at Setter by chance and had found herself tantalized by the mystery. How could such a substantial house have disappeared so completely from Shetland's history? It didn't show up in any of the early maps or the records. She hoped the dig might provide an answer. Paul, her supervisor, had first thought that there might have been a fire to wipe away traces of the dwelling, but they'd found no evidence of that.

Hattie, who had been given to obsession since she was a child, found herself haunted by the place. In her imagination she lived there, in fifteenth-century Shetland, when the islands were still culturally closer to Norway than to Scotland and Whalsay's loyalties were to the other Hanseatic ports, to Lubeck and Hamburg rather than Edinburgh or London. She saw the sailing ships arriving into Symbister and her husband, the merchant, counting out gold coins to pay his men for the goods he was importing from Europe, and the money he was paying the islanders for their salt fish and dried mutton. In her daydreams it was spring, but the sun was shining and the island was green.

Did the skull Evelyn had found belong to the merchant or to his wife? They were starting to find more bones in the second trench and perhaps they already had enough evidence to know. There were times in the early morning, as the damp penetrated her body, when she thought the dreams were driving her mad. *And it's not just me,* she thought. *The dig's getting to Mima too.* Their last conversation had been pretty weird.

At seven o'clock she began to get dressed, still sitting in her sleeping bag, pulling on the layers of clothes she would need to stay comfortable during the day. On top of the T-shirts she wore the hand-knitted sweater Evelyn had made for her birthday.

The Bod was one of a string of bothies spread across the islands, places for backpackers to stay. This was an old croft house and it just contained four beds, a table and a camping stove. There was a shelf with some pans, cutlery and crockery, an open peat fire. The Bod had one cold tap and they had baths and washed their clothes at Mima's house, or more often at Evelyn's. Evelyn was almost as passionate about the project as Hattie, and often invited them to Utra for dinner. She mothered them. Hattie thought she had her eye on Sophie as a potential daughter-in-law. Sophie was easygoing and pleasant, she ate everything Evelyn put in front of her and she laughed at Sandy's jokes. Hattie knew Sophie would never marry Sandy – she had wealthy parents and ambitions of her own, which didn't include being a policeman's wife in Lerwick – but she might have sex with him for her own amusement. That was the way Sophie was.

Sophie didn't wake until Hattie had lit the camping stove and made coffee. Then she stretched extravagantly, blinking in the light of the Tilley lamp. Hattie watched her through the open bedroom door. Sophie always slept naked and now sat quite comfortably, apparently not feeling the cold at all, with her breasts exposed, her long tawny hair falling around her shoulders. Hattie envied her. *I was never that comfortable with my body*, she thought, *not even as a child. Why would any man want to sleep with me?* Sophie, her legs still encased by the sleeping bag, looked like a mermaid or the figurehead of one of the sailing ships that in Hattie's imagination had brought goods to trade with her merchant husband.

Hattie would have liked to ask who was in the Pier House the night before. *Who did you stay up drinking with?* But as usual the words stayed inside her head.

'Is there anything for breakfast?' Sophie asked. 'I'm starving.'

Sophie was always starving. She ate like a horse without putting on weight. A natural athlete, she loped across the island at a pace that left Hattie breathless and panting, and she could work all day without seeming to get tired. Recently she'd been recruited by Anna to take her place in the Whalsay women's rowing team. Hattie had watched her practising with the group, bending and pulling on the oars, collapsing in laughter at the end of the session. *Why can't I be like that?* Hattie thought now. *I'm scared of the world and I always have been. I can't blame Paul Berglund for that.* The image of her supervisor slid into her brain, filled it with his size and his strength. She felt a return of the old panic and forced herself to breathe slowly, to retreat to her dreams of the merchant house and her island lover.

'I'm starving,' Sophie repeated.

'There's bread,' Hattie said. 'Some of Evelyn's marmalade.'

'That'll keep us going until elevenses at Mima's.' Sophie stepped out of her sleeping bag. Hattie was embarrassed by the sight of the girl's naked body, but fascinated too. She couldn't help looking at it, at the flat belly, the golden pubic hair, the muscular shoulders. She turned away quickly and began to slice bread.

Usually Sophie was full of chat about what had happened in the bar the night before, the island gossip, news of any overseas trawlers that had put into Symbister during the day, men she fancied, but this morning she seemed subdued and got dressed in silence. She opened the main door of the Bod and looked outside.

'God,' she said. 'Do you think this fog will ever clear? It's getting me down. Don't you long for sun and a clear blue sky? It's spring. In the south there'll be green leaves and primroses.'

'At least it's not pouring with rain. I left my spare coat at Mima's last night and the other one is still wet.' But Hattie found the mist disturbing too. It slid across the island, changing her perspective and challenging her ideas about the landscape and its history.

She spread marmalade thinly on to a slice of bread, folded it in half and forced herself to eat it. There'd been a stage in her life when food had become a source of conflict between her mother and herself. Her mother had decided Hattie was anorexic, panicked and dragged her off to a specialist clinic. Being Junior Minister for Health made Gwen James sensitive about things like that, sensitive at least about what the press might write if they got the idea that Hattie was unnaturally thin and her mother doing nothing to address the problem. Hattie hadn't been able to understand the fuss; not eating had been a symptom of her problem, not the root of her illness. Occasionally she got engrossed in her work and forgot to eat. So what? Now she remembered meals as a duty – like taking regular medicine – to keep her mother off her back. She was never hungry and seldom took any pleasure from food, even after a day's work on the dig when Sophie was ravenous. It astounded her that people could waste time planning what they would cook, that a meal out was considered a treat.

Sophie had already finished breakfast and was brushing her hair, her one vanity. It hung halfway down her back, the colour of a barley stalk. Now she tied it back into a long loose ponytail at the nape of her neck. 'We'd better go,' she said. 'I suppose we can't really be late with the boss on the island.'

The boss. Their supervisor, Paul Berglund. Another obsession from an earlier period in Hattie's life. Now she realized the obsession had turned into an unhealthy paranoia. Sophie knew nothing of this; she hadn't picked up on the antagonism between them. To Sophie, Paul was just 'the boss', someone who turned up occasionally to lay down the law about their methods, treated them to a decent meal out in a restaurant in Lerwick if he was in a good mood, signed off their expenses. She couldn't know that Hattie was counting the days until he left.

Hattie didn't think Paul would have allowed her to set up the project if he'd been supervising from the start. But he'd only joined the department the year before. She remembered the meeting at which he'd been introduced to her and Sophie. 'You'll have heard of Paul Berglund,' the head of department said. 'You couldn't wish for a better supervisor.' Paul had shaken Hattie's hand, said how pleased he was to be working with her and given no sign that they'd met before. His hand had been cold and dry; hers was sweaty. She'd muttered something about feeling unwell, fled the office and thrown up in the nearest ladies' toilet. Perhaps he expected her to dump the project, find another subject for her PhD.

But she hadn't left – the dig on Whalsay had been her idea from the start – and she had made sure that he had no excuse for excluding her. Now the merchant's house mattered more to her than escaping from him. Her record-keeping was impressive and though she wasn't as physically strong as Sophie, her fieldwork was deft and thorough. Whenever she was in Paul's presence she felt tense. She watched him, always aware of the space he took up, of his position in the room.

'Paul Berglund was in the bar after you left,' Sophie said. They'd left the Bod and were on their way to Lindby. They couldn't see much beyond the field on each side of the track. Sheep were darker shades in the mist.

'Oh.' Hattie tried to sound unbothered. She didn't want to hear about him.

'Yeah, he was drinking whisky. I've never seen him pissed before. Not that pissed.'

I have, Hattie thought, and shivered inside her fleece. 'Anything else happen after I'd gone?' She wanted to move the discussion away from Berglund.

'Not really. I was chatting to Sandy, but he left before I did. He had to get home to his mammy. I mean, what is he like? He still acts like a fourteen-year-old.' She shifted the straps of the rucksack on her shoulders. 'I do see him as a bit of a challenge, though. I'm sure he gets up to all sorts of mischief in Lerwick. It would be fun to see if I can get him to misbehave here, on his mother's doorstep.'

Hattie didn't know what to say about that. She supposed Sophie could look after herself, but in her opinion all games around sex were dangerous. She would be quite pleased though if Sophie and Sandy hooked up with each other for a while.

They'd reached the dip in the land that led to Setter, the most sheltered spot on the island. The merchant had chosen the land for his grand house well. Hattie wondered if it had the same name then, something similar perhaps which had become corrupted over the years. They always called in on Mima before they started work, both as a courtesy and because she'd put on the kettle and bring them out tea if she knew they were there. The house seemed unusually quiet. Mima liked Radio Two, the chat of Wogan and singing along to the ballads she recognized. Sophie opened the door and called in but there was no answer.

'She's not there.' Paul Berglund appeared from the back of the house, squat, short-necked, looking more like a soldier than a professor of archaeology. Hattie couldn't work out what he could be doing there. He didn't usually arrive on site so early. And if he'd been drinking the night before, shouldn't he still be in the hotel nursing a hangover? 'Come into the house,' he said as if he owned the place. 'Sit in the kitchen in the warm.'

Something awful's happened, Hattie thought. *What's he done now?*

She held back so Sophie walked into the house first. Usually they would have taken off their boots, but Paul was beckoning them in and they were used to following his instructions. He'd been cutting up an apple with the knife he always carried on site. It lay on the table and Hattie thought again what a cheek it was that he should make himself so at home. In the kitchen the cat wound itself round her legs and almost tripped her up. She picked it up and it hissed.

'Mima's dead,' Paul said. His voice was quiet but matter-of-fact. 'The police were here earlier. They called me at the Pier House Hotel first thing this morning and asked me to meet them. There was a dreadful accident late last night. Some guy out after rabbits hit her by mistake.' He paused. They were all still standing. 'I think it would be better for you not to work today, out of respect for the island. Take the day off. I'll give you a lift into Lerwick if you like. I'm going anyway, to catch the ferry south this evening. I need to get home.'

'Cool,' Sophie said, then must have realized how that sounded. 'I mean about the lift into town and the day off. Not Mima. We'll really miss her. I mean, what a shit thing to happen.'

Hattie could tell the only thing Sophie would miss was the tea in the morning and the home baking, sitting in front of the Setter fire when it was raining outside. She didn't care about a dead old lady.

'What about you, Hattie?' Paul said. 'Do you want to come too?'

'No, I'll stay here.' She must have spoken more sharply than she'd intended because they both stared at her. She'd been wondering about his sudden decision to go south. They'd been expecting him to stay for another week. The undergraduates were still on holiday for Easter. 'I'll go to see Evelyn and tell her how sorry we are, ask if there's anything we can do.'

And before either of them could stop her she stooped to put the cat on the floor and was out of the house and on her way to Utra. Halfway there she realized her eyes were streaming with tears.

Chapter Ten

Perez wasn't sure what to make of the hysterical girl who turned up at the door of Evelyn Wilson's house. At first he mistook her for one of the island children; she might have been fifteen or sixteen, certainly not old enough to be a postgraduate student. Even after Evelyn had introduced her and she had calmed down sufficiently to talk more rationally, he still thought of her as a girl. Her voice was breathy, high-pitched. The voice of a well brought-up child.

She was small and thin. Big dark eyes and very black hair, cut short so the eyes looked even bigger. They were ringed by grey shadows, which made her look exhausted. He wished she wasn't so sad, caught himself wondering how he could make her feel better, then stopped himself. 'It's not your responsibility. It's a sort of arrogance, thinking you can change the world.' Fran's words, spoken with exasperation and affection, repeated often enough that they came into his head in situations like this.

Hattie leaned against the doorpost to take off her work boots and looked as if she didn't have the strength to stand upright. Without the boots she seemed even more frail. Perez had the fancy that without them on her feet to anchor her to the floor she might float into the air.

Evelyn helped the girl to a chair, automatically moved the kettle on to the hotplate. Hattie reached across the table towards Sandy, not quite touching his hand. 'I'm so sorry,' she said. 'I know you were close to your grandmother. She talked about you all the time.' In her confusion she seemed not to notice Perez.

'You shouldn't have had to hear like that,' Evelyn said. 'One of us should have come to the Bod to tell you. What a shock it must have been! But we've all been so busy here and it never crossed my mind. How did you find out?'

'From Paul. He was waiting for us when we got to Setter. He said it was an accident, but I don't understand.'

'Sandy's cousin Ronald was out shooting rabbits. He won't admit it but he must have fired across the Setter land. He couldn't have thought Mima would be out on a night like that. What other explanation is there?' Evelyn stood quite still for a moment, then turned to pour water into a brown earthenware teapot which she covered with a striped cosy and put at the back of the Rayburn. She sat at the table next to Hattie. 'I'm very sorry, my dear, but she was wearing your waterproof. You won't be able to use it again. We'll replace it for you.'

'No.' It seemed to Perez that she hadn't heard more than the first couple of sentences. She was frozen with shock and couldn't take in the information. Not all at once. 'There's no need for that. Of course not.' She turned to Evelyn. 'Are you sure that's the way it happened? How could Ronald not see the jacket? It's bright yellow.'

'It was very dark,' Evelyn said. 'The mist came down again last night.'

'I don't understand it,' she said. She began to cry again.

Perez found a clean handkerchief in his pocket and handed it over to her. She seemed to see him for the first time and stared, startled. 'My name's Jimmy Perez,' he said, though Evelyn had introduced him when she'd arrived. 'I work for the police. We have to ask questions, to be satisfied about the accident.'

Hattie blinked quickly like a camera shutter clicking. Perez had the impression of thoughts and images fizzing in her head. 'If I hadn't given Mima the coat,' she said, 'perhaps she wouldn't have gone out.'

'That's plain stupid,' Evelyn said. 'Don't you dare think like that. We all wonder if there was anything we could have done to prevent it. It's natural after a tragedy like this but does no good at all.' She stood up. Perez watched her take an old biscuit tin from a cupboard. When she lifted the lid he smelled cheese scones, another memory of home. She split and buttered them and set them on a plate, poured the tea into mugs.

'Why *did* you give Mima your coat?' Perez asked.

She had just picked up her tea and stared at him over the mug. 'It was yesterday afternoon,' she said. 'It was pouring with rain. We came in drenched to dry out before going back to work. Mima admired my jacket when she took it out to dry. She'd been so kind that I said she could have it. I had a spare in my rucksack.'

'Aye,' Evelyn said. 'That's how it was. I was there.

She was so pleased with it. "How fine I'll look going out in that! The hens won't know me." You know how she carried on, Sandy?'

Sandy nodded. They sat for a moment in silence, then Evelyn became all efficient and businesslike:

'You mustn't think this will affect the project. Not at all. Everything will carry on just as before. Setter will come to Joseph when everything's sorted out with the lawyers. We haven't even thought what we'll do with the croft just yet, but you can continue with the dig as soon as you like.'

Perez looked at Sandy. Was Evelyn speaking for the whole Wilson family? But Sandy said nothing.

'I'd rather you didn't work on the dig today,' Perez said quietly. 'Today the Fiscal might need to visit. It's her decision whether any action needs to be taken and how we should proceed.'

'Will Ronald be charged?' Hattie asked.

'That's not a decision for me.'

'The weather's so bad,' Sandy said, his first contribution to the discussion, 'that you wouldn't want to be working this morning anyway.'

'Oh I would!' Hattie said immediately. 'I hate it when it's too wet to work. It's fascinating, addictive I suppose. You understand that, Evelyn.'

'What exactly are you looking for?' Perez thought she looked quite different when she spoke about her work. Her face lit up, and the grey shadows around her eyes seemed to disappear. Another young woman driven by her work, just like Anna Clouston.

'Local archaeologists picked up signs of a dwelling on that site in the sixties, but nothing much happened with it. According to Mima, although most of the Setter land is fertile, nothing much would grow just there – she said her mother had called the mound there a trowie knowe. You know the myths about the trows, the little people. It was supposed to be a hole in the ground, a place where they kept their treasure. Mima explained them to me, told me some of the stories.'

Perez nodded. He'd been brought up on stories of trows too, small malevolent creatures who lived in the islands and ruled their kingdom with magic and decorated their houses with glittering jewels and gold.

Hattie continued: 'Everyone assumed that it was a croft that had gone out of use before the first Ordnance Survey map. They thought perhaps the present house developed from it. Or that the remains composed some sort of outbuilding. Then I came to Shetland on a working holiday with Sally Walker, one of my lecturers. We took a closer look at the Setter site and thought the house looked more substantial than had been assumed. I was looking for a postgraduate project and it seemed perfect. Sophie's taking a year out after graduating and agreed to come and help. Sally left on maternity leave and didn't feel she could continue to supervise me.'

The words came out in a rush. *Nerves?* Perez wondered. *Or is it just passion for her subject?* 'And now Paul Berglund's in charge?'

'He's my supervisor. Yes.'

She doesn't like the man, Perez thought. Then he saw her face freeze again. *No*, he thought with surprise. *It's more than that. She's scared of him.*

'And what have you found?'

'Well, we've still got a long way to go, of course, but we did a geophysical survey and there certainly seems quite a grand building on that site. The excavation we did last season bears that out. I think it could be a merchant's house. We know that Whalsay was an important trading point within the Hanseatic League. That was a community of ports around the North Sea, a sort of medieval EU. The mystery is that there's no record of the house, or of the man who lived there. It's frustrating. It would be wonderful to put a name to the man who built it. We've just got a couple of months left here to see if there's enough evidence to justify funding for a full-scale dig. I suppose the bones might tell us something. They've gone for carbon dating, but I'm assuming they're fifteenth-century. There's nothing in the context to suggest otherwise.'

'Sandy told me about the skull.'

'We found it in a trench outside the walls of the house. We've found other bones there too, presumably from the same individual. It's strange because you'd expect a body to be buried in a graveyard at that period. I've spoken to people at the university. They say it might be the body of a drowned man washed up on the shore. Strangers didn't always get a proper burial: the superstition was that drowned men belonged to the sea. But Setter's quite a distance from the shore, and that doesn't really make sense to me. I'd like to think we've found my merchant.' She looked up at him. 'I hope we can go on with the work tomorrow. Time's already running out.'

He didn't answer directly. 'Who's testing the bones?'

'Val Turner, the Shetland archaeologist, came in when we realized what we'd found. She's sorted them out, sent them to the lab in Glasgow to date them.'

He supposed it was a coincidence. Two deaths in one place, separated by hundreds of years. Corpses growing from the same garden. Places couldn't be unlucky, could they? 'How was Mima when you were with her yesterday?'

'She seemed in fine form. Didn't she, Evelyn?'

'Oh aye. Just the same as usual.' Evelyn reached across the table and poured more tea.

'She didn't object to you digging up her land?' Perez asked. There wouldn't be many Shetland landowners who'd be glad of that intrusion.

'Not at all,' Hattie said. 'She was really interested. And interesting. She said when she was growing up in Whalsay there'd been a legend about a big house that had once been at Lindby, built by the son of a fisherman. It's the sort of folk tale that might have its root in reality.'

'Aye well.' Evelyn stood up briskly. 'You don't want to believe everything Mima told you. She was a great one for stories. She might have remembered a few snatches from what her grandmother told her and made up the rest. I'd never heard anything about a big house at Setter. She was a bit of a romantic, was Mima.'

'That's what I liked about her, I think,' Hattie said. She broke off a piece of the scone on her plate and crumbled it in her fingers. Perez thought she'd just taken the scone to be polite. None of it had got as far as her mouth. She looked up suddenly and frowned. 'Mima seemed shocked when we found the skull. Didn't you think so, Evelyn?'

'Maybe she'd started to believe her own scary stories,' Evelyn said. 'Maybe she thought it was the work of the trows.'

Perez thought Hattie was going to say more about the skull, but she changed the subject. 'I hope Ronald doesn't get charged,' she said. 'Mima wouldn't have wanted that.'

Perez wondered why it seemed to matter to her so much. She'd only been here for a couple of months. Whilst she'd obviously been fond of Mima, the other people in the drama could hardly be more than names to her. 'How well do you know him?'

She shrugged. 'I've seen him a few times in the bar of the Pier House Hotel. He did history at university and knows a lot about the myths and legends of the islands. He seems quite interested in the project and last season he came out to visit the site a few times. We've tried to involve local people. That's a prerequisite of work in Shetland. Val Turner insists that we explain what we're doing to the community and include them as much as possible. Anna seems keen too.'

'Poor Anna,' Evelyn said. She stood up and took the empty mugs to the sink for washing up. Perez expected her to elaborate, but suddenly she turned back to Hattie. 'Where's Sophie? You should have brought her in for some tea. Sandy would have been pleased to see her again.'

Perez watched Sandy turn pink. Even when you'd grown up mothers had the knack of embarrassing you. His own was just the same.

'Sophie's gone into Lerwick for the day.' Hattie's voice was bland but Perez thought he could hear a trace of disapproval. 'Paul's going south on the ferry tonight and he's offered her a lift into town.'

'He didn't mention earlier that he was leaving

Whalsay.' Perez didn't know why Berglund should, but it seemed a strange omission.

'We weren't expecting him to go yet either. He said something had turned up at home.' Now that she wasn't talking about her work Hattie had that closed-down look again and the shadows had come back.

'Perhaps we should try to catch him before he leaves,' Perez said. 'Thanks for the tea and the breakfast, Evelyn.' Sandy was already on his feet, anxious for an excuse to escape his mother.

Though the fog was still as dense as before, Perez was glad to be out of the croft kitchen too. As they walked to the car he could hear Evelyn urging more food into Hattie. 'Look at you, child. You're all skin and bone.'

The Pier House Hotel was a square stone building close to the ferry terminal. There was nobody behind the desk in reception and Perez wandered through to the bar, where a skinny middle-aged woman in a pink nylon overall was pushing a Hoover across the faded carpet. The room was panelled with brown, varnished wood and was shabby and depressing. In the evening, with a crowd in, a fire in the grate and artificial light, it might look welcoming. Now it was hard to imagine anyone wanting to spend time there.

Perez yelled at the woman but she had her back to him and she couldn't hear. He tapped her on the shoulder, could feel the sharpness of her bone through the sticky nylon. She switched off the machine.

'I'm looking for one of your guests. Paul Berglund.'

'Don't ask me, hen. I only do the cleaning. And

keep the show on the road.' An incomer from Glasgow. She grinned to show that she was happy enough with her role there. 'I'll fetch Cedric for you.' She disappeared into a back room and returned with an elderly man with a stoop.

'Is Paul Berglund here?' He couldn't work out why he felt it so important to speak to Berglund again before he left Shetland. Perhaps it was the way Hattie had looked when she talked about him.

The landlord was going to ask who Perez was, then he saw Sandy who'd wandered in from the car and realized he must be police. 'He checked out earlier. He's been back since to pick up his stuff. You've just missed him. That lassie from the dig was with him.'

Outside they could see the ferry was already moored at the pier, a dark shape in the mist. From here Perez couldn't tell if it was disembarking or being loaded with cars. He drove far too fast down to the jetty, but by the time they arrived the boat was sliding away towards the opposite shore.

'What do you want to do?' Sandy peered out into the mist.

'Nothing.' They'd be able to trace Berglund if they needed to speak to him. Besides, Perez was sure the death would go down as a terrible accident. Mima had been an old woman and there was nobody to make a fuss on her behalf. 'I'm going back to the office and I'll talk to the Fiscal. You'll go and get some sleep. Take a couple of days' compassionate leave. I'll see you back at work after the weekend.'

Suddenly Perez was eager to leave the island. He wasn't sure he could make sense of the place while he was still there. He'd been aware for so long of the Whalsay myths: its wealth, its friendliness and its traditions. Now, surrounded by fog, he knew it was quite different from anywhere else in Shetland, certainly from the bustling town of Lerwick and the self-contained remoteness of Fair Isle. But he couldn't define it. Perhaps it didn't matter. If Mima Wilson's death turned out to be an accident, what did it matter what Perez thought of the place where she'd spent her life? But Perez thought it *did* matter and that he needed to be away from Whalsay so he could think about it more clearly.

Chapter Eleven

Perez had offered Sandy a lift back to Lerwick. 'If you want to go back to town, that is. You're too tired to drive. You can come back to Whalsay and collect your car another time.' For a brief moment Sandy was tempted to leave Whalsay. Usually he did what Perez told him, not because he thought his boss was always right but because it was the easier course of action. And how good it would be to drive away and leave the mess surrounding his family behind. An afternoon's sleep followed by a few pints with the boys in The Lounge in Lerwick and he'd feel fine again. What good was he doing on Whalsay anyway? His mother would deal with all the practical details of arranging a funeral for Mima and he was in no position to provide the reassurance Ronald needed.

But he told Perez he'd stay for another night on the island. It was an instinctive feeling that it was the right thing to do. His father wouldn't have run away in this situation and ever since he was a boy, more than anything Sandy had wanted to be like his father. Now he saw Perez give a brief nod of approval too and that reinforced his sense that he'd made the right decision. He watched Perez drive into the ferry and waited until it had moved out of the harbour. He felt suddenly bereft.

His car was still on the jetty where he'd left it after driving down to meet his boss. He switched on the engine and the clock on the dashboard lit up. It wasn't midday yet. It always amazed Sandy how much Perez could pack into a small space of time. If you met him you'd think the inspector was kind of slow. It was his way of thinking before he spoke so you knew that when the words came out they were just the ones he'd intended. But Perez wasn't slow at all. There was a sort of magic in his asking the right questions the first time, picking up the clues in a situation, knowing when it was time to move on.

As he drove past the Pier House Hotel on his way back to Utra he saw that Ronald's car was parked outside. Sandy jammed on the brakes, felt the car slide on the greasy road then pulled in too. Getting pissed at lunchtime wasn't going to help the man. Sandy thought he might not have Perez's brains but he knew that much.

The woman in the pink overall had finished cleaning the bar but the place still had that smell of last night's beer mixed with furniture polish, the smell of bars everywhere before customers arrive and start drinking. Cedric Irvine stood polishing glasses. He'd owned the Pier House for all the time Sandy could remember. He'd served the boy his first under-age pint, winking as he slid it over to him. There'd never been a Mrs Irvine, just a series of live-in barmaids and housekeepers who, it was rumoured, satisfied all his needs. The skinny Glaswegian was the most recent. Nobody was ever quite sure what the relationship was between Cedric and these women. When one of the regulars got sufficiently drunk to ask, Cedric would only shake his head and say that gentlemen never spoke of these things. 'And neither will you if you hope to set foot in this establishment again.' That was how he spoke. Sandy thought there was something of the preacher about him.

Now Cedric looked up from his work and gave Sandy a smile of welcome that was more than professional. He nodded to the corner of the room, where Ronald sat in front of a pock-marked copper table. The man had finished his pint and was halfway through his whisky chaser.

'He needs a friend,' Cedric said. 'It's never a good thing drinking on your own. Not like that. Just drinking to get drunk.'

'He feels dreadful.'

'So he should. Mima was a good woman.'

'It could have happened to any of the boys.' Sandy had seen it before. The young men would get fired up on beer, then jump into cars and vans and roar across the island with their shotguns to try for rabbits or geese or anything else that took their fancy, as likely sometimes to hit each other as what they were aiming for. They were lucky there'd been no other accidents. On a number of occasions Sandy had been with them, whooping and cheering them on, behaving like a moron. It didn't only happen in Whalsay. Whenever men got together and drank too much they made fools of themselves. Never again, he thought. How would he feel if he'd been the one to kill Mima? But he knew that if he were with a gang of his friends he'd get dragged along on other foolish escapades. He'd never been able to stand up to them.

Cedric had pulled Sandy a pint of Bellhaven. Ronald

still hadn't noticed that his cousin had come in. The whisky glass was empty now and he was staring out of the window into space.

'Give me another pint for him,' Sandy said. 'Then I'll take him away for you, before anyone else comes in and there's a scene.'

He carried the pints across to the table. At last Ronald looked up. Sandy thought he'd never seen the man look so ill.

'I thought we'd already done the wetting of the baby's head.'

Ronald glared. 'Leave the baby out of this.'

'I take it Anna doesn't know you're here,' Sandy said. 'She'd kill you.' He regretted the words as soon as they were spoken, but Ronald didn't seem to have heard them.

'I can't see how it could have been me.' It came out as a cry. He'd changed into a shirt and a tie. Perhaps it was his way of paying respect, but it made Sandy see him as a different person. The sort of person Ronald might have become if he'd stayed on at the university for that last year and got his degree. Someone who worked in a museum or a library. When they'd talked about careers at primary school Ronald, to the astonishment of the rest of the class, had announced that he wanted to be an archivist. Where had that come from? Not from Jackie and Andrew.

Ronald continued: 'There were times when I was reckless with a gun, but not last night. Last night I knew where I was and what I was doing. But it must have been me. No one else was out there last night. Am I going mad, Sandy? Help me here. What can I do?'

'We can get you away from the Pier House for a

start,' Sandy said. 'It'll do no good for people to see you in here so soon after what happened. Finish your pint and I'll take you back.'

Ronald looked at the full glass, pushed it away from him so the beer slopped on to the table. 'You're right,' he said. 'I shouldn't be drinking at all. I'll give it up. It won't bring Mima back but I'll not do that to anyone else. I've got the bairn to think about now. And it'll make Anna happy. Maybe. You have it Sandy.'

But suddenly Sandy couldn't face the beer either. They walked out of the bar leaving the glasses untouched on the table.

They stood together at the cars. The mist was still so low that they couldn't see much beyond the harbour wall. The fishing boats with their huge winches and aerials turned into the silhouettes of sea monsters with spiny backs and serrated jaws.

'What's Anna up to?' Sandy asked.

'She's at home. The midwife was going to visit. I'd only be in the way.' Sandy was surprised by the bitterness in Ronald's voice and wondered what it must be like to live with a woman who made you feel that way. His mother was desperate for him to marry someone with brains and an education but that was the last thing Sandy wanted.

Ronald continued. 'I wish I could be at work myself. Usually I hate it, but just now it would be good to have a few weeks in the Atlantic after the white fish.'

Sandy couldn't understand that either – working at something you hated, even if the money was so good. He supposed there'd been pressure from Ronald's family for him to take his place in the boat. And how would they be able to afford that huge house without the money it brought in?

'You don't mean that, not with the baby just home.' Though Sandy thought babies brought out the worst in women. All the female relatives would be crowding into the bungalow, cooing and gurgling, sharing stories of labour and the cowardice of men. He could understand why Ronald had taken himself off on his own with a gun the night before.

'Will you be OK on your own?' Something about the way Ronald was talking made Sandy picture him holding a shotgun under his chin and blowing his head off. It couldn't happen that way, of course – Ronald's shotgun was in Perez's boot on the way to Lerwick – but in Shetland suicide wasn't hard to arrange if you wanted it badly enough. There were cliffs to jump from, water to drown in.

'Sure.'

'Do you want to come back to Utra for a meal? You could ask Anna to come too. Mother would be delighted to see the bairn.'

'And have Auntie Evelyn reliving what happened last night and enjoying every minute of it? No thanks.'

'We could take a drive up to the golf course. Just for a laugh. Catch up on the old times.'

For a moment Sandy thought Ronald was tempted, but the man shook his head and got into his car. He was probably close to the limit for driving, but this wasn't the time for a lecture. He followed his cousin as far as the turning to the Clouston bungalow and then continued on his way home.

In the yard outside his house he met his father on his way in for the midday meal. All the time Sandy was growing up Joseph Wilson had worked as a joiner for Duncan Hunter, a Shetland businessman. Joseph had put up with being treated like shite and ordered around as if he was an apprentice and not a craftsman, just for the sake of a pay packet at the end of the week. There'd been times when he had to stay out in Lerwick to get the work finished. The croft had been a kind of hobby, fitted in after the regular work was done. There'd been little time left over to spend with his sons.

A couple of years before, Joseph had given up working for Hunter and taken on the croft full-time. Sandy wasn't sure now how he managed for money – Evelyn had never worked – but that wasn't the sort of thing he could discuss with his parents. The new arrangement seemed to be working out fine. Evelyn liked the idea of having a husband who was his own boss and Joseph had always been happier as a farmer than a builder. Maybe they'd managed to save some money when Joseph was working for Hunter.

Recently Perez had taken up with Hunter's ex-wife and Sandy didn't know what to make of that. He teased Perez about having a woman in his life again and Fran seemed a fine woman, but in his opinion anyone who'd been involved with Hunter was trouble.

It was lambing time and Joseph had been up on the hill to check his ewes. Many of the islanders didn't bother so much. Mostly the hill ewes could manage on their own, and now there was no subsidy for headage it didn't even matter if they lost a few lambs. But Joseph was conscientious and this time of year he walked miles.

His father had heard the car on the track and waited

for him outside the house. 'Aye, aye.' This was Joseph's form of greeting to the whole world. Sandy thought if the Prime Minister arrived on his land he'd say the same thing. He stood at the kitchen door watching as Sandy crossed the yard. He was wearing a blue boiler suit splashed with creosote.

Sandy couldn't think what to say. He wished he had Perez's gift with words. Now phrases floated around in his head and all he could come up with was 'We'll miss her. I'm sorry.' He touched his father's shoulder, which was as close as they got to physical contact. He knew Joseph had adored Mima. Once Sandy had heard his mother say to his big brother Michael, exasperated because of something Mima had done, 'She's a poisonous old witch. I'm sure she's put a spell on your father.' And sometimes that was how it seemed. Joseph would drop everything to fix a slate on her roof or hoe her vegetable patch.

A brief moment of pain crossed his father's face, then he made an attempt at a smile. 'Aye well, maybe that's the way she would have chosen to go. She never minded a bit of drama. It would have been quick. She'd never have been able to stand illness, hospital.' He paused. 'I thought she had a good few years yet in her though.'

That was his father's way. Things he couldn't change he made the best of. He said there was no point in taking on the world. He'd never win. Besides, he had Evelyn to do that for him. All Joseph needed to keep him happy was football on the television and a few beers in the evening. He'd worked all over Shetland for Duncan Hunter. Now he'd be quite content if he never left Whalsay again. Evelyn had always been ambitious on his behalf, with her plans for the house, the croft and her sons. Sometimes Sandy thought she might be happier if she moved away, to Edinburgh maybe, to be close to Michael and his family, that Whalsay was just too small for her.

Inside the house she seemed content enough now. Perhaps like Mima she enjoyed a bit of drama, needed it to make her feel useful. She was sitting in the old chair, feeding the lamb from a bottle. Before she realized they were there, she was talking to it in nonsense language as if it was a baby. When she saw them she put it back in the box, ran her hands under the tap and stood at the Rayburn to stir a pan of soup. 'Reestit mutton,' she said. 'I had some in the freezer and I know you like it. I was thinking of Mima while I was heating it through. It was her favourite too.' Joseph went to wash at the sink. She came up behind him, turned him to face her and pecked his cheek. Sandy was still taking his shoes off. 'Are you ready for some lunch too, son? Has that nice inspector of yours gone?'

'He's away back to Lerwick to see the Fiscal. I'll take a small bowl of soup.'

'He thinks a lot of you, I can tell. I'm proud of both my boys.'

'Have you told Michael about Mother?' Joseph sat himself at the table, laid his hands flat on the oilskin cloth. The fingers were fat and red. Sandy remembered again the day they'd struggled to kill the pig, the noise that seemed to drill into his skull before the poleaxe silenced the animal, the blood.

'I rang him at home this morning but he'd already left for work. Some early meeting. I caught Amelia as she was on her way out and left a message with her for him to call me. He was on the phone a few minutes ago. She'd only just managed to get through to him.'

Or she couldn't be bothered trying. Sandy thought his sister-in-law was a stuck-up cow. Nice arse, but when it came to a wife he wanted more than that. He thought Michael could have done better for himself.

His mother was still talking. 'He wanted to know when the funeral was. I said we couldn't make plans until we know when your Inspector Perez will release the body. Michael will definitely come. He's not sure about Amelia and Olivia.'

Sandy knew fine well Amelia and the baby would stay in Edinburgh. She had her work for one thing, and that mattered more to her than the family. She'd brought Olivia to Whalsay once when she'd been just a couple of months old and she was still on maternity leave, and then there'd been nothing but complaints and anxieties. She'd gone home earlier than expected. 'Oh, I couldn't dream of missing baby massage. It's the best way there is to bond.' Sandy couldn't understand how his mother, usually so clever and on top of things, could be taken in by it all. But he made no comment. This wasn't the time for a row.

He watched his mother ladle out three bowls of soup and his father stand to cut the bread. Suddenly he couldn't bear the thought of Setter without his grandmother. He wasn't optimistic like his father. Despite what he'd said to Perez, he couldn't believe it was for the best.

His mother wouldn't stop talking. She got that way at times of stress. Now she was rattling on about Setter and pushing Joseph to make plans for the land and the house. Sandy wasn't really listening to her and he wasn't sure his father was either. He was eating the soup, lifting his spoon with mechanical regularity, chewing and swallowing as if his life depended on tipping the steaming liquid into his mouth.

'I've told the lasses from the Bod that they can carry on with their work once the police say it's OK. That's all right, isn't it, Josie?' No answer. None needed or expected. 'I wondered if the Amenity Trust might be interested in buying the house, in renting it at least. The boys won't want to live there.' Her voice continued, but Joseph's spoon was still. 'Michael won't leave Edinburgh now and Sandy has his flat in Lerwick. It would make a fine visitor centre once the excavation's finished.'

Now Sandy was listening too. He was about to protest when he caught his father's eye across the table. Joseph gave a brief shake of the head unnoticed by his wife. A look that said, *Don't worry, son. It'll never happen. Don't argue over it now. Just leave it to me.*

Chapter Twelve

After the midwife went, Anna Clouston sat in the window of the living room and looked out over the water. She carried James with her and sat with him lying lengthways along her knee. It was unusual for her to be alone with him and she felt that he was a stranger; she couldn't believe it was the same child she'd been carrying in her body for nine months. Perhaps that was because they'd had so little time on their own since they'd come back to Whalsay from the hospital. The house had been full of well-wishers, people bringing presents and cakes and casseroles. And then, this morning, the police had come.

Anna had struggled to adapt to living on Whalsay. It wasn't the isolation that was the problem; that she relished. She liked the drama of living on the island. It was the feeling that she had no privacy, that her life was no longer her own and she was crowded with people telling her how to run it. What was most difficult was finding that she'd become attached to a family so entirely different from her own.

Her parents had started a family in middle age. Anna's father was a junior civil servant, bookish, reserved and a little distant. She had the feeling he'd been bored at work and had felt undervalued. His work had been routine and he wasn't the sort of man to put himself forward for promotion. Her mother taught in a primary school. Anna and her sister had been brought up in a family where money was saved, thrift was encouraged and academic achievement was valued but not flaunted. Treats were only obtained after hard work. It was a suburban, respectable life of church-going, music lessons and weekly visits to the library. Nobody put their elbows on the table at mealtimes. Restraint was taken for granted.

Of course at university she'd met people from different backgrounds but she'd come out at the end with her view of the family intact – represented by the smell of the Sunday meal as her mother lifted it out of the oven, the sight of her father dead-heading roses in a late-summer garden, her sister dressing the Christmas tree with the faded baubles brought out each year. Anna had imagined that she'd replicate it in her turn, with a few minor changes: certainly she'd be more assertive than her mother – you wouldn't catch her cooking a roast dinner every Sunday – and she'd marry someone a bit more exciting than her father. But the basic pattern would be the same. What other was there?

Then she'd met the Whalsay Cloustons and realized there was quite a different model of family life. Their house was always full of noise, the radio playing, Ronald's mother Jackie talking and the gossip of cousins, aunts and neighbours who regularly dropped in. Restraint didn't feature. If Jackie decided she needed a new outfit, kitchen or car, she had it. There was no question of saving up first. Once Anna had asked where the family money had come from in the first place. *Cassandra* was only a few years old and she had been bought from the proceeds of the old trawler. 'But before that?' Anna had asked. 'How did your father get his first boat?'

'Hard work,' Ronald had said. 'It was hard work and the willingness to take a chance.'

Anna could imagine Andrew would have been a risk taker when he was young. She'd seen photos of him, big and strong, his head thrown back in laughter. Then he'd become ill and Jackie had wanted her son to give up college and take his father's share on the boat. She'd got her own way there too. Anna had thought that Ronald was different, thoughtful, less spoiled. Now it seemed he was just the same as the rest of them, determined to have his own way, whatever the consequences. Thought of his selfishness made her angry again. She could feel the tension in the back of her neck and her arms. How could they maintain their life on the island after this?

James stirred on her knee and stretched his hands towards her, fingers opening like the petals of a flower. His eyes were still shut, the skin around them wrinkled. *How will you grow up here?* she thought. *Will you be spoiled too?* And she thought that he would drain the life out of her, just as she felt Ronald was doing.

She felt very tired. They'd been invited to a meal at Jackie's house. 'You won't feel like cooking,' Jackie had said. 'Besides, we haven't celebrated the baby properly. You must come here.'

It hadn't occurred to her that Anna and Ronald might like some time on their own, so soon after the birth of their child. Jackie had a knack of transferring her own desires into the wishes of other people: she loved entertaining, so they would be grateful to be entertained. Ronald hadn't seen any problem with the plan. He found it impossible to deny his mother anything. 'We don't have to stay long,' he'd said when the invitation had been made and Anna had been less than enthusiastic. 'And it'll be great to have a proper meal, won't it?'

The baby whimpered and Anna undid her shirt and put him to her breast. She'd expected feeding to be difficult; she'd never been a particularly physical person. But she had lots of milk and the baby guzzled so greedily that the thin white liquid dribbled from the side of his mouth and ran down her skin. Sometimes she felt that he sucked her dry. She looked at the clock and wondered where Ronald was. He'd put on his smart clothes and gone out before lunchtime. She'd assumed he'd gone to pay his respects to Mima's family, wondered what sort of mood he'd be in when he got home.

The phone rang. She reached out to answer it, hoping it would be Ronald telling her he was on his way home. A quiet afternoon had relaxed her. Perhaps it might be possible to put things right between them. But it was Jackie sounding excited, eager.

'I was checking on the time you'd be able to make it up to the house this evening.' Jackie always called it 'the house,' as if it was the only dwelling in Lindby.

Anna, cradling the baby with one arm, felt an ache of disappointment. She wasn't sure she could keep up the pretence of happy families. She'd hoped Mima's death might mean the cancellation of the meal. The rituals and proprieties surrounding death were taken seriously on Whalsay. 'Whenever's best for you,' she said. 'We're looking forward to it.' And perhaps it would be better to have company tonight. Otherwise she and Ronald would spend all evening going over the incident of the night before and she might say something unwise, something she'd really regret.

She replaced the phone and heard Ronald open the door into the house.

'We're in here,' she said.

Outside, the light seemed to have faded early and she only saw him as a shadow standing just inside the room.

'Look at you two,' he said. He was still wearing his jacket, but he'd loosened his tie at the neck. She hardly recognized him in the smart clothes. He was speaking to himself and his accent was more pronounced than when he talked to her.

How can we get on? she thought. *We don't even share the same language. We come from different worlds. I don't know him at all.*

'Have you been to see the Wilsons?' she asked.

'No. I bumped into Sandy, but I wouldn't know what to say to Joseph.'

'You look so smart,' she said. 'All dressed up like that.'

He paused, then shrugged. 'A gesture of respect, maybe. It didn't seem right to be wearing my working clothes today.'

He came further into the room and squatted beside her chair. He stroked her hair and watched while she prised the baby's mouth from her nipple with her little finger. She lifted James on to her shoulder and rubbed his back, then held him out to her husband.

'He probably needs changing,' she said.

'We can do that, can't we, son? We can manage that.' He was murmuring into the baby's hair.

'Jackie's just phoned to sort things out for tonight.'

'Are you all right with that?' He looked at her over the baby's head. 'We can always cancel if you can't face it.'

'It'll probably do me good to get out.' She smiled at him tentatively. 'I'm sorry I've given you such a hard time. It was the shock. I haven't been much support.'

He shook his head. 'No. I deserved it all. I've been a fool.'

Oh yes, she thought, *you've certainly been that*. But she knew better than to speak out loud.

Later they wrapped the baby in a blanket and carried him up the hill to the big house in his Moses basket. It was the first time Anna had been out that day and she enjoyed the feel of the drizzle on her face. As soon as they walked through the door she realized there would be the new lamb of the season to eat. The smell of it reminded her again of her parents' home, the calm lunches after church, her father drinking sherry and reading the Sunday papers. Then they were engulfed by Jackie's hospitality; she hugged them both and would have had James out to play too, if they hadn't said they hoped he would sleep.

Through an open door Anna saw that the table had been set in the dining room to show this was a special occasion; there were candles already lit and the napkins had been elaborately folded. After Mima's accident it seemed tasteless, as if they were celebrating her demise. Usually they ate in the kitchen, even if a crowd of guests had been invited. Andrew had been dressed in a shirt and dark trousers and Jackie wore a little black frock, rather stylish and simpler than her usual taste. Anna felt lumpy and under-dressed. She hadn't bothered changing and there was probably baby sick on the back of her top. She wondered if Jackie's understated wardrobe was a gesture towards acknowledging Mima's death.

Apparently not, because she seemed in determinedly party mood.

'We'll have champagne, shall we?' she cried. 'I've got a couple of bottles chilling.' She led them through to the kitchen and there on the table were bottles of very expensive champagne sitting in an ice bucket. Anna wondered if she'd bought in the bucket especially for the occasion – Jackie had taken to internet shopping with gusto. But probably not. Champagne was routinely drunk in the Clouston household for every birthday and anniversary. Jackie put her arm round her son. 'Come on now, Ronald, open a bottle for me.'

Anna thought Ronald was going to object. She saw him tense within Jackie's embrace, then wriggle free from her. But in the end the habit of fulfilling Jackie's expectations was too strong for him to refuse. Entering into the spirit of the occasion, he wrapped the bottle in a white napkin to stop it slipping in his hand, twisted the top and gave his mother a brief grin, more like a grimace, when it made a louder pop than he was expecting. But he wouldn't accept a glass when she was pouring it out.

'You'll have a beer, then? Your father never liked this stuff. All the more for you and me, Anna, eh?'

'I'm not drinking,' Ronald said. 'Not after what happened last night.'

Jackie was going to push the matter, but stopped herself just in time. Anna saw the effort that took. The older woman turned away and took a can of Coke from the fridge, handed it to her son.

'Let's not talk about that,' Jackie said. 'Not tonight. This is supposed to be a party.' She poured herself another glass of champagne and led them into the dining room.

They didn't talk about Mima again until they started the pudding, and then it was Jackie who raised the subject. Anna had found herself enjoying the meal. The wine had relaxed her. She must even have become a little drunk, because she realized she was laughing too loudly at a joke Jackie had made. That would never do. She put her hand over her glass when Ronald next offered the bottle to her. *Perhaps everything will work out*, she thought. *Perhaps I can make it work*. Jackie too had been drinking heavily throughout. Her face was flushed with the cooking and the responsibility of encouraging them to enjoy themselves.

'She won't be missed, you know.'

'What do you mean?' Ronald was poised with a spoon in one hand.

Jackie looked up at him. 'Mima Wilson. She could be a dreadful old gossip. And it was an accident. You mustn't blame yourself.'

'Don't say that.' Ronald's voice was steady.

There was a pause while Jackie composed herself. 'No, you're right. We mustn't speak ill of the dead.' She flashed a look across the table to Anna. *We'll humour the boy. He's upset.*

Since the stroke Andrew had spoken with difficulty. Sometimes it took him a long time to work out the words in his head and then to get his tongue round them. Occasionally a whole sentence came out at once, surprising his audience and himself. That happened now.

'She was a good-looking woman,' he said. 'When she was younger.' Then seeing them all staring at him, he added: 'Jemima Wilson. I'm talking about Jemima Wilson.' He retreated into a shocked silence.

'Oh aye, she was bonny,' Jackie said bitterly. 'And didn't she know it. When she was middle-aged she was flirting with men half her age.'

Anna wondered if Andrew had been one of Mima's younger men. There was an awkward silence.

'I always liked her,' Ronald said quietly. 'When we were bairns she told great stories.'

'Oh, the bairns liked her right enough. They were round her place like bees at a honeypot.' Jackie seemed about to continue but stopped short.

There was a moment of silence. Perhaps they were all replaying their memories of Mima.

Andrew coughed, then came out with another of his surprise sentences. 'A man died because of Jemima Wilson.' He looked around the table to make sure they were listening. It seemed to Anna that he was desperate they should believe him. 'A man died because of her.'

Satisfied that he had their attention, he added; 'Well, now she's gone to join that husband of hers. They were two of a kind. A match made in heaven.' A pause and a strange choking laugh. 'Or in hell.'

Chapter Thirteen

As he drove carefully off the ferry at Laxo, Perez had a momentary stab of shame. He shouldn't be so delighted to have escaped Whalsay and Sandy's family and the upset that always follows unexpected death. Grief he could deal with. What he found more difficult to handle were the selfish reactions, inevitable but distasteful, that came in its aftermath. The first was greed, because even if the deceased person weren't wealthy there would usually be something to squabble over. Then came guilt, because greed seems inappropriate after the death of a loved one and because relationships, especially between family members, aren't perfect. At least one of Mima's survivors would have thought at some time, *I wish you were dead*. Not really meaning it perhaps, but thinking it all the same. Now the thought would have come back to haunt them.

He drove south down Shetland mainland towards Lerwick with the radio on. Fran said his concern for the people he met through work was a sort of arrogance. 'I love the fact you care about them, but you're not a priest after all. Let people take responsibility for their own pain. Why do you think you can help them when their own friends can't?' Now he tried to take her advice, to forget Sandy's grey, exhausted face and the tension in Evelyn's back as she bent over the stove. Instead he sang along, very loudly, to the Proclaimers. The mist lifted a little as he approached the town and there were streaks of pale sunlight reflected from the dock as he drove past the ferry terminal.

He decided he would go home for lunch. He felt a need to talk to Fran and Cassie and he couldn't do that from the office with its noise and interruptions. He lived in a narrow, old house built right on the waterfront, so you could see the high-water mark on its outside wall. By now the mist had cleared sufficiently for the island of Bressay to be visible. It was the warmest day of the spring so far and he opened the living-room window to let in the sound of the gulls and the tide, the salt-laden air.

He was missing Fran more than he thought he would. He hadn't told her, of course. She would despise it and think it was a sign of his easy emotion. Whenever he phoned she was full of the people she'd met, the shows she'd seen, the galleries she'd visited. Sometimes he worried that she wouldn't want to come back. It occurred to him now that the Whalsay women he'd met had that in common with Fran. Sandy's cousin and father were content with life on the islands, but Evelyn and Anna looked at the world outside and wanted more. It seemed to him that in their demands for change they might spoil the place they claimed to love.

He'd bought a second-hand filter-coffee machine at one of last summer's Sunday teas. He folded the filter paper and spooned in the coffee, waited for the delicious smell as the coffee dripped through. Fran envied his ability to drink strong black coffee all day and still sleep at night. He realized she was in his head whatever else he was doing, a backdrop to all his other thoughts.

He dialled the number of her parents' house, but there was no answer and he replaced the receiver when the answering service clicked in. He didn't like the idea of them picking up his message and listening to his stumbled words in an accent that must be all but unintelligible to them.

It had become an obsession that he should ask Fran to marry him. The idea had come to him as a fleeting whimsy the summer before, but now it had returned and wouldn't let him go. If he suggested that they live together he knew she would agree at once. They'd known each other for more than a year and he spent as much time in her house at Ravenswick as he did in his own place. She'd said recently, making a joke of it but obviously wanting to test his reaction, 'If we sold both homes we'd be able to buy somewhere with a bit more space.' He'd been non-committal and he knew she'd been disappointed but too proud to let on.

He had no moral objection to their living together and he couldn't care less what people – even his parents – thought, but still he was haunted by the idea of marriage. It was to do with permanence and stability; he knew that Fran wanted another child and he was terrified of being the cause of a fragmented family. There was a less noble motivation too. Fran had married Duncan, hadn't she? If she refused Perez, wouldn't that mean she loved him less than Hunter, with his affairs and his wild parties? Perez was tortured by the possibility of rejection, but couldn't let the idea go.

He poured another mug of coffee then called Fran's

mobile. He wanted to talk to her and was willing to put up with a background noise of laughter and traffic. She answered almost immediately.

'Jimmy? How lovely to hear you.'

'Is it convenient?' Why did he always sound so formal when he spoke to her on the phone? He might have been talking to one of his colleagues.

'Brilliant timing. We've come to an exhibition at the Natural History Museum. Mum and Dad have taken Cassie off to look at dinosaurs and I've sneaked off to grab a decent cup of coffee.' He could imagine her face lit up with enthusiasm, wondered what she was wearing. He'd like to picture that too. Would she think it weird if he asked her?

'I'm at home,' he said. 'I've sneaked off for a quick coffee too. And I wanted to talk to you in peace.'

'I wish I was there.'

Come home then. Get on the first flight from Heathrow to Aberdeen and I'll book you on to the last Loganair. You could be back this evening.

Because that was racing through his mind and he was thinking about the practicalities of the plan – he supposed she would need to pack her bags, so after all there wouldn't be time – he realized suddenly that there was a silence between them. She was waiting for a reply. 'You don't know,' he said, 'how much I miss you.'

In his head the haunting, ludicrous chant. *Marry me. Marry me. Marry me.* She would despise him and think him sentimental all over again.

'Oh well,' she said. 'It won't be long. Less than a week now.'

'I was worried that you might be enjoying yourself

so much in the city that you wouldn't want to come home.'

'Oh God no, Jimmy. Never think that. I can't wait to get home.'

Then his stomach tipped like it did in a storm on the *Good Shepherd* and he felt sixteen again and in love for the first time. But that had to be enough for him, because Cassie and her grandparents arrived and Cassie demanded to speak to him, to tell him everything she'd learned about Tyrannosaurus Rex.

In the office the talk was all about the death of Sandy's grandmother and speculation about how the accident might have happened.

'I was at school with Ronald Clouston,' one said. 'He was always sort of absent-minded, but you'd have thought he'd be more careful around guns. He never was one of the really wild boys.'

'According to Sandy he liked a drink.'

Perez listened to the conversation and wondered how long it would be before people forgot that Ronald Clouston had shot Mima Wilson on a foggy night in Whalsay. The rumours would follow the man round for years, wherever he went; even if no criminal charge were brought the story would stay with him until he died.

To avoid getting drawn into the gossip, he picked up the phone and set up a meeting with the Procurator Fiscal. Before going over to her office he jotted down some notes on a scrap of paper. He still wasn't sure what angle she would take. He didn't want to make light of the accident, of Ronald's folly in going out with a gun in the fog after having taken a few drinks. But he hoped he'd be able to persuade her it was reckless, not criminal.

He found it hard to explain the role of the Fiscal to English colleagues. Even Fran couldn't grasp it: 'But what does she do?' Perez always said she was a cross between a magistrate and a prosecuting lawyer, but Fran didn't even get that. All she understood was that the Fiscal was his boss.

Rhona Laing, the new fiscal, was a cool fiftysomething with a cutting tongue and a designer wardrobe, which seemed completely out of place in Shetland. Rumour had it that she flew south to Edinburgh every month to visit her hairdresser. Perez never believed Shetland stories, but he could almost believe the blonde hair was natural and the way it was cut took ten years off her age. Her passion was sailing. She'd come to Shetland on a yacht from Orkney and fallen in love with the islands. In an unguarded moment at the opening of the new museum, she'd told him that from the sea Shetland looked like paradise. He'd wanted to ask what she thought it seemed like from the land, but by then she'd been swept away to meet more distinguished guests. She lived alone in an old schoolhouse near the marina in Aith, and managed to keep her past and her present entirely private. All that anyone knew about her was that she owned a catamaran, the biggest and most expensive sailing vessel in the islands.

Perez didn't know quite what to make of her. She was efficient and organized, but rather ruthless, he always thought. There were rumours in the islands that she had political ambitions. She would like to be a Member of the Scottish Parliament. Certainly, he thought, she would like the power.

She got up from her desk when he came into the room and they sat in easy chairs across a small table. A moment later her assistant brought in coffee.

'You're here about Jemima Wilson.' She poured the coffee, turned her flawless face to him.

'It looks like one of those unfortunate accidents. A man out for rabbits with a torch after dark. He couldn't have known the elderly woman would be wandering round outside. We still don't know why she was there.'

'Lamping for rabbits is illegal,' she said.

'Aye, but everyone does it, and we've never yet taken anyone to court.'

There was a moment of silence. He could hear the tapping of a computer keyboard in an outer office. A phone rang.

'When I first moved here I was asked to give a talk to a group in Bressay,' she said. 'I asked the organizer what people would think of having a Fiscal who was a Lowland Scot and a woman. He paused for a while and then he said, "Folk won't consider you to be the enemy." Another pause. "No," he said. "Rabbits are the enemy."' She looked up and smiled. 'He was only half joking.'

'So you won't be popular if you prosecute.'

'For lamping, no. A death is a different matter. There is the question of recklessness.' She was wearing a cream trouser suit. Now she crossed her legs at the ankles and he saw the slim flat shoes that matched in colour exactly. 'To be reckless, Mr Clouston must have considered it a possibility that Mrs Wilson would be outside her house that late at night.'

'Mima was known for keeping indoors after dark,' Perez said.

'In that case I don't see that we have a crime here.' She looked up at him and smiled. 'What do you think, inspector?'

'I certainly don't see Clouston as a criminal.'

'But?' She gave a frown, not of impatience exactly, more of surprise. She had thought her decision on the matter to his satisfaction as much as hers.

'He claims not to have been shooting over Mima Wilson's land.' Perez wished she hadn't picked up on his hesitation, the slight emphasis on the man's name. After all he'd got what he'd come for.

'A natural response, surely. He must have been devastated to discover what he'd done. In similar circumstances we'd all want to avoid the guilt, to persuade ourselves we weren't responsible.'

'Perhaps.'

She looked at him. It was hard to imagine this immaculate woman managing her boat single-handed in a force-eight gale, though he was aware of the strength of character that allowed her to enjoy the experience. 'Tell me what's troubling you, Jimmy. Off the record.'

'I wish I knew what Mima Wilson was doing outside in that weather. And I'd be happier if Ronald Clouston admitted to shooting over her land.'

'What are you saying, Jimmy? That someone else killed the woman?' Somewhere in her voice he picked up a hint of sarcasm, almost of derision, but there was no sign of that in her face.

'Clouston says he was out on his own last night. He's not trying to lay the blame elsewhere.'

'So if someone else did kill Jemima Wilson, it wasn't an accident. Is that what you're saying, Jimmy? You can't seriously expect me to open a murder investigation just on the slight possibility that Clouston didn't fire close to the house. You know how much that would cost the taxpayer.'

Now that the words were spoken Perez realized that the possibility of a conspiracy had been at the back of his mind since he'd first seen the scene of the shooting. He'd dismissed it as ridiculous, melodramatic. 'I can't see why anyone would want to kill her,' he said. 'She's Sandy Wilson's grandmother. She's lived in Whalsay all her life. A bit of a character by all accounts, but not a natural victim. I only have reservations because I don't understand how the accident happened.'

The Fiscal paused, sipped her coffee. 'We are sure that it was Clouston's gun that killed her?'

'With a shotgun it's impossible to tell. It's not like a rifle, where each weapon leaves an individual trace on the bullet. We'll track down the ammunition used, but my guess is that everyone on Whalsay will use the same when they're out after rabbits.'

She leaned back in her chair. Despite the expensive make-up he saw the fine lines on her forehead, the wrinkles at the corners of her eyes.

'I don't have enough here to put it down as anything other than accidental death,' she said at last. 'Anything else would cause unnecessary distress to the deceased woman's family and the sort of hysteria in the community that doesn't help anyone. I couldn't justify it.'

He nodded. There was no other decision she could have taken.

'We're agreed that we won't charge Clouston? It wouldn't be popular in the community.'

'Oh yes,' he said. 'We're agreed about that.'

'As for your reservations about the details of the shooting, I understand them. Perhaps the best course of action would be a discreet inquiry. Nothing formal at this stage. We'd have a post-mortem anyway in a death of this kind. Let's see what you turn up in the next week or so. Keep me informed.' A clever decision, he thought. She was covering her back. If Mima's death did turn out to be murder, she would be able to show that she hadn't dismissed the idea out of hand.

He nodded again. She hadn't been in Shetland long enough to understand that discretion in a matter like this was almost impossible. There was no privacy. Nothing went unnoticed. She'd set him on a course of action that he'd be unable to fulfil to her satisfaction. And he'd lacked the courage to tell her.

At the door he paused, remembering another detail.

'A skull was found on Setter land a couple of weeks ago. Val Turner reported it to Sandy. He did tell you?'

She raised her eyebrows. 'Do you think that's relevant?'

'I don't know.'

'It's old,' he said. 'Just a fragment of skull. Part of an archaeological dig. A coincidence.'

Chapter Fourteen

Sandy woke from a deep sleep. He heard the sheep outside and smelled baking and immediately realized that he wasn't in the cramped and messy flat in Lerwick, but at home at Utra croft in Lindby. His mother baked most days, even when she and Joseph were alone in the house. Having Sandy there gave her an excuse. He lay for a moment looking around the familiar room. His mother had tidied it after he'd left, taken his posters off the walls, removed the dartboard, put up fresh wallpaper and different curtains. He'd remembered to get rid of the stash of pornography, hidden under the bed since he was a teenager, before he'd allowed her into the place, smiled despite himself at the memory of his smuggling the pile of magazines out of the house in a couple of Somerfield carrier bags. How pathetic was that! She always made him feel like a fourteen-year-old. Now the room was clean and anonymous and even the smell was different. Evelyn had decided that this was where the baby would sleep whenever Amelia and Michael came to stay from Edinburgh. It wasn't his space any more. He looked at his bedside clock. Eight o'clock.

If he had a day off in Lerwick he'd be straight back to sleep, but in Whalsay it was different. His mother was here, with her expectations and her judgement and her baking. You'd think he was still a peerie boy the way he cared what she thought of him. He wondered if he'd ever escape her.

He stretched and stumbled towards the bathroom, but already his mother had heard him.

'Sandy! The kettle's just boiled. Will I make you some tea?' She'd never got it into her head that he preferred coffee in the morning.

'Not yet. I'm going in the shower.' His voice was more aggressive than it needed to be. Their relationship was made up of these tiny stands for independence; he was certain she never noticed them and that made the exchanges even more frustrating. Standing under the new power shower, he wondered about his father's relationship with Mima. Had he felt the same resentment when Mima called on him to kill her hens when they stopped laying? Sandy thought it hadn't been the same at all. Joseph had loved Mima and delighted in her company. They had laughed at the same jokes. Sandy was sure Joseph told Mima things he'd never have confided to his wife. Sandy had spent his life finding ways of not talking to his mother about anything important.

In the kitchen he felt the same mix of irritation and affection. Evelyn was standing at the table rolling out pastry, the sleeves of her sweatshirt rolled to her elbows. She'd be making a fruit pie because she knew it was his favourite. She had so much energy. Maybe she felt trapped here on the island. Maybe she'd sacrificed all her own ambitions to be here, bringing up her two boys, keeping the family together while Joseph was working for Duncan Hunter. It couldn't have been easy for her struggling over the finances, watching Jackie Clouston and the other fishing wives with so much money that they didn't know how to spend it, knowing that if she'd been born into a different family, or married into one, she'd have been wealthy too. He knew there were times when she brooded about it.

'There's tea made,' she said. Then with a frown, remembering, 'Or would you prefer coffee? I can easily do that. The kettle's not long boiled.'

'Tea's fine.'

He poured the tea and helped himself to a bowl of cereal, found a clear corner of the table.

'Would you be able to phone that nice Inspector Perez today, sort out when we can fix a day for the funeral?'

So Michael can arrange to get up here, he thought. *So she can show her fine eldest son off to the whole island, with his fancy suit and his hand-made shoes.* And it occurred to him then that his relationship with his mother was troubled because she cared so much more for Michael than she did for him. *I'm jealous,* he thought, astounded. *That's what all this is about. How could I have been so dumb that I didn't realize?*

'Perez might come to Whalsay,' he said. 'It depends what the Fiscal said.'

'You mean he could be here to arrest Ronald?'

Sandy shrugged. She didn't have to sound so pleased at the prospect. *But she's jealous too,* he thought. *Jealous of Jackie and the flash house on the hill and the new BMW every year and the trips to Bergen on the boat. After Andrew's illness you'd have thought she'd have realized there was nothing to be jealous about, but she just couldn't help herself. She doesn't really want Ronald prosecuted, she only wants Jackie's nose put out of joint.*

'Where's Dad?'

'He's gone over to Setter. That cow still needs milking and the hens and the cat need feeding.'

'I'll wander over. See if he needs a hand.'

He thought she was going to say something to stop him. Perhaps she wished the two of them got on as well as Sandy did with his father. But she stopped herself. 'Why not?' she said. 'The rain's stopped and the mist has lifted. It's a fine day for a walk.'

By the time he reached Setter, his father had finished with the animals. Sandy found him standing in the kitchen. He waited in the doorway and looked in. His father looked lost in thought and it seemed like an intrusion to blunder in, but he felt kind of foolish just waiting outside. At last Joseph saw him.

'It's hard to think of this place without her,' the older man said. 'I keep thinking she'll come up behind me, full of mischief and gossip.'

'How did she keep track of everything that was happening in the island?' Sandy had wondered about this before. His grandmother knew about his friends' escapades and love affairs before he did. No wonder Evelyn had talked about her as a witch. 'She didn't go out so much towards the end.'

'She made it to the Lindby shop every couple of days,' Joseph said. 'People were always coming to visit her. Cedric called in every Thursday to chat, but it wasn't only her own generation who liked her company. Besides, she could smell a scandal like other folk smell rotten eggs.' He looked around the room, seemed to be scoring the details on to his memory. The postcard from Michael and Amelia's last foreign holiday propped on the dresser, the religious sampler which perhaps she'd stitched as a child, that seemed out of place in any room where Mima had lived, the enormous television, the dirty glasses by the sink. The photograph of Joseph's father that had been taken during the war, looking young in his Norwegian jersey. They both knew Evelyn wouldn't rest until everything had been dusted and scrubbed and tidied away.

'Do you still think of this house as your home?' As soon as he'd spoken Sandy thought that was a daft sort of question. Joseph had lived in Utra since he'd married. Utra had been in Evelyn's family and had been a tumbledown wreck when they'd moved in. Joseph had made a home almost from nothing.

But his father considered before speaking and then it wasn't a direct answer. 'It wasn't easy growing up here,' he said. 'My father died while I was still a baby and Mima was never the sort of island wife to have a meal on the table when I got in from school and clean clothes for me to put on each morning. I learned to look after myself pretty quickly. But it was a happy time. She was full of stories. She said it was us against the world.' He laughed. 'She always did have a dramatic turn of phrase. I grew up with tales of my father, about how well off we'd have been if only he'd lived. "He promised me the earth. Fine clothes and a fine house." She loved telling stories; it was a mix of real island characters, make-believe and myth. I could have listened to her for hours, though sometimes I'd have preferred to do it with a full belly.'

For the first time Sandy could see what had attracted his father to Evelyn. She'd make sure there was dinner ready for him when he got in from work and the house was always clean, the clothes washed and ironed.

'Why do you think she went out that night?'

'Why did Mother do anything?' Joseph laughed. 'I'd known her all my life and she was still a mystery to me.'

Sandy thought that was too easy and was just about to push it, when there was a tap on the open door. He saw the two lasses from the dig standing outside. Sophie was wearing a shirt that was open at the neck and one size too tight around the chest. She had on shorts with walking boots and thick socks; that should have made her look like a geek, but her legs were long and brown and shapely. He tried not to stare. He didn't want to get attracted to a girl with a brain. It was Hattie who spoke.

'We wondered if it'd be all right to get on with our work. The police don't mind, but we'll understand if you'd prefer it if we left it for a while. I mean I suppose you might rather we stopped the project all together.'

Sandy could tell that was the last thing she wanted. He'd chatted to her a couple of times in the Pier House Hotel, when he was there visiting the boys. She was always on the edge of the crowd and her work was all she could talk about, all he could imagine her being passionate about. He remembered her leaning over the table towards Ronald Clouston, giving him a lecture about Iron Age tools. Sandy thought it was good to have the lasses in Lindby. They brought a bit of life to the place. 'What do you think, Dad?'

His father frowned.

Sandy wasn't sure if he'd even heard the question. 'Dad?'

'I don't know,' his father said. 'Things are different now. We don't know what'll happen to the croft.'

Sandy wondered then if Joseph dreamed of selling Utra and moving back here, to the house where he'd been so happy as a child. He couldn't see his mother going along with that! It would mean leaving behind her new kitchen and bathroom and starting all over from scratch.

'But they can carry on with their work?' he said. 'At least until you decide? You know how Mima liked having them around the place.'

His father hesitated again and Sandy thought he would refuse. But at last he smiled. 'Of course,' he said. 'Of course. Why don't you show us what you've been doing out there?'

Perhaps Joseph just didn't like having the strangers standing in his mother's kitchen. Certainly outside he seemed more friendly and helpful to the young women. It was Sandy who found it weird to walk right past the spot where he'd found Mima lying in the rain. The memory of her stick-thin body distracted him and he missed most of the conversation. When he tuned in again Hattie was describing what they were doing.

'It's just a couple of exploratory trenches. At this stage there won't be any more disruption than this. If we find anything really interesting we'd apply for funding to extend the dig, but of course we'd need your permission to do that. Mima had already given it in principle. The initial results have been fascinating.

And Evelyn thinks it would be a great boost for the island.'

She looked at Joseph anxiously. Sandy could tell she was hoping for reassuring words from him. *Of course you must go ahead with your dig. Mima's death won't change anything. I can see how important it is.*

But the man frowned again as he had in the kitchen.

'Is this where you found the skull?'

'Yes, in this practice trench here. Outside the wall of the main house. It's gone off to a lab in Glasgow for dating. I hope we can date it at fifteenth-century. That would fit in with my theory about the place. Of course it could be older. We know there's been a settlement in Lindby since the Iron Age. But it was quite near the surface so we don't think it's that old.'

'Could it be younger?'

'I suppose so, but it seems unlikely. There's no record of a more modern building here.'

Joseph was quiet for a moment.

'I think it's too early to be making any decision about the future of the dig just yet. There's no rush, is there? We can talk about all that later.'

Sandy wondered why his father, usually so easy-going, especially if a pretty lass was around, should be so discouraging about this. There were no crops in that part of the croft and it wasn't needed for grazing. What would it matter if a dozen people came to make holes all over it? Joseph was sociable, he loved a party, a few new folk to chat to. Again he wondered if the man had his own plans for Setter and what they might be.

Sandy's phone rang. It was Perez calling from his

mobile. Sandy walked away from the group so he could talk without being overheard.

'I'm at Laxo,' Perez said. 'I've just missed a ferry. I wondered if it was worth bringing my car or if you'd be able to meet me in Symbister.'

'I'll meet you.' Sandy felt his mood lift. He had an excuse to run away from the family for a while, even if it was just to the end of the island. It was only as he was driving down towards the pier that he thought Perez's arrival on the island might be a bad sign and that he could be here to arrest Ronald Clouston.

Chapter Fifteen

Hattie's feelings were spiralling out of control. She loved being in the islands but whenever she imagined Mima lying in the rain, shot by Ronald Clouston, she started to cry and she couldn't stop. Her imagination was a curse.

Perhaps she was ill again. Depression had first appeared when she was at school, but then it had been insidious, almost gentle, so for some time the people around her hadn't recognized what had been going on. When her mother had finally bullied her into seeing her GP, he'd prescribed medication, talked about stress, said it was unlikely to happen again. But at university there'd been a major breakdown and there'd been a couple of short episodes since.

It usually started with an obsession, an inability to let go of one thought or idea. At eighteen it had all been about her schoolwork, the individual project that was submitted as part of the history course. She'd been relatively relaxed about the other subjects. She'd wallowed rather in T. S. Eliot's 'The Waste Land', but her English teacher had told her anxious mother that many adolescents did that. No, it was her work on a nineteenth-century almshouse close to her home that had taken over her life and her dreams. She'd stumbled on to the original records by chance through a friend of her mother's, and from reading the first page of neat and tiny writing she'd been hooked.

The idea of the essay had been to set the records in their social context, to explore the conditions that had allowed the formation of the houses and how their establishment fitted in with the political debate of the time. But it was the individual stories that had captivated her. She had felt herself living under the humourless regime of the almshouse trustees, saw the world through the residents' eyes. Before she became ill enough to need a doctor she had the sense to change her university application from history to archaeology. It was the specific and the human that fascinated her, not the political or strategic. What could be more grounded than digging in the earth?

Somehow she completed her examinations and submitted her dissertation. It was when school broke up for the summer and the familiar routine of revision and writing was over that she lost any sense of perspective. Then she heard the old women in the almshouse talking to her and couldn't let them go.

The depression had come back big style at the end of Hattie's first year at university. She stopped eating and her mother wheeled her off to see a specialist. But then it had been Paul Berglund rather than her academic work that had triggered the illness. At school she'd had no time for men or sex, watched the antics of her friends as if *they* were the mad ones with their dressing up and flirting, the parties and the desperation. Falling for a man seemed just as ridiculous to her as getting excited about food. Then in her first long vacation she'd volunteered on a dig managed by Professor Berglund. It had been a hot summer, day after day of clear skies and sunshine. They'd camped out in a barn quite similar to the Whalsay Bod. The team was full of oddballs and eccentrics and Hattie had felt wonderfully at home. Here, she was no weirder than the rest of them. In the evening they went to the pub and drank pints of beer and rolled home singing.

The site had been surrounded by fields of ripening corn and her first view of Paul had been of him striding down the side of a field towards them. He'd been wearing a yellow T-shirt, slightly ripped at the neck. Because of the angle of the field she hadn't been able to see his legs. He was a bull-necked, blunt northerner quite different from anyone she'd ever met before. None of her mother's friends were so forthright or so rude. So *this* is what all the girls at school were going on about, she'd thought. Paul Berglund had become her obsession. Later, when she returned to London she lost her mind completely. She found herself unable to sleep. The events of the summer continued to haunt her. Images flashed into her head with the jagged brilliance of a drug-induced trip. Again she couldn't bring herself to eat.

She'd been admitted to an enlightened NHS psychiatric hospital that ran a residential unit for teenagers. She supposed her mother had pulled strings to get her in. By that time she was hardly aware of what was happening. The stated cause of admission was the eating disorder, which had become the focus of her mother's concern. An eating disorder was fashionable, almost commonplace among the children of the high-powered women with whom Gwen James worked. But quite simply, Hattie thought she'd been mad. She developed paranoia, heard voices again, this time loud, controlling, battering into her brain. She couldn't trust anyone.

The unit had twenty-four beds and had an old-fashioned emphasis on talking and shared activity. They took pills too, of course, but the other treatments seemed just as important. The place was run by a nurse called Mark who was a little overweight, with a soft doughy face and thinning hair. Perhaps his unappealing appearance was part of his strategy. He was so sympathetic that if he'd been at all good-looking all the young women would have fallen in love with him. As it was they could treat him as a favourite uncle or adored older brother. Hattie had regarded the unit as her sanctuary. She still considered some of the other patients as her friends. She had few others.

Mark had taught her strategies for avoiding stress and for taking control. He told her she wasn't to blame for what had happened, but that she found harder to accept. He encouraged her to put her thoughts into words. When she first left home for university she'd developed the habit of writing a weekly letter to her mother. A letter was less demanding than a phone call, but it still kept Gwen off her back. Now, in the unit, she continued the practice. There was nothing of any importance in the letters – certainly she didn't confide in Gwen as she had in Mark – but she enjoyed passing on the details of life in the hospital. Her mother replied with chatty notes about the House, anecdotes about the neighbours in the Islington street where Hattie had grown up. Letters seemed their most effective means of communication. In their letters they could persuade themselves that they liked each other. Stranded in the unit, Hattie looked forward to receiving them.

She was discharged from hospital in the middle of the autumn and came home to prepare for her return to university. Her tutor was understanding – she was so bright, he said that she'd have no problems catching up with the academic work. On the last day of October her mother drove her back to the hall of residence and left her there, Hattie thought, with some relief. Now Gwen could return to her real passion, politics. She convinced herself that the stay in hospital had cured Hattie for ever. The illness would never come back.

Now Hattie knew she had developed another obsession. She'd returned to Whalsay full of hope and dreams. Then Mima had died and everything had become more complicated. Perhaps she *was* ill again, though she didn't recognize this as depression. She was suffering from the same symptoms as before – the difficulty in sleeping, a reluctance to eat, the inability to trust her own judgement – but it didn't feel at all the same.

It had been very different when she'd first arrived back in Whalsay. Then the summer had spread ahead of her, full of possibilities.

Mima had realized how happy she was. Two nights before she'd been shot, she'd called Hattie into the house. She'd poured glasses of whisky, put them on a tray with the bottle and a little jug of water. It had been unusually mild and they'd sat outside on the bench made of driftwood that stood by the kitchen door, the tray on the ground between them.

'Now what has happened to you over the winter? You look like the cat that got the cream.'

'Nothing's happened. I'm just pleased to be back in the island. You know how much I like it here. It's the only place I feel quite sane. It's the best place in the whole world.'

'Maybe it is.' Mima had gathered her cat on to her lap and given a little laugh. 'But what would I know? I've never lived anywhere else. But maybe it would be good to see a bit of the world before I die. Perhaps you'll dig up a hoard of treasure in my land and I'll be able to travel like the young ones do.'

Then she'd looked at Hattie with her bright black eyes, quite serious. 'And it's not so perfect here, you ken. Bad things happen here the same as everywhere else. Terrible things have happened here.'

Hattie had taken another drink of the whisky, which she thought tasted of peat fires. 'I can't believe that. What are you talking about?'

She'd expected gossip. Mima was a great gossip. She thought there'd be a list of the usual island sins – adultery, greed and the foolishness of bored young men. But Mima hadn't answered directly at all. Instead she'd gone on to talk about her own youth. 'I got married straight after the war,' she said. 'I was far too young. But my man worked with the men of the Shetland Bus and we got used to seeing them taking risks. You'll have heard about the Shetland Bus?'

Hattie shook her head. She was dazed now by the whisky, the low spring sun in her eyes.

'It was after the Germans had invaded Norway. Small fishing boats were used to carry agents in and bring folk out. They called that the Bus. It was run from the big house in Lunna. There were a few Whalsay men who helped and they got close to the Norwegian sailors. I'm never sure exactly what happened. Jerry never liked to speak about it and he wasn't quite the same afterwards . . .' She stared into the distance. 'We were all crazy then.'

Hattie had thought Mima was going to explain, but she had wrapped her arms around the cat, poured herself another dram and laughed. 'Certainly more mad than dee!'

'I hope it didn't upset you too much to see the skull in the practice trench.' Hattie had remembered Mima's white face, the way she'd fled into the house. 'It's not that unusual, you know. Old bones turning up at a dig. I suppose we're used to it and we're not squeamish any more.'

'I'm not squeamish!' Mima's voice had been almost brutal. 'It was a shock, that was all.' Hattie hoped she was going to explain further, but the old woman pushed the cat from her lap and stood up. It was clear Mima was ready for her to go: 'You'll have to excuse me. There's a phone call I must make.' And Mima had stomped into the house without saying goodbye. Hattie had heard her voice through the open door. It sounded angry and loud.

Now Mima was dead and Hattie would never find out what had so disturbed her. Setter felt quite different without Mima there. Even from outside it was different. Before, they'd have heard the radio, Mima singing along or shouting at it if she disagreed with one of the speakers. Sophie saw Sandy through the window as they were walking past and it was her idea to go in.

'Come on,' Sophie said in her loud, confident, public-schoolgirl voice. 'We'd better go in and tell him we're here. Besides, he might have the kettle on.' They hadn't seen Joseph at that point and could hardly turn round and go out again when they realized Mima's son was there.

Then Hattie had brought up the matter of the dig. So eager to please, so apologetic, the words had tumbled out. And Joseph had frowned and refused to give any sort of commitment about the future of the project. At least that was how it had seemed to her. She thought she might be banished from Shetland and never allowed back. *Why didn't I keep my mouth shut?* she thought. *Why didn't we just sneak past the house and go on with our work?*

After Sandy's phone had rung he and his father left Setter. Hattie watched them go and it was only as she felt her pulse steady at their departure that she realized how anxious the men had made her. She was kneeling in the main trench, carefully easing her trowel around what could have been the base of a stone doorpost. The soil was a slightly different colour here and she wanted to dig in context. Sophie had gone to turn on the outside tap so the water would run into the flot tank. She was planning to wash the soil from the second trench, allowing the soil to float off and the more dense fragments to sink and be collected in the net beneath. Sophie called over from the tank: 'Did you get the impression that Mima's son doesn't want us here?'

Hattie was surprised. She'd got exactly the same impression but had wondered if she was being paranoid again.

'Yes,' she said. 'Yes, I did.'

Sophie stretched her arms above her head to ease the tension out of her muscles. 'I don't think we have to worry about him throwing us off the croft. Evelyn's all in favour of the project and none of the men in that family stands up to her.'

Hattie looked up at her and considered. 'Do you think so? Joseph seems very easy to manage, but if there was something he really wanted I'm sure he'd get his own way in the end.'

Sophie gave one of her wide, easy, slightly predatory smiles. 'All the men on this island are easy to manage. Don't you think so?'

Hattie didn't know what to say to that. She disapproved of Sophie's relationships with the island men. Sophie continued: 'I mean what they really want is a bit of fun. The women here take themselves so seriously.'

Hattie thought some of the Whalsay men must want more than fun, but she didn't answer. As she looked back into the trench the pale sun caught something softly metallic.

Hattie leaned forward on the kneeler. She could smell the soil, felt it damp through her sweater where she must have propped herself on her elbow. She trowelled back the soil around the object. Sometimes it felt that the trowel was an extension of her arm, more sensitive even than her fingers. She could be as delicate as she would be with a brush. Sophie must have sensed her excitement because she jumped across the trench so she could get a better view without blocking the light. Hattie could tell the other woman was holding her breath and realized she was too. Now Hattie did take a brush and cleaned the object that stood in relief proud of the soil.

'What do you think?'

'A coin.' Sophie looked down with a huge grin. For a moment the tension between them evaporated.

'Similar to the ones they found at Dunrossness?' It had been in Hattie's mind from the moment she'd seen it. At a dig in the south of Shetland mainland, a dwelling had been validated by the discovery of a store of medieval coins.

'Absolutely.' Sophie grinned again. 'I'd say you've found your merchant's house. And I think the boss will be in on the next plane.'

And now, Hattie thought with relief, *I'll be able to stay in the islands for ever.*

Chapter Sixteen

Perez walked off the ferry to Whalsay after the cars had driven down the metal ramp. This should be a pleasant task – he'd be telling Ronald Clouston that no charge would be brought against him – yet he felt a gloom settling on him as he walked past the two huge fishing boats moored at the pier. A strange sort of claustrophobia. Though he'd grown up in Fair Isle and that was smaller than Whalsay, here he felt trapped, as if it was hard to breathe. Perhaps that was because from Fair Isle there were low horizons in every direction; even on a very clear day the Shetland mainland was no more than a smudge to the north. From Whalsay the Shetland mainland seemed a close and oppressive presence. The low cloud just made it worse.

A couple of men stood outside the fish factory, smoking and chatting. Perez didn't recognize the language. Something eastern European, Polish or Czech. He was distracted for a moment, wondering what they made of Whalsay and if the island's famous friendliness extended to them. He thought it probably would. Sailors were the most open-minded people he knew; they travelled the world and came into contact with strangers all the time. It was the people left behind who distrusted incomers.

Sandy was waiting in his car. He seemed anxious, jumpy, and Perez realized he'd read his boss's arrival as a bad sign. He assumed that Perez was there to arrest Ronald, that he'd be involved in taking his cousin into custody.

'The Fiscal doesn't think there's enough to charge Ronald. She'll take no further action.' Perez settled himself in the passenger seat and waited for a response.

It took a moment for Sandy to take in the information, then there was a huge smile. No words. He couldn't find anything to describe how he felt. Perez waited for him to drive off, but he seemed incapable of smiling and driving at the same time.

'Well? Shall we go and tell him?' Perez said.

Sandy switched on the engine. 'He's not at home. He's at his mother's house. I saw him go in as I came down the road to get you.'

'We'll go there then, shall we?' Perez found himself interested to meet Jackie Clouston, Evelyn's rival. He couldn't help his curiosity. Fran laughed at him, told him he was like the old woman in Ravenswick who sat by the window watching the cars go past, who knew all her neighbours' business. Perez dressed up his nosiness and his fascination with gossip as work, Fran said, but really he was just a voyeur. She was right, of course, but he had been charged by the Fiscal to make discreet enquiries into Mima Wilson's shooting. Now he had a licence to be inquisitive.

The house had been built in the last ten years and stood on its own land on a slight hill away from Ronald and Anna's bungalow. If *she* were the curious sort, Jackie would see everything that went on there from the windows at the front of her home. The building was two storeys high with a porch held up by moulded pillars and a roof of green tiles. In Shetland terms it was enormous and would have been more in place in a suburb of Houston or a gated estate in the south of England. Perez wondered briefly how it had managed to get planning permission and which architect had actually designed something so tasteless.

'They knocked down the old house and built on the same site,' Sandy said. 'Ronald and Anna lived here too while they were waiting for their place to be finished.'

'There'd be plenty of room.'

'Aye. It's a grand place for a party.'

It seemed a poor excuse to put up such a monstrosity.

Jackie had seen them coming and had the door open before they had the chance to ring the bell. She was small, wiry and energetic, with dyed blonde hair so tightly curled that it might have been a wig. Perez guessed she was older than Evelyn. She wore a white T-shirt in Lycra with diamante letters on the front. Perez didn't want to stare at her chest to read it and by the end of the visit was still not sure what it said. Her jeans had more diamante on the pockets. Her sandals were gold. In the house the central heating was full on and even with the door open the heat was overwhelming. Perez was still dressed for the ferry and began to sweat.

Jackie seemed to know exactly who he was and why he was there. 'Ronald's in the kitchen,' she said. 'The baby's finally gone to sleep, so Anna thought she'd do some work and he decided to keep out of her way.' She paused briefly for breath. 'Whoever would have thought you could make a business out of teaching people to knit and to spin? It's always seemed an old-fashioned kind of pastime to me and it's so easy, with the internet, to buy clothes in. But Anna says it's a big business in America. In my day it was enough for us to look after the house and bring up the bairns, but now all the women want work of their own. It doesn't seem right so soon after the baby was born.' She paused again. He wondered if she was remembering the time when Andrew was skipper of a trawler and Ronald was a boy.

'Thanks,' he said. He didn't want to encourage the flow of words. He understood that Jackie was nervous on behalf of her son, but her tension was having an effect on him. He suddenly felt an irrational panic, as if the woman's stress was contagious.

The kitchen was the size of his house, with chunky units built of orange pine, a six-hob range cooker and a huge stainless-steel fridge. Jackie pointed out the main features of the room with pride. 'We've just had it done.' Her speech was rapid, clipped. It reminded him of the regular metronomic click of knitting needles. 'The old one was looking kind of tired.'

Ronald sat at the table reading a newspaper. Not the *Shetland Times,* one of the more intelligent nationals. When he saw them come in he got to his feet. He appeared to Perez like one of the rabbits he dazzled and then shot, terrified but unable to move. Next to him was an older man.

'This is Andrew,' Jackie said. 'My husband.'

The man waved a hand at them. He was a giant, tall and big-boned, with frizzy grey hair and a full grey beard. Perez could tell Andrew Clouston wasn't well, but wasn't sure how he knew. Something about the stiffness of the gesture, the brief moment of panic in the eyes at seeing a stranger in the house. The fact that he was wearing slippers and a cardigan rather than working clothes during the day. Jackie stroked his shoulder. 'There's nothing to worry about. He just wants to speak to Ronald.'

'Perhaps Ronald and I could talk on our own.' Perez thought the house was sufficiently large to allow half a dozen confidential interviews. It wasn't that he felt the need for privacy, but he wanted to escape the woman's words for a while.

'You can use the office,' Jackie said. Ronald seemed to have lost the power of speech.

The office was on the ground floor just off the lobby. There was a desk with a PC, printer and scanner. Perez shut the door behind him and leaned against it. He nodded to Ronald to take the chair.

'The Fiscal's decided not to proceed with the matter,' he said at once. 'You won't be charged.'

Ronald stared at him, speechless.

'She couldn't get a conviction to any criminal charge at this point.' Perez went on. 'It'll go down as an unfortunate accident.'

'But I killed a woman.'

'You couldn't have known she would be outside. You had every reason to think she'd be in her house, not wandering about on her land. That means you weren't criminally reckless.'

'I feel as if I should be charged with something,' Ronald said. 'Not murder – I honestly didn't know she was there – but it doesn't feel right to kill someone and for nothing to happen.'

'It's the law.'

'I must go home and tell Anna,' Ronald said. 'She'll be so relieved. I don't think either of us has slept since it happened, and that's nothing to do with the baby. She was worried about it affecting her business. She wants us to be more independent here. My parents are brilliant – I'm the only child and they'd give me everything I wanted. But she doesn't like that. She says we should stand on our own feet. And besides, she says the fishing's precarious. We still make a good living from it, but maybe she's right and it won't go on for ever.'

Perez wondered if Ronald had any opinions of his own. He might be a bright man but he seemed incapable of independent thought. 'Do you enjoy the work?'

There was a second's pause. 'I hate it. I'd be glad if the seas were all fished out and there'd be no reason to leave harbour.'

'You have a choice,' Perez said mildly. 'You were at university. You could have finished your degree.'

'My father had a stroke. It's a family business. There was nobody else.'

'Your family could have found someone.'

'That wouldn't be the same. Besides . . .'

Perez said nothing, waited for him to find the words to continue.

'Besides, the money's addictive. I'm not sure how I'd take to being poor. I earn more in a month than some of my old schoolfriends do in a year. I grew up living comfortably and I want that for my children.' His mood suddenly lightened. 'So I'll have to hope that Anna's business becomes a roaring success, won't I?

Then she can support the family and I can go back and take my degree.'

'I'm still not quite sure how the accident happened,' Perez said. 'Now you've had some time to think about it, perhaps it'll be clearer in your mind.'

'No,' he said. 'I've been running it over and over again in my head to work out what must have happened and I still don't understand it.' His relief at finding out that he wouldn't be charged had already evaporated. He seemed pleased for Anna, but still haunted by what he'd done.

'All the same, I would like you to take me through it again.'

'Is there any point now?' Ronald looked up at him. 'Mima's dead. I killed her. I accept that.'

'I still have to make a report, tie up the loose ends.'

'I went out to shoot rabbits. I'd had a row with Anna so I wasn't in the best of moods. It was dark and murky. I shot a couple from the car then went out with the flashlight into the field. I didn't think I was anywhere near Mima's place, but I was thinking about Anna and what I should have said to her. About how I shouldn't have been so scratchy. She was still tired after giving birth. Moody. Hormonal. It wasn't easy for her. I never thought giving birth would be . . .' he paused to search for the right word, '. . . as violent as that. You know how it is when you've had an argument, you rerun everything in your mind.'

Perez reflected that he and Fran didn't argue much. He'd never liked rows, didn't see the point of them. Sometimes that frustrated her. 'Don't just agree with me! Stand your ground and fight!' But usually he did agree with her. He could see her point of view and was happy to concede that she was right.

'You're sure you didn't see anyone else out?'

'No one else was shooting.' Ronald looked out of the window. Following his gaze, Perez had a view of the bungalow where he and Anna lived. Anna came outside and hung a basket of washing on the line, just as Mima had done the day before she was shot.

'But there were people about?' Perez persisted. He could understand why Ronald just wanted the nightmare of Mima's death to be over but he couldn't let it go. And it wasn't something Ronald would wake up from.

'A car went down the road while I was shooting over the field.'

'You have no idea who it belonged to?'

'It was dark, man, and I had other things on my mind.' The tension was starting to tell again. 'I saw headlights and heard an engine. Nothing more.'

'Which direction was it going?'

'I don't know! Does it really matter?'

'Was it coming from the Pier House, or away from Lindby?'

'Not from the Pier House. The other way.'

So, Perez thought, *not drinkers on their way home from the bar.*

'Who else shoots regularly in Whalsay?' he asked. He tried to keep his voice relaxed and easy.

'Most of the men do. We're all trying to keep down the rabbits. What is this about?'

'It's the sort of thing I need to say in my report. Better me asking the questions than a lawyer in the court.'

'I'm sorry.' Ronald looked straight at Perez again. 'I know you're only doing your job. I should be grateful. Ask whatever you like.'

'Nah, I've done for today. Go and tell Anna the news.'

Ronald grinned. 'Thanks, I will. I'm going out tonight, fishing with one of my friends. Not on the big boat, but one of the inshore ones. I wouldn't have wanted to leave her alone with this hanging over us. At least now she'll be able to focus on the baby and her work. She's setting up a website for her business. And she still has knitting orders to complete.'

Perez thought that sounded like a phrase Anna would use. *I need to focus on my work.*

Ronald stood up and left the office. He didn't wait for Perez to follow, but ran straight out of the front door of the house. Then he began to bound down the hill to the bungalow, like a boy running just for the pleasure of it.

'Ronald, is that you?' Jackie emerged from the kitchen, saw Perez alone in the office and frowned. 'What have you done with Ronald?'

'I've done nothing with him. The Fiscal has decided not to press charges. He's gone to celebrate with his wife.' It wasn't his place to tell the woman, but she'd find out soon enough. He was surprised Ronald hadn't called in to tell her. Even more surprised that Sandy had managed to keep his mouth shut.

She stood very still. Suddenly Perez realized that the gaudy clothes, the silly hairdo, the talking had been her way of fending off the possibility of her son's disgrace, to keep up appearances in front of her husband. It would have hurt her just as much as Anna to see

Ronald in court, his picture in the *Shetland Times* in a suit and tie waiting for the case to be heard. 'Thank God,' she said, her voice so low that he could hardly make out the words. Then, quietly triumphant, 'This will stop the talk on the island. Evelyn Wilson will have to watch what she says about us now. There'll be no more spreading of stories and lies.'

Sandy had walked into the hall to see what was going on. He heard the words and blushed.

Chapter Seventeen

They went for lunch at the Pier House Hotel. Fish and chips served in the bar, blessedly free of smoke since the ban. Perez had been surprised at how law-abiding Shetlanders had been when the smoking ban came in. Especially on the outer islands where there was little danger of being caught by the police. On the smaller isles few people even bothered with MoTs or vehicle licences. He remembered as a boy the police flying in to Fair Isle after a birdwatcher had fallen to his death from the cliff. As the plane came in to land all the cars on the place were driven into barns or hidden by tarpaulin. By contrast this law was generally observed.

'Will my grandmother's body be released for the funeral now?' Sandy was halfway through his second pint. His resolution to give up strong drink hadn't lasted long. Perez had ordered coffee and was surprised at how good it was.

'Aye, I don't see why not.'

'Only my mother wants to start making the arrangements. My brother will need to come up from the south. He doesn't like dragging himself up here but he can hardly get out of visiting at a time like this.'

'Do the two of you not get on?'

Sandy shrugged. 'I was always closer to Ronald when

we were bairns. Michael was my mother's favourite. Maybe I was jealous.'

Perez wasn't sure what response to make to this. Sandy didn't usually show so much insight.

'It *is* all over?' Sandy went on. 'I mean the case.'

Again Perez thought Sandy was being uncharacteristically perceptive. 'The Fiscal doesn't see any case to answer.'

'It's just you were a long time with Ronald this morning. I mean, it doesn't take half an hour to tell a man he won't be prosecuted.'

'I want to be sure in my own mind that it was an accident,' Perez said.

'You're saying Ronald meant to shoot her?' The words had come out as an outraged shriek. Sandy looked around him and was relieved to see that the bar was empty. Even Jean from Glasgow had disappeared into the kitchen.

'I'm saying there are problems with his version of events.'

'He's not a liar,' Sandy said. 'Never has been.'

'Have you seen much of him since you left home?'

'Not so much. It's not like when you're at school, is it? We each have our own lives to lead. But he wouldn't have shot Mima. Not on purpose. She was as much a grandmother to him as she was to me.'

Perez hesitated, reluctant to put into words the idea that had taken root in his mind and had been growing since the conversation with the Fiscal. He looked around to check that the bar was still empty and kept his voice low: 'Someone else could have shot Mima. Put the blame on Ronald.'

'That's what Rhona Laing thinks?' Sandy seemed astonished.

'She's not prepared to dismiss the idea out of hand. It's one explanation for the facts, for Mima being outside on a night like that, for Ronald's certainty that he wasn't shooting over the Setter land. But she doesn't want any sort of fuss made.'

'In case she upsets her friends in high places.' Everyone in Shetland knew about Rhona Laing's political ambitions.

'Aye. Something like that.' Perez paused. 'You said Mima asked you to call in the next time you were in Whalsay. Did she give you any idea what she wanted to discuss?'

'No.' Sandy looked up at him. 'You think she realized she was in danger?'

'I'm just considering possibilities.'

'What will you do about it?'

For a moment Perez thought. What in fact could he do? He could only afford a limited time in Whalsay and from his office in Lerwick he had no chance of getting any sort of sense of what was going on here. It might only be a short ferry ride from Shetland mainland but this was an enclosed community and it took an insider to understand what was going on.

'Do you have any leave to take?' Perez knew Sandy always had leave. He was famous for it. He managed to carve out time for himself from his official working day and always complained at the end of his leave year that he still had holiday to take.

'Aye, a few days.' Sandy was suspicious. They'd had arguments about this before. Perez on the warpath. 'If you've been out on the piss and wake up with such a hangover that you can't face work, take it as holiday. Don't invent imaginary dental appointments.'

'Maybe now would be a good time to use them up. Stay here. Help your mother sort out the funeral. Ask a few questions . . .' Perez looked at Sandy, just checking that he understood what Perez was asking.

'But I'm involved,' Sandy said. 'They're all family. You said yourself I should have got out as soon as the investigation started.'

'This isn't an investigation,' Perez said. 'You're making informal enquiries. Mima was your grandmother. It's hardly surprising that you're interested in how she died. But be discreet. The Fiscal was absolutely clear about that.'

'The Fiscal asked me to follow this up?' Sandy stared back. The Fiscal had never been particularly complimentary about his abilities as a detective.

Perez was saved the necessity of lying, because they were interrupted by the arrival of two young women. He recognized one as the archaeologist who'd turned up, distressed, at the Wilson house. The other was taller, stronger, with long corn-coloured hair, a wide mouth, freckles. She was talking, almost dragging Hattie behind her into the bar.

'Come on. A find like that, we can take a bit of time off to celebrate.'

'After what happened to Mima, I don't feel much like celebrating.' Hattie seemed even thinner. 'Anyway we should keep this quiet. We don't want treasure hunters turning up at the site hoping to make their fortune.'

'This is Shetland. Do you really think you're going to keep this a secret? And Mima would have been *so* excited. It was always what she wanted, wasn't it? For us to find something really spectacular on her land. Besides, we have to eat, don't we? I feel as if I've been living off sandwiches for months. You can't work a dig on an empty stomach.'

'I thought Paul bought you a meal in Lerwick yesterday.'

'Only a bowl of soup in the museum coffee bar before his meeting with Val at the Amenity Trust. I fancy a huge steak. So rare it's almost breathing.' Sophie saw Sandy, waved at him, grinned. 'And a mountain of chips.' She pulled her sweater over her head. Her T-shirt rode up at the back, revealing a firm brown torso. The legend on the shirt read: *Archaeologists Do It In Holes*. 'Hi, Sandy. Is it OK if we come and sit with you?'

Sandy had been staring at Sophie with a stunned fascination, now he looked at Perez.

'Why not?' Perez said. The curiosity was kicking in again, though he found Hattie more interesting than her friend. 'Can I get you both a drink?'

'Oh please.' Sophie gave a shiver of anticipation. Perez thought he'd never met anyone quite so physical. Like a small child she communicated her thoughts through her body. 'A large red wine.' Then, sensing her friend's disapproval, 'Don't look at me like that, Hat. It's not as if we can get much done this afternoon. Really we need to wait for guidance from Paul and he won't be here until tomorrow. And you must feel like celebrating. It's what you've been dreaming of since the project started.'

'What's happened?' Perez thought he'd have to continue the conversation. No good leaving it to Sandy, who was still staring, his mouth half open. Sophie was wearing a sleeveless vest with a scoop neck showing a lot of cleavage. Soon he'd be drooling.

'Go on, Hat, you tell him. It's your find.'

'Let me get you a drink first.' Perez stood up.

He thought Hattie would refuse. He sensed a real tension between her and her colleague. He couldn't understand why Hattie had come. But at last she gave a quick smile. 'All right then. Beer. A half. Sophie's right: we are celebrating and Mima *would* have been excited.' She sat on the bench seat and unlaced her boots, slipped them off so she was sitting in her stockinged feet. She pulled her feet underneath her and looked, Perez thought, like a trow, one of the mythical small men he'd heard stories about since he was a child.

When he returned with the drinks and Sophie had ordered food, Perez repeated his question. 'So, what's happened?'

Hattie took a deep breath. 'I can hardly believe it. We've been hoping that the dwelling on Mima's land would turn out to be something grander than a croft and maybe we've found the proof. Look, let me put it in context . . .' She leaned forward. 'In the fifteenth century Shetland was a strong member of the Hanseatic League, a trading partnership, but there was a problem. The merchants in the islands were mostly German incomers. As the trading policy became more isolationist, the Germans left and there was nobody to take on that role. My thesis is that some of the more important Shetlanders became traders in their own right. There's evidence that happened in Shetland mainland, but nothing so far here in Whalsay.'

She paused and looked at Perez to check that he was following. He nodded. Her voice was very precise, almost as if she was presenting to an academic audience. Perhaps she didn't know how to speak to anyone else.

'The remains of the building at Setter are bigger than you'd expect for a croft, but there could be reasons for that. Perhaps there were extensive outbuildings, a workshop. The foundation stone we've found is even, dressed, it's not the rough boulders you'd expect to make up the wall of a croft, but that hasn't provided the proof I was looking for. Today though we made a find that would suggest the inhabitants were much wealthier than they'd have been as crofters. This is a big deal. For me at least. I mean it kind of proves my theory. It makes the whole project worthwhile.' She gave a sudden wide smile that lit up her whole face. 'It means I can get funding to extend the project. We should be able to do a full-scale dig over a number of years.'

'So what did you find?' Sandy managed to drag his attention from Sophie's body.

'Silver coins. Half a dozen of them. Beautiful and quite intact. I came across one by chance and the others soon after. It's likely that the floor would have been made of wood, rather than beaten soil, though of course there's no trace of that now. We can't tell how the coins got left there. Maybe they slipped through the cracks in the floor and into the hole in the foundation. Maybe they were hidden there. We might find more.' Hattie took another breath. 'Two silver coins of the same age were found during a dig at Wilsness, Dunrossness, in Shetland mainland. In the dunes close to the airport. Those coins confirmed the interpretation of that building as a merchant's house. I'm hoping that this find will do the same for me.'

'Where are the coins now?'

'We've taken them to Evelyn. She's locked them up in a drawer in her desk. Val Turner, the Shetland archaeologist, will come in later and Paul Berglund will be in too.'

The little Glaswegian came out with food for Hattie and Sophie. Perez watched Sophie slice her steak with complete focus. He thought she was like a man. She didn't like to concentrate on more than one thing at a time. But now she'd started Hattie was happy to continue talking. 'We'll get an expert to look at them of course. I mean they could be more modern, but they look like right to me and Sophie thought so too as soon as she saw them. We're both familiar with the Wilsness coins. But we do need Paul's advice about what we should do next.' She stopped abruptly and forked a tiny piece of lasagne into her mouth, frowned as she chewed.

'When's Mr Berglund coming in?'

'Professor Bergland,' Hattie corrected him. 'Tomorrow or perhaps the next day. He'd hardly got home when he got our call. He needs a bit of time to sort things out at home. He's got a young family.' Perez thought she seemed subdued. Did she resent her supervisor coming in and taking over her project? Or the fact that he hadn't left immediately to return to Whalsay?

'Are these coins worth anything?' Sandy asked.

'They're invaluable.'

'But if I was to try and sell them on the open market?'

'You mean money?' Hattie seemed startled by the question.

'Aye, money.' Sandy looked at her as if he was tempted to add, *What else would I mean?*

'I don't know. If they were sold at auction to a collector perhaps they would.'

She seemed uncertain; the whole concept of private collection and trading in artefacts was strange to her. Perez felt a rush of sympathy. She seemed too frail and innocent to be living alone here in Whalsay. Sophie the Sloane Ranger was no sort of guardian. How would Hattie survive in the big world outside? He wanted to ask if she kept in touch with her parents. He imagined a protective mother who'd had to find the courage to let her daughter go, but who had sleepless nights about her, who held her breath every time the phone went in case there'd been a disaster. Because somewhere in Hattie's history there must be illness or tragedy, he thought. No one got that haunted look if they'd had a happy childhood.

Curiosity led him to form a question about her family in his head. *Your parents must be very proud of you. Will they get a chance to visit the islands?*

Then he heard Fran's voice, had a very clear picture of her tipping her head to one side, a half-smile, her nose slightly wrinkled as it was when she meant to tease. *What business is it of yours, Jimmy Perez? You're a policeman, not a psychotherapist. Let the poor child alone.*

So he said nothing. There was a moment of awkward silence at the table. Sophie picked up a piece of creamy fat which remained on her plate and bit into it with sharp white teeth. She looked around her.

'Now,' she said, 'which of you lovely men would like to buy me another glass of wine? I thought this was supposed to be a party.'

Chapter Eighteen

Outside the Pier House, Hattie and Sophie stood briefly before separating. Hattie had only drunk two halves but felt disengaged and a little woozy. She wasn't used to eating a big meal at lunchtime.

'The boys have promised me a look round one of the big ships,' Sophie said. 'I'd like to see what it's like inside and they might not ask again. Don't suppose you want to come?'

'Who's going to be there?'

'Oh, you know, the usual *Artemis* crew.'

Hattie shook her head. The way she was feeling a boat would make her sick, even if it were moored at the harbour. Anyway, she never knew what to say to most of the fishermen with their unintelligible voices and their stories of adventures at sea. Besides, she had other plans.

'They said I could go out with them sometime,' Sophie said, looking out towards the Shetland mainland. 'There's a spare cabin I could use. It's got a DVD, everything. Do you think they'd take me for a spin today? The sea's flat calm.'

She turned back to Hattie, a challenge as well as a question in her look.

'You should be careful,' Hattie said. 'You'll get a reputation.'

Sophie laughed, her head thrown back, so Hattie could see her long neck, stretched even further, much paler than her face.

'Do you think I care about that? It's not as if I want to make my life here.'

'Shouldn't you be here when Paul gets in?' Hattie was thrown by the thought that she might have to deal with Paul on her own. She felt a return of the old panic.

'Oh, I wouldn't really want to go.' Sophie grinned, so Hattie realized the woman had just been winding her up. 'But don't expect me back until the morning!'

She grinned again and loped away quite steadily, though she'd had twice as much to drink as Hattie. There was a rip in her jeans and the flesh of her thigh showed through. It reminded Hattie of the fat on the steak Sophie had just eaten. Hattie watched her walking away down towards the harbour. There were times when she hated Sophie for her beauty, her easy way with men, her thoughtlessness. There were times when Hattie wanted to lash out and slap her.

It seemed to Hattie that the walk down the island had a hallucinatory quality. Phrases and ideas came into her mind with no logic or reason.

April is the cruellest month.

Living in the south of England, that had never made sense to her in a literal way. Spring was a time of gentle rain and imperceptible growth. Now she thought of the last ewes lambing untended on the hill with the ravens circling above, Mima lying on the sodden ground at Setter. She repeated the phrase under her breath to the beat of her footsteps.

She wasn't used to drinking in the middle of the day. Perhaps that was it. She hadn't slept the previous night, consumed by a recurring paranoia that the shot that had killed Mima might really have been meant for her. The implication of that was so shocking that now she couldn't bring herself to consider it in any detail and she allowed her thoughts to float away from her.

Instead she tried to relive the moment of finding the silver coins in the Setter dig, from glimpsing the first glint of metal. The scene was so close to what she'd dreamed of that she found it hard to believe in the reality of it. Still walking, keeping the rhythm of her feet on the road and the words of T. S. Eliot at the back of her mind, she took her hands out of her pockets and looked at them. Under the fingernails she saw the soil in which the coins had been buried. In that one moment, the instant of rubbing the earth from the dull silver, she'd justified the project, established a future for herself in the islands. *Unreal*, she thought. *It's unreal*.

She decided to walk on to Utra. She'd ask Evelyn to open the drawer of her desk and show her the coins. There was a British Museum website with images of coins and she wanted to check it out, see if there was anything similar to her find. Evelyn had a computer with internet access. Hattie thought if she didn't do something constructive, in her present state she'd go crazy, maybe even manage to convince herself that the find was a dream; in the past after all she'd muddled fantasy and reality. She wished Mima were still alive; she'd always helped Hattie get things in proportion.

As she walked down the track that led to Utra, she passed an elderly couple. The old man was pushing a wheelbarrow with a hoe and a fork balanced on the top. The woman carried a plastic carrier bag containing something so heavy that one shoulder was lower than the other. Hattie didn't recognize them. They stopped; the man smiled and said a few words of greeting. He only had one tooth and Hattie couldn't understand a word he said.

'Good-afternoon!' She grinned, lifted her hand. 'Good-afternoon!'

The old woman said nothing. Further along the track, Hattie swivelled back to look at them, but they'd disappeared. She told herself that they'd turned off. Perhaps they were working in one of the planticrubs, the old woman with her grey skirt and her wellingtons, the old man with his gummy smile. But she wasn't entirely sure that they existed at all. Perhaps they were ghosts, like the merchant's wife at Setter and her powerful husband, conjured up by her own imagination.

Evelyn was real enough. She was standing at the kitchen table cutting meat. The knife was small with a sharp, serrated blade. There was a pile of fat and bone pushed to one side of the wooden chopping board. It made Hattie feel ill.

'I thought I'd do a casserole,' Evelyn said. 'There was some of last year's mutton left in the freezer. It needs using. Sandy's taken some leave from work to help with the arrangements for the funeral. I never know what time he'll be in to eat.'

'Can I do anything towards the meal? We're not

working this afternoon.' Hattie hoped the activity might stop the whirling thoughts.

'You can peel the carrots if you like. I won't ask you to do the onions. They're big strong ones and they'll have you crying like a baby.'

'I don't mind.' Hattie thought you couldn't make up tears, the stinging of the eyes, the taste of salt in the mouth as they ran down your face. But she sat at the table next to Evelyn and began to peel the carrots, aware of how slow and clumsy she was. She knew the older woman was watching.

'Would you and Sophie like to come for dinner?' Evelyn looked up from the growing pile of meat. 'There's plenty, and you can't just go back to the Bod on a night like this.'

'I don't know . . .' Hattie set down her knife.

'Of course we must celebrate! It's a dream come true. I wish I'd been there with you when you came across that first coin. This is just what we need before we put together a funding application for a big dig. I'm so thrilled for you. It's much more exciting than the piece of old skull.' She tipped the meat into a bowl and, using the same knife, cut an onion in half. A smear of blood was transferred to the white semicircle. She held it face-down on the board and chopped it very fast into translucent slices.

'Would you mind if I used your computer?' Hattie asked. 'There are some museum websites with images. Until Val gets in, I thought I might check the coins out, see if I can identify them. And I'd like to take another look at them.' Hattie wished she could have the feel of the coins on her fingers again; she wondered what they would smell like and imagined the sharp metallic scent of blood.

'Why not? Just let me get this in the oven. I'd be interested in what you can find out too.' Evelyn shook oil into a heavy pan and threw in the vegetables. Hattie saw her eyes were glistening. The onions must have made her cry.

'Mima would have been so excited,' Hattie said.

Evelyn stopped stirring; the wooden spoon was still in her hand. 'We have to make plans,' she said. 'When we have the information back about the skull and the coins we'll call a meeting. Perhaps something grand in the new museum in Lerwick. Or even better we could arrange something on the island. Show the folk from town what great work's going on here in Whalsay.' She shut her eyes briefly and Hattie saw that this was a woman with big dreams too. She was imagining a glittering evening, with all the important Lerwick folk in Whalsay, wine and canapés and Evelyn at the heart of it. 'We can turn Setter into a museum now, a celebration of Whalsay history. Wouldn't that be a fine thing? We could name it after Mima.'

'I'm not sure that would be what she wanted.' Hattie paused, remembered conversations in the Setter kitchen, drinking tea. 'She said she wanted a young family to move into the house when she died. She was always teasing Sophie and me. "Find a nice island lad and settle down here. You can rent this place when I'm gone. The boys won't want it. Bring up your bairns in Lindby."'

'Aye well,' Evelyn said. 'Mima was a great one for telling other folk how to live their lives.'

She scattered flour over the meat in the bowl and tossed the mutton in it with her fingers until all the pieces were covered, then tipped it all into the pan. There was a smell of searing flesh and the oil hissed and spat. She pushed at the meat with a wooden spoon to stop it sticking.

How competent she is! Hattie thought. *I'd never know how to turn a dead animal into a meal.* There was a sweetish smell coming from the pan, which made her feel again that she was going to throw up.

'I'm not sure what plans Sophie has for this evening,' she said. 'The boys were going to show her around *Artemis*. It's just come back from Lerwick.'

'She's a fine boat.' Evelyn tipped a jug of water over the stew, continued stirring while it thickened and came to the boil. 'Call Sophie's mobile and ask her. They won't feed her on board.'

'I will.' Hattie made no move to find her phone though.

'I wonder how Anna's getting on with the baby,' Evelyn said. She'd put the pot in the oven and turned, her hands still in the oven gloves. 'She wasn't getting much sleep last time I saw her. Maybe we should take a walk down to the bungalow. Anna was talking about working on her website if she got the chance. It would be good to put something up about the coins. The folk keen on signing up for her workshops would be interested in hearing about the project. And maybe you'd like to see the baby.'

Hattie thought that was the last thing she wanted; she'd much rather go back to the Bod and begin her plans for the project.

'You could write something about the dig for her

site,' Evelyn went on, 'It might persuade folks to book up. It'd help put Whalsay on the map.'

'We can't do that yet!' Hattie felt anxious just at the thought of it. She looked up at Evelyn in horror. 'We should keep the find secret for as long as we can. If word gets out you'll have a bunch of people trespassing on the site, looking for buried treasure. It could damage the project.' She had the image of geeky men in grey anoraks with metal detectors marching all over her dig.

Evelyn seemed not to have heard her. 'Maybe we should take the coins to show Anna. She has a digital camera. I'd love to have a photo of them.'

'Not yet. Paul Berglund should be coming in tomorrow. I think I should wait and see what he says.'

'Maybe you're right. I wouldn't want you to get into trouble with your boss. And it would be good to keep a bit of mystery about them, before we show them to the public.' Evelyn put the knives and chopping board in the sink to soak. 'Come on then. Let's go and look at your treasure.'

The desk was in the living room and locked with a small brass key, which Evelyn took from her jeans pocket. Hattie had put the coins into a clear plastic box. They were small and dull. They were in the box just to prevent the need for their being handled, but Hattie longed to touch them. 'Imagine them being in Mima's garden all the time,' Evelyn said. 'All those hundreds of years.'

Hattie shut her eyes for a moment and resisted the temptation to lift the lid of the box and put in her nose to sniff the coins. 'I can't do any more until Paul comes in tomorrow,' she said. She replaced the coins in the desk on top of a file containing the Amenity Trust documents and a chequebook.

'I'll need someone else to countersign the cheques for the project,' Evelyn said. 'Mima used to do it. If we're going to expand the project it might make sense for you to be a signatory.'

Hattie wondered how the woman could discuss Mima's death so dispassionately. She still felt herself falling apart whenever she thought about it. What would it feel like to know that you were dying? To be lying in the grass in the rain knowing there was no one to help you or hold you? But perhaps a farmer's wife who helped slaughter animals took death in her stride. It was all part of her competence.

Later, after they had looked at the British Museum website, they walked to the Cloustons' bungalow. Evelyn insisted and Hattie didn't know how to stand up to her without appearing rude or stand-offish. They found Anna in the workshop, not in front of her computer. She had switched on the light and for a moment they stood outside and looked in through the long window, watching what she was doing. She had no sense that they were there. There was no sign of Ronald.

It seemed to Hattie a terrible intrusion, to be staring in at her. The baby was in his basket on one of the big trestle tables. Next to him, some cloth was soaking in an old tin bath. Anna was carding some fleece, preparing it for spinning, combing it between the carders with strong easy movements. The process seemed very complicated to Hattie; she could work out the theory but knew she'd be useless in practice. The fleece was combed between flat hardboard sheets pierced with thin nails. Anna moved the untangled fleece from board to board, then pulled it free of the nails and curled it into a loose roll. Now it was ready for the spinning wheel. *Another competent woman*, Hattie thought. *I can't even peel a carrot with any sort of skill.*

Then Anna noticed them through the window. Their presence had obviously startled her. She stared at them sharply before waving them to come in. She met them at the workshop door and there was a moment of awkward silence. Hattie almost expected her to send them away.

'You've heard about Ronald?' She kept her voice low, though there was no one to hear except the baby. 'The police have decided to take no further action. They've accepted Mima's death was an accident.'

'He's a lucky man,' Evelyn said.

'I know that, and so does he. He's going out fishing with Davy for the night. I told him it would do him good to get away for a while.'

Hattie found the atmosphere in the bungalow almost unbearable. *I'm going to faint*, she thought.

'At least we can go ahead and organize the funeral now.' Evelyn walked ahead of Anna into the workshop. 'The Fiscal has agreed to release the body.'

'Ronald wants to be there,' Anna said, 'but he's not sure what Joseph would feel about that.'

'Joseph's an easygoing sort of man. He's not one to bear a grudge.'

'Thank you.' Anna reached out and touched Evelyn's shoulder. 'I hope this doesn't change things between us.'

There was a brief pause before Evelyn said, 'Of course not. Why should it?'

Hattie had the impression that suddenly Evelyn was very pleased with herself, but she couldn't work out why. She'd never been any good at picking up unspoken communication. Sometimes she felt lost, a stranger in a foreign country, only half understanding the language. *I shouldn't be here*, she thought. She had to control an impulse to turn and run away.

'Have you heard about the find at Setter?' Evelyn took a seat at the table where Anna had been sitting.

No chance of keeping it secret then! Hattie didn't know what to say. She thought Evelyn had used her as an excuse to be there. She wanted to make her own excuse and leave, but couldn't think of a way of doing it with any sort of dignity.

'Tell me all about it.' Anna leaned against the trestle and Hattie could see the swelling around her belly where the baby had been. Hattie mumbled an explanation of the significance of the coins. The baby started crying, a griping grizzle as if he was in pain. Anna lifted him out of his basket, rocked him in her arms. Suddenly she held him out to Hattie, a kind of challenge. 'Would you mind taking him while I tidy this away? He's got colic and he'll scream the place down if I put him back in his basket.' She gave a tight little smile. 'Actually he's been driving me mad today.'

Hattie found the baby in her arms before she could object. She held him gingerly, slightly away from her body. He seemed very light and fragile. She had a moment of panic when she imagined herself dropping him; in her imagination she deliberately opened her arms wide and he slipped from her grasp and his head cracked on the floor like one of Mima's big white eggs. There'd be a puddle of blood. The picture was so vivid that she was surprised that there was no sound, no crying and shouting, but the two island women were chatting about the next forum meeting and seemed to take no notice of her. The baby smelled very sweet. When the time came to hand him back, Hattie wanted to protest and to hold on to him. Perhaps after all it wouldn't be so terrible to be a mother.

Evelyn seemed to have forgotten her decision to invite the archaeologists to supper, and Hattie was pleased. She couldn't bear the thought of another meal in the Utra kitchen, forcing herself to eat to keep Evelyn happy. She knew Sophie wouldn't be back for hours. She'd be in *Artemis* with the boys, drinking and flirting, the nearest she'd get to her wild London social life here in Whalsay. Hattie wondered what else she'd be getting up to.

She started walking down the road towards the Bod. It was the beginning of dusk, what Shetlanders called 'the darkenin'', but there was still light enough to make out the colours of the stone in the wall and the peat on the hill. She began to think of Mima again, recalled their conversation sitting outside the house of Setter, Mima's anger and her loud words shouted into the telephone.

Chapter Nineteen

Perez woke early. He'd been dreaming about Fran, turned and panicked when he found the bed next to him was empty. He lost the details of the dream on waking but was left with a sense of unease, a premonition of danger that he knew was ridiculous. He had to lose the notion that life away from the islands was risky. He'd seen too many parents reluctant to give their children the freedom to move away. Another week and Fran and Cassie would be home.

But he couldn't return to sleep. He found himself running over the details surrounding Mima's death. It was absurd to let the incident haunt him. Ronald must have killed the old woman in a freak accident. Any other explanation seemed so melodramatic that it was ludicrous. The Fiscal had been right. He didn't really believe Sandy's stay in Whalsay would result in fresh information. He thought they would be left with the worst possible outcome: not really knowing what had happened. He would have to live with that, but knew he would find it hard to stomach.

He'd heard Sandy talk about Mima so much that he felt he knew her well. In fact he'd only met her once, at Sandy's birthday party on Whalsay. He remembered a tiny, bird-like woman with a surprising belly laugh.

She'd matched the men drink for drink but apart from flushed cheeks hadn't shown any sign of inebriation. It hadn't affected her ability to dance the most intricate of steps.

He wondered what there was about her that might have invited violence. Had that sharp tongue provoked one of the Whalsay folk to kill her in a rage? Or was it something she knew? Something she'd seen? But perhaps, after all, her death was simply an accident and he should accept this most obvious explanation. What was it in his nature that forced him to question the accepted version of events? Fran said he was too sympathetic to be a cop, that he always saw the best in people, but he knew that not to be true. Everyone was capable of violence, he thought, even of killing a harmless old woman. He was capable of it himself.

Perez got out of bed and went to the kitchen to make tea. It was too early for the heating to have come on and the house was cold. He imagined the damp seeping in through the stone walls, could almost smell it. He opened the curtains and sat in the window seat looking out at the harbour, drinking coffee. Eventually he came to a decision and set off for the ferry terminal.

Paul Berglund was one of the last passengers off the Aberdeen ferry. If the archaeologist had left earlier Perez might have missed him. Some people ignored the bright voice on the PA system announcing the arrival of the NorthLink to Lerwick, they stayed in their bunks and had breakfast in the cafeteria before making their way ashore. Berglund sauntered down the gangplank almost as soon as Perez arrived. Perez wasn't sure what he would have done if Berglund hadn't disembarked now. Would he have waited in the cavernous terminal until the stragglers emerged? How could he justify that?

Berglund could have been a squaddie home on leave. His hair was cropped and he carried about him the sense that he could look after himself in a fight. That at least was how he came across to Perez. It seemed an odd image and Perez thought he shouldn't make up his mind about the man without knowing him. He had no reason to think of Berglund as an aggressive man. The academic was wearing jeans and a Gore-Tex jacket, heavy trainers. He carried a small rucksack, in one of its pockets was a small archaeologists' trowel and in the other a big knife in a sheath. Perez supposed they were tools of the trade. He wondered what excuse he could give for being here to meet Berglund. It seemed a disproportionate gesture.

'Mr Berglund.' As soon as he spoke he realized he'd got the title wrong. Berglund was a professor. But Berglund stopped and turned slowly, curious but not offended. At first he didn't recognize Perez and seemed confused. Not far away a family was welcoming back a young man, a student, and there was a lot of noise. Everyone was there – both parents and a couple of children. The returning teenager seemed embarrassed by the attention, the hugs and the shrieking voices.

'I'm sorry to trouble you,' Perez said. 'I wonder if I could have a few words. It won't take long. It'll save me a trip to Whalsay.'

Now Berglund did recognize him. 'Of course: you're the detective.' A pause and a frown. 'What's happened now?'

It seemed a strange question. Perez wanted to ask, *What were you expecting to happen?* 'I just need to complete my report for the Fiscal. Routine. I'm sure you understand. She's satisfied Mrs Wilson's death was an accident, but as you were on the island when it happened . . .' It sounded an unconvincing explanation to Perez, but Berglund shrugged and nodded his agreement.

They had breakfast together in a small and steamy cafe by the harbour. Bacon rolls and tea in thick china mugs. There was nobody to overhear them. Berglund shrugged off his heavy coat and Perez saw he was wearing a hand-knitted sweater in a pattern he didn't recognize.

'That's not Shetland, is it?' Small-talk because he wasn't quite sure how to begin.

If the archaeologist was surprised by the question it didn't show. 'No, my grandmother's a great knitter.'

The pattern of the sweater and the name made Perez think Berglund's family must be Scandinavian.

At first he seemed nervous, almost jumpy. Perhaps it was just a natural reaction to being questioned by the police. He talked too much about the dig at Lindby and the find of coins the girls had made. 'Hattie will be pleased. It's her commitment that set the project going. She's a strange young woman. Obsessive. There are times when I worry about her. I hope this will take the pressure off a bit. She doesn't need to justify herself now.'

It was warm in the cafe. The condensation on the window meant there was no view outside.

'Have you known Hattie long?' It had come into his mind. Of course it had no relevance to the inquiry, but perhaps he could form a proper question while Berglund answered.

Berglund considered for a moment. 'I've been supervising her since the beginning of her project.'

Was that a real answer? But Perez thought he couldn't justify following it up. Berglund's personal life was none of his business.

'How did you get on with Jemima Wilson? I take it you knew her?'

'She was a joy,' Berglund said. 'So many landowners can be a real pain. They don't want the hassle or the disruption of a dig. Or they expect compensation. Mima loved having the girls at her place. I think she was glad of the company.'

'Even though she had her family close by?'

'They're all men.' Berglund was beginning to relax. He'd eaten half his bacon roll, almost finished the tea. 'She had a son and two grandsons. Not quite the same. She told me once that she'd always wanted daughters.'

'It seems an odd kind of thing to say to a stranger.'

'I called round one evening with a bottle of Scotch to thank her for her help. We had a few drinks and we started chatting. We got on surprisingly well. I had the feeling that if I'd been thirty years older she'd have seduced me. She must have been wicked when she was young.'

'She has a daughter-in-law,' Perez said.

'Ah, that's not at all the same, apparently. I have the impression that Mima had never really taken to Evelyn. Perhaps that's always the way with mothers and sons. I'm an only child and sometimes I think my mother was always faintly disappointed that I felt the need of a wife at all. She should have been enough for me.'

My mother wants me to find a wife, Perez thought.

She wants a grandson to carry on the family name. What will Fran make of that when she finds out? It seemed to him a terrible kind of pressure and he wondered if that had something to do with his reluctance to propose to her. Would Fran think it was all about keeping a Perez in Shetland?

'Did Mima ever tell you what she had against Evelyn?'

'Evelyn won't let Joseph be himself. I think that was the essence of it.' Berglund drank the dregs of his tea. 'All the man wants is his croft and his friends. A beer or a few drams in the evening. A good dance once in a while with a band to play. Evelyn was interested in making him an important man in the community.'

'Evelyn's an important woman in her own right, isn't she? I had the impression that she'd supported your project, and according to Sandy she's managed to bring funds for other community events into Whalsay.'

'Oh, I've got nothing against the woman. She's been helpful to us.'

'What else did Mima say about her?'

'What is this about, inspector? It's just gossip.' But he grinned and continued without waiting for an answer. 'Mima thought Evelyn was spending all Joseph's money. "Why on earth does she want a bigger kitchen? What's wrong with the old one? She'll bankrupt the lot of us." That sort of thing.'

'When did you last see Mima?'

'The afternoon before she died. Late afternoon, after the girls had gone back to the Bod. The weather was so bad that they'd left early. I was planning to leave on the first ferry the following day so I went to say goodbye. She made me tea, cut us each a slice from one of Evelyn's cakes then got out the whisky. To keep out the cold, she said, though it was always warm enough in her kitchen.'

'How did she seem?'

Berglund looked up sharply. 'What possible relevance could her state of mind have if she was killed in an accident?'

'We have to rule out all the other possibilities.' Again Perez thought how unconvincing he must sound.

'She wasn't suicidal, if that's what you mean. The idea's ridiculous. I've never met anyone more full of life than Mima Wilson. She'd want to stay around just to cause mischief.'

'Can you remember what you discussed?'

He frowned. 'The girls. I told you they'd become like members of the family. She felt very protective of Hattie. "She's too wrapped up in the work. What she needs is a fine young man to give her something else to think about. Don't you think so Paul? Bring her a couple of boys up here to help on the dig." I told her times had changed and young women wanted careers as well as families now. She said Sophie had a bit of spirit about her. She reminded Mima of herself at that age. Fond of a party.'

'Anything else?'

'She was going on about Evelyn again. By that time I'd had two whiskies and in the warmth of the kitchen I was finding it hard not to drop off. She said something like, "That woman's gone too far this time. I'll have to sort it out. Make sure I arrange things so Joseph doesn't get hurt."'

'Do you know what she was talking about?'

'Not really. Like I said, I wasn't exactly giving the conversation my full attention. I assumed it was about island politics of some sort. I don't know Evelyn well but she seems to build alliances then fall out with people. That sort of thing happens in the university too. I try not to have too much to do with that either.'

Perez still found it hard to think of Berglund as someone who worked in a university. His speech was too blunt and he was too big. University professors should be skinny and use long words.

'This discovery Hattie made—'

'Wonderful,' Berglund interrupted enthusiastically. 'It's just what she needs at the beginning of her career. And fascinating. Nobody had any idea there was a house of such proportions on Whalsay. Hattie seems to have an instinct for domestic archaeology. I'm still not sure how she got it so right.'

Perez supposed the fact that Mima was shot just days before the coins were found by the students was a coincidence. He disliked coincidence, but he couldn't see how the two events could be related. Not if things had happened that way round. Then there was the skull. Could the discovery of an ancient body have triggered these events in the present? Of course not, but he wished he knew more about it.

'There's no possibility that Hattie could have found coins on an earlier visit?' He kept his voice tentative. The last thing he wanted to do was question the student's integrity without good reason. But if Mima, or any of the other islanders, had known there was something of value on her land it would bring a new perspective to her death. It seemed to Perez a more natural order of events.

'Why wouldn't she tell anyone? Hattie and Sophie always work on the site together. There are all sorts of health and safety constraints that prevent solo work. Besides, she's not a thief, inspector. She's passionate about the project. There's no way she'd remove objects from the merchant's house at Setter without recording them properly.'

'Of course,' Perez said. 'It was a foolish idea.'

But he was wondering if anyone else had been rooting around on the site, if any other objects of value had been found there. He imagined the misty, rainy night. Perhaps Mima heard something from her house or went out unexpectedly late to shut up the hens. Of course if the intruder came from Lindby she would recognize them, even from the faint light seeping out of the back of her house. She'd grown up there. Everyone was familiar to her. Islanders had been encouraged to take an interest in the dig, but Mima wouldn't expect anyone there once the students had left. Had she challenged the person? Shocked them into violence?

He realized Berglund was staring at him. The archaeologist wasn't a man for quiet contemplation.

'Is that it?' Berglund asked. 'Can I get back to Whalsay now? I'm interested to see the coins for myself.'

'Of course.' Perez though was lost in thought. Would Hattie have noticed if someone had been visiting the site when she wasn't there? And what might the intruder have already found? He remembered the conversation between Sandy and Hattie in the Pier House Hotel, Sandy's questions about the value of the coins. Perhaps other people would believe them worth stealing. He should find out if there was a black market in objects like this.

Later, in his office, he tried to call Val Turner, the Shetland archaeologist. He thought she would know if the coins had any sort of value. She'd put the Whalsay dig into context for him and because she could have had nothing to do with Mima's death it would be possible to talk to her more freely than to Paul Berglund. But she wasn't in and he had to leave a message on her answering machine.

He'd just replaced the receiver when his phone went. He expected it to be Val and was thrown to hear the breathy, little-girl voice of Hattie James.

'I wonder if it might be possible to speak to you.'

'Of course,' he said.

'No, no. Not on the phone.'

'Were you planning to come into Lerwick in the next couple of days?'

'No, no,' she said again, frustrated because he didn't seem to understand her. 'That wouldn't be possible. My boss has come in today.'

'You'd like me to come there to talk to you?' At last he could see what she wanted from him. The idea of returning to Whalsay filled him with an unexpected dread. He liked the island, what he knew of it. Why was he so reluctant to return? Why the clammy claustrophobia of impending imprisonment? Perhaps it was the fog, the lack of any recognizable horizon. Or the twisted family ties that seemed to pull him in too, so he lost his objectivity. He was tempted to suggest that she speak to Sandy, but he thought she needed careful handling, and even the new, perceptive Sandy would frighten her off.

'Oh, please.' The relief in her voice was palpable.

'Is it urgent? Could it wait until this evening? Shall we meet in the Pier House at six?'

She paused. 'No,' she said. 'Come to the Bod. I'll make sure I'm on my own there.'

Chapter Twenty

Sandy stood at the north end of the island and watched the small fishing boat approach. This was nothing like the *Cassandra*, the huge pelagic ship owned by the Clouston family. When that went to sea it was away for weeks, far out in the north Atlantic. It landed its catch in Denmark and then went back to the fishing grounds again. There were stories all over the island about how much it had cost when Andrew bought it just before his stroke. A fortune, they said. But as long as Sandy could remember the Cloustons had had money. This boat belonged to Davy Henderson, had just been on a short trip and was already on its way home. It had been kind of Davy to take Ronald with him. It would have done him good to get away from Whalsay, even for a short while.

The wind blew his hair across Sandy's eyes. He'd driven up the island to Skaw because he needed to get away from Utra for a while. A little way inland was the most northerly golf course in the British Isles, green and manicured despite its exposure to the weather. He came occasionally with Joseph to play and his father was pretty good, though they never took the game too seriously. Now he wished Davy had asked him to go out on the boat too. He wasn't much of a sailor but it would be worth a few hours of discomfort to get away from his family and the discussion of the funeral.

He wanted his grandmother to have a good send-off, of course he did, but she wouldn't have wanted all this fuss. She'd have been happy just to know all her friends were there in the kirk. The place she'd been married. The kirk was on a spit of land to the west of Whalsay known as the Houb. It was surrounded on three sides by the sea, and Mima always said that being there made her think of her sailor husband: it was a bit like being in a ship. She'd have wanted lusty singing during the hymns and a bit of a party afterwards. Nothing else would have mattered to her. Now his mother was wound up about getting rooms ready for Michael, Amelia and the baby, planning the food as if she was preparing for a thirty-day siege, working herself into a state about who else they should invite.

He relived the scene at breakfast. His mother had been at the kitchen table, drinking her second cup of tea, surrounded by lists. Lists of food and drink and people who should be told. Joseph had had the sense to make himself scarce and was already out on the croft, checking the ewes.

'Do you think Paul Berglund would want to come?' His mother's question had come out of the blue, sharp, underlaid by a barely controlled hysteria.

'I don't know.' Sandy thought it unlikely. Why would someone with a life want to go to the funeral of an old lady he barely knew?

'He's a professor,' Evelyn said.

'What has that to do with the price of fish?'

'I was thinking Michael might get on with him.'

'Michael will get on just fine with Ronald and the

rest of the lads.' But was that true? The last time Michael had been home it was like he was a different man.

Sandy sat on the grass and watched the boat come in against a stiff south-easterly breeze. It was one of those bright and gusty days: one minute there was sunshine and the next a bit of a squall would come up. At least the fog had cleared. He wished his mother could relax more. When she was relaxed she was a lovely woman. He'd thought with his father working at home and both of the boys gone she'd be able to enjoy herself, become less tense. He didn't know what to do to help her. Once, confiscating cannabis from a couple of German students who'd been camping on Fetlar. he'd wondered flippantly if that might provide an answer. Chill her out a bit. Years ago he'd gone to visit Michael at Edinburgh University and someone had made hash cakes. He laughed at the thought of slipping some dope into his mother's baking, wondered what Michael would say about the idea. Once he'd have laughed too, but now Sandy wasn't so sure. That evening when they'd sat round with his friends in the student house, candles lit, music in the background, was probably the last time they'd really talked.

Maybe he should suggest to his mother that she should see a doctor. His understanding about women's health was sketchy, but perhaps this anxiety, these swings in her mood were to do with her age. Wasn't there a pill she could take? Like the cannabis but legal? He knew he'd never bring up the subject with her though, partly because he would be too embarrassed and partly because he was scared of what her response might be. It was pathetic, but she could still terrify him when she was angry.

Something positive had come out of the discussion over breakfast: he was going to move into Setter when Michael and Amelia came up from the south. His mother had agreed as soon as he'd suggested it. Sandy knew she was worried he'd show himself up in front of Michael's smart wife, though she made out it was because they needed his room for the baby. It occurred to him that she might like Joseph to move out too, in case Amelia got upset by his drinking, his table manners and his limited conversation. He hoped so. He and his father would get on fine together there.

The boat was getting closer, bucking and twisting where the tides met. Sandy thought he'd drive down to the harbour at Symbister and wait at the Pier House for the boys to come in. They'd been out all night but they might be ready for a few pints before they hit their beds. He knew he was supposed to be making discreet enquiries into Mima's death and he didn't want to let Perez down, but everyone was entitled to some time off.

Besides, perhaps he might learn something from sitting with the boys in the bar. That was how Perez worked, after all. The inspector listened to folk talking, just throwing in a question occasionally, like tossing a pebble into a pool and waiting to see what the ripples stirred up.

Sandy was in the Pier House Hotel with the gang of men. Davy was there, but there were boys from the pelagic boats too. By now it was mid-afternoon. Sandy had had a couple of pints while he was waiting for his friends to come in, but they'd already caught him up and now they were steaming. They were laughing and joking because Sophie had come to look round the big boat the day before. One of the older men had said it was bad luck having an Englishwoman aboard. There were lots of superstitions about the fishing – words you shouldn't say, rituals to follow – but Sandy had never heard that one before. Ronald wasn't in the bar. Sandy had asked Davy where he was, but the man just made a gesture with his thumb to show that Ronald was well under Anna's control. 'These days he seems to spend all his free time with that stuck-up wife of his. He's as daft about the new baby as a lassie. Anyway, he says he's given up the drink.'

The men gathered at the bar looked at each other and began to laugh. Sandy felt excluded. It was as if they were sharing a joke he couldn't understand. Because he lived in Lerwick he didn't really belong here any more.

'Aye well,' Sandy said, aware that his words weren't as clear as they should be. 'If I'd shot a woman, I'd stop drinking too.'

There was a brief lull in the conversation then, before someone shouted to Cedric for more drink and the talk moved on.

Soon after, Sandy decided he would leave. It didn't feel right to be here drinking when Perez thought he was working. He shouldn't let his mother get to him in this way, niggling away at him until he was as tense as she was. He should be more like his father and just let her panic wash over him.

After the dark of the bar it was a shock to come out

in to bright sunshine, to realize that it was still daytime. A couple of bairns ran up the street ahead of him, whooping and laughing until a pretty young woman came out of a house near the High School and called them in to their tea. He decided he would leave the car where it was and walk back to Utra. On the way he'd call into the Clouston house and see how Ronald was.

At first it seemed that the bungalow was empty. He opened the front door and everything was quiet. Then he thought perhaps the baby was asleep and Anna was resting. He didn't want to shout in case he woke them so he closed the door quietly and started to walk back up the path.

'Sandy!' It was Anna. She was leaning out of the workshop window. 'Sorry, I didn't see you. I was dyeing some yarn. Come on in.' Ronald had explained to Sandy about Anna's ambitions to set up courses in spinning and knitting. It seemed odd to him: an Englishwoman presuming to teach other folk the traditional island crafts. He would have understood if that had annoyed his mother, but she'd said very little about it.

He went into the large room that was already kitted out for students. She lifted a hank of yarn out of a big old pan with a pair of stained wooden tongs. The wool was a sludgy green colour. He couldn't imagine anyone choosing to wear it.

'What do you think?' she said. 'It's a new recipe. Lichen. Pretty, isn't it?'

'Aye.'

He was surprised to see her working so soon after the baby was born. Amelia had taken to her bed for what seemed like weeks after the birth of his niece.

Evelyn had gone down to Edinburgh to help out, to cook and clean and shop.

'Is Ronald in? I ken he was out with Davy earlier, but he's back now, isn't he?'

'He was,' Anna said. 'But he went up the road to see his mother.' Sandy thought Anna still sounded angry. He had a picture in his head of a pan of soup standing on the Rayburn and ready to boil over. He thought that was how Anna was feeling: ready to boil over at any minute. It couldn't be easy having a mother-in-law like Jackie living just up the hill and a baby crying and keeping you awake all night. 'She phoned to say that Andrew's had a bad day. Ronald went a while ago though, so he shouldn't be long.' She paused. 'Do you want to wait? Can I get you some tea?'

Sandy wondered if his mother would have been more pleasant and easy to get on with if she'd had a little business of her own like this, if she hadn't been forced to live her life through her sons.

'Aye,' he said. 'Why not?'

He followed her when she walked through to the kitchen, carrying the sleeping baby with her in a basket. She was talking about some of the emails she'd had from women wanting to book on her course. Their enthusiasm seemed to have excited her. Sandy had never seen her so lively, so lit up.

'There was one from Idaho who said she'd knitted Shetland patterns for twenty years and never thought she'd actually make it to the islands.' Anna turned from pouring out tea to look at him. 'You and Ronald were very lucky to grow up here, you know.'

Sandy supposed that was true, but now he was

just looking for an excuse to leave and to get back to Lerwick.

She stood with a mug in each hand. 'Shall we take this outside? The sun's still quite warm out of the wind.'

They sat on a white-painted seat, their backs to the house. Sandy felt suddenly awkward. He'd never been on his own with Anna before and didn't know what to say to her. After her chattering in the kitchen, it seemed quiet; there were just the noises he didn't usually notice, the sheep and the gulls, the wind rattling a bit of loose wire on the fence.

'How is Ronald?'

It must have sounded abrupt to her because she seemed startled and hesitated before she replied.

'Obviously he's pleased the police have decided to drop the case against him, but he's still upset.'

'Only natural.'

'Perhaps now he'll think a bit before he goes out with the boys, drinking, behaving like a lunatic. Perhaps he'll realize how much he has to lose.'

Then it seemed to Sandy that Anna was almost pleased that Mima was dead because it had pulled Ronald back into line. She'd always have that one moment of foolishness to hold against him. *Just remember what happened last time when you didn't listen to me.* What was it with island women that they had to control their men?

He set down his mug on the path.

'Maybe Ronald didn't kill Mima,' he said.

'What do you mean?'

He realized he'd been a fool to open his great mouth. What could he say to her now? But as he'd spoken he'd thought it was probably true. Ronald was no fool. He wouldn't have shot Mima no matter how dark and foggy the weather.

'Nothing,' he said 'Nothing official. I just don't believe it happened the way everyone thinks. There could have been someone else who was responsible.'

Anna looked up at him astounded. He mumbled an excuse and walked away before his great stupid mouth let him down all over again.

Chapter Twenty-one

Perez didn't tell Sandy about Hattie's phone call or that he was coming into Whalsay to meet up with her. He was hoping he could reassure her and leave again before word got out that he was there. He assumed that she wanted to talk to him about the dig. On the phone he'd sensed she had something to confess, something that was making her feel sheepish, uncomfortable with herself. It would likely be some irregularity she wouldn't want Paul Berglund and the university to know about. Perhaps there *had* been earlier finds on Setter land and she'd had her own reasons for not telling her supervisor about them. It would be easy enough to set her mind at rest if the matter had nothing to do with the old woman's death.

Although he hadn't been looking forward to the trip, when he arrived at Laxo the weather lifted his spirits. The fog had cleared. The breeze blew the water into little white peaks and even on the ferry he could feel the sea moving beneath his feet. Billy Watt was on duty again and they stood on the car deck chatting. Billy had married late and had a little boy. 'Eh, man, it's fantastic. The best feeling in the world. You should try it.'

I should, Perez thought. He imagined what it must

be like to hold his own child in his arms. *Do men get broody? Is this how women feel?* He told himself it was just the time of the year. Spring. All those new lambs on the hill. He should concentrate on the case.

'I'm meeting one of the lasses from the university in the camping bod,' he said. 'Can you tell me how to find it?'

So when he drove off the ferry at Symbister he knew exactly where he was going and he didn't have to ask. He pulled into the side of the road and walked down past a couple of empty houses until he reached it. He looked at his watch. Five to six. He was pleased; he didn't like to be late. Many of the Shetlanders he knew had a relaxed attitude to time and it always irritated him.

He expected Hattie to be waiting for him. There'd been desperation in her voice on the phone; although she'd said it wasn't urgent he knew she'd been eager to talk to someone. But there was no response when he knocked at the door. Ten minutes later he was feeling uneasy. He looked inside. It seemed quite primitive: a bare floor, a camping stove and a pile of assorted plates, cutlery and tins on a wooden shelf. Equipment for use with the dig was stored there too: a theodolyte, camera and tripod, surveying poles. On the table a pile of pink sheets of thin paper that seemed to be used for recording finds. There was no sign of Hattie and no explanation for her absence. He walked into the house in case she'd left a note for him and once inside couldn't help looking around. Beyond the kitchen there was a bedroom with four bunks, two against each wall, the lower of each made up. One was tidy, the sleeping bag straightened for use, clothes folded on a plastic chair at one end. The other, which he presumed was Sophie's, was a mess.

'What the hell do you think you're doing?'

He turned, startled and embarrassed. The inside of the house was in shadow and the figure was silhouetted in the doorway.

'I was looking for Hattie.'

'In our bedroom?' Sophie stood accusingly where she was, blocking his exit.

'I'm sorry,' he said. 'I didn't know. We'd arranged to meet here. I thought she might have left a note.'

She said nothing, though just the way she was standing made it clear what she was thinking. *Yeah, right!*

He walked towards her and her image came into focus. 'Look, I'm sorry to have intruded. There must have been a misunderstanding. Just tell me where she is and I'll leave you in peace.'

Still she stood her ground. She was almost as tall as he was. She wore a sleeveless vest under a denim jacket. Her stomach was flat and firm. She had the poise he associated with film stars and models. He wondered how she and Hattie got on away from the dig, what they could have to say to each other.

'What do you want her for?' Her tone was amused, but he was left in no doubt that she expected an answer.

'I think that's between her and me.'

'I haven't seen Hattie since lunchtime.' At last Sophie did step aside to let him past and they stood together in the sunshine.

'Where was that?'

He thought she was going to question his right to

put the question but after a pause she answered. 'We were at Utra. Evelyn invited us for a meal. Paul was there too – his first chance to look at the Setter coins. Afterwards he wanted to talk to Hattie about her PhD. I suppose they were planning what should happen next, the focus of the next phase of the project.'

'You weren't involved in that discussion?'

'No, I'm just the hired labour.'

He couldn't tell what she made of that, whether it rankled. 'Where did they have the meeting?'

'I'm not sure. I left them at Utra.'

'What were you doing this afternoon?'

'I went back to the dig and carried on working for an hour. I expected Hattie to join me there.'

'But she didn't?'

'No. I presumed Paul had taken her back to the Pier House for a celebratory drink. I thought, *Sod them!* and I packed up early. I've been visiting a couple of the fishing boys.' She seemed edgy and out of sorts. Perez wanted to ask whose house she'd been in, but it probably wasn't any of his business.

'Hattie doesn't strike me as someone who would enjoy an afternoon in the bar,' he said, keeping his voice light, hoping it didn't sound like an interrogation. The day before when they'd been there, Hattie had been jumpy, nervy even after a couple of drinks.

'No, definitely not her scene. She doesn't do pleasure. He should have asked me instead.' Sophie grinned, but Perez thought she was finding it hard to keep things light. 'But he's her supervisor, isn't he? Her boss. She wouldn't have the guts to tell him it wasn't her thing.'

'Yes,' Perez said. 'He seems to me like a man who

usually gets what he wants.' But if he hoped this would encourage Sophie to give her own opinions of Berglund he was disappointed. She shrugged and said she'd had a hard day. All she wanted now was to sit in the sun with a nice cup of tea. Or maybe a can of lager.

'So you have no idea where I could find Hattie now?'

'Sorry, I haven't a clue. And it's no point me giving you her mobile number. Her phone doesn't work anywhere on the islands.'

'If she comes back tell her I'm looking for her.'

'Sure,' Sophie said. 'Sure.' But he thought she was a mischief maker and he didn't know how much he could trust her.

He found Berglund sitting alone in the bar of the Pier House Hotel. There was a tray of coffee on the table in front of him and he was scribbling notes on an A4 pad. Perez saw that the writing was large and spidery and quite unintelligible. The place was empty apart from Berglund and Cedric Irvine, who was sitting behind the bar reading the *Shetland Times*.

'What can I get you?' The landlord recognized him from the day before, gave a knowing smile. Perez thought he would probably have as much information as anyone about what had been going on in the island. He wondered if Sandy had thought to talk to him about Mima.

'Coffee,' Perez said. 'Strong and black.' Cedric nodded and disappeared.

Berglund waved at him. 'I thought you weren't coming into Whalsay today.'

'Something came up.' He sat at the same table. 'Did the Setter coins live up to expectation?'

'Absolutely. They're in fine condition too.'

'I'm looking for Hattie.'

Berglund raised his eyebrows. 'What do you want with her?'

Perez smiled. 'Just a chat. More loose ends.'

'I presume she's in the Bod.'

'I've just been there. Sophie said she was with you.' This was becoming ridiculous. He didn't want to play hide-and-seek throughout the island, looking for a neurotic girl. He had better things to do with his time.

'We had a quick chat earlier just about where she should take the project from here, but I haven't seen her for a couple of hours.'

Cedric came over with Perez's coffee. Perez waited until the landlord was engrossed in the newspaper again before continuing.

'You didn't bring Hattie in here?'

Berglund pulled a face. 'Good God, no. Earlier on the place was full of men from the trawlers. It was pretty rowdy and Hattie's a sensitive sort of flower at the best of times. We just walked along the shore below Utra. It was quite sheltered there, very pleasant.'

'Did she say where she was going when she left you?'

'She was going to walk on a little way, just to collect her thoughts, plan out in her own mind how she should organize the work at Setter. I thought she would go back to the dig later. Sophie was already there. I came here. As I said, it was pretty wild in the bar. I sat in my room to make some phone calls – we need to get the coins validated, but I have other work at the university too.'

Perez sipped at his coffee. He supposed Hattie had regretted the phone call to the police station as soon as she'd made it and was hiding from him, too embarrassed to face him. People often behaved irrationally in their relations with the police. The sensible thing would be for him to go back to Lerwick. But he could still hear the desperation in Hattie's voice when she'd called him. Even if she'd changed her mind about confiding in the police, perhaps he could convince her that she needed to talk to someone. Fran would understand if he missed the call to Cassie tonight. He left the Pier House without discussing his plans with Berglund.

Perez walked to Setter along the edge of the loch. He stood for a moment looking out over the water, and a red-throated diver flew in. It was the first diver he had seen that spring. He supposed later it would breed there. It called. Fran had once said that the cry made her think of a lost child desperate for help. He'd laughed at her then, but now he knew what she meant. The old folk called the diver 'the rain goose', and the superstition was that its arrival predicted storm or disaster.

Setter looked just as unkempt as on his first visit. There was the same pile of rusting junk by the side of the house and the nettle patch and untidy hens were still there. The scabby cat was sunbathing on the roof of the byre. Perez wondered what his father would have made of Mima Wilson; he set great store by keeping his Fair Isle property tidy and would have disapproved of her wild ways and her drinking. He knocked at the door. He thought he heard a sound inside, but when he tried the door it was bolted from the inside. He looked through the window into the kitchen. Sandy's father was sitting in the one easy chair. He had his head in his hands and he was weeping. Perez knew he couldn't intrude on an old man's grief. He looked quickly over the site of the dig to check that Hattie wasn't there and then he walked away.

Chapter Twenty-two

Perez missed the last ferry home and ended up taking a room at the Pier House Hotel. He'd expected a quick trip into the island, to be home in time for supper, and now felt stranded there. Marooned. But he knew he wouldn't sleep much if he did get back to Lerwick. He wanted to be here if Hattie turned up. He'd sat with Evelyn for most of the evening while she phoned all her neighbours. Nobody had seen Hattie since Paul Berglund had walked away from her on the shore. If she was still in Whalsay she wasn't with anyone who'd known her in the past.

Joseph arrived just as Perez was leaving. 'Should we organize a few of the men to walk over the hill?' he said. 'Maybe the lass has fallen, broken an ankle.'

Perez hesitated. It was dark now. And Hattie was last seen on the shore. Why should she be wandering over the hill? In the end it was Sandy who answered.

'Should we not wait until the morning when it's light? We don't know that she didn't leave the island, and she'd hate a fuss.'

Perez called in at the Bod again on his way back from Utra and was surprised to find Sophie still there. He didn't have her as the sort of woman to spend a whole evening in on her own. She was lying on the bed reading a book, a can of lager in one hand, and didn't move when he knocked; she just shouted for him to come in. Now the sun had gone in, it felt cold in the stone building but she didn't seem to notice. Her rucksack was beside her on the floor with clothes spilling out.

'Is there still no news?' Now she did seem almost concerned. At least she did look up from her book. 'It's not like her. She doesn't usually do much except work.'

'I wondered if you had a phone number for her mother.'

'No. I don't think they keep in touch a lot.' She set down the novel and twisted her body so she was lying on her side, facing him. 'Hattie's mum's a politician, more worried about her work than her daughter. Hattie didn't say so, but that was the impression I got.'

'What about her father?'

Sophie shrugged. 'He's never mentioned at all. But we don't really go in for girly heart to hearts about our families.'

'How has Hattie been lately?'

'Well, she's always been kind of weird. I mean intense. Mostly on digs you work hard during the day then party in the evenings. I think she'd keep working all night given half a chance. And she definitely has a problem about food. Most people eat like a horse on a dig – it's hard physical work. She hardly swallows enough to keep a sparrow alive. But towards the end of last season she lightened up a bit. Maybe the place was getting to her, helping her to relax. When she came back this time she seemed full of the joys of spring.'

'Finding the coins must have made her feel she doesn't have to put in so much effort.'

'You'd have thought so, wouldn't you? But since Mima died she seems to have gone super-weird again. Withdrawn. I've had enough of the mood swings. And I'm not sure archaeology is my thing after all. I'm hoping to persuade my parents to invest in a little business for me. An old schoolfriend is opening a cafe bar in Richmond and she's looking for a partner. More my scene. I mean, a girl needs some fun. I told Paul this afternoon that I was resigning.'

'Did Hattie know you'd decided to leave?'

'Well I didn't tell her. I didn't want to provoke one of her sulks. I thought Paul would do it when he took her off on her own this afternoon.' She pointed to the overflowing rucksack. 'I was making a start with the packing. Now I've decided to leave I want to go as soon as possible.'

Had the news that Sophie had resigned been enough to push Hattie over the edge, to make her hide or run away? Perhaps. She could have seen it as rejection of a sort. It hadn't prompted Hattie to phone him though. She'd done that before her meeting with Berglund.

Back at the hotel, Perez found Berglund still in the bar, still working. He'd moved on to whisky, was sitting with a glass in one hand and a pen in the other.

Perez took a low chair on the other side of the table. 'Sophie tells me she's resigned.'

'I know, it's a bugger. I don't know who we'll find to replace her at this stage.'

'What did Hattie make of the news?'

'She seemed pleased. She said she'd just as soon work on her own. I have the feeling the girls haven't got on so well this season. I'm not sure how that would play with our health and safety officer though, especially as Setter is empty now.'

'You didn't think to tell me about this when I was looking for Hattie earlier?'

'It didn't seem important. Besides, I'm still hoping I can persuade Sophie to change her mind. Haven't you found Hattie yet?'

The question was an afterthought. He seemed curious but hardly concerned. *Am I the only person to be worried about the girl?* Perez thought. Even Sandy had thought he was overreacting. But Sandy had his own concerns at the moment: a grief-stricken father and a funeral to prepare.

'No. I thought I should check with her family in case she's left the island. I don't want to organize a full-scale search if she's not here. Do you have a phone number?'

He expected Berglund to resist, but perhaps thought of the search, the publicity it would bring to the university, made him suddenly co-operative. 'I'll have it in a file on my laptop. Give me a few minutes and I'll get it for you.'

Perez made the phone call from his room. Gwen James answered immediately. 'Hello.' A deep voice, rich, pleasant on the ears. Perez had a picture of a dark woman, full-breasted, singing jazz in a shadowy club. Ridiculous. She was probably skinny, fair and tone-deaf.

He introduced himself; found himself stuttering, trying to explain, to hit the right note. 'There's no real cause for concern at this point. But I wondered if you'd heard from Hattie.'

'She called me this afternoon.'

He felt a brief moment of relief. 'Did she tell you she planned to leave Whalsay?'

'She didn't tell me anything. I was in a meeting and my phone was switched off so she left a message. She just said she'd call back. She wanted to talk to me. Of course I tried to phone her when I was free but I couldn't get through on her mobile. She often has no reception there. Perhaps she borrowed a phone to call me, or used a public box.' There was a moment's silence. 'I can't help worrying about her, inspector. In the past she's had mental-health problems. She's not good when she's under stress. I thought the island would be perfect for her. Safe, relaxing. And she did seem to have a great time last year. But on the phone she sounded quite ill and panicky again.'

It was as if she was blaming Shetland, as if the place had betrayed her trust.

'Is it like her to take herself away if she's feeling upset?'

'Perhaps. Yes, you're probably right. She preferred to be alone even as a child. Crowds always sent her into hysterics.' She paused, then added quickly, 'I don't think I can come up. Not at short notice. I have to be in the House tomorrow. I'm not sure how I'd explain my absence. The last thing Hattie needs if she's unwell is a pack of reporters on her trail.'

She seemed completely in control. Perez remembered what Fran was like when she'd believed Cassie to be missing: so desperate that she could hardly speak.

He wondered if this woman suspected where Hattie might be, if that was why she seemed so calm.

'Hattie wouldn't have gone to her father?'

'I don't think so, inspector. We divorced while Hattie was still a toddler and he's never taken much interest in her welfare. He's a journalist. The last time I heard he was in Sudan.'

'Is there anyone else she might have contacted if she was feeling ill? A nurse or a doctor?'

'I really don't think so. It's possible, I suppose, that she could have phoned the unit where she was treated as an in-patient. I'll check. If they've heard from her I'll get back to you.' She paused again. 'You will be discreet, won't you, inspector?'

In the hotel he talked to Billy Watt, one of the regular workers on the ferry that ran from Whalsay to Shetland mainland. By now the bar was closed. Berglund had taken himself to bed without waiting to hear if there was news of Hattie and Billy had come along as a favour. He couldn't get there earlier because his son wouldn't settle. 'He's teething,' Billy said, a great grin on his face. 'Poor little man.' They sat in Perez's room, drinking coffee.

'I think she might have left Whalsay on an afternoon ferry. Have you seen her about? Little, very dark. Would you recognize her if she went out with you?'

'I don't know her, but we don't take that many foot passengers. I'd remember if she came out while I was working. There was no one like that on my shift.'

'What time did you start?'

'Four o'clock this afternoon. There were two ferries working today like there usually are. Just because I didn't see her doesn't mean she didn't leave the island.'

Perez was wondering what could have scared the girl so much that she'd run away. *I should have persuaded her to talk to me on the phone*, he thought. *I should have dropped everything and come to Whalsay immediately. She had three hours to wait between leaving Paul Berglund and seeing me. What happened that she couldn't bear to wait three hours?*

'I'll talk to the rest of the crew,' Billy said. He sat on the windowsill of Perez's room at the front of the hotel and looked out to the trawlers moored in the harbour. Further out to sea a buoy was flashing. 'Will it wait till the morning now? I wouldn't want to bother them if it's not desperate. Some of them are working the early shift tomorrow.'

She's an adult, Perez thought. *Twenty-three. An intelligent young woman.* 'No,' he said. 'It'll wait until the morning.'

He expected Billy to make an excuse and leave, but the man sat there drinking the last of the instant coffee made using the kettle in the room. When Perez offered him another one he accepted. Perez was glad of the company. At least with Billy here he could keep Hattie's disappearance in some sort of perspective. When the crewman left, his imagination would run wild.

'You know what I'd do if I wanted to leave the island without anyone seeing me?' Billy set his mug on the floor beside him. 'I'd get a lift in a car. Specially in the small ferry, most folk just stay in their cars on the way across. We don't notice the passengers when we're taking the money. You register there's someone sitting there, but you never really look at them. There were a few of those today.'

'Who might have given her a lift?' Perez was talking almost to himself. 'And where would she go once she got to Laxo?'

'Depends what time she got there,' Billy said. 'Sometimes there's a bus to Lerwick connects with the ferry.'

Perez thought perhaps he'd seen the bus when he was driving north out of town. Was it possible that their paths had crossed? Perhaps Hattie had been sitting in the bus, hunched in the seat, staring out of the window. If she didn't turn up in the morning he'd have to talk to the bus driver. He wondered if someone in Whalsay had a photo of her. Either Sophie or Berglund would surely have a picture. He didn't want to have to call Gwen James again. *All this is an overreaction. Hattie might be an adult but she's immature, overwrought. She's upset because Sophie couldn't face working with her any more. She's like a kid in the playground, burying her head in her hands and hoping the bullies will go away.*

He was reassured by the idea that she'd got a lift and left the island, that she was safe and well on the NorthLink ferry, going south to meet her mother. Sandy had been right. There was no need to make a fuss. He'd give Joseph a ring and tell him to hold off the search until he'd spoken to the ferry company in the morning.

Now Billy did stand to go. 'Let's hope the bairn is still asleep, eh?' Perez was so obsessed with thoughts of Hattie that it took him a moment to realize he was talking about his son.

Chapter Twenty-three

Sandy woke very early to a beautiful morning. There was sunshine and very little wind. The house was quiet, not even his father was up. He got out of bed and decided this was the earliest he'd been awake for years, maybe since he was a bairn, unless he was called out to some emergency at work. It was all this healthy living, he thought. It was no good for a man. It was making a mess of his body clock. In the kitchen he made coffee and drank it outside. Through the open door he heard the sound of the cistern refilling upstairs. He didn't want to talk to either of his parents, so he set his mug on the doorstep and walked away from the house.

Without thinking he found himself on the way to Setter. His head was full of the missing Hattie. He thought Perez was right and she'd just run away. There were times when Whalsay got to him like that. He just wanted to turn his back on the place and never come home. And Hattie was such a frail and nervy young woman. Pretty, with those big black eyes, and he could see that some men would find her attractive. Men who wanted a woman they could look after and protect. But Sandy thought life with Hattie would be kind of complicated and he liked to keep things simple.

When he got to his grandmother's croft, he let the hens out before going into the house to have a piss and make another cup of coffee. There were signs that someone had been in the kitchen: a half-full bottle of Grouse and an unwashed glass, an ashtray full of cigarette butts. That would be his father. Sandy knew Joseph came to Setter to escape Evelyn and to remember Mima in peace. The kitchen had a squalid feel to it that made Sandy feel miserable. He hated to think of his father sitting alone here, smoking, drinking and grieving.

Outside the sun was still low. It glittered on the sea, a silver line at the horizon mirrored again on the loch at the end of the field. A twisted, woody lilac bush, bent by the wind, was coming into bloom close to the house. Over the water, a scattering of gulls was making a terrible racket and in the clear morning light they looked very white against the sky. He remembered Anna's words: 'You're lucky to have been born here.' He supposed on a day like this the place *was* kind of perfect.

He walked across the field towards the dig, his coffee mug still in his hand, and paused as he always would now at the spot where he'd found Mima's body. Would it be such a terrible thing to give up his work in Lerwick and take over Setter? He was good with beasts and it would make his father awful happy. If he sold his flat he could bring some cash and some energy into the place, make a real go of it. But even as the thought came into his head, he knew it was impossible. He'd end up hating his family and the island. It was better to stay as he was and just come every now and again to visit.

By now he'd reached the practice trench where his mother had found the skull. He peered inside. What was he expecting? More bones, growing out of the ground, an elbow maybe, bent like a huge potato tuber? Or a row of toes? Of course there was nothing, except the earth scraped flat by his mother's trowel.

He sauntered on to the deeper trench where the medieval house had stood, where the silver coins had lain hidden for hundreds of years. He knew he was putting off his return to Utra. He couldn't face the stoic good cheer of his father or his mother's restless energy. He had a hazy recollection of television documentaries. What if he found a whole heap of coins, gold and silver, jewellery maybe? He had a picture of a pile of rubies and emeralds glinting in the morning sunshine. Wouldn't that be considered treasure trove? Wouldn't it make enough money so his parents could take a holiday, so they wouldn't have to work quite so hard to keep up with the Cloustons and the other fishing families? He checked himself: he was making up fairy tales in his head again. As a child he'd been told stories of the trows who hoarded shiny, glittering objects, but it would never happen in real life.

But as he approached the rectangular hole in the ground, for a moment it seemed as if the childish fantasy was being played out in real life. The sunlight was reflected from an object within it, a dull gleam that might be buried treasure.

He looked down, excited although he knew how foolish he was being, and saw Hattie James lying at the base of the trench. She was on her back and she stared up at him. Her face was marble white in the shadow. She was dressed in black and the image had the washed-out look of a photographic negative. Even the blood looked black – and there was a lot of blood. It had spurted into wave-shaped patterns on the bank of the trench and seeped into the soil. It was on her hands and her sleeves and on the big brutal knife with which, it seemed to Sandy, she'd slit her wrists. The cuts weren't made across the wrists, but were deep, lengthways slashes, almost up to her inner elbow. The sunlight continued to reflect from the knife blade and made a mockery of the earlier image he'd formed in his head.

He couldn't take his eyes off her face, the sight and shape of it were swimming in front of him. He realized he was about to faint and leaned forward, forcing himself to stay conscious. He turned away, then had to look back to check it wasn't some awful nightmare. He couldn't phone Perez until he was certain. Then he went back to the house to call the inspector's mobile.

Perez answered immediately, but when Sandy explained in a stuttering sort of way what he'd found, there was a complete silence.

'Jimmy, are you there?' Sandy felt the panic taking over. He couldn't deal with this on his own.

And when Perez did reply his voice was so strange that Sandy could hardly recognize it.

'I was at Setter last night,' Perez said. 'I looked across the site, but not in the trenches. I should have found her.'

'There would be nothing you could do.'

'I persuaded myself that she'd gone out on the ferry,' Perez said. 'I should have been more careful, brought people out to do a proper search. She shouldn't have had to be there on her own all night.'

'She would have been dead by then,' Sandy said, and again: 'There would be nothing you could do.' It seemed odd to him that he had to reassure his boss. Usually Perez knew what to do in every situation; he was the calm one in the office, never flustered and never emotional. 'Will you come over? Or is there someone I should call?'

'You'll need to get a doctor to pronounce her dead.'

'Oh, she's dead,' Sandy said. 'I'm quite sure of that.'

'All the same,' Perez said. 'We need it official. You know how it works.'

'I'll get Brian Marshall. He'll be discreet.'

'I'm on my way then.' Just from the way the inspector spoke those words Sandy knew Perez was blaming himself for Hattie's death and he always would. He wished Perez didn't have to see the white face in the shadow of the trench, the long, deep cuts to the white inner arms, the blood that looked like tar. He would like to protect his boss from that sight.

While they waited for the doctor to arrive, they stood by the edge of the pit that Sandy now thought of as Hattie's grave. Perez was in control again, quite professional.

'I recognize the knife,' he said.

'Does it belong to the girl?' Sandy had assumed that it did. Surely if you were going to kill yourself you would use an implement familiar to you. You wouldn't drag a stranger into your suicide by using someone else's knife.

'No, it's Berglund's.'

'He must have left it here on the site,' Sandy said.

'They put all the equipment in the shed close to the house overnight.'

'For the time being we treat this as a suspicious death,' Perez said. 'Keep everyone out. And I want the knife fingerprinted.'

'But she killed herself.' Sandy thought that was obvious: the posed position, the slit wrists. This was an overwrought lassie with a vivid imagination and a taste for the dramatic.

'We treat it as suspicious death.' This time Perez's voice was loud and firm. Sandy thought it was the guilt getting to him. Hattie had asked the inspector for help and now he felt he'd let her down. Sandy couldn't think of anything to say to make things better.

Perez looked up at him. 'How would she know to cut herself in that particular way? Most suicides fail because they make tentative slashes across the wrists.'

'I don't know,' Sandy said, almost losing his patience. 'She was a bright lass. She'd look it up. There are probably sites on the internet.'

There was a moment of silence then Perez turned away from the trench. 'Your father was here last night,' he said. 'He was at Setter. That was one of the reasons I didn't stick around. He looked upset.'

Sandy didn't answer that either. He knew his father would never hurt anyone and that Perez was feeling so bad about the girl's suicide that he was looking for someone else to blame.

Chapter Twenty-four

The Fiscal was wearing a soft suede jacket and a cashmere sweater in pale green. She'd put on wellingtons before coming on to the archaeological site, folding her trousers carefully into them so they wouldn't be creased when she came to take off the boots. The three of them looked down at the girl in the trench. Perez could hardly think straight; ideas and pictures were dancing round his head. He struggled to hold himself together in front of the Fiscal. He'd had to notify her formally of another suspicious death, but he wished he'd had more time before she turned up. He hadn't thought she'd be here on the first ferry.

'Have we had a doctor to declare life extinct?' the Fiscal asked. She carried a hardback notebook and a slim silver ballpoint. Throughout the discussion she was making notes.

'Aye.' Sandy got in first in his eagerness to gain her approval. 'Brian Marshall came along earlier.'

'Did he hazard an opinion as to cause of death?'

'Everything consistent with suicide.' Sandy again.

'But he said there'd need to be a p-m. before we could come to a real decision.' Perez almost felt that he was defending Hattie. This grotesque show, so tasteless and flamboyant, didn't seem her style at all.

'I don't suppose he could tell us anything about the time of death?'

'Nothing that helps,' Perez said. 'We know she was last seen at about four o'clock. I'd arranged to meet Hattie at six in the Bod and she didn't turn up. That could mean she was already dead by then, but not necessarily. Sophie was working here until about four-thirty and claims not to have seen her.'

'Where was she seen at four o'clock?'

'On the footpath close to the shore.' Perez was finding it easier to think straight now. If he could just focus on the facts he might see this through without making an idiot of himself. 'I phoned round all the Lindby folk last night. Anna Clouston saw her making her way back towards the Bod. Hattie and her boss had been walking along the beach before that. He was congratulating her on making a significant find at the Setter dig, but he also told her that her assistant had resigned. She'd found Hattie difficult to work with and she'd decided to ditch archaeology anyway. I have the impression Sophie doesn't need to work for a living and this wasn't much more than a passing fad.'

'So the assumption is that the woman killed herself after some sort of disagreement with her boss.'

'I don't think there was a disagreement. Berglund passed on the news of Sophie's resignation. Hattie didn't seem too unhappy about working the site alone.'

'All the same . . .' the Fiscal broke off and looked up from her notebook for a moment. 'You say she had a history of mental illness?'

'According to the mother when I spoke to her last night.'

'There must have been an implied criticism in

Sophie's decision to leave, don't you think? Sophie obviously didn't enjoy working with Hattie. That would have been hurtful to a sensitive young woman.'

'Perhaps.' Perez hoped she could tell by the tone of his voice that he didn't agree.

'Any previous suicide attempts?'

'We didn't go into that sort of detail. But she did say she'd been treated as an in patient in a psychiatric hospital and the mother was obviously worried about her.' *Though not worried enough to come to Shetland to see for herself.* 'Her colleagues both say that since Mima's death she's become more isolated and withdrawn. Even her success at the dig doesn't seem to have raised her mood very much. They'd found some silver coins to validate her theory about the building. Everyone expected her to be very excited. She was – she talked to me about her plans for the future of the project – but she still seemed troubled. Mima Wilson's death seems to have affected her deeply.'

'You'd met her, then. Couldn't the resignation of her colleague have pushed her over the edge?'

'Unlikely, I'd have thought. She seemed very self-contained to me. I had the impression that she preferred to be alone. Her boss didn't seem to think that Sophie's wanting to leave had upset her very much.'

The Fiscal seemed to come to a decision. 'We need to talk to the mother before we commit ourselves on this. If the girl has attempted suicide before, we don't want to turn this into a full-blown murder inquiry. That'll mean bringing the team in from Inverness.'

Which had implications for budget, not to mention the Shetland tourist trade. The Fiscal wouldn't make herself popular with the politicians if she called it as murder and it turned out to be something less dramatic. And at the moment she was very keen to keep in with the politicians.

'I'm worried about the coincidence,' he said. 'Two sudden deaths, one explained as an accident, another as a suicide. I can't accept it.'

'That *had* crossed my mind too.' Gently sarcastic. *I'm not a fool, Jimmy.* Her voice hardened. 'But I won't be drawn into conspiracy theories. She was a depressive young woman. This looks like a classic adolescent suicide.'

'She was twenty-three,' Perez said. 'Hardly an adolescent.'

The Fiscal stretched. It was as if he hadn't spoken. 'Yes, the most likely cause of death is suicide and that's how we'll play it for now. Is the mother coming into Shetland?'

Perez paused, remembering the phone call he'd made to Gwen James earlier, the silence on the other end of the line, broken eventually by a single sob. 'Not immediately. She says she can't face it. Not yet. I have the feeling that she would hate to break down in public and that she'll be hiding out in her own home for a while.' How did he know that? He wasn't sure but he thought it was true.

The Fiscal frowned. 'We need some background on the girl's medical history. You'll have to talk to her, Jimmy.'

Again Perez remembered the earlier call. 'I'm not sure that's a conversation we could have on the phone.'

The Fiscal considered for a moment. Perez thought she was weighing up the cost of a trip south against the value of providing good customer service to a politician. 'Get yourself to London to talk to her, then. Get this afternoon's plane south. Give me a ring when you get back.'

Sandy shuffled his feet, making the shingle scrunch and shift. Perez knew what was going on in the Whalsay man's head. *Take me too.* He wasn't sure if Sandy had ever been to London; perhaps once on a school trip. He pictured him wandering around the streets, staring up at the buildings he'd only ever seen in films or the television news. Sandy looked up at Perez and caught his eye. Pleading. Perez read the expression exactly. He'd sensed the tension in Utra. Sandy was desperate to escape, even if only for a couple of days. But there was no way he could justify both of them being away from Shetland.

Perez took a risk, knew he would probably come to regret it later. It was as much about showing Rhona Laing that he wouldn't be bossed around as giving Sandy a chance.

'I wonder if this is a job Sandy could do. It would be fine experience for him.'

Fran was in London. If Perez went himself he'd have the opportunity to spend the night with her. But she'd want to introduce him to her friends. He knew how it would be. Some trendy wine bar, loud voices discussing topics about which he had no knowledge and no opinion. He'd show her up. So this was about cowardice too.

Rhona Laing raised her eyebrows. 'This is a sensitive job, Jimmy. The woman's a politician.' Sandy wasn't exactly famous for his tact or discretion. Or his brains.

'I think he's ready for it. We'll talk it through before he goes. And I want to be here.'

She shrugged. 'Your call.' Leaving him in no doubt that he'd be the one to get the blame if Sandy screwed up.

Perez caught Sandy's eye again and saw pure terror. This wasn't what he'd had in mind at all. He'd imagined going along with Perez for the ride, a night in a London hotel on expenses, a bit of sightseeing, not being left with full responsibility for the interview, not having the wrath of the Fiscal on him if he made a mess of things. 'Go and get your bag packed. I'll call in to Utra when I've done here and we'll discuss the approach you should take.'

Sandy scuttled away.

Perez walked with the Fiscal to her car. 'I really don't think that was one of your most sensible decisions,' she said sharply. 'I'm not sure he'll even get as far as London without a minder.'

'I think I've under-estimated him in the past. He's shown a lot of sensitivity on this inquiry. Besides, Gwen James will be good at handling questions from sophisticated interviewers. She does it all the time in the Commons and with the media. I hope Sandy's simplicity will get under her guard.'

The Fiscal looked at him as if she didn't believe a word, as if Perez were mentally ill himself, but said nothing.

News of Hattie's death had got out around the community, as Perez had known it would. A small group of onlookers had gathered at the gate, drawn by the drama rather than by any sense of involvement with the dead woman. She was one of the lasses working on the dig; that was all. Even Evelyn only thought of her as part of the project. Mima was probably the only person on the island to have really known her.

When the Fiscal drove off the people started to drift away and Perez saw Sophie on the edge of the group.

'I'm sorry,' he said. He could see that she'd been crying. She wasn't the sort to cry easily and he was surprised by the display of emotion. He watched the other people walk back to the road. Most of the islanders had cars there. Jackie Clouston scurried back on foot to her mansion on the hill. Had she left Andrew alone to check what was going on?

Sophie sat on the grass beside the track. She was wearing combat trousers and a university sweatshirt, walkers' sandals. Her toes were wide and brown. 'I feel dreadful. There I was slagging her off yesterday, and all the time she was planning to kill herself.'

'You had no idea anything like that was in her mind?' He sat beside her.

There was a pause. Perez thought she was preparing to say something significant, but she seemed to decide against confiding in him and only shook her head. 'I never knew what she was thinking at all.'

'You won't be able to work here. Not for a while at least.' He still thought the Setter land should be treated as a crime scene. 'When were you planning to leave?'

'I thought I'd stay until after Mima's funeral,' Sophie said. 'I decided when I heard what had happened. Hattie would like me to be there for that.'

In Utra Sandy was in a state of terminal panic. Joseph was nowhere to be seen. His mother was ironing a shirt for him and there was a pile of underpants on the kitchen table. Evelyn was obviously proud that her son had been chosen for the mission but was ratcheting up the anxiety. Edinburgh she could understand. Michael had been to college there and lived there. It represented sophistication. London was a different world, alien and violent. A place of hooded gangs and foreigners.

'You'll only be away a night.' Perez took a seat.

'Where will I stay?'

'I'll get Morag to book somewhere for you. And I've fixed up for you to meet Hattie's mother in her home. It's in Islington. Not far from the Underground. I'll show you a map. She's been told about her daughter's death. Don't worry, man. This time tomorrow you'll be on your way back into Sumburgh.'

I'm not sure I can do this. He didn't have to speak the words. Perez knew what he was thinking.

Evelyn finished ironing the shirt and hung it on a hanger on the door. She folded up the ironing board and propped it against the wall. Then she left the room with the underpants in one hand and the hanger in the other. They could hear her banging around in Sandy's bedroom. She obviously considered him incapable of packing for himself.

'Look,' Perez said. 'The woman's a mother who's just lost her daughter. That's all you have to concentrate on. Forget about what she does for a living. Imagine how Evelyn would be feeling if your body was washed up on the shore.'

'Guilt,' Sandy said after a pause. 'She'd be wondering what she could have done to prevent it.'

'And Gwen James will be feeling just the same. You

don't want to make her feel bad about what's happened. She'll be guilty enough without you adding to it. Your role is to get her to talk about her daughter. Don't ask too many questions. Just give her time and the sense that you're really listening to her. She'll do the rest.'

'Couldn't we suggest she fly up here? Then you could talk to her.' Sandy had the air of a man desperately clutching at straws.

'I did suggest it and I'm sure she will want to come up. But she says not now. She prefers to be in her own home. And I prefer you to see her there, on her own territory, where she'll feel most comfortable. You can do this, Sandy. I'd not send you to London if I didn't think you'd do it well.'

Perez left Sandy to get ready and went outside to find Joseph. The older man was in the barn doing something to the insides of an ancient tractor. When he saw Perez he wiped his hands on an oily piece of cloth. He looked very pale.

'This is a terrible business. Two deaths on Setter land.'

'Nothing to do with the place, surely,' Perez said.

'I don't know. That's how it seems.'

'You were there last night.'

'How do you know that?' The older man looked up, startled. It was as if Perez had performed some sort of conjuring trick.

'I saw you through the window. You looked upset. I didn't want to disturb you. What time did you get there?'

'I don't know. After my tea.'

'Did you go outside? Down to the dig?'

'No.'

'Did you see anything? Hear anything?' Perez looked at Sandy's father. In the gloom of the barn it was hard to tell what he was thinking.

'No,' Joseph said. 'I just go there some nights to drink and forget. I didn't hear a thing.'

Chapter Twenty-five

Sandy arrived at Heathrow at the height of the rush hour. He'd never liked the idea of the Underground, even before the bombings were all over the television. It seemed unnatural being shut in a tunnel, not being able to see where you were going. Anyway, he'd had a look at the map on the back of the A–Z Perez had loaned him and it all seemed too complicated for him to work out. He couldn't make sense of the different-coloured lines. Instead he got the direct bus to King's Cross. That was where it terminated, so there should be no danger of getting out at the wrong place. Perez had asked Morag to book him into a Travel Inn in the Euston Road. Sandy would check in and collect his thoughts before he went to speak to Gwen James. He was still astonished that his boss had trusted him to do the interview, felt extreme pride and extreme fear in the space of a minute.

The bus was full of people. Sandy looked to catch someone's eye and start up a conversation with a local, a person who would be able to reassure him when he reached his destination. But they all seemed exhausted after their flights; they sat with their eyes closed. Those who did talk weren't speaking English. Whenever he went to Edinburgh or Aberdeen, Sandy had the same reaction of claustrophobia for the first couple of days. It was being surrounded by tall buildings, the sense of being shut in, of not being able to see the sky or the horizon. This was just the same but the buildings were even taller and closer together and there was a feeling that the city was endless; there would be no escape from it.

Coming into the city centre, he had the odd flash of excitement when they passed a street name he recognized, a signpost to a famous monument, but it didn't last. He was here for work. This was one interview he couldn't get wrong. He peered out into the streets looking at the people who were walking past. Perez's woman, Fran Hunter, was in London at the minute. He'd feel happier if he could glimpse just one familiar face. Of course he knew it was impossible. What was the chance of seeing her among all those thousands of people? But it didn't stop him looking.

Walking to his hotel he had to push against the flow of people hurrying to King's Cross and St Pancras Stations. He felt he couldn't breathe. If he stood still for a moment they would flatten him, walk right over him without hesitating, without stopping to find out what was wrong.

In the hotel the receptionist struggled to understand his accent, but the room was booked and he was given a plastic card instead of a key. It seemed a very grand room. There was a big double bed and a bathroom. He looked out over the Euston Road at the line of traffic and the pavements heaving with people. He was so high up that the only noise was a dull hum, a background roar like waves on the shore on a stormy day, the sound Mima had called 'the hush'. He turned on the television so he couldn't hear it. He had a shower and changed into the shirt his mother had ironed for him. She'd folded it carefully in his overnight bag and it was hardly creased at all. *I should be nicer to her*, he thought. *She's looked after me so well. Why can't I like her more?*

It took him a while to find the kettle hidden away in a drawer, but then he made himself a cup of tea and ate the little packet of biscuits. He didn't feel like eating a proper meal. Perez had said he could get something on expenses, but he'd wait until after the interview. He wanted to phone Perez to tell him that he'd arrived safely, then decided that would be pathetic. He'd wait until he had something to report.

The road was less busy when he went out to find Gwen James's place. He decided he'd risk the Underground. It was only a few stops and Perez had marked the route from the Underground station on the map. He didn't have change for the ticket machine and had to queue at the office; he was ridiculously pleased with himself when he found the right platform for his train.

He arrived at Gwen James's flat far too early and walked about the streets waiting for time to pass. It was dark and the streetlights had come on. Some of the basement flats had lit windows so he could see inside. In one, a beautiful young woman dressed in black was cooking dinner. It seemed unbelievably glamorous to Sandy, the sight of the slender young woman with her shiny hair down her back, a glass of wine on the table beside her, cooking a meal in the city flat. There were trees down each side of the street; the leaves were new and green in the artificial light. On the corner of the road music was spilling out of a pub. The door opened as a man in a suit came out and Sandy heard snatches of laughter.

He stood outside Gwen James's flat and took a deep breath. There were two bells. Beside hers was a handwritten label – *James*. The writing was in thick black ink and italic. He rang it and waited. There were footsteps and the door opened. She was tall and dark. If you were into older women – and Sandy wasn't really – she was attractive. High cheekbones and a good body. She carried sophistication about her and seemed completely at home in this city. It occurred to Sandy that in twenty years' time the young woman he'd seen in the basement flat would look like this.

He introduced himself, trying to speak slowly so she'd understand him first time and he wouldn't be forced to repeat himself. Perez always said he had a tendency to gabble, and she wouldn't be used to the accent.

'I was expecting Inspector Perez.'

'I'm afraid he couldn't leave the islands.'

She shrugged to show it was of no real consequence and led him into a living room that was as big as the whole of Sandy's flat. The colours were deep, rich browns and chestnuts with splashes of red. She lit a cigarette, inhaled deeply.

'I gave up when I joined the Department of Health,' she said. 'But I don't think anyone would criticize me now.'

'Don't you want someone with you?' If there was a death in Whalsay, folk gathered round the relatives. This seemed an unnatural way to grieve.

'No,' she said. 'I really don't want to become a spectator sport.' She looked at him through the cigarette smoke. 'Did you know my daughter?'

'Yes, my mother Evelyn was involved in the archaeological project. My grandmother lived at Setter, the croft where they were digging.'

'Mima? The old woman who died?'

'Yes,' he said. 'She got on very well with Hattie.'

'Hattie wrote to me about her. I was pleased she was making friends on Whalsay, but jealous too in a way. My daughter and I always had a very strained relationship. It seemed sad that she was closer to a stranger than she was to me.'

'I don't think that was true.' Sandy knew families were tricky. Look at his relationship with his mother. 'My grandmother got on with all the young folk in the place.' He paused. 'Did Hattie write to you often?'

'Once a week. It was a habit she developed after she left home. A duty. I think she found it easier than talking to me on the phone. She started when she went to university and continued even when she was quite ill in hospital. She kept it up ever since. We got on quite well by letter. Things only became difficult when we met in person.'

Sandy wondered fleetingly if he should try writing to *his* mother. 'I don't suppose you kept her letters?'

'I did actually. Isn't that sad? I have them all in a folder. When I feel especially lonely I re-read them. And do you know, she probably thought I just glanced at them then threw them away.'

Sandy didn't know what to say so he kept quiet. That was what Perez did. 'Just give her time and sense that you're really listening to her.'

'Would you like to see them?' Gwen stubbed out the cigarette and looked at him through narrow eyes.

'Very much.'

'Shit,' she said. 'I don't think I can do this entirely sober. Will you have a drink with me?'

He nodded. It wasn't even as if he wanted a drink now, though he could have used one earlier. He didn't want to break the mood.

'Wine?'

He nodded again.

She came back into the room with a bottle of red wine and two large glasses, which she held by the stems between her fingers. She uncorked the wine and left it on the low table beside him, then went out again. When she returned she was carrying a folder full of letters. She sat on the sofa beside him, so close that he could smell her perfume and the cigarette smoke that remained in her hair.

'This is the most recent. It arrived yesterday. That was why I was so surprised when she phoned me. We didn't communicate by phone very often, and what new could she have to say?'

'Did you keep the envelope?' Sandy asked.

'No.'

'I wondered when it was posted.'

'Oh, I can tell you that. Just the day before I got it. I was impressed – it had come all that way.'

She handed him the sheet of paper. It was A4, white, unlined. It seemed to him that the writing was very neat. He thought it was a strangely old-fashioned way for someone so young to keep in touch with her mother. He always phoned home and even Evelyn used email.

Dear Mum

It's been a very odd week. On Tuesday there was a terrible accident. Mima, who lives at Setter where the dig is based, was shot. It's hard to imagine a tragedy like that on a place like Whalsay. Apparently one of the islanders was out after rabbits and she was hit by mistake. She was wearing my coat. I can't help feeling responsible. You'll say that's the old paranoia coming back and perhaps you're right. Her death has unsettled me. Don't worry though. I'm fine, keeping on top of things. And yes, I am eating.

Then today we made a tremendous discovery on the dig – silver coins which prove that I was right about the building there. There's some talk about recreating the house as it would have been in the fifteenth century, but that's a long way off. Sometimes I'm not sure that I'm up to carrying it through, then I think it would be the most exciting project in the world. And I'm here at the start of it.

How are things going with you? I heard you on the Today programme earlier this week and thought you kept your cool very well. Look forward to hearing from you. See you soon.

Love, Hattie

'What do you think?' Gwen had almost finished her first glass of wine.

Sandy's mind went blank and he forced himself to come up with a response. 'She doesn't sound so depressed.'

'That's what I thought when I first read it, now I'm not so sure. "Sometimes I think I'm not sure that I'm up to carrying it through". Perhaps that means she was thinking about killing herself.'

'No,' Sandy said. 'It means she was making plans for the future. That's what it sounds like to me.'

'If you're right, something must have happened between her writing the letter and phoning me. Don't you think so? Or at least she came to see events in a different way.'

Sandy didn't know what to think. He had very few opinions of his own. He said nothing.

'I mean, this letter is quite calm. But by the time she phoned me she sounded really distressed.'

'Have you saved her message on your mobile?'

'Yes.' She fumbled in her bag and pulled out her phone.

'I'd like to take the SIM card with me, let my boss hear it. And there are other things we could learn. Like where she was calling from. It might help.' He wasn't sure he could face hearing Hattie's voice now. Not in this room with her mother listening. But Gwen James hadn't taken any notice of him; she was already pressing buttons.

'Mum! Mum! Where are you? Something dreadful's happened. I can't believe it. I think I was wrong about Mima. I need to talk to you. I'll try later.' The voice was high-pitched with panic. Sandy remembered Hattie sitting at the table in the Utra kitchen, smiling at something Evelyn had said. She'd been upset when she'd learned Mima was dead, but this was quite different. This was real distress.

'Had Hattie ever tried to kill herself?' he asked. 'I know she was ill in the past.'

'No,' Gwen said listlessly. She was still staring at her phone. 'Once she said she wished she was dead but that's not quite the same, is it?'

'No.'

'When I read the letter I thought she was OK. Upset about the old woman but basically fine. I've lived with anxiety about my daughter. Some people think I'm hard-hearted because I don't talk about her, because we didn't live together. It would have been easier to have her here where I could keep an eye on her, but she needed her own life. Sometimes I don't think about her for a whole working day; then I feel guilty. I dreamed that one day the anxiety would stop, that I could stop worrying about her. There'd be some magic new medication or she'd find a man to love her and take care of her. Over the winter it seemed that had happened. Shetland had worked some sort of magic. She still had her bad days, but she seemed calmer, almost happy.' She paused, breathed in a sob. 'Now I'd give anything to have the worry back.'

Sandy held his glass and sipped the wine. He wished he could say something to make it easier for the woman. Perez should have come. He would have known what to say.

'Do you think Hattie killed herself?' Gwen's question came at him so hard and fast that it made him blink.

'No,' he said without thinking. Then, blushing, realizing what he'd done, 'But you mustn't take any notice of me. That's just my opinion and I get things wrong all the time.'

She looked at him. 'I'm grateful that you've come all this way.'

'My family is from Whalsay. If you'd like to come back and see where she stayed, we'd be happy to show you.'

Standing outside the flat on the pavement with the woman's SIM card in his pocket and the file of letters in a supermarket carrier bag, Sandy thought he hadn't achieved a lot. What would Perez say? And the Fiscal? All that money to send him and really he'd not found out much at all. He couldn't face the rattle of the Underground, the blank faces. He looked at the map under a streetlamp and walked through the mild city night all the way back to his hotel.

Chapter Twenty-six

Perez watched the ferry carry Sandy away from Whalsay on his way to London and thought this must be what his own parents had felt when he was twelve and he was sent off from Fair Isle to stay in the hostel at the Anderson High School in Lerwick: responsible for his loneliness and as if they'd deserted him. All day whenever his phone rang Perez thought it would be Sandy, stranded somewhere, or lost in the city.

He found Berglund still in the Pier House Hotel. He seemed to have taken up residence at the table by the window, turning the place into his office, filling it with his laptop computer and his piles of paper.

'You'll have heard about Hattie?' Perez said.

'Yes, what a waste! She was such a talented girl. I've never been able to understand suicide.' There was an academic interest in his voice but no real regret.

'Your knife was found by her body.'

'Really?' He looked up sharply from the computer screen. 'I hadn't even realized it was lost.' He gave a shiver of distaste.

'We'll need to keep it for forensic examination.'

'Oh, I don't want it back. I'd never feel able to use it again.'

'When did you last see it?'

'I can't remember. I certainly had it yesterday morning on site. I suppose I must have left it there. Or I could have dropped it while I was walking with Hattie.'

'Did you see her pick it up?'

'Of course not, inspector. I'd have expected her to give it back to me, wouldn't I?' He gave a little laugh, as if he could hardly believe the detective's stupidity.

Perez drove from Symbister to Lindby and the big Clouston house. Jackie was outside, cleaning the windows of the lounge, polishing them with a dry cloth, so vigorously that you'd think she'd make a hole in the glass. She turned round, suddenly aware that she was being watched.

'I know,' she said. 'One storm and they'll be covered again with salt. But it's good to get the view, at least for a while. Everyone said Andrew was daft to rebuild his house here, where it's so exposed, but we wouldn't like to be lower down. We like the sea all around us and a bit of a view.'

'I don't want to disturb you.'

'You're not. I was just looking for something to do. A distraction, you know. Another death on the island . . . It's hard to take in. I didn't really know the lassie working in Setter but it's a shock all the same. Come away inside.'

He expected to see Andrew in his usual chair in the kitchen but it was empty. Jackie saw that he was wondering about her husband. 'Ronald's taken him out for a peerie drive. Up to the golf club so he can have a bit of company with his friends, then they might call in at the sailing club or have a drink at the Pier House. He's not been well the last few days. It gets Andrew down, not being able to get out with the boys on the boat. He was the one who made all the decisions. Now he feels kind of powerless. It's not a physical thing so much; he just gets frustrated. Anna wanted Ronald to make a start on her garden today, but I said to him, "That can wait. Your father's more important than planting a few beans and tatties."'

Perez wondered what Anna had made of that. But he just nodded. 'Can we go through into the other room? Enjoy the view now the windows are so clean?'

'Aye,' she said. 'Why not? I usually sit in the kitchen, but you go through and I'll bring the coffee in to you.'

It was a big square room the width of half the house. There was a marble fireplace and the furniture was large and shiny: two sofas covered in grey satin, a highly polished sideboard and a couple of gleaming occasional tables, a gilt-framed mirror on the mantelpiece. The photographs were posed and covered in glass. There was one of Jackie and Andrew's wedding, Andrew looking very grand in a morning suit, a giant standing next to his little wife. There was a shot of the house when it was first built, Ronald's official school photos. The room seemed cold and impersonal. Perez wondered how often it was used. He sat on a chair looking out through the long window. He could see the whole of the southern point of the island, from the new bungalow where Anna and Ronald lived, along the boulder beach to Setter where Hattie's body had been found.

Jackie bustled in with a tray: the best china, milk

in a jug and real coffee in a pot, a plate with home-made biscuits. What else did she do besides baking and housework? He thought she must get bored here in the giant show-house. Did looking after her husband take up all her time?

She seemed to guess what he was thinking. 'When we built the new house, I thought I might take in paying guests. Not so much for the money but because I'd enjoy the company, meeting folks from all over the world. That's one of the reasons why it's so big.'

'Sounds like a good plan. Especially with Anna running the workshops. It would save her having to put people up in the Pier House or in the bungalow.'

'Aye well, Andrew doesn't like the idea. Not now. Since the stroke anything out of his usual routine upsets him. He couldn't face meeting strangers.' She shook her head, dismissing the dreams she'd had once.

Perez poured coffee, waiting a moment to enjoy the smell. 'Did you see Hattie James yesterday?'

'No. I didn't really know her. We weren't on visiting terms. Evelyn took it on herself to look after the lasses, but that's the sort of woman she is. She has to poke her nose in everywhere, especially when money's involved. She's not the saint everyone makes her out to be.'

'How would money be involved?' He was genuinely curious.

'They'd surely get a fee for the dig at Setter.' He sensed there was something more she wanted to say, but she snapped her mouth shut.

Perez left the subject alone. He thought he should defend Sandy's mother, but really how much did he know about the woman, except that she was hospitable? He found the bickering between the cousins depressing. Suddenly he was back in Fair Isle, at a Sunday-school lesson in the hall, him a child of seven or eight, listening to a gentle, elderly woman talking about a love of money being the root of all evil. 'The love of money, you see. Not the money itself. It's when money takes over our lives that things start to go so badly wrong.' *Is that what's happening here?* he thought. *It's not the wealth itself that's soured relationships between these two families. It's the bitterness and envy that surrounds it.*

'So the lasses from the dig never came in here?'

'No. Once we used to have grand parties and invite most of the island. We'd push back the furniture; someone would start playing music. Grand times. Then the house would be full of young people. Ronald would bring in his friends from the High School and all the boys from the boats would come along with their wives and kiddies. Andrew was a great one with the accordion. There'd be songs and dancing. But Andrew can't deal with big numbers of visitors these days. He finds it a strain just with the family.'

'Of course.' Perez helped himself to more coffee. 'You must miss the old times.'

'Oh,' she said. 'You'd never guess how much.'

She looked down towards her son's bungalow. Perez thought her head was full of fiddle music, memories of parties and laughter. Had she expected Anna to take on her role as hostess and party giver? Was she disappointed in the daughter-in-law who seemed more interested in building a business than having a good time?

'Hattie and her boss went for a walk along the

shore here yesterday afternoon,' he said. 'You have a great view from the house. Maybe you saw them?'

'Andrew wasn't so good yesterday. Sometimes he gets an idea in his head and he can't let it go. He worries away at it and it drives him crazy. I had to call Ronald in to calm him down.'

'What was it that troubled him?'

'It was the accident with Mima. Something about the shooting took him back to when he was young. He's a good few years older than me and he can remember Mima's husband. Andrew's father worked with Jerry Wilson building little inshore boats to go out to Norway on the Shetland Bus. The boats they made were used by the Norwegian resistance and agents in the field. It was a long time ago. Mima's man died years ago, not so long after the war ended, when I was a very young bairn, so what could he have to do with the accident? But sometimes that's the way Andrew's mind works. Things that happened when he was a peerie boy seem more real than what went on yesterday.'

'So you didn't get the chance to look at the view of the shore? You won't have noticed Hattie and Paul Berglund out here?'

She flashed him a smile. 'Yesterday I didn't get the chance to go to the toilet without Andrew standing at the bottom of the stairs and asking where I was. Ronald managed to calm him down a bit when he got here. He's good with his father, more patient than I am.'

'Perhaps you saw her later, when she was on her own.'

'No,' Jackie said. 'I didn't see her at all.'

'But you saw the Fiscal come in this morning? I noticed you with the others.'

'I saw the crowd gathering when I was upstairs making the bed. I went down to Setter to see what was going on. Pure nosiness. That was the first I heard the girl was dead. I couldn't stay long. Andrew was in the house on his own.' She looked up at him. 'How did the lassie die?'

'I'm sorry,' he said gently. 'It's not something I can discuss.'

'No,' she said. 'I don't suppose you can.' She paused. 'They're saying it was suicide.'

'Really, at this point we don't know.'

'What must her parents be going through?' Jackie said. 'We'd do anything to protect our children but we can't save them from themselves.' She smiled at him. 'Do you have children, inspector?'

He shook his head automatically. *But surely I do. Cassie feels like my daughter. How would I feel if she was so desperate that she jumped into a hole in the ground and slit her wrists?*

Chapter Twenty-seven

Sandy was surprised when Perez was at Sumburgh Airport to meet him. He'd left his car there and he could have driven north fine by himself. After a few beers and a meal in the hotel in London he'd slept like a baby until his alarm clock had woken him and in the morning the city hadn't seemed quite so daunting or closed in.

It helped that he had something physical to bring back to Perez in the form of Hattie's letters and the SIM card from her mother's phone. He'd made some notes about the conversation too, but he didn't trust himself much with words. At least he wasn't coming back empty-handed.

In the plane he'd looked out for the first sight of Sumburgh Head and landing there he felt relief at being back safely without having messed up in any dramatic way. Then he saw Perez waiting for him in the terminal, leaning against the wall by the car rental desk, and he felt nervous all over again.

'What's happened?' His first thought was that Gwen James had been on the phone to complain about him. Sandy wasn't sure what he might have done wrong, but that had never stopped him getting into bother. Then he worried about his family.

'Nothing.' Perez grinned. 'I was just curious to hear how you'd got on. I got a lift down from Val Turner. We had a meeting in Lerwick. She's flying south for a day for a conference.'

'What did you have to talk to her about?'

'I wanted to ask her about these bones the girls have been digging up at Setter. Everyone's assumed that they were hundreds of years old, but we don't really know that's the case. If they were more modern we'd look at the recent deaths in quite a different way. Three bodies in the same bit of land. Even the Fiscal would have to accept that was more than a coincidence.'

'What did Val say? If the body was recent, surely there'd be more than a few bones left.'

'I suppose so. It doesn't make sense. It's probably coincidence. It just seems odd. Both women had a connection with Setter and there's evidence of another burial there too . . .' His voice tailed off and he shrugged. 'Take no notice. I'm probably making too much of it.'

Sandy thought Perez would never have talked to him like that a few months ago, never have taken him into his confidence. There was a moment of the same sort of panic he'd felt before setting off to London. How could he live up to these new expectations? 'There were always strange stories about Setter,' he said tentatively.

'What sort of stories?' Perez looked up sharply.

Now Sandy wished he'd kept his mouth shut because he didn't really know, not the details. He half remembered tales of ghosts and the dead walking at night.

'Some folk didn't like to go out there after dark. Old folk. It's all forgotten now.'

'Would your mother know the stories?'

Sandy shrugged. *Even if she did, she wouldn't tell you. She'd be frightened of looking foolish.* He changed the conversation. 'So what did Val say about the bones?'

'She thought they must be ancient. Another theory down the drain. But she's fast-tracked them for testing and she'll let me know as soon as she can.'

The airport was quiet and they sat drinking coffee at one of the tables outside the shop.

'Have you read all the letters?' Perez was watching an elderly couple in conversation with the guy at the check-in desk. Sandy followed his gaze. They were holding hands. Gross, he thought. At their age they should keep that sort of thing for their own home.

'No. Only the most recent one.' *Of course*, Sandy thought, *I should have looked at the letters. Perez would have stayed up all night reading them, worrying at them. He wouldn't have got pissed on expensive lager in the hotel bar and fallen into a drunken sleep.* In the plane on the way home Sandy had read a glossy men's magazine with a topless model on the cover; he hadn't really given a thought to the case.

But Perez made no comment. 'What was your impression of Gwen James?'

'Like you said, she felt guilty. She'd done what she thought was the best for her daughter.' Sandy found himself wanting to show Gwen in a good light. 'She didn't want to intrude on Hattie's life but you could tell she cared about her. I mean, work obviously takes up a lot of her time but that didn't stop her worrying.'

'Does she think Hattie killed herself?'

'She says that Hattie talked about wishing she was dead when she was very depressed but she'd never attempted suicide. And she doesn't think Hattie was so depressed at the moment. All winter in the university she'd been positive, looking forward to getting back to work in Whalsay. The last letter seemed to be about plans for the future. It was only the phone call that really worried her.'

'And we can listen to that?'

'Yes, I've brought back the SIM card.' Sandy had checked his pocket at least a dozen times to make sure it was still there. Now he took it out and gave it to Perez, pleased to be relieved of the responsibility. 'I said she could have it back once we've finished with it. It's the only record she has of Hattie's voice.'

'Of course. You did well to persuade her to let you have it.'

They'd finished their coffee. Sandy had the impression that there was something else Perez wanted to say. They sat for a moment in silence.

'Should we go then?' he said at last. He'd never had Perez's patience.

Again there was a moment of hesitation. It came to Sandy that Perez was as reluctant to go back to Whalsay as he was. It was the muddle that made things difficult. Should they treat the deaths as crimes or not? Were they on the island as part of the community or as investigating officers? The Fiscal would only support them if it suited her and at the moment she was keener on pleasing the politicians.

'Aye,' Perez said. 'We can't sit here and drink coffee all day.'

Sandy was going to say that Perez was lucky. At least he didn't have the funeral of the decade to live through on the following morning. Then he thought that might sound childish and ungrateful and it didn't tie in with his new adult image. And it might sound disrespectful to Mima too. He was proud that he was learning when to keep his mouth shut.

Sandy had expected Perez to come all the way back to Whalsay with him but the inspector asked to be dropped at his house in Lerwick. He said he didn't need to be in Whalsay; he had other work to do and he should let the Fiscal know how the interview had gone with Gwen James. He'd come back to the island when there was word on the date of the bones.

In Utra, Sandy's mother hardly seemed to notice he'd returned. Michael and his family were due in on the last plane from Edinburgh. Sandy had thought she'd be full of things to say about Hattie, but the girl's death seemed to have slipped from Evelyn's consciousness, pushed out by essentials like what the baby might eat for breakfast and whether Amelia could possibly cope with towels that didn't match the bedlinen. Sandy was surprised that the whole family would make the trip from Edinburgh to Whalsay. He wondered what his sister-in-law hoped to get out of the trip. Did she think Mima had anything worth leaving?

Joseph had made himself scarce too. Evelyn said he was in Setter making sure the Rayburn was lit and the house fit for Sandy to stay in.

'I'll go and see if he needs a hand.' Sandy had bought a bottle of single malt at Heathrow. He tucked it into the inside pocket of his jacket and walked down the track towards Setter. The weather was fine and still. He thought in London it would never matter what the weather was like and which way the wind was blowing.

Joseph was squatting in front of the Rayburn. The fire had gone out. He was plaiting twisted pages of newspaper and laying kindling on top of it. He heard Sandy come in and smiled when he saw who it was.

'There's a pile of peats in the yard. You'll not go cold at least.'

Sandy took the bottle from his jacket with the air of a conjuror. 'You'll take a dram.'

'Aye well, maybe a small one. Can't go back drunk with Michael and his wife about to arrive. What would your mother say?'

They smiled conspiratorially.

'Well,' Sandy said, 'if it gets too much for you over the next day or two you can always hide away here.'

Joseph put a match to the paper and the kindling flared and caught. He set a peat on top of it, then another. The smell of peatsmoke filled the room, caught Sandy's throat and reminded him so vividly of Mima that he had to blink to be sure she wasn't there too.

Sandy turned away and brought two tumblers from the cupboard on the wall, rubbed the dust away with a tea-towel hanging on the range, poured out the whisky. His father shut the Rayburn door. They clinked glasses, a silent toast to Mima, and settled to drink.

'Did you hear they'd found some more old bones after Mother dug up the skull?' Sandy thought his father would surely know. He never seemed to be listening to gossip, but he had Mima's genius for sniffing out what was going on in the island. 'They could belong to an ancestor of ours. What do you think?'

'I think they should stop digging up the Setter land.' The voice was hard, quite unlike Joseph's. Sandy looked up, shocked. He'd never heard his father talk like that before, even when he was a boy and he'd misbehaved. Joseph continued: 'I think if they hadn't been mucking around here my mother would still be alive.'

'Why do you say that?'

'Two deaths in a week,' Joseph said. 'When was the last time anyone died from anything other than natural causes on Whalsay?'

Sandy wasn't sure his father was expecting a reply, said nothing.

'Well?' Joseph demanded.

'I don't know.'

'I've been trying to think,' Joseph said. 'My father was lost at sea. That was more than fifty years ago. I can't mind any accidents since then. And now two people dead in a week. I never liked the idea of strangers rooting around in the ground and I wasn't the only person in the island to feel that way. Mima was an old woman but she wasn't ready to die. The English lass was a child. Now you say they've dug up a pile of bones.'

'Not a pile,' Sandy said. 'And old bones. Likely hundreds of years old.'

'I don't care. I'll go and see that Paul Berglund tomorrow morning before the funeral. I'll tell him I want them to leave. I don't care what arrangement he made with Mima. This is my land now. It shouldn't be disturbed.'

Sandy sat, feeling the heat come off the Rayburn

and the whisky in his throat, wondering what he could say to make his father less miserable. It wasn't like him to be superstitious. Why hadn't he realized his father was so upset? Joseph would never let on what he was feeling, but Sandy should have known Mima's death would have hurt him more than he was showing.

'I'll speak to Berglund,' he said at last. 'You'll have enough to do tomorrow.'

'Your mother won't like it.' Sandy expected another sly conspiratorial smile, but Joseph was quite serious. 'You know she has plans for this place.'

'A fancy museum, with her in charge,' Sandy said. 'Aye well, she'll have to find herself another project, something else to fill her time.'

'It hasn't been easy for her, living with me. I was a poor sort of catch as a husband. We never had as much money as the other families in Lindby.' Joseph reached out and poured himself another dram. Michael and the Edinburgh wife were forgotten. 'You should be easier on her. She hated it when we couldn't give you things the bairns from the fishing families had.'

'You've always looked after her well enough,' Sandy said. 'We never went short.' Outside it was already starting to get dark; it was still early in the year and the sun was low in the sky.

'That was down to her more than me. She was a magician with money, always had a way to make it stretch.' Despite the warmth still left in the day, Joseph reached his hands out towards the range. His face was a shadow.

'What do you plan to do with Setter?' Sandy asked. As he did with Perez, he felt his relationship with his father was different from how it had been in the past, more equal. He was being taken more seriously. And he thought if he could bring his father back to practical matters the man might be more his old self. 'I wondered if you'd consider moving back here.'

'Oh I don't think I could do that!'

'Why not?'

'You can never go back. Never relive your life.' Joseph drained his glass, paused. 'I wondered if you'd want Setter. I always thought I'd make a good crofter out of you. You've got a way with the beasts.'

'No!' Sandy realized he sounded horrified and that his father would be offended, but he could think of nothing worse. To live where his mother could always find him, to have his life the subject of island speculation, his girlfriends scrutinized. To have his skills always measured against those of his father. 'I have thought about it,' he said. 'But it wouldn't work. I've got my job. I love it.' As soon as the words were spoken he knew they were true.

'Of course,' Joseph said. 'It was a stupid thought.'

'I'll see Berglund in the morning, tell him we want the place to ourselves for a while.'

'Aye, you do that.' Joseph got up. He walked towards the sink to rinse his glass under the tap.

'Leave it,' Sandy said. 'I'll see to it later.' He stood too. They faced each other. There was a moment of silence.

'We'd best get back,' Joseph said at last. 'Your brother should be here soon. Evelyn will be sending out a search party.'

They walked together through the dusk to Utra and arrived just as Michael's hire car appeared at the end of the track. The stars were coming out.

Chapter Twenty-eight

The day before Mima's funeral, Anna took the afternoon ferry to Lerwick to pick up her dress from the dry-cleaner's. It had been loose round the waist before she became pregnant and it still fitted now. This was her first trip there with the baby. She felt self-conscious pushing the pram down the street in Lerwick, like she was an impostor, a little girl playing at mummies and daddies. She still didn't quite believe in her role as mother.

She was pleased to get out of the house. You'd have thought Ronald would be happy that he wasn't going to get charged with Mima's killing, but he seemed more moody than ever. Anna always enjoyed a trip into town and today she decided she'd turn it into a treat, with good coffee and a scone in the Peerie Cafe and a browse around the Shetland Times Bookshop. She was almost feeling like her old self again and the baby had stopped squawking, for this afternoon at least.

On her way into the cafe she bumped into a woman she'd met at a seminar the year before. Organized by the Shetland Islands Council, it had been for first-time entrepreneurs. Jane was setting up her own computing business. They had coffee together and time passed quickly as they chatted, first about the baby of course, but soon after about plans for their respective businesses. Jane was a southerner too, a little older than Anna, and she'd never had children. She said she found being self-employed very lonely. She was thinking of looking for a partner.

When Anna had first come up with the idea of the Fibre Workshops she'd considered asking Evelyn to come into partnership with *her*. She'd thought it would be good to have one of the Whalsay women on her side and Evelyn's background, her voice and her stories would bring an authentic flavour to the enterprise. But in the end Anna hadn't wanted to share control of the project with anyone. Evelyn had been disappointed, Anna had been able to tell that, but she'd still been generous in her support. She'd let Anna use her knitting patterns and copy her recipes for the dye. Evelyn had even tried to raise some funds for the business from the Shetland Islands Council. That hadn't worked out in the end – money was a lot tighter than it used to be, Evelyn said – but it had been kind of her to try.

Anna didn't discuss any of this with Jane: she didn't think the woman would understand that she preferred to work on her own. But at the end of the afternoon they exchanged email addresses and promised to keep in touch.

When she got home Anna felt almost elated and over supper she talked about the meeting to Ronald.

'That's good,' he said. 'I'm glad you had a fine afternoon.' But she sensed he was preoccupied with his own thoughts. He wasn't listening to her at all.

'What is it?' she asked. 'Something I can help with?'

He shook his head without speaking.

She felt another little stab of impatience. Why wasn't he stronger and more decisive? She could forgive him almost everything except his weakness.

On the morning of the funeral she dressed carefully. As soon as she got up she took her dress from its plastic wrapper and laid Ronald's suit on the bed. He'd disappeared early to the big house after another summons from Jackie. She went to have a bath and saw the suit was still there when she came back to the bedroom. Sitting in front of her dressing-table mirror to fix her make-up, she could see its reflection, reminding her that Ronald was still not home. Soon the neighbour who had offered to mind James would be here. Anna thought it would be embarrassing if Ronald hadn't appeared before the woman arrived.

She didn't usually bother with make-up, but today she wanted to show that she'd made an effort to look good. It was the only way she could face meeting all those people. Besides, her confidence could do with a boost too. She'd felt so lumpy and awkward in the last stages of pregnancy. She glanced at her watch again, although she knew quite well what time it was and wondered when Ronald would get back from his parents' house. In another half an hour they would have to leave for the kirk. His lateness was making her feel tense. Where was he? She suspected he might have changed his mind about going to Mima's funeral. *I shouldn't have let him go up to the big house*, she thought. *I shouldn't have let him out of my sight*. Anger began to bubble inside her. He always managed to let her down.

She began planning what she should do if he didn't turn up. Should she go to the funeral alone? Then she heard the front door and felt the usual mix of fury and relief. She looked at her watch again. They'd just have time to make it.

He came into the bedroom. He was flushed. She thought he'd run down the hill.

'My father won't come,' he said. 'I don't know what's wrong with him. He's been in a state all week, but never this bad. My mother won't leave him.'

'We'll just have to go on our own then.' Anna thought this might be a blessing in disguise. She'd rather have Ronald to herself. They'd be more discreet, just the two of them. Much better than turning up mob-handed. Jackie was always fierce in defence of her son and capable of causing a scene. Anna turned to look at him, wondering if he planned to use his father as an excuse not to be at the funeral, but he was already getting undressed.

'Do you think I've time for a shower?'

'If you're quick.'

Still in front of the mirror, she watched him coming out of the bathroom with the towel wrapped round him. She would have liked to take him into her arms and dry him, but she felt quite shy and instead watched him secretly, pretending to brush her hair. There was a knock on the door and she left him alone and went to let the neighbour in.

They crossed the spit of sand that attached the land where the kirk had been built to the rest of Whalsay. Theirs was the last of a line of cars. The kirk was packed with people. There were folk here from other communities on the island, from Symbister, Skaw and Isbister as well as from Lindby. Looking for spare seats, Anna saw the blonde girl from the dig and the university professor sitting together; the pews were so full that they were pushed against each other, their shoulders touching. The girl was wearing black jeans and a black V-neck sweater. The story on the island was that her parents were very rich, so Anna thought she could have been able to come up with something more suitable to wear than that. The professor wore a suit and a black tie. At least he'd come prepared.

Evelyn and Joseph sat in the front seat with Sandy and his brother Michael. Anna had only met Michael once. Evelyn had brought him down to the bungalow when he was visiting, keen to show off the successful son who'd made it big in Edinburgh. Now Anna thought he looked rather strained, his shoulders hunched, his hands clasped as if he was praying. Sandy stared ahead of him like a small boy trying very hard not to cry.

People had stared when she and Ronald walked in. There were nudges and whispers. Ronald had paused beside her, but she'd taken his hand and they carried on walking, both looking straight ahead of them. They found seats next to an elderly couple she only knew by sight. She often saw them together, casting peat or working the planticrub on the hill close to Setter.

When the first hymn began Anna found herself crying. She wasn't in the least musical – she couldn't hold a tune or play an instrument – but sometimes music touched her in that way. Now, standing in the middle of all these people, the noise swelling around her, she found herself sobbing. Ronald gave her his handkerchief, took her hand in his and stroked the back of it with his thumb. After the first verse Anna told herself she must still be reacting to the hormones and managed to pull herself together. She thought Ronald would find her emotion out of character and rather embarrassing.

After the service they stood in the graveyard. It was neat and ordered, the grass mown. The sun was still shining and the water surrounded them on three sides. The gannets had returned to the islands after a winter at sea and were diving straight into the bay, looking very white against the grey water. She turned back to the group around the grave and watched the small coffin being lowered into the ground. She found it impossible to imagine that the real Mima was lying inside.

Her breasts were heavy with milk and she thought about James waiting for her at home. She realized she would be buried here. Her life was all mapped out and nothing would get in her way. She and Ronald would have more children. The children would be baptized in this church and later they would marry here. If there were a daughter, Ronald would walk up the aisle with her to give her away. Anna would become a real Whalsay wife, with a kitchen full of grandchilden.

People were starting to drift away now. They had been invited back to Utra for tea. Anna knew that the tea would be too much for Ronald and that anyway they probably wouldn't be welcome. They would go straight home. She would need to feed James. Evelyn left very quickly. Anna knew how she would be, filling kettles, taking the clingfilm off the scones and the cakes, an apron over the Sunday-best dress. Joseph and his sons remained standing next to the grave.

She was about to take Ronald's arm and lead him away. She was proud of the way he'd held things together. She knew he'd never wanted to be there and she wondered if she'd been right to insist.

But without her noticing he'd moved away from her and gone to talk to Joseph and the boys. He held his hand out to Michael. She couldn't hear what he said. Michael hesitated for a moment, looked at his father and his brother and then took the offered hand. Anna remembered Evelyn telling her that he had become quite religious after his marriage. Amelia's influence. Perhaps he felt it was his duty to forgive. Then Sandy had his arm around Ronald. Both men seemed to be close to tears. Joseph kept his distance, but didn't seem hostile.

'It'll be all right.' She realized that she'd actually spoken the words under her breath. There was nobody close enough to hear and she repeated them a little louder. This had been a terrible week but they'd got through it. With Mima's burial out of the way, they'd be able to put the awful events behind them.

As she waited for Ronald to finish talking to Michael and Sandy, Sophie and Paul Berglund came up to speak to her. It seemed they'd walked to the kirk. Sophie looked so pale and drawn that Anna thought she must be sick. Then she remembered that the girl's friend had died too. Sitting through the service must have made Hattie's suicide seem very real. Anna was convinced that the police would decide the death was suicide. What else could they think it would be?

'We wondered if we might have a lift back?' Berglund said. 'You don't mind, do you?'

'Look, it's OK.' Sophie's hair was blowing about her

face. 'We can walk. We don't want to put you out. Perhaps you're going back to Utra.'

'No. We have to get back for the baby. He'll need feeding.' Anna thought again how poorly the girl looked. She couldn't believe Sophie was capable of walking all that way in such a state. Sophie had always been so fit. Anna had recruited her into the Lindby women's rowing team and the student loved the exercise and got out of the boat after a race beaming, hardly sweating. But Sophie was young. Perhaps she thought it was OK for an old woman to die violently, but not a person of her own age. 'If you don't mind waiting till Ronald's finished talking to the boys we'll take you back. Where do you want to go? The Bod or the Pier House?'

'The Pier House,' Berglund said before Sophie could speak. 'We both feel like a stiff drink.' He put his arm around Sophie's shoulder. Anna supposed he could just be comforting her because she'd had such an upsetting few days, but it didn't seem like that. It seemed more intimate and proprietorial.

Ronald waved to her and started walking to the car. She would have liked to ask him how he was feeling, what the Wilson men had said, but it was awkward with the strangers there. They drove to Symbister in silence.

On impulse at the hotel, Anna got out of the car to say goodbye to the visitors. She reached out and put her hand on Sophie's shoulder.

'Hattie must have been ill,' she said. 'Why else would she do something like that? Come in to the bungalow whenever you want to. It would be good to have the company.'

Sophie nodded. There were tears in her eyes again and she seemed unable to speak. Berglund held her close to him again and led her into the hotel.

Chapter Twenty-nine

Perez wasn't there for Mima's funeral. He'd explained his decision to Sandy the day before. 'It's not a lack of respect. Please tell Evelyn that. I'll be thinking about you all. But it'll be a distraction to have the police there.'

And Sandy had nodded, understanding how it would be. There'd be gossip enough over the means of Mima's dying. Perez's presence would just give the congregation something else to talk about.

Instead Perez sat in his room in the Pier House and read Hattie's letters to her mother. Without any real decision having been made, it seemed he'd taken up residence in the hotel. He'd come back there the evening before after his meeting with the Fiscal. In the morning when he came down to breakfast Jean, the skinny Glaswegian, grinned at him. 'Still here then?' Now she knew what he liked: a big pot of very strong coffee, scrambled eggs, brown toast. She'd say, 'Do you no' fancy something more substantial this morning?' But teasing him, not expecting a different order.

Before starting to read the letters, Perez went into the kitchen to find her and asked if she'd be kind enough to make him some coffee to take into his room.

She was on her own; Cedric Irvine would be at the funeral. He could tell the woman would have liked him to stay and chat to her, but he was eager to get back to the letters. She had only been on the island a short time and he didn't think she could have much to tell him. It occurred to him again that he should talk to Cedric about Mima, but because he'd be at the funeral it would have to wait.

The letters were kept in chronological order, though Perez didn't read them that way. Sandy had told him that Gwen James treasured them, that she'd missed Hattie when she went off to college and would have found it easier to keep her daughter at home, protected. Perhaps Perez had misjudged the woman. His parents had thought it was in his best interests to send him away to school in Lerwick at the age of eleven. But really, he thought, they'd had no choice.

He dipped into the letters in a disorganized, irrational way. He'd read them in order later, but now he wanted a flavour of what Hattie had to say. The first few he came to had been written from a psychiatric hospital. They were short, rather incoherent, written on cheap lined paper, and the handwriting was quite different from the rest of the scripts – sprawling, the words slanting away from the lines. At first it was clear Hattie resented being there. *Please, please let me come home. I really don't need this. I can't stand it. I want it all to end.* Was this the reference Sandy had mentioned to her wishing she were dead? Later in her stay as an in-patient they became more chatty. *We all went to the swimming pool in town today. I haven't been swimming in ages and enjoyed it a lot. The minibus broke down on the way back to the unit. We had to walk back and Mark led us like a bunch of schoolkids along the main road. I almost expected him to tell us to get into pairs and hold hands.* As her mood improved her handwriting changed, became tidier, more controlled.

There was a gap of two weeks. Perez assumed that she'd moved home before her return to university and there was no need to write to her mother then. He wondered how they'd got on. He wished he'd had the opportunity to meet Gwen James, so he could picture the household more clearly. Had there been long meaningful talks every evening? Or had both women found it easier to pretend that nothing much had happened in Hattie's life, that the girl's absence from home had been perfectly normal, like a holiday job or a trip away? Had Gwen continued to lose herself in her work?

Perez went right back to Hattie's first few weeks at university, before the breakdown and the hospital admission. The paper was plain A4, but the letters were handwritten, not printed from a PC. She never missed the weekly letter. Perez was surprised by the discipline: most students surely led disorganized lives, they went to parties, gigs, had hangovers and last-minute essays to complete. But perhaps Hattie's life at university was unusually ordered. It was clear that she was ambitious and determined to do well academically. The university letters were mostly about her work. If she had any social life she didn't tell her mother about it. He read each one carefully, looking for references to friends who might be contacted for information about Hattie's state of mind, but those who were mentioned were talked of in passing as colleagues. It seemed unlikely that Hattie had kept in touch with any of them.

He had almost given up hope of learning anything from the letters apart from an insight into Hattie's life. He finished the coffee and stood up to stretch, looking down at the harbour. Everything there was unusually quiet. The ferry was making its way towards Laxo, but no other boats were moving. He supposed that most of the island would be at the funeral. Then, reading a letter from an address he didn't recognize, he saw a familiar name.

It was dated at the end of June and came in Hattie's first long vacation, the summer before the stay in the psychiatric unit. The tone was happy and enthusiastic. Perez thought how relieved Gwen James must have been to read it. *I'm loving every minute of the experience. This is definitely what I want to do with my life. Paul Berglund, who's in charge of the dig, came on to the site today and seems delighted with the way things are going. He took us all out to the pub after we'd finished for the day. Had a bit of a hangover the next morning!*

There was no other reference to Berglund in that letter. Perez thought if that was their only contact, the professor could be forgiven for not recognizing a student who'd helped as a volunteer. However, two weeks later he was mentioned again.

Paul took me out to dinner to thank me for my help on the project. He's such a nice man and the best in his field in the country. I'm even thinking of changing my course so I can work in his department. I don't want to lose touch after he's given me so much help.

Perez's attention was caught by the sound of a car outside his window. It was Ronald Clouston's enormous four-wheel drive. He wondered if the funeral had been so difficult for him that he was coming into the bar to drown his sorrows. But Ronald didn't get out of the car. Berglund and Sophie got out of the back seat, then Anna emerged from the front. Perez couldn't hear the conversation. Anna got back in beside her husband and the car drove off. Berglund and Sophie came into the hotel.

Perez was eager to talk to Berglund. When he had asked him how long he'd known Hattie, why didn't he mention meeting her as an undergraduate? But he didn't want to ask him in front of Sophie. He went back to reading the letters.

Hattie didn't mention Paul again and there was no other reference to her changing courses so she could work with him. Perhaps her stint as a volunteer was over, because again there was a gap in the letters to her mother. The next ones came from the hospital. He wondered what had changed so dramatically in her life to turn her from an excited young woman to a depressive who needed in-patient treatment.

When she returned to university she never regained the excitement of her time on the dig managed by Paul Berglund. The news was conveyed in a flat, unenthusiastic way and it was all about her academic work. The handwriting was tight and cramped. She didn't talk about how she was feeling but Perez could sense her unhappiness. She might not be ill but she was very sad. He found the text hard to read. He imagined her in her small cell-like room in the university hall of residence, quite alone, writing to her mother every week because it was what she always did.

The street was very quiet outside, so Perez heard the door of the hotel and the footsteps walking away. He looked out of the window and saw Sophie hurrying off. Her back was towards him so he couldn't see her face.

Berglund was in the bar. No one else was there, not even Jean, but she must have been there earlier to serve him because he was holding a large glass of red wine. Perez supposed that Sophie had joined him for a drink but the empty glasses had been cleared away.

'Inspector, can I get you something?' He was still wearing his suit, but he'd taken off his tie and undone the top button of his shirt.

Perez would have liked another coffee, but he didn't want to call the barmaid in. This was a conversation he didn't want anyone listening to. He shook his head and sat down.

'The church was full,' Berglund said. 'Mima must have had a lot of friends.'

'I wanted to talk about Hattie.'

'Of course.'

'Another funeral you'll have to attend.'

Berglund seemed shocked. 'I suppose I will. Someone will have to represent the university. That makes it seem horribly real. I presume her mother will deal with the details once the body is released. I'd planned to phone Mrs James tomorrow, to offer our condolences and see if we can help in any way.'

'You gave me the impression that you hadn't met Hattie before you started supervising this project.'

'Did I?' Berglund frowned. He didn't have much of a neck and now he tucked his chin towards his chest so it disappeared altogether. It gave him the look of a cartoon bulldog.

Perez looked at him but said nothing, waiting for an explanation.

'I met her when she was an undergraduate,' Berglund said. 'A few years ago. That hot summer. She was volunteering on a dig I was managing in the south of England.' He stopped speaking, stubborn, challenging Perez to ask more detailed questions.

'Why didn't you tell me you'd met her previously?' Perez kept his voice pleasant. If the man felt threatened he might stop talking altogether.

'It slipped my mind. I've worked with a lot of undergraduates over the years. Then when I did remember I didn't want to make too big a deal of it. I thought you might misinterpret the incident, take it out of context.'

'You took her out to dinner,' Perez said. 'One evening in that hot summer, you asked her to go out with you. Just her, not any of the others. Tell me about it.'

Berglund hesitated. Perez thought he was deciding how much he would have to give away. At last he started talking and it was almost as if he was telling a story.

'She was a pretty little thing. I suppose she was still attractive when she was working in Whalsay, but here she could be so earnest. Back then she seemed happier, funny, full of life. Yes, I invited her out to dinner. A couple of times, actually. A spur-of-the-moment decision that I went on to regret. I was married and I had a small child. But after a long day in the field I wanted someone to share a beautiful evening with. I like female company and my wife was two hundred miles away. That was all.'

'Did she know you were married?'

'I didn't tell her but it certainly wasn't a secret. The other volunteers would have known.'

'What happened?'

'The first time, nothing. We shared a meal and I dropped her back at the site. The next time was more intimate. We had a meal in the pub where I was staying. The windows were open and there was honeysuckle in the garden. I remember the smell of it. We shared a bottle of white wine. Then we went to bed together, inspector. Not a crime. I wasn't even her teacher and she was a consenting adult.'

'She was young and very naïve.' Not a judgement, a comment. Perez wished now he'd asked for a drink. His hands were on the table in front of him and he didn't know what to do with them.

'As you say she was young and naïve. She read more into the encounter than I'd expected. Most students are more sexually experienced than I am. She was an exception.' He paused. 'She was nineteen, I was thirty-five. She fancied herself in love with me.'

'Did she make life difficult for you?'

'Not particularly. There was one embarrassing encounter, then she left the dig. I never expected to see her again. Then I changed jobs and found myself supervising a colleague's postgrad student while she was on maternity leave. Hattie.'

'Did you recognize her?'

'Of course, inspector. I don't make a habit of sleeping with my volunteers. But she made no sign that she knew me, so I assumed that was how she wanted to play it.'

'She never mentioned the previous relationship?'

'It wasn't a relationship, inspector. It was a one-night stand.'

'Did you know she'd suffered with depression?'

'No, but I'm not surprised. In our previous encounter and in her work there was a lack of proportion. She took herself too seriously. I can see that might have been a symptom of her illness.'

'She had a spell in hospital after her encounter with you.'

There was another, longer pause. 'I'm sorry. I didn't know.'

'You and Hattie spent some time together on the afternoon before she disappeared. Was any of this mentioned then?'

'Absolutely not, inspector. It was a professional conversation between colleagues. Just as I explained earlier.'

'Is it significant, do you think, that she used your knife to kill herself?' *If that is what she did.*

'You think she still felt rejected by me? That the suicide was some sort of romantic gesture?'

Perez sat for a moment looking at the man on the other side of the table. Berglund seemed almost flattered by the notion and that made Perez feel ill. He thought Berglund had deceived him. He was missing something and he hadn't been told the full story, but he wasn't sure which questions to ask. He couldn't face reading any more of Hattie's letters just now. He went back to his room and phoned Fran. She asked about the inquiry but he refused to talk about it. He wanted her to tell him about Cassie and about everything they'd been doing. He wanted her to make him laugh.

Chapter Thirty

It seemed to Sandy that the funeral service in the kirk passed in no time, like a kind of dream. The place was full of people. The tradition was that it was mostly men who came to a Shetland funeral and when a woman had passed away there were fewer people in the congregation, but today the kirk was packed and there were as many women as men. He wasn't sure why that was – more because they didn't want to miss out on the drama, he thought, than that they'd miss her. She'd always had more male friends than women. Sandy remembered sitting there in the front row and thinking that Mima would have liked the singing. She'd always been one for a great tune. Joseph hadn't said anything throughout the service, but Sandy could hear his mother's voice speaking the Lord's Prayer and in the hymns. She had a high, piping voice that could keep a tune but that still wasn't very pretty. Sandy thought he'd like to marry a woman with a pretty voice.

Then they were outside in the sunshine watching the coffin being lowered into the ground. There was a crowd of gulls fishing from the point below the kirk and he wondered if that meant there was a shoal of mackerel there; that led him to think about Mima frying fresh mackerel on the Rayburn at Setter when he was a boy. She'd roll it in oatmeal and throw it in the pan. When he came to again the service was over and it was just him and his father and brother standing by the grave. His mother had gone back to the house to prepare the tea and the people left behind were hanging around, wanting to give their condolences, but not liking to intrude either. The breeze blew at the women's skirts and messed up their hair.

Ronald came up while they were still standing there. Sandy could tell folk were watching, wondering what the response of the family would be. Michael had said hard words about Ronald when he'd arrived on the island, his big hire car packed with so much stuff for the baby you'd think he was staying for a month: 'Completely irresponsible. He should have known better than to take out a gun after he'd been drinking. I can't believe the Fiscal intends to let him get away with it.' Sandy had thought it sounded more like Amelia speaking than Michael. She'd let slip at one point that she thought the family should sue if the Fiscal refused to prosecute. Now Sandy was worried there might be a scene and that Michael would shoot his mouth off in that pompous, arrogant way he sometimes had about him these days. But seeing Ronald, he seemed to come to his senses. Ronald said how sorry he was. He looked grey and gaunt to Sandy, worse even than when Sandy had found him in the bar the morning after Mima had died. Michael must have realized he meant it, because he took his hand and smiled. It was the old Whalsay Michael, not the new one who lived in Edinburgh and never took a drink.

Back in Utra, Sandy felt more himself. He would have liked to go upstairs to change out of his suit but the baby was in his room having an afternoon nap, so he had to leave it on. He had clothes in Setter and he could have gone there to change, but it didn't seem right to leave the house. His mother would have been cross anyway if he'd come back in jeans and a sweater and he didn't think he could face her scolding today. There'd been some talk of having the tea in the community hall, but Joseph had wanted people back to the house. There were folks in the living room and the kitchen and a few of the boys were standing in the yard having a smoke. Amelia must have taken the time while the baby was sleeping to get her smart clothes on. She was wearing a suit in grey and black and little black shoes with heels. Sandy thought she was very keen that people should admire her, even though she made a show of covering herself up with an apron once they'd all had a chance to see what her clothes were like. She helped Evelyn to hand out the tea and the sandwiches and was polite to everyone to show what a good Christian she was. Later, when the baby woke up, she brought her down and showed her off. Evelyn was flushed with the pleasure of the occasion and you'd have thought it was a baptism they were marking, not a funeral.

Sandy couldn't stand it any more and went through into the living room where the men were gathered and his father was handing out drams.

'Tell me,' one of the men said, 'what plans do you have for Setter?' It was Robert who was a skipper of the pelagic boat *Artemis*. He was a big man in his fifties with a face that was red even before he'd started drinking. 'I'd give you a good price for the house.

My Jennifer's getting married next year and it would suit her fine.'

Joseph looked at him sharply. 'It's not for sale.'

'I'd give you the market value. Cash in your hand.'

'Not everything has a price,' Joseph said. 'I've told you, Setter is not for sale.'

Robert shrugged as if Joseph was mad, and turned away to talk to his friends. Sandy watched Joseph pour himself another drink and tip it quickly into his mouth. He wished all the people would go home so his father could grieve in peace.

It was almost dark by the time the visitors had all gone, and the lights were on in the house. Michael and Amelia were upstairs trying to settle the baby. Evelyn was at the sink rinsing the dishes for the machine. Sandy put the kettle on and offered to make them tea. He was relieved that it was all over. Soon he'd get back to Setter. He thought Perez might drop by to tell him what he'd found out from Hattie's letters. Joseph brought a tray of empty glasses through from the living room. He looked more tired than Sandy had ever seen him, more tired than when he'd been travelling out on the first ferry every day to work for Duncan Hunter.

'I'll just light a fire in there,' Joseph said. 'A day like this, a fire would be kind of comforting.'

'Do that.' Evelyn looked round from the sink and smiled at him.

The fire was made and they sat in there drinking tea. The weather had changed and there was a rattling of rain against the window. Drawing the curtains, Sandy thought the wind had gone northerly; a north wind always brought the weather into this side of the house. The baby was quiet now, but Michael and

Amelia hadn't reappeared. Evelyn took up her knitting. She found it impossible to sit and do nothing, even on a day like today.

Suddenly she seemed to make up her mind about something.

'Robert spoke to me,' she said. 'He wants you to sell Setter to him.'

'I know.' Joseph looked up from his tea. 'He spoke to me about it too.'

Sandy could tell his father was angry, though there was nothing in his voice to give him away. It was quiet and even.

'You won't sell it to him, will you?' Evelyn continued to knit, the needles clacking a background rhythm to her words.

'I won't. I told him: Setter is not for sale.'

Evelyn seemed not to hear the last words, or perhaps she already had her own speech prepared in her head and nothing would stop it coming out. 'Because if you are going to sell, I think we should approach the Amenity Trust. We need the money right enough, and I think they would give us a decent price. The coins the lasses found would give the place an even greater value, don't you think?'

'Don't you listen to a word I say, woman? Setter is not for sale.' It came out as a cry. Not so loud but much louder than he usually spoke, the words passionate and bitter. The sound was so shocking that the room fell silent. Even the knitting stopped. Looking around the room, Sandy saw Michael in the door, frozen and horrified.

Sandy didn't know what to do. Occasionally his father teased his mother about her projects and her meddling into other folks' business but he never raised his voice to her. Sandy hated what was going on in his family. For the first time he began to think he would find it hard to forgive Ronald for killing Mima. He hoped Perez was right and someone else was responsible. Someone he would feel it was OK to hate.

In the end it was his mother who put things right. She set down her knitting and went up to his father and put her arms around his shoulder. 'Oh my dear boy,' she said. 'I'm sorry. I'm so sorry.'

Over Joseph's head she motioned to her sons to leave them alone. Sandy thought his father was crying.

Embarrassed, Sandy and Michael stood in the kitchen. Sandy longed to get out of the house. 'You've not been into Setter since you got back,' he said. 'Would you like to come? See the old place?'

'Aye. Why not? Amelia's asleep on our bed. She finds this sort of family occasion exhausting.'

Sandy bit his tongue. Another sign of his greater maturity.

They walked to Setter despite the wind, which made it feel like winter again, and the sudden showers of rain. Sandy felt more awake than he had all day. The range was still alight in the kitchen. Sandy brought in peat from the pile outside and set it beside the Rayburn to dry for later. Without thinking he poured a dram for both of them.

'Sorry,' he said. 'Mother tells me you don't drink any more.'

Michael smiled. 'Oh, don't believe everything she tells you. I make an exception for special occasions.'

'It seems so strange in here without Mima, don't you think so?'

'When I was growing up,' Michael said, 'there was one time when I believed Mima was a trowie wife. Did you ever hear those stories?'

Sandy shook his head. The trows were part of Shetland folklore, but he'd never believed in them, even when he was a peerie boy.

'Maybe it was before you started school. It was one of those crazes that start suddenly then disappear. They said she was a trowie wife and she'd put a spell on her husband and made him die. For a couple of weeks I wouldn't come here on my own. Then the kids had something else to talk about and I forgot all about it. Until now.'

'Are you saying it was a trow killed Mima?'

Michael laughed out loud. 'A trow named Ronald? I think he's kind of large, don't you?'

Sandy was tempted to tell Michael that maybe Ronald wasn't the culprit but things between the men seemed easy now and he didn't want to spoil that.

'Mother's right about Setter,' Michael said. 'Father should sell it.'

'He'll never do that.'

'I don't think he'll have any choice,' Michael said. 'How much do you think he makes from the crofting? I doubt Duncan Hunter gave him a pension plan and he's not getting any younger.'

'They manage OK.'

'Do they? I don't understand how.'

They sat for a while in silence. Sandy offered Michael another dram but he shook his head. 'I should get back and see how Amelia's getting on.'

Sandy would have liked to ask about Amelia. *What possessed you to take up with a woman like that?* But what good would it do? They were married with a bairn. Michael would have to make the best of it.

'Will you find your way back?'

Michael laughed again. 'Oh, I think I'll manage.'

The first thing Sandy did when he was on his own was to change out of his suit. Then he began to think of what Michael had said about their parents' income and the implications of it. It kept him up late into the night. Once he got up to make coffee, but the rest of the time he sat in Mima's chair, thinking. He would have liked to discuss his thoughts with Perez. Perez would likely reassure him that he wasn't on the right track at all. He was Sandy Wilson and he always got things wrong. But Perez must have thought Sandy would want to be on his own on the evening of his grandmother's funeral and he never turned up.

Chapter Thirty-one

Perez woke the next morning to the sound of his phone ringing. Again his first thought was of Fran and Cassie and their safety in London. The voice was English and female, and at first he didn't recognize it. Suddenly he lost control of his imagination; gothic images of spilled blood and smashed limbs flashed into his head. The woman was a nurse in accident and emergency, he thought. Or a cop, specially trained to break bad news.

'Inspector Perez, I'm sorry to call you so early.'

He struggled to sit upright in the bed and to clear the nightmare pictures from his mind.

'This is Gwen James, inspector. You asked me to contact you if Hattie had been in touch with the psychiatric nurse who looked after her when she was ill at university.'

At last he felt he had a grip on the conversation. 'And had she?'

'Not recently, I'm afraid, but the nurse thought you'd find it interesting to talk to him. He didn't feel he could discuss Hattie's case with me.' Her voice was tight, clipped. Perez thought she'd had a battle over that. She'd demanded information and the nurse had stood up to her. A brave man.

She waited impatiently while he found paper and

pencil to write down the man's number. The bedroom was cold. He'd found it stuffy and airless after his discussion with Berglund the night before and had switched the heating off. Shivering, he got back into bed to complete the call. Despite her apparent impatience, in the end Gwen was reluctant to end the conversation.

'Did you find Hattie's letters useful, inspector?'

'Thank you. Very. We will get them back to you as soon as we can.'

'When you have news about the circumstances of Hattie's death, you will tell me?'

'Of course,' he said. 'Of course.' He switched off the phone before she could ask any more questions.

It was too early to contact the nurse. He'd wait at least until nine o'clock. In the dining room Jean was just laying the tables for breakfast. 'Could you not sleep?' she said as she snipped the top from a carton of juice and poured it into a jug. He wondered when *she* had the chance to rest. She was still behind the bar when the last customer left at night and the place always looked clean in the morning. 'Cedric is still in his bed. He stayed up last night drinking to Mima. He was always very fond of her.'

'Did he ever go to visit her at Setter?'

'Aye, every Thursday afternoon. To talk over old times, he said. To flirt, more like. Mima was a dreadful old flirt.' She hurried away to make his coffee.

Cedric appeared just as Perez was finishing the meal. He looked bleary-eyed and grey.

'Paul Berglund didn't go out on the early ferry, did

he?' Perez asked. He supposed he'd finished with the academic, for the moment at least, but he didn't want the man slinking away without his knowing.

'No, he'll be down later, I'm sure. He doesn't usually get up so early.'

'Did Mima have a good send-off?'

'I suppose she did. I didn't stay long at Utra. All those people sitting round saying fine things about her. They had little enough good to say about her when she was alive. I came back here to have a few drams to her memory in peace. I'll miss her.' Cedric looked up at Perez. The flesh around his eyes was soft and creased like folded suede. 'It seems a strange thing, two bodies on an island this size. What are you doing here, Jimmy? What's going on?'

Three bodies, Perez thought. *There are the bones they found on Setter too*.

'I'm working for the Fiscal, enquiring on her behalf into the sudden death of Hattie James.'

'Aye, right.'

'Is there anything you can tell me, Cedric? Anything I need to know about Mima Wilson and Setter? Anything strange been happening there?'

'Not these days, Jimmy. Not for sixty years at least.'

'What happened sixty years ago?'

'These are old men's tales. You don't have time for these.'

'Try me.'

Cedric paused, then he seemed to make up his mind to speak.

'Three men from Whalsay were involved in the Shetland Bus.' He looked at Perez to check the inspector knew what he was talking about. 'You know it was mostly the Scalloway men that kept the boats repaired and in good order to put to sea. But when Howarth, the naval officer in charge, decided the Norwegians needed small boats to be dropped off with the agents, so they could make their own way up the fjords, he came to Whalsay to get them made. It was skilled work; the inshore boats had to pass for Norwegian. Men's lives depended on it. There was young Jerry Wilson, who was just a schoolboy, too young to get called up into the services but the best sailor of his generation. My father, who was called Cedric Irvine like me. And old Andy Clouston, the father of Andrew.'

'So Mima's husband, your father and Ronald's grandfather?'

'Exactly that. Though Jerry hadn't married Mima then. They were walking out together but too young to wed.'

Perez said nothing. Cedric would want to tell the story in his own way and Perez had told him he'd have time to listen. He tried not to think of the nurse's phone number scribbled on the pad in his room or to speculate about what he might have to say.

Cedric began to talk. 'There have always been tales about Setter. There were odd kind of bumps in the land where the dead lass started digging. Crops never did well there. The bairns thought it was a trowie place and even the grown-ups believed Mima was something of a witch.' He paused, closed the flaps of skin over his eyes.

'What did that have to do with the Shetland Bus?'

'They say there's a Norwegian man buried there. That was the story I grew up with, though my father always denied it. An agent who'd passed information to the Germans and got some of his people killed.'

'And the Whalsay men meted out their own form of justice?'

'That's what people say. One of the men that died was a close friend of Jerry Wilson. He was in a Whalsay-built boat when he was captured. My father would never speak of it, but there were rumours when I was growing up.' Only now Cedric opened his eyes very slowly. He paused a moment before continuing. 'I did hear they found some bones at Setter. The piece of a skull, I heard, and others besides.'

'Those were old bones,' Perez said. 'Older than that.' *But are they?* he thought. *I don't really know that. Sixty years is a long time. Would we be able to tell the difference? Wouldn't bones from a body buried during the war look just the same as ones buried hundreds of years ago?*

'There you are then,' Cedric said, suddenly becoming jovial. 'Like I said, they were all just stories.'

'How did Jerry Wilson die?' Perez asked.

'At sea. A fishing accident. He was taken in a freak storm. Mima was heartbroken. They'd been sweethearts since they were children.' Cedric paused again. 'She was wild even as a child. Setter was her house, not Jerry's. She lived there as a bairn with her grandmother. Her parents both died when she was quite young. Jerry moved in with them when they got married, and when the grandmother passed away they had the place to themselves. It caused some jealousy. Two young people with their own croft. Mima was never liked on the island, especially by the women. She never made any effort to fit in. Things were different then: folk had to work together to make any sort of living. The men went out to the fishing and the women were left to do most of the work on the crofts. Mima was strong and fit – she could cast peat and scythe hay as well as a man – but she was never what they'd call now a team player. If she didn't feel much like working she'd stay at home in front of the fire.' Cedric stopped to pour himself a cup of coffee from the pot on Perez's table.

'Then when Jerry was drowned and she was single again she was a threat to all the island wives. She was a bonny young girl with her own house and her own land and they were scared their husbands would run off with her. She was still in love with Jerry though – with his memory, at least. She had plenty of offers but she never married again. She enjoyed her independence too much for that.'

'I'm surprised so many people turned out for her funeral if she wasn't so well liked.'

'Oh,' Cedric said, 'folk wouldn't want to miss it. She was a kind of celebrity in her day. And the young ones all liked her. It was her own generation who had the problems.'

'How did she get on with Evelyn?'

Cedric shot him a sharp look under the hooded lids. 'Let's say they never exactly saw eye to eye. After Jerry was drowned Joseph was all Mima had. She used to call him her peerie man. She wasn't going to take kindly to anyone who stole him away. Mima should have married again. She didn't have the temperament of a single woman.'

'Were you one of the ones to propose to her?'

Cedric laughed again. 'I knew better than to ask her. She'd have thought I was a poor thing after her

Jerry. Everyone in Shetland knew he was a handsome man.'

'Do you think the things that happened all those years ago could have any bearing on Mima's death?'

'Of course not,' Cedric said. 'How could it?'

Perez looked at him, not sure if he really meant what he said, but Cedric turned away and walked back into the kitchen.

Mark Evans, the psychiatric nurse, said he needed to be sure Perez was who he claimed to be: 'Mrs James is in the public eye. I don't want her hassled by a load of reporters. You do understand?' He had a soft, slow voice and an accent unfamiliar to Perez. Rural. Perez wondered if he'd grown up on a farm; that would give them a point of contact, but he didn't feel he could ask. Instead he gave the man the number of the police station in Lerwick. 'They'll confirm my mobile number.'

Then he waited, looking out over the harbour, for his phone to ring again. After the deserted feeling of the day before, the place was back to normal. There were cars queuing for the ferry and a couple of fishermen were getting a small trawler ready to go out to sea. He supposed Jerry Wilson's Norwegian friend had sailed a boat of a similar size to Norway.

His phone rang, interrupting daydreams of wartime adventures, grey seas and huge waves. He'd never been physically brave and he didn't think he'd have had the courage to volunteer for the Shetland Bus.

'I was so sorry to hear that Hattie's dead,' Mark said. 'I remember her well.'

'I wondered if she'd been in touch with you recently, but Mrs James said not.'

'No. She might have contacted another professional though. Her GP should have records. Even when she was ill she was unusually self-aware. I think she'd have realized she needed help. If she was so desperate that she committed suicide.'

Perez picked up an uncertainty in his voice. 'Were you surprised to hear she'd killed herself?'

'I was. She was a very intelligent young woman. I thought she'd taken on board the strategies for coping with her depression. And she understood that medication would help her. She never refused to take it. Was there an event that distressed her, something very serious that provoked the suicide attempt?'

'Not that we know.' Perez paused. 'We've not ruled out the possibility of other causes of death. I'm looking into the matter for the Procurator Fiscal. I'm grateful that you've taken the time to talk to me.'

'I thought you should know that four years ago Hattie was a victim of a criminal assault,' Evans said. 'It might not be relevant, but it seemed important to tell you.'

'We have no record of that.' As he spoke Perez hoped that was true. They had checked Hattie's name against the criminal records. That was standard procedure but if she'd been a victim would that fact have come to light?

'She never reported the matter to the police,' Evans said.

'Why not?'

'A number of reasons. She'd suffered a severe bout of depression a couple of years earlier. There had been occasions of psychosis. She didn't think she'd be believed. Perhaps she even felt she was responsible. She wouldn't even talk to her mother about it.'

In his quiet, reassuring voice Evans described the incident, as he understood it had taken place. He was clearly angry. When he'd finished, Perez could understand why.

'You realize there's no proof,' he said. 'They might not have got a prosecution even then.'

'I do realize that,' Evans said. 'I probably shouldn't have told you. It's very unprofessional. I couldn't discuss it with Mrs James. I just wanted you to know. After all, Hattie's not here to tell you herself.'

Chapter Thirty-two

Sandy woke early. He was lying in Mima's high double bed. His mother had given him clean sheets to put on it, but the blankets had belonged to Mima. They smelled of peatsmoke and damp like the rest of the house. The sheet was wrinkled uncomfortably underneath him. He'd never quite got the hang of making beds the old-fashioned way. He liked fitted sheets and a duvet.

On the wall in front of him there was a photograph he hadn't noticed before. Two women walking down a dirt track. It was taken on Whalsay but before any of the roads had been made up. On their backs they had the rush baskets or kishies that were used for carrying peat and they were so full that he could see the peat piled behind their shoulders. They were wearing old-fashioned bonnets and skirts below their knees, heavy boots. And as they walked they were knitting; the wool was held in apron pockets, their elbows were close to their bodies. They smiled towards the camera, poised for a moment, but you could tell the needles would begin clacking again as soon as the shot was over. Sandy wondered if they were knitting just for the fun of it, or because raising peat was boring, or because they were so busy that this was the only time there was in the day to provide clothes for their children. Or if they did it to make money. It was the sort of thing his mother might do, Sandy thought. Not exactly like the women in the old photo, but working at several things at once, because Evelyn liked to be active and because she needed to hold the family together.

He lay for quite a long time staring at the photograph. He didn't think either of the women was Mima. She'd been much better-looking than they were and she'd never been a knitter. 'I don't have the patience for it,' she'd said when he'd asked as a child why she didn't knit like the other grandmothers. Then he thought about his father who'd gone to school in dirty clothes because Mima didn't have the patience for washing either. Sandy didn't think now he'd have preferred Mima as his mother; at least Evelyn had always fed them well and kept them clean.

Michael and his family were going south on the afternoon plane. Evelyn and Joseph were travelling down to the airport in Sumburgh to see them off. Sandy thought that might give him a chance to go into Utra and have a look round the house without his parents asking questions. His uneasiness about what had been going on there had grown in the last few days. Michael's words about their parents' future had brought it into sharper focus. He thought that was what had made his father so tense too – a vague anxiety that things weren't quite right.

In Mima's kitchen he made himself coffee and dialled Perez's mobile. He hadn't seen the inspector at all the previous day and he felt disconnected from the case. He'd enjoyed being at the centre of things during the investigation, responsible for making things happen. The inspector's number was busy. He took his coffee outside. He felt the stirrings of hunger. His mother would be cooking breakfast for the whole lot of them in Utra but he didn't think he could face that: the bairn grizzling, Michael talking about how well he was doing at work, Amelia being saintly. He went back inside, found an old packet of Bourbon biscuits in the cupboard and tried Perez's number again.

This time it was answered. 'Sandy. How are things?'

'Well enough.' He had wanted to discuss his concerns about the situation at Utra with Perez, but now he couldn't find the words to do it. Besides, this was probably something he should deal with on his own.

There was a brief pause before Perez spoke again. 'Did Mima ever talk about the Shetland Bus?'

'Not to me.' Of course Sandy had heard the stories but the old folks' reminiscences had never meant much to him. All that seemed so long ago that it was no longer relevant. They could have been telling tales about trows. He wondered why Perez was interested now.

'Apparently your Uncle Andrew's father helped build the little inshore boats that the Norwegian vessels carried across the North Sea.'

'Aye, I did hear that.'

'Would Andrew know anything about it, do you think?'

'I should think he would. He was always interested in anything to do with the sea.'

'Would he tell you what he knows?'

'He might. Some days he talks better than others.

He minds things that happened long ago better than stuff that went on yesterday.'

'Would he still talk to you if I was there too?'

'Aye, I think he would.'

'We need to ask him if there's a Norwegian man buried at Setter.' Perez went on to explain why the question should be asked, but Sandy wasn't much clearer about what that could have to do with Hattie and Mima dying. All the same he was glad he had something constructive to occupy his time this morning. It gave him an excuse to stay away from Utra until everyone there had left for Sumburgh; he wouldn't have to put on a show that he was sorry Michael and Amelia were leaving so soon.

His Aunt Jackie must have seen them coming up the hill because she had the door open before they arrived.

'Come in,' she said. 'Come in, come in.' He wondered why she was so pleased to see them, and then remembered how sociable she'd been before Andrew was ill. The house was always full of people. When they'd been bairns they'd gathered at the Clouston house; Jackie would welcome them all in no matter the noise or the mess they made. She even liked them around the place when they were teenagers, drinking cans of lager and playing loud music. Andrew had bought them a full-size snooker table. It must be hard for her now. She and Andrew had built this grand new house which was perfect for parties, and she rattled around in it with nobody to talk to.

They went into the kitchen and she had coffee made and a plate of flapjack on the table in no time.

Andrew was sitting in his usual chair in front of the Rayburn.

'I'm sorry we couldn't make it to the funeral,' Jackie said. 'Andrew was having a bad day. He didn't want to leave the house. But I heard it went off very well.' She didn't ask what Perez was doing there, but shot suspicious glances towards him.

'Aye,' Sandy said. 'Very well.' Now he was here he wasn't sure how he could explain Perez's presence or engage the big man in conversation. Jackie often acted as if her husband weren't in the room, or as if he were deaf. He turned to his uncle. 'Are you feeling more yourself today?'

Andrew stared, then nodded briefly.

'Look,' Jackie said. 'While you're here would you mind staying with your uncle while I get to the shop? I've run out of flour and I wanted to get some baking done. I don't like to leave him on his own.' She looked again at Perez. 'That is if you've nothing you need to ask me.'

'No,' Perez said easily. 'We were just wanting to talk to Andrew. Chat about the old times. Nothing important at all. You get yourself away.'

Sandy knew this was a good thing, because they'd be able to talk to his uncle without Jackie overhearing, but he couldn't help being nervous. Perez would expect him to persuade Andrew to confide in them and he wasn't sure it would be that easy. Folk said Andrew's intellect hadn't been affected by the stroke, just his speech and his short-term memory, but Sandy thought he'd become quite a different man. Before the illness Andrew had been loud and strong and fierce. Competitive. Sandy remembered him on the golf course, swearing because he'd made a mess of a drive. Sandy had been a bit frightened of his uncle when he was a boy.

There was a moment of silence. Then they heard Jackie slam the front door and the roar of the Audi as she drove it down the track to the road.

'This is Jimmy Perez,' Sandy said. 'He's my boss. You don't mind him listening in while we talk?'

There was a pause, a brief shake of the head.

'Your father knew the men on the Shetland Bus? He built boats for them?' Sandy had just bitten into a piece of flapjack, it was more crumbly than he'd been expecting and the oats fell out of his mouth as he spoke. He felt himself blushing, wondered what Perez would think of his clumsiness.

Andrew continued to stare at him then nodded.

'Did he ever talk to you about it?'

'They built the yoals the Norwegian men used once they got to their country.'

'Responsible work,' Perez said. 'They'd have known the Norwegians' lives depended on it.'

Andrew stared at him and nodded again. 'The Whalsay men took the yoals out into open sea to test them.'

'It must have been scary, out there in a tiny boat.'

'They were young,' Andrew said. 'Reckless. They thought they'd live for ever. And they were all pals together.' He stumbled occasionally over a word, but he knew what he wanted to say.

'Jerry was with them too. Mima's Jerry.'

'He was just a boy. More reckless than anyone, my father said.'

'You've heard they found some old bones at Setter?'

This time the silence lasted so long that Sandy thought Andrew hadn't heard him.

'They don't tell me things any more.'

'The lass from the university found them.'

'The one that died?' This time the response was immediate and so sharp that Sandy was surprised. He hadn't thought Hattie's death had registered at all with his uncle.

'She found a skull,' he said. 'At least my mother found it while she was working there as a volunteer. Then I believe it was the other one, Sophie, who found some bones.'

There was a pause. Andrew raised a mug of cold coffee to his mouth and slurped it.

'My boss seems to think the bones could come from that time,' Sandy said. 'That they might belong to a Norwegian man. Did your father ever talk about that?'

Now Andrew turned towards Perez. 'Why do you want to know? Why are you still here if the woman killed herself?'

'Oh, you understand how it is,' Perez said. 'There are forms to fill in, boxes to tick.'

Andrew nodded, apparently reassured. 'Fishing got that way too in the end.'

'So did your father talk about the dead Norwegian?'

Another pause. Andrew seemed deep in thought. 'He mentioned it.' There was a brief grin, which reminded Sandy of how his uncle had been before the illness. The life and soul of any gathering, a teller of jokes, a dancer. He could fill a room with his laughter. He could drink more than any man on the island and still stay standing. 'After a few drinks he'd talk about the war.'

'What did he say?'

'That he was shit-scared every time he went out to test a yoal. That maybe he owed his life to Jerry Wilson.'

Sandy had a sudden flash of intuition. It was something in Andrew's voice. 'Is that why he kept quiet about the dead Norwegian?'

Andrew looked up at him. 'Has someone been talking?' Again a reminder of the old Andrew, who had a fearsome temper when he was roused.

'No.' *I've just learned a few skills from Perez.* 'Will you tell me what happened?'

'How would I know? I wasn't there.'

'You'll remember your father's stories.'

'Maybe they shouldn't be told.'

'Two people have died,' Sandy said. 'It has to stop. And folks will go on thinking Ronald shot Mima if we don't find out what happened.'

'They'll soon forget.'

'Will they?' Sandy demanded. 'Will his wife?'

Andrew sat in silence again for so long that Sandy thought Jackie would soon be back from the shop.

'I only know what my father told me,' Andrew said at last. 'I can't say if it's true. I think it's true but I can't be sure.'

'I understand that. Old stories. Who knows what to believe?'

'They say that Jerry Wilson shot a Norwegian lad.'

'I heard that. It was because he'd betrayed some Shetland boys to the Germans.

'No,' Andrew said. 'That was the story they put about on the island when folks started asking questions. But that wasn't what happened. Not according to my father.' Throughout the conversation Andrew's speech had become more fluent, but now he stopped.

'So why *was* the Norwegian shot?'

'Because he was Mima's lover.' There was a sudden pause. Andrew seemed surprised that he'd spoken the words. He continued in a rush. 'And one day Jerry found them together. The Norwegian had come into Whalsay to try out one of the new yoals. He was stranded there because of the weather, or because there was a problem with a boat. I don't know. My father never said that part. Just that Mima had been flirting with him all day and they ended up in bed in the Pier House. Jerry was out in the Lunna House to talk about future operations and he wasn't expected back. Then he came back and he found them in bed together.'

'But Jerry went on to marry her.'

'He didn't blame her. Not so much at least, though the marriage was never as fantastic as everyone made out. That was what my father said. She was only a girl, too young to understand what she was about. Jerry blamed the Norwegian.'

'So he took him out and shot him?'

'That was what my father said. Jerry was never . . .' Andrew paused to find the right word, '. . . stable.'

'And he buried the body at Setter?' Sandy didn't get that bit. Why Setter, where Mima and her grandmother lived? Was it to be a constant reminder to his new wife that he wouldn't be messed with?

'That was the story.' Andrew leaned forward and very carefully set his mug on the table. Sandy saw that his hand was shaking. 'One of the stories.'

Sandy looked at Perez, wondering if he wanted to

continue the interview, but the inspector nodded for him to go on.

'I don't understand why Mima allowed the dig on her land,' Sandy said. 'She must have realized there was a chance the body would be found.'

'She didn't know,' Andrew said. 'She might have guessed but she didn't know.'

They heard the sound of Jackie's car approaching the house. Andrew didn't register it. Sandy reached out and took another piece of flapjack. This was his breakfast, after all, and he felt he deserved it. Jackie opened the door and came in laden with carrier bags.

'Thank you,' she said. 'I hope you've not had such a boring time. Andrew doesn't have much to say for himself these days.'

Chapter Thirty-three

Berglund had hired a car from Bolt's in Lerwick. It was still parked outside the Pier House. Perez could see it from his bedroom window. He phoned Bolt's office and asked how long they expected Berglund to keep it.

'He's travelling south on the NorthLink this evening. He'll drop it off in the car park at the terminal at around four-thirty. That was what we arranged, at least.'

Perez wished he had a reason to keep Berglund in Whalsay, but there was no way he could justify it. It was possible that the Setter project would be abandoned altogether now without Hattie to champion it. Rhona Laing was determined that Hattie's death was suicide and that the use of Berglund's knife had no significance. And perhaps she was right. The professor had been on the island when Mima was shot, but what reason could he have for killing an old Whalsay woman? He didn't even have access to a shotgun as far as Perez knew. Hattie was a different matter. Perez could understand why the man would want her dead, and he was the last person to see her alive. But was it possible that the two deaths were unconnected, coincidental? He wondered if he should ask Berglund to stay, at least if he should arrange a more formal interview before the man left. But if he did that he'd be showing his hand. Berglund was a clever man. Better at the moment to let him think his secret was safe.

Perez continued to sit at the window, waiting for the moment when he saw Berglund drive down to the pier and on to the ferry. He wanted to be sure the man was off the island. He had almost an hour to wait before that happened, but Perez didn't become restless or bored. He valued times of inactivity. He could think more clearly then. In his head he considered the characters playing out this drama in Whalsay. Were any of them capable of killing two people? There were occasions when his stillness drove Fran crazy. Sometimes she'd scream at him, laughing but irritated too. 'How can you just sit there? What is going on inside your head?' He was never quite sure how to answer. *Stories*, he thought. *I just tell myself stories*.

His mind left the inquiry, drifted back to Fran and again to marriage. Would she laugh if he proposed to her? It would seem an old-fashioned concept to her and quite outdated. Ridicule would almost certainly be her response.

When the ferry sailed off he got up. He went to the shop in Symbister and bought bread rolls, cheese, ham, fruit and cakes. There were other customers there and they fell silent until he left, when he was aware of a sudden buzz of conversation behind him. He turned back to the shop to buy a couple of cans of beer and was amused that the silence returned. He put his purchases in his car and drove to the Bod to see Sophie. With Berglund out of the way he supposed he'd find her alone.

She was sitting inside the bothy at the Formica

table, seemed to be filling in some sort of form. He could see her through the grimy window. Remembering the time she'd found him there uninvited, he was careful to knock and wait outside until she called him in. She seemed disappointed. 'Oh, it's you.'

'Who were you expecting?'

She hesitated. 'I thought Paul might call in before he left.'

'No,' Perez said. 'He's already gone. I saw him go off on the ferry.'

'I'm tidying up the paperwork for the project before I leave.' Sophie turned round in her seat. 'There's no point my hanging around here. I might as well go back to London. It was what I planned anyway.'

'So you'll be running a cafe bar in Richmond?'

She grinned up at him. 'Maybe. That's one of the options. I'm not going to rush into anything. Maybe I'll just take some time out.'

Perez was going to ask what she would do for money, but he saw that was no real concern for her. He didn't think he'd met anyone before who didn't have to work for a living. Duncan Hunter was probably the richest person he knew, but he still worked.

'Will you stay with your parents?'

'In their house. Daddy's just gone off to Hong Kong for six months. Something about one of the businesses. So they're not there.'

'You don't want to be with them?' He thought despite the confidence and the loud voice she could use some support.

'Why would I want that?' Her voice was scathing. 'I'm a grown-up. I'm not going to run away to Mummy every time I feel a bit miserable. Besides, all my friends are in London.'

'Why are you miserable?'

She stared at him as if he were completely mad. 'Why do you think? The person I've been sharing my life with for two months just killed herself. But don't worry. A couple of decent nights out and I'll be fine.'

'Is that what you believe? That Hattie killed herself?'

'Of course. What other explanation is there?'

He didn't answer directly. 'I've got a picnic,' he said. 'Let's go up the island and have a bit of a walk.'

Again she stared at him as if he was a madman.

'It's all right,' he said, though he wasn't quite sure why she might need reassuring. 'I just want to go somewhere we won't be disturbed or overheard.'

They parked near the golf clubhouse. Again the weather was unusually mild: a gusty breeze blew startling white clouds and there were moments of bright sunlight. There were no other cars there and the golf course seemed deserted. They walked right to the end of the island and sat on rocks looking out to the Skerries, the inhabited island which stood very clear on the horizon.

'I've lived all my life in Shetland and I've never been there,' Perez said. He handed her one of the cans of beer and spread the food on a flat rock. A red-throated diver flew over their heads calling. *Last time I heard that sound*, Perez thought, *was just before Hattie's body was found*. Although he knew it was superstition, he felt uneasy. What terrible thing would happen now? He turned his attention back to the Skerries. 'Maybe I should pay a visit one day.'

Sophie tugged on the ring pull of the can. 'What is all this about?' she said. 'What do you want from me?' She was wearing shorts again and the big boots, a loose sweater with holes in the elbows. No bra, he thought. She leaned forward with her arms on her knees.

'What do you think of Paul Berglund?' Perez asked.

He pulled apart a crusty roll and cut a piece of cheese off the block of Orkney cheddar with his penknife, handed the makeshift sandwich to her.

'I've always found Paul OK,' she said. 'He's been all right to me.'

'Really?'

'Yeah. You could have a worse boss. He can be a good laugh.'

'What about Hattie?' He broke off a piece of chocolate and put it in his mouth. He thought she sounded defensive. 'Was he all right to her?'

Sophie didn't reply. A gull swooped down, scavenging for bits of food. A curlew shouted in the distance.

He went on. 'Did Hattie tell you about Paul? Maybe warn you about him? Did she think the two of you were getting close and want you to know how he'd treated her?'

She stared out to the islands on the horizon. 'Paul hasn't done anything wrong,' she said. 'He wouldn't have.'

'Did he tell you that?'

She didn't answer.

'Something made Hattie kill herself,' Perez said. 'If that's what happened, she used his knife to do it.'

She turned away from him. 'I hate it here,' she said. 'Everyone knowing each other's business. At first it was OK. Different from anywhere else I've ever lived. The boys from the boats were good fun, they know how to party. Now I can't stand it. Once the fog rolls in you feel as if the world outside doesn't matter at all. People here lose any sense of proportion. Tiny incidents that happened years ago fester and take over their lives.'

'What incidents?'

She shook her head in frustration that he didn't immediately understand.

'There's nothing specific. Just a feeling that the islanders can never break free from their history. That they have no free will. Or that they won't allow themselves any.'

'Go home then,' he said. 'There's nothing to stop you. Just leave me your address.'

She'd pulled out a piece of heather and was tearing the tiny dead flowers off the stalk one by one. Perez thought it might take more than a night of clubbing and drinking to make her feel happy again.

'Did Hattie talk to you before she died?' he asked.

She turned, startled. 'Of course she talked to me.'

'So you got on OK?'

A brief hesitation. 'Boarding school's great practice for this sort of work,' she said. 'You have to muck in together.'

He wasn't sure that was a real answer. *I went to boarding school*, he thought. *If you can call the hostel at the Anderson High School a boarding school. I'm not sure it taught me much.*

'Did she talk about Paul Berglund?' he asked. 'About what happened when they worked together before?'

'Paul says it's all rubbish. She just had a teenage crush.'

'What did *she* say?'

'Was it true then, all that stuff about Paul?' Sophie looked at him; her eyes seemed huge. 'You could never tell with Hattie. Sometimes I thought she was mad. She came up with such odd ideas.'

'Like what?'

Sophie shook her head, unwilling to be specific. 'I don't know. She just let her imagination run away with her.'

'But she did talk to you about Paul?'

'Yes, she thought he was hitting on me. She was warning me off. I told her I was a big girl and I could look after myself.'

'I think she was telling the truth about Paul,' Perez said. 'But there's no evidence and he'll never be charged, if that's what's concerning you. I just need to hear what she told you.'

Sophie finished the beer and crushed the can with her fist. She told her story looking out to sea in a flat, unemotional voice. Throughout, there was no eye contact.

'It was at the end of her first year at university. She'd already had some sort of stress-related illness after A levels. I guess she was that sort of person. An obsessive. Then in the summer vacation she worked as a volunteer on a dig in the south.'

She paused but Perez said nothing. He knew all this, but Sophie had to tell the tale in her own words.

She continued: 'That was where Hattie met Paul. She fell for him. I mean absolutely head over heels.

She admitted that to me. He was married but when's that ever stopped anyone?'

Now Perez did interject. 'Did she know he was married?'

'Maybe not. She was so naïve, it probably never occurred to her. He must have been flattered. She was young, bright, quirky. He took her out a couple of times. Enjoyed her company but wanted more. Men do always want more . . .' She paused again and continued to stare into the distance. Perez wished he knew what she was thinking about. 'One evening, they both got drunk. He invited her into his room for coffee. She went, expecting coffee, maybe a kiss and a cuddle. Like I said, she was very naïve. Paul expected more than that.'

'He raped her,' Perez said.

'No!' she said and now she did turn towards him, shocked. 'Not rape. That sounds horrible.'

'Rape is horrible.'

'They were both drunk. He misread the signals. She never actually told him to stop. Not really. Not so he understood.'

And perhaps that was true, Perez thought. Hattie had so little confidence. After a while perhaps she had just given in and let the man do what he wanted, too scared to shout and make a fuss. And afterwards she'd blamed herself instead of him. And the anger had eaten away at her and made her ill. Had it turned to paranoia here in Whalsay? Had she been scared it would happen again? Did she imagine him watching her, waiting for his moment? But everyone said she'd been happy until Mima's death. It didn't quite make sense.

He didn't want Sophie to think he was blaming her. He looked out at the water too, at the reflected sunlight shifting with the movement of the waves and the wind-blown shadows.

'Are you having a relationship with Berglund?'

'No!'

Perez had an image of the two archaeologists as he'd seen them the day before, standing together outside the Pier House after Mima's funeral, both dressed in black. Berglund had put his arm around Sophie's shoulders, but she'd resisted and walked away. He thought she was telling the truth. He stood up, starting to feel cold. Despite the brightness of the light there was still a chill in the rock where they sat.

'Have you discussed her allegations with Paul?'

'I couldn't help it. It was while we were in the kirk before Mima's funeral. We got there early. Everything was so solemn and dreary. I couldn't just sit there in silence. We were the first people there. There was nobody to overhear. And I had to know what he had to say for himself.'

'What *did* he have to say?'

'He laughed it off, said she was a screwed-up kid with a serious crush on him and she didn't know what she wanted.' She hesitated. 'Then he warned me off: "Don't go spreading rumours about me, Sophie. I've got a lot to lose."'

'Do you think Hattie discussed it with him when they had their meeting?'

'I don't know.' Sophie's attention seemed to be wandering now, or perhaps she was feeling the cold as much as he was. 'Paul didn't say anything about that to me.'

Did he warn Hattie off too? Perez thought. *Or did he take more drastic action to stop her talking? As he'd said, he had a lot to lose.*

'Do you think Hattie killed herself?' The question came out unplanned, but he found that he'd caught his breath while he waited for the answer.

'Of course,' she answered, looking at him as if he were a little mad. 'What else could have happened? Though . . .'

'Yes?'

'I'd have thought she'd have left a note. She was always writing. It was the best way she communicated, how she made sense of things.'

He knew he should find Sandy and that the Fiscal would be waiting to hear from him, but despite the cold now he was reluctant to move. He thought Sophie had more to tell him, that he'd mishandled the situation. He hadn't asked the right question. But Sophie had grown impatient. She got to her feet too and strode across the cropped grass of the hill back towards the car, past the loch where the clouds were reflected in the water and where soon the diver would build its nest. He was left to follow.

Chapter Thirty-four

When Sandy came back to the house after letting the hens out and collecting the eggs, Perez was waiting for him. The door was unlocked, but Perez was standing outside as if he had all the time in the world.

'Your car's still here,' he said. 'I didn't think you'd be gone long.'

Sandy thought Mima would have enjoyed having these visitors to Setter. She'd have taken to Jimmy Perez, poured whisky for him and told him her stories. Today the inspector was the one with the stories to tell.

'Let's stay outside,' Perez said. 'Make the most of the weather.' So they walked down past the site of the dig with its tape and its poles and its mound of earth, to the dyke that marked the end of Setter land. Perez wondered again what would happen to the site now. Would the trenches be filled in and the spoil heap flattened? Would the land then remain undisturbed for ever? He talked about Paul Berglund and Hattie James and what had happened when they worked together on another dig in Sussex.

'Do you believe what the psychiatric nurse said?' Sandy wasn't sure what he thought of the incident. Rape to him was a city crime, a stranger attacking a woman after dark in some alley. Two people having sex in a hotel room was something different. But he knew Perez well enough not to say so.

'Yes.'

'It doesn't really give Berglund a motive for killing Mima though, does it?'

'Unless Mima had found out what he'd done,' Perez said. 'She might have threatened to go public. Or she could have tried to persuade Hattie to tell us. You said Mima liked the girl and that they were close. She was a strong independent woman. Hattie might have confided in her. Berglund could lose his job even if it never came to court.'

'I don't really see it,' Sandy said. He thought Perez always made things more complicated than they really were. 'He wouldn't be daft enough to use his own knife.'

Beyond the dyke there was one fat old ewe with rheumy eyes, chewing on the long grass, and two tiny lambs, still unsteady on their feet.

'What did you make of our conversation with Andrew?'

'I'm not sure,' Sandy said. He still didn't like to commit himself in front of Perez. The inspector was used to working on serious crimes with bright men from the south, not inexperienced local cops like him.

'Did Mima ever mention meeting a Norwegian man during the war?'

'No, and it's just the sort of story she'd have enjoyed telling. Kind of saucy and dramatic.' Sandy wasn't sure he believed any of it. Andrew's memory was unreliable and some days the words weren't very clear.

'According to Andrew she never knew the man

had been killed,' Perez said. 'But she must have been aware of the rumours that were going round. Cedric told me one version and there were probably others. Maybe she didn't want to make herself the subject of gossip. No more than she already was.'

'You can't think that something that happened all that time ago has anything to do with an old woman being shot on Whalsay today?' Sandy thought Perez was mad to be distracted so much by the past.

'Probably not.'

'I was wondering . . .' Sandy paused. He didn't want to make a fool of himself.

'Yes?'

'Berglund. Is that a Norwegian name?'

'Scandinavian, certainly.'

'Another coincidence, do you think?'

'You're thinking he could be a relative, a grandson maybe, who's come in after revenge?' Perez was amused but not altogether dismissive.

'I don't know. Perhaps not revenge, but information. He could have been asking questions and stirred things up.'

'It's worth checking,' Perez said. 'I'll do that when I'm back in the office. I'm going home this afternoon. I can't really justify staying another day and the Fiscal needs to know what's going on. You know what she's like.'

'Will you tell her everything? About my grandmother and the Norwegian?'

'Of course. She's very discreet, you know, whatever we think of her. She has to be.'

Sandy shot a quick look at Perez to see if he was mocking him, but he seemed quite serious. 'I just don't like the idea of it,' he said. 'Folk talking about my family in that way.' He turned and began to walk back to the house. He was wondering what Joseph would make of it. Or had he always known what had happened sixty years before? Perhaps he should talk to his father before word got out.

As they approached the house, a car drew up and Ronald Clouston climbed out. He hadn't noticed them and when he did he seemed startled. Like a great awkward schoolboy caught out in mischief. Sandy thought perhaps Ronald had hoped to speak to him alone.

'Aye, aye,' Sandy said. His father's greeting. 'Are you coming in? I have to get to Utra in a while to see Michael off, but not just now.'

'No.' Ronald stood with his hand on the car door as if he was ready to make a get away. 'I can see you're busy.'

'I'm just going,' Perez said.

'No,' Ronald said again. 'I'll get off. I've got things to do.' He got into the car and drove away.

'What was all that about?' Perez asked.

'Folk get kind of shy when the police are about.' Sandy wished Perez hadn't been there. Maybe he'd give Ronald a call later and find out what he'd come for. He could tell that Ronald had wanted to talk to him and had lost his nerve at the last minute. He turned to his boss. 'What do you want me to do?'

'Can you bear to stay in Whalsay for a little while?'

'Aye, I suppose so. I'd like to get home soon though.'

'I'm hoping we'll have it all cleared up in the next few days.'

Sandy wondered if Perez had any real reason for

saying that or if it was wishful thinking. He repeated his question. 'What do you want me to do?'

'Do you think you could get Sophie to talk to you? She spent all that time with Hattie. She might know something that doesn't seem at all important to her. You're more her age and she knows you socially.'

'I can try.' Sandy had a sudden vision of how it would be if he got Sophie to talk, if he discovered a fact that moved the case forward. How pleased and proud Perez would be! 'I'll go to the Bod this evening, maybe take her to the Pier House for a drink.'

'I wondered if she has a relationship with Berglund. She says not, though, and I don't know why she should lie, unless she's worried about getting him into trouble.'

Sandy was tempted then to talk to Perez about his anxiety about his parents, but he decided that was his problem. If he discussed it with Perez it would become official and until he was sure what he was dealing with there was no question of that.

At Utra they were all just about ready to leave for the airport. Michael's big hire car was packed with luggage and Amelia was standing in the yard, obviously impatient to be off. She was wearing very tight jeans, a jersey with a scooped neck, a little jacket. Michael was fixing the baby into her seat in the back.

Evelyn came hurrying out of the house. 'There you are,' she said. 'Amelia was just thinking we should leave without saying goodbye to you. I told her there was plenty of time. Sumburgh's not like those big airports in the south where it takes an hour to check in.'

Sandy couldn't tell whether Evelyn was more irritated by him or by her daughter-in-law.

'Well, I'm here now.'

Michael turned round. He took Sandy in his arms, gave him a great bear-hug. 'Now you're the great traveller and you can find your way to London on your own, there's no excuse for not visiting.'

'I will,' Sandy said.

Amelia was already in the passenger seat. As the cars drove off she waved to Sandy. A little flutter of the hand, as if she were a film star, or the Queen. Sandy waited until both cars were well on their way to Symbister before he went into the house.

Inside there were signs of the hurry there'd been in getting Michael's family ready to leave. The washing-up had been done, of course – Evelyn would never leave the house with dirty pans in the sink, but they were still piled on the draining board and not dried. There were crumbs on the floor and the waste bin was full.

Now he was here, Sandy wasn't sure what he was looking for. He sat down at the table and forced himself to think clearly. He needed reassurance, that was all. He couldn't understand how his parents had managed to renovate the house on their limited income. He wanted to check that they weren't in debt. That had been his nightmare: that they'd borrowed foolishly to allow his mother to compete with the pelagic fishing families. He knew the stress that came from owing money. He was crap about finance and in the end he'd cut up his credit card because he couldn't face the monthly bills; he still remembered the tightness in the pit of his stomach when he'd realized how much he owed.

The tension between his parents could be caused by anxieties about money. He preferred to think it was about that. Any other cause – sex: that one of them had fallen for someone else – was simply horrible. They were old and they were his parents; he couldn't contemplate it. He wondered if he was overreacting. Perhaps the two deaths so close to home had made him jittery and caused him to blow trivial arguments out of proportion. Then he remembered his father yelling at his mother after Mima's funeral. Joseph had never raised his voice to Evelyn throughout their marriage, even when he was exhausted after working all day for Duncan Hunter. Sandy wasn't overreacting. Something was wrong between them.

Then came the difficult part. He forced himself to order his ideas and take the next logical step. If his parents had problems with money, was it possible that one of them had shot Mima for her house and her land? Not Joseph. He could tell how upset his father was. Besides, he'd been made a good offer for the house already and he'd turned it down. Evelyn then? Sandy had known all along that this was where the thinking would end up. Evelyn had never particularly got on with Mima. She could shoot well enough and there was a shotgun in Utra. But if the couple had no money problems, then there would be no real motive. That was why Sandy was lurking in Utra like a thief or a spy.

He knew where his mother kept the bank statements: in the drawer in the sideboard in the living room, where the lasses had put the silver coins before the man from the university had taken them away. It was locked, but the spare key was hanging from a hook in the larder along with all the others. Evelyn had always been the one to look after the family finances. Even when his father had worked for Hunter she'd sorted out the bills and the invoices and filled in Joseph's tax returns. Sandy could remember her sitting at the table every month, going through the bank statements, frowning when she saw how little they had to live on until the next paycheque.

He found the key and unlocked the drawer. The statements were neatly clipped together in the blue file he remembered. He looked immediately at the balance and felt a wild relief when he saw it was in credit. He scanned back over the past twelve months. No problems. Little excess in the pot, but no debt. He wondered if Evelyn could have taken out a loan, but there was no sign of that and the paperwork would be in the drawer too. *How could I have doubted her?* he thought. *How could I have even considered for a minute that she would be capable of murder?*

He looked at his watch. It was almost six o'clock and he felt suddenly ravenous. He hadn't had any lunch. He felt like celebrating. He thought he'd go down to the Pier House for his supper, maybe have a couple of pints. Some of the boys might be in and they could play cards, talk about the old times. Davy Henderson should be around. Maybe Anna had relented and let Ronald out for the evening. Then he remembered that Perez had asked him to talk to Sophie. He locked the drawer and hung up the key again, making sure everything was as it had been before. He hated the idea that his parents might know he'd been snooping.

On the way to Symbister he stopped by the Bod. The Pier House would be quiet this early and they'd have the chance to talk. It wasn't such a chore; Sophie was good company. She had a knack of making every man she was with feel special, attractive. He wondered whether he could persuade her to open up. If he'd made more effort to get to know Hattie, perhaps she'd have felt able to confide in him too. But when he knocked on the door there was no answer. He looked inside. All the archaeological equipment was still there in a heap at one end of the living room, but Sophie's personal belongings seemed to have gone.

In the Pier House, Cedric was behind the bar, staring into space. He'd looked the same age since Sandy had been a boy, but recently he seemed to have got older. His responses were slower.

'Have you seen the lassie from the Bod?'

Cedric turned his head to look at Sandy.

'Aye she was in earlier. She took the ferry out. I was down at the pier to meet Jean. Sophie was all loaded up like a packhorse with that huge rucksack. She seemed pleased to be away.'

Sandy phoned Perez and told him what had happened. Perez went very quiet, but he didn't seem to think Sandy was to blame for allowing the girl to leave. It occurred to Sandy that Hattie might be travelling to Aberdeen on the same ferry as Sophie, but she'd be in the anonymous Transit van that the undertaker used to carry bodies for post-mortem, and Sophie would be in the bar.

Chapter Thirty-five

When Perez arrived back in Lerwick, he called in to his office. It had a sleepy feel: most of his team were taking Easter leave. He phoned the Fiscal's secretary and learned she'd be in a meeting for most of the afternoon. He made an appointment to see her first thing the following morning. He was looking forward to getting home early, sticking some clothes in the washing machine, cooking a meal for himself. In the meantime he began to wonder about the best way to track down the nationality of Berglund's family.

Although he'd planned a quiet evening at home, when he got there he couldn't relax. He found it impossible to stop thinking about Sophie, rerunning in his head the conversation on the cliff by the golf course. She was right about the note. Of course not all suicides left notes, but Hattie was a writer. If she were planning to kill herself she'd have written a considered letter to Gwen James explaining what she was doing. There wouldn't have been a panicky phone call. Suddenly he wanted this over. Soon Fran would be home. He didn't want her to arrive back in the middle of an investigation, to find him distracted and exhausted.

In the end he ran himself a bath. His bathroom was

thin and narrow, the bath old and deep with scarred enamel. The room filled with steam and condensation ran down the window. It didn't matter. The house was damp anyway, what difference would it make? He lay back, trying to let go of the case, but the possible scenarios, the shifting relationships, swirled into his head and out again. He was half asleep. *A Dance to the Music of Time.* Who had written that? He saw the Whalsay folk past and present waltzing in and out of his consciousness. A Norwegian sailor and a screwed-up young archaeologist, an ambitious businesswoman and an old man disabled by a stroke. How did they all fit together? He shut his eyes and felt he was floating towards a solution.

The phone rang. He wanted to leave it, to continue with his thoughts, but it could be Fran. He'd found it difficult to talk to her away from his own surroundings and now he was desperate to hear her voice. He climbed out and grabbed a towel – he always thought his house on the shore gave him privacy, but he'd been caught out before when a canoeist or sailor floated close to his window. The phone stopped just before he reached it. She would leave a message, he thought. And he'd call her straight back, before she rushed out to meet her friends at some experimental piece of theatre, some gallery opening or smart restaurant.

But when he pressed 1571 to pick up the message he heard quite a different woman's voice. It was Val Turner, the local-authority archaeologist. 'Jimmy, I've got an initial report back on the Whalsay bones. I'll be in the office for half an hour if you want to give me a ring.'

He went back into the bathroom but now the water seemed grey and uninviting, his contemplations ridiculous. He pulled out the plug and got dressed.

Instead of phoning Val back immediately he called Fran's mobile. There was no reply and he left a message. When he rang Val, she picked up her phone straight away. 'You've just caught me, Jimmy. I was just about to leave.'

'Have you got time to meet up? I'd be happy to buy you dinner. A thank-you for rushing through the analysis of the bones.' After all, he thought, he needed company. It would do him no good to sit in on his own, brooding. And he still had questions about the dig. The laundry could wait for another day.

'Ah,' she said. 'You don't know the favours I've had to call in to get that done so quickly. I've never known it happen in under six weeks.'

'I owe you, then. Shall we see if they can squeeze us into the museum?'

'Fine,' she said. 'Half an hour?'

She was there before him in the upstairs restaurant, sat at a table for two looking over the water. It was only just starting to get dark; the nights were drawing out. She was sitting over a glass of white wine and there was another for him.

'I didn't get a bottle,' she said. 'I'm driving and I presume you are too. Is that OK?'

'Of course.'

'Now, the bones . . .' She grinned. She knew how much he needed the information.

'Just tell me. How old are they?'

'Most are old,' she said.

'How old?'

'Given the unusual circumstances, I sent four pieces of bone for dating. Three of them returned dates that fell between 1465 and 1510, and it's probably one individual, not several people. So they're not contemporary. They can't have anything to do with the recent deaths in Whalsay. The age fits in perfectly with Hattie James's theory about the building. Fifteenth-century. Like the coins.'

So not the dead Norwegian. Is that old story from Mima's youth just a distraction?

Val Turner was still speaking. 'I wish I'd been able to tell her. Perhaps if she'd known absolutely that she was right about the age and the status of the house she wouldn't have killed herself.'

If she did *kill herself*, Perez thought. But he didn't say anything. It would take one chance remark to start a rumour. It suited him fine for the time being if people thought Hattie's death was suicide. Then he took in the importance of Val's first words.

'You said *most* of the bones were old. What did you mean by that?'

'There's one piece that seems more recent than the rest. I've asked them to check it. It's probably an error.' She seemed suddenly aware of the effect her words had on him. 'Really, it happens. You shouldn't take it too seriously.'

'Do you know whereabouts on the site it was found?'

'I'll be able to check. Hattie was a meticulous record taker. I'll talk to Sophie.'

'Sophie's gone home,' Perez said.

'Then I suppose she's left the paperwork with Evelyn.'

'How well did you know Hattie?' he asked.

'I'd met her several times, obviously,' Val said. 'The dig's part of post-grad research, but it's on my patch. Ultimately it's my responsibility that it's carried out to a professional standard.'

'What will happen in Setter now?'

'I'm hoping the university will take it on, make a large-scale project of it. We'd certainly support that. Whalsay would be a good place to have a reconstruction open to the public. There are some enthusiastic local volunteers.'

'Evelyn?'

'You know her? Yes. She's a dream to work with. It's amazing the way she's found her way round the grant system.'

'I understood Joseph Wilson wasn't so keen to have the dig on Setter land, and he's the new owner.'

'Really?' Val didn't seem too bothered. Perhaps she thought Evelyn would always get her way.

'What's the next step in the process?'

'Public consultation,' Val said. 'And Evelyn's taken care of that too. She's planning an event in the community hall in Lindby to explain about the coins and the remains to the island. Next week. She asked if we could host it here in the museum, but we wouldn't have time to organize it. Will you be able to come along?'

Fran will be back by then, he thought. *It might be something she'd enjoy.*

'Why the rush?' he asked.

Val laughed. 'Evelyn doesn't really do patient.'

'Doesn't it seem a little tasteless, so soon after Hattie James's death?'

'The idea is that it'll be a memorial for her too. A celebration of her work. Evelyn's invited her mother, the MP.'

'Has Gwen James agreed to come?' Perez was surprised. The woman had refused to come to Shetland when her daughter had first died. Why would she turn out for something so public? But perhaps that was the point: the public domain was where she felt most comfortable.

'Apparently.'

Perez looked out over the water, where examples of traditional Shetland boats were moored. He thought they could be in a ship themselves here, something large and grand, one of the cruise ships that put in to the islands in the summer. 'Is she expecting Paul Berglund back?'

'Presumably. Now Sophie's gone, he's the only person left to represent the university. I need to be sure the site's going to be properly written up. That's down to him.'

They sat for a moment in silence.

'What did you make of Hattie?' Perez asked. 'You must have met her a few times.'

'She was very bright, passionate, meticulous. She would have had a brilliant future in archaeology.' Val broke off as the food arrived. 'This is going to sound really sexist, but I thought she needed a man in her life. Someone to share things with. Someone to stop her taking herself too seriously.'

Perez said nothing.

'There's something else though,' Val went on. 'Something about the bones. The bones that *were* accurately dated. It'll fascinate you.'

He looked up. His thoughts were elsewhere. Back in Whalsay, with a beautiful young woman lying in a trench, close to where those ancient bones had lain for centuries.

Val didn't seem to notice. 'They're part of the body of a man. We found enough of the pelvis to establish the gender. He didn't die a natural death. He was murdered, killed by a stab wound. That's what it looks like, at least. The ribs have shattered. We'd not have been able to tell from the skull. We'll never know why he was killed, of course, though it's fun to guess.'

Now he was starting to be interested. 'What do you think might have happened?'

'Hattie's theory was that a local man took over the role of merchant in Whalsay. He'd suddenly acquire wealth, status. I'd guess that wouldn't make him very popular with his neighbours.'

'You think he was killed so people could steal from him?'

'That,' she said, 'or because they were jealous of him. They were poor and he was rich. Envy, the green-eyed monster, perhaps that was what finished him off.'

Val Turner hurried away as soon as the meal was finished but Perez stood for a moment outside before driving home. Through the long plate-glass windows he could see the reconstruction of the top of a lighthouse that stood in the museum, the huge glass dome and the workings. Once, the flashing beams had guided ships away from a rocky shore. *Throw some light my way*, he thought. But he felt he was groping towards a solution. Being away from Whalsay had given him some perspective and the conversation with Val had brought an even sharper focus.

Chapter Thirty-six

Sandy made no attempt to move back to Utra even though his room was free. He even took it upon himself to milk Mima's cow. Early in the morning and late in the afternoon he would sit on the box in the shed, wipe the udders with the cloth he'd brought out from the house and watch the liquid squirt into the bucket. After the first few tries, with his father watching and grinning, it had come easily to him. Maybe it was like riding a bike, he thought, one of those skills that, once you learned, you never forgot. He remembered Mima teaching him when he was a child, laughing at his first tentative attempts to get milk to come. 'You'll need to be firmer than that boy. Squeeze and pull. They'll not come off in your hands. That's more like it.' It had been one of the few things he'd managed better than Michael. Sitting here this morning, the smell was exactly the same. Cow and muck and the rich sweet smell of the new milk. There was the same sense of achievement too when the pail was full.

Later he took the churn round to Utra. His father was out on the hill. Sandy could see him in the distance as he walked down the track to the house. Evelyn was in the kitchen at the table, poring over sheets of paper. More lists. He'd thought all that was over after the funeral, but now it seemed she had other plans; there was something else for her to organize. At first she didn't talk about it. She took the milk and poured half into a jug to go in the fridge. The rest she set to stand in the kitchen.

'I thought I'd make some soft cheese,' she said. 'Do you mind, Sandy, we used to make it when you were bairns?'

'What's all this?' he asked, nodding towards the paper, the ruled columns, the round handwriting.

'We're having a do in the Lindby Hall,' she said. 'A sort of memorial for Mima and Hattie. And to give folk a chance to see the silver coins and hear about the project. The press will be interested too. I can organize the catering.'

Sandy thought that was his mother all over. Once she'd made up her mind about something there could be no delay. It had to happen immediately. The timing seemed in poor taste to him. What was the hurry?

'What does my father say about it?'

'He thinks it's a good idea.'

'Really?' Sandy was astonished. The last he'd heard, Joseph hadn't even wanted the dig on Setter land. Wouldn't all these visitors want to see where the coins had been found? His father was a private man. He would hate all the fuss and the disruption to his routine.

'He understands how much it means to me.' Her face shut down with that closed, obstinate look she could have sometimes. He knew there was no point questioning it. She shuffled the papers into a pile and slipped them into a clear plastic envelope. He thought again she should have had a career of her own, a business to use up all that energy. She looked up at Sandy.

'When are you planning to get back to Lerwick?'

'I'm not sure,' he said vaguely. 'I've got some leave to take.'

'So you'll be here for the evening when we show off the coins. I was thinking Friday would be a good day. It's fine that you'll be here. Hattie's mother is going to come. It'll be nice for her to see a friendly face. Can I put you down to meet her at the airport?'

'Does she know what she's letting herself in for? She's not even buried her daughter yet.' Sandy thought these island events could be daunting for anyone. He couldn't face them without a couple of drams and a few cans in his belly. He remembered Gwen James in her London flat, chain-smoking, guilt-ridden. How would she deal with the curious islanders, the intrusive questions? Then he remembered she was a politician and probably capable of putting on a show.

'I spoke to her this morning,' Evelyn said. 'She said she wanted to see where Hattie died.'

'Would she rather not do that without an audience?'

'I explained what we were planning.' The stubborn tone had returned. 'It was her decision. She didn't have to agree.'

But it would suit Evelyn's purpose, Sandy thought, to have the woman there. An MP, something of a celebrity, to give the Setter project a bit of credibility, almost a touch of glamour. Sometimes he was shocked by how ruthless his mother could be. She would make a fine politician herself.

'I've booked her a room at the Pier House,' Evelyn

went on. 'I said she could stay here but she didn't want to put us out.'

At least, Sandy thought, the woman would have her own space to escape to. He wondered if Perez knew what his mother had planned and what he would make of it.

'Who else have you invited?' he asked.

'Everyone who's been involved with the dig. Paul Berglund, of course.'

'Will he come?'

'I'm not sure. He said he might have other commitments.'

I bet he has.

'But I've talked to his head of department at the university and said how important we feel it is for him to be there.'

Sandy found himself grinning. His mother could be as persuasive as a bulldozer. Where had this drive and nerve come from?

'And what did the university say?'

'They were sure Professor Berglund would find time in his diary for such an important occasion, especially as it would be dedicated to one of his students.' Evelyn looked up and caught his eye. For a brief moment they shared the conspiratorial laughter.

'I'd have liked Sophie to be there,' Evelyn said. 'Did you hear that she'd gone south?'

'Aye, I had heard that.'

'It was all very sudden. She didn't even drop in here to say goodbye, and that seems kind of rude. I don't suppose you have an address for her, her mobile phone number?'

'No, Mother, I don't.'

His mother seemed about to press the point, but thought better of it. 'I suppose the Cloustons will be there,' she said. 'You can never keep Jackie away from any sort of party.'

Sandy went out on to the hill to look for his father. Walking over the heather he thought the week in Whalsay had made him a bit fitter. He didn't feel the strain in his legs or that dreadful heaving in his lungs that came sometimes when he followed his father up the hill. In town he never walked anywhere and he lived off takeaway food. He thought with longing of sweet and sour pork, the batter all crispy, the sauce rich and thick with sugar and pineapple. What was so great about feeling fit?

He found Joseph squatting over a dead newborn lamb. It had already been picked over by ravens and hooded crows.

'It was tiny,' Joseph said. 'It was never going to survive. Maybe the smallest of twins.' He straightened and looked along the ridge of the hill. 'I thought you'd be away back to Lerwick now the funeral's over.'

'Perez said I should take some leave. I've got plenty owing and I can't carry it forward after the end of April.'

'Your mother will be pleased to have you around.'

'Yeah, right!'

'Really,' Joseph said seriously. 'She misses you.'

'She misses Michael right enough.' But he couldn't help feeling pleased and hoped it was true. 'What's all this about a big do in the hall to show off the project at Setter?'

Joseph didn't answer immediately. Sandy thought he was choosing his words carefully. For a moment his father reminded him of Jimmy Perez.

'Do you fancy a coffee?' Joseph said. 'Your mother made up a flask for me.' He pulled a Thermos from his pocket, then took off his coat and laid it on the grass. They sat together, both looking north-east up the island.

'Couldn't you talk her out of it?' Sandy took a swig from the cup they were sharing. The coffee was strong and very sweet.

'I didn't try too hard,' his father said. 'You know how she is once her mind is made up.'

'She always listens to you.'

'Not this time.'

'I don't want to her to make a fool of herself.' Sandy's voice came out louder than he'd expected. The wind flicked the words away and he could hear the panic in them, the underlying thought: *I don't want her to make a fool out of me.*

'Oh, between us I think between us we can keep her under control.' There was an attempt at humour, but it didn't quite work. Joseph's words were serious and matter-of-fact.

'Is anything wrong, Dad? Anything I can help with?'

For a second Sandy thought his father would confide in him. A curlew called and in the distance he could hear the barking sound of a raven. Then Joseph screwed the cap back on the flask and stood up.

'What could be wrong? We're all upset because of the accidents. Two deaths. Terrible bad luck. There's nothing wrong between your mother and me.'

Sandy remembered his last conversation with his father at Setter. Then Joseph had spoken of the deaths as more than 'terrible bad luck'. He knew his father was lying, but he was grateful for the lie. If his parents were having problems, Sandy didn't really want to know.

They were on their way back to Utra, walking at a stiff pace down the hill, so Sandy could feel his breath coming in tight little bursts, when Joseph spoke again.

'I was thinking maybe your mother has been right about Setter. Perhaps we should consider selling it.'

Sandy stopped in his tracks and bent over. It was as if someone had thumped him in the stomach, winding him.

His father didn't seem to notice. Now he'd started talking it seemed he couldn't stop.

'We're neither of us getting any younger. We need to think about our future. What do I need with another house? Neither you nor Michael will ever live there. I've taken most of the Setter land into Utra anyway. It's only a building.' He realized that Sandy wasn't with him and stopped for him to catch up. 'But I'll not sell it to Robert,' he went on. His voice was defiant. He shouted his words into the wind. 'I'll not sell it to that rich bastard so he can put his fancy daughter in there. We'll do as your mother says. We'll offer it to the Amenity Trust. They can make a museum out of it. Something to the memory of Mima Wilson. A house in her honour.'

Sandy had straightened his back. He walked down the hill towards his father. His legs felt weak and he had to concentrate so he didn't trip.

'What made you change your mind? You said you didn't want strangers walking all over it.'

'It's my house,' Joseph said. 'I can do what I like with it.'

'I ken that fine. But something's made you change your mind. What's happened?' Then came the same question and this time he hoped his father would give him the truth: 'Is there anything I can do to help?'

As he spoke, Sandy was still further up the hill than his father and looking down at him. Joseph wasn't an old man; he was wiry and strong. But from this perspective suddenly he seemed small.

'No,' Joseph said at last. 'There's nothing you can do to help.'

Chapter Thirty-seven

Perez spent most of the day in the office, glad of the routine, the familiar paperwork. He spoke to a local historian who'd written a book on the Shetland Bus, and put in a call to the Norwegian Embassy. Later he had a meeting with the Fiscal. They drank tea in her office, discussed depression and date rape as they sipped Earl Grey and nibbled shortbread biscuits. The horrors of her work never seemed to affect her.

'Well, I think we can put the girl's death down to suicide now,' the Fiscal said. 'She must have been under considerable stress, working with a man who had once assaulted her. She even used his knife to kill herself. That works for me as a final communication, to him and to us. She held him responsible for her misery. And now you say she discussed the rape with her colleague just before she disappeared; that confirms our original decision.'

Perez could see it would make life easier for Rhona Laing if they could tidy away Hattie's death like that. Two tragedies on Whalsay, one accident, one suicide, only connected in that Mima's death had made Hattie feel lonelier and even more depressed.

He sat for a moment in silence. The Fiscal waited. She hadn't been in Shetland long, but she was used to his ways and she was a patient woman when she had to be. Eventually though she'd had enough.

'Well? Don't you agree?'

'I think there was more to it than that. I don't understand why she should phone me if she intended to kill herself. There was something she wanted to tell me, something about Mima's killing.'

'You believe she was murdered?' There was something close to ridicule in the Fiscal's question.

'Almost certainly.'

'Are you sure emotion isn't getting in the way here, Jimmy? Guilt, perhaps, because you didn't do a proper search of Setter when you had the chance?'

'I believe both women were killed,' he said. 'I just can't prove it yet.'

'I can't dither over a decision for much longer,' she said.

'No.'

'How long do you need?' Dithering was bad for a politician's reputation, but so was making the wrong call on a suspicious death. She set her cup carefully on its saucer. 'How long do you need, Jimmy? I can't keep the case open indefinitely.'

'Somebody knows what's been going on there,' he said. 'Not just the murderer. In one of the houses in Whalsay a friend or a relative is keeping a secret. It's that sort of place.'

'So, how long, Jimmy? I really can't give you more than a few days.'

'I hope,' he said, 'that's all I need.'

'You have a suspect in mind?'

He nodded but he didn't speak. She looked at him

with curiosity but didn't press the point. At this stage she didn't want to know.

'If I don't have something by the end of next week, we call Hattie's death as suicide. I can't turn it into an accident, however kind that would be for her mother. Then we can get through the inquest and release the girl's body back to her family.'

He nodded again, but he was already preoccupied. He needed proof. He didn't have time for long conversations, for allowing the truth to emerge over time. He worked well that way, was much more patient than the Fiscal. But now he'd have to make things happen. He had to precipitate a crisis. He wasn't sure how he could do that without putting other Whalsay folk at risk.

On his way home he stopped at the Co-op for food, but walking down the aisles he was still thinking of the case. The case and Fran, who was always with him.

The problem with the Whalsay investigation was that so much was going on there. It was hard to unpick the actual causes and connections. Like Fair Isle knitting, he thought. Four different coloured threads, tangled together in the working to make a pattern. It was difficult to follow the line of each yarn, to decide how much impact each colour had on the overall effect.

In the house, he poured a glass of wine, fried a salmon steak quickly on each side, drained spinach and potatoes. *Shit*, he thought, *I forgot to buy a lemon*.

He'd finished the meal without really tasting it when there was a knock on his door. He put his plate to soak in the sink before going to answer it. Walking down the hall there was a moment of excitement when he imagined that perhaps Fran had come home a few days early. Would he find her there, standing in the street, looking up at his window, stamping her feet impatiently, waiting for him to answer? He pictured her wrapped in her jacket against the drizzle, the blue scarf with the silver threads tied at her throat. But it wasn't Fran. It was Sandy, leaning against the frame, obviously drunk and desperate to talk. Perez stood aside to let him in.

He was apologetic in the snivelling way that drunks are – if they don't become violent. 'I'm sorry, Jimmy, I've let you down. But I couldn't stand it there, I had to get out.' After that he became incoherent. He was red in the face and his nose was running. Perez sat him in the living room and made him coffee.

'Where have you been?' Perez's immediate fear was that Sandy had been shooting his mouth off in a bar in town, telling all the world about events in Whalsay. It was only eight o'clock. When had he started drinking?

'In The Lounge with a few of the boys.' He must have been sufficiently aware to see the alarm in Perez's face. 'But I didn't talk about the case, Jimmy. I wouldn't do that!' He slurped the coffee, pulled a face as he burned his tongue. 'I just made out I was fed up being stuck out there with my folks, that I was glad to be back in town. You can't blame me for having a few drinks.'

'What's happened at home?' Because something must have happened, Perez could tell that. Sandy had been calm enough when he'd got back after the trip to London. He'd done well there. He'd proved the Fiscal wrong.

Sandy set down his mug and put his head in his

hands. 'I don't know,' he said. 'I don't know what's going on.'

'What time did you leave Whalsay?' Perez thought if he kept to the facts, Sandy might drop the drama and come up with a rational explanation.

'This afternoon. I had a pint in the Pier House and I knew I wouldn't be able to stop at the one drink. You know how it is sometimes. I couldn't get pissed in there. Davy Henderson was coming into Lerwick so I got a lift down with him. I phoned up a few of the boys.' He looked up at Perez, belligerent and defensive at the same time. 'I'm on leave. I can do what I like.'

'Do your parents know where you are?'

'I haven't told them.'

'For Christ's sake, man, there've been two deaths on the island. They'll be frantic. Give them a ring and at least let them know you're safe.'

'Mother will have been on the phone to Cedric, trying to track me down. He'll have told her I went out on the ferry.' He was sulky as a child.

'That's not good enough and you know it.'

'Look, I don't care! This is all their fault.'

Perez looked at him. Earlier in the week he'd thought Sandy had matured. The man had dealt with Gwen James with sensitivity, come back with more information about Hattie than Perez had expected. Now he was like a toddler throwing a tantrum over a lost toy, blaming his parents for his misery.

Sandy met his eye. He must have realized how disappointed Perez felt because his tone changed. 'OK, I'll phone them.'

Perez carried the coffee cups into the kitchen. Through the wall he heard Sandy's muffled voice, still defensive and angry, but he couldn't make out the words. When he returned to the room the conversation was over. He drew the curtains and waited for Sandy to speak. That was why the man was here, after all. Why else would he have turned up on the doorstep in such a state?

'My parents are going to sell Setter,' Sandy said.

Perez nodded. 'It makes sense. They wouldn't want to leave the house standing empty, and doesn't Joseph work most of the croft anyway?'

'You don't understand. My father doesn't want to sell. He hates the idea. He didn't even want the dig to go ahead. And now there's this grand do in the hall. Mother says it's about showing folk the coins found on the land, but it'll be about persuading the Trust to buy the house. If the sale goes ahead, they'll be digging up all over the land, maybe even knocking down Mima's house to put up some sort of replica. And my father just says, "Fine, go ahead."'

'What are you worried about, Sandy? I don't really see the problem. It's your parents' house now. Their decision.'

'I want to know why he changed his mind.' It came out as a shout, so loud that Perez thought the neighbours would hear through the wall. 'He's not a man to change his mind.'

Perez sat still and waited for the rest.

'Someone's put pressure on him,' Sandy said. His voice was quieter but still intense.

'Your mother, maybe. She's a woman used to getting her own way. Nothing sinister in that. You know how excited she is about the history.'

'Not my mother. She's all bluster and talk, but he takes the decisions in the house.'

'What then?'

'Blackmail,' Sandy said. 'I wondered if that could be it. He needs the money to pay someone off.' He looked at Perez, desperate to be told that it was a crazy idea. He was Sandy Wilson and he got everything wrong.

But Perez didn't speak for a moment. He was considering the possibility seriously. The scenario he'd dreamed up to explain the Whalsay deaths didn't involve blackmail, but perhaps it could fit in with the facts. At this point anything was possible.

'What might Joseph have done that he could be blackmailed? You're not saying he killed Mima?'

'No!' Sandy said immediately. 'Not that. Not deliberately.' He paused. 'I've been going over and over it in my head. Wild ideas. Just churning round and round and making no sense at all. I thought the drink would give me some peace from it.'

'Let's look at them then. The wild ideas.'

'My father could have killed Mima by accident. A mistake. Hattie saw him and so he killed her too. You said yourself he was at Setter the night she died.'

'But he was in his house the whole of the evening of Mima's death, watching television. Your mother confirmed it.'

'Of course she did. She'd lie for us all.'

Perez smiled. 'So she would. What's the next wild idea?'

'Could the killer have mistaken Mima for Hattie? They were both small and slight and Mima was wearing Hattie's coat. Mima was out in the field next to the dig – Hattie would have had more reason to be there.'

'It's something I've thought about,' Perez said. 'But what reason could your father have for killing Hattie?'

'None at all. He hardly knew her. Another crazy idea.'

'Pretty crazy.' But Perez thought Sandy wasn't doing badly. The ideas the man had come up with had floated around in his head too. 'Anything else?'

'Nah,' Sandy said. 'That was about as far as I got.' He gave a self-deprecating grin. 'Not much of a detective, huh? Maybe I should give up policing and take up crofting after all.'

'I think perhaps you're overreacting about the sale of your grandmother's home. Hardly surprising. You were very fond of her.'

'Things aren't right at home,' Sandy said suddenly. 'I hate it.'

'Joseph and Evelyn are under a lot of strain. Things will sort themselves out when this is all over.'

'Will it ever all be over?' Sandy was almost sober now, but gloomy. 'I'm not sure how anyone on Whalsay will cope if we don't find out what happened.'

'They'll cope if they have to,' Perez said. He thought the islanders had suffered worse than this. The fracturing of a community during the fifteenth century. The huge storm that had killed half the male population of Whalsay at the end of the nineteenth century, when boats out to the fishing had capsized under freak waves. The murder of the young Norwegian from the Shetland Bus during the war. 'But I want to know. Not for them but for me.' He looked at Sandy. 'What are your plans for the rest of the night?'

Sandy shrugged. 'I was going to stay in town but I'll only carry on drinking. Maybe I'll get home.'

'It's still early. We'll get a ferry. I'll give you a lift back.' Perez looked at the man. 'That is if you're sure you're OK to go home?'

'Aye,' Sandy said. 'You're right. I've been a fool. My father's not a murderer.'

Perez was going to say Sandy hadn't been a fool at all, but that wasn't what the man wanted to hear.

Chapter Thirty-eight

Sandy stumbled down the road towards Setter. Perez had offered to take him right up to the house, but Sandy thought he'd put his boss out quite enough tonight. He'd already made a fool of himself. It was a dark, damp night, much like the one when he'd found Mima. He ignored the picture of the woman's body, hardly more than a pile of cloth-covered bones lying in the rain, that forced its way into his head, tried to concentrate instead on avoiding the pot-holes and not falling flat on his face in the mud.

As he rounded the bend in the track he saw there was a light in the house. Had he left it on? He didn't see that he could have done: it had been early afternoon when he'd gone down the island to the Pier House. And this wasn't the white glow of the strip light in Mima's kitchen, with its plastic case greasy and filled with dead flies. This was flickering and red.

Sandy broke into a run and he was already wheezing when he got to the house. He opened the door and the heat hit him, scorching his face. There was thick smoke that stung his eyes and made him choke. He tried to push his brain into gear, to remember the training he'd been given in fighting fire. The blaze had started in the kitchen and still hadn't taken hold of the rest of the house. It was licking up the paint on the cupboards and the wooden panels under the window were alight. There was a towel on the table and he threw it over the flame on the cupboard, smothering the fire, hitting out the air from it. He filled the washing-up bowl with water and threw it over the flames by the window. There was a hissing, but the wood was still burning. He filled the bowl again. This time the fire was doused. He was left heaving for breath, his heart pounding.

He heard a nose outside. A strange kind of cry, like an animal in pain. He stood at the door and looked out. Anger stopped him feeling frightened. Anger and stupidity.

'Who is it?' he yelled. 'What the fuck are you doing out there?' He wanted to hit someone, to smash in the face whoever had desecrated his grandmother's home.

A figure moved out of the shadow of the cowshed. His father stood in front of him. He looked small and old. For the first time Sandy saw how like Mima Joseph was physically. The same small frame and wiry strength.

'Did you see him?' Sandy demanded. 'Did you see who did this?'

Joseph didn't speak.

'You stay here,' Sandy said. 'The fire hasn't long started and there wasn't a car. I might catch him.'

'It was me.'

Something in his father's voice stopped Sandy short. He'd started to move down the track, but now he turned back.

'What are you saying?' Sandy was still wearing his

jacket and felt bulky, huge even, looking out at his father.

'I set fire to your grandmother's house.'

They stared at each other. Sandy knew he should make sense of this, but he couldn't. Even when he was sober as a judge he would never make sense of it. The drizzle had stopped and there was a faint fat moon showing through the mist.

'I don't want to go inside,' Sandy said. 'Not with the kitchen the way it is.' He walked round to the back of the house, past the dig to the dyke looking over the loch. The moonlight was reflected on the water. He didn't look behind him but he knew his father was following. They leaned against the dyke to talk, not looking at each other.

Sandy had questioned suspects in his time. It was a part of the job he enjoyed. When he was taking statements from offenders or witnesses he was the boss, in control. It wasn't like that for much of his life. Now he wished his father would take the lead, but Joseph just stood there in silence.

'Why would you do that?' Sandy asked at last, not loud, not in his bossy police voice, but with a kind of desperation. 'Why would you set fire to your own house?'

'Because I couldn't face anyone else living here.'

'Is this to do with that Norwegian?' A sudden idea. If he weren't still a bit pissed Sandy didn't think he'd have had the nerve to bring the subject up.

'What do you know about him?'

'I know that your father found him in bed with your mother, took him outside and shot him.'

'There isn't much else to know,' Joseph said, and

then, in a quiet voice. 'And I'm not even sure that story's true.'

But Sandy wasn't ready to listen to that. 'How did you find out about it?' he demanded. 'Did Mima tell you when you were a boy?' He wondered what it would be like to discover that your father was a murderer. How would Mima pass on that bit of information? Would she tell it as a bedtime story along with the tales of the trows?

'She didn't tell me at all.'

'Who did then?'

'It was always going to come out,' Joseph said. Sandy shot a look at him. The moonlight turned his beard and his hair to silver. 'You can't keep a good story like that a secret on a place like this. It was while I was at school. The little school here in Whalsay. There was a scrap. You know how boys are. Andrew Clouston came out with it then. A fit of temper, a way of hurting me. He was never much of a fighter when he was young. He was a good bit older than me but a coward. He must have got the tale from his father, old Andy. I ran straight out of the schoolyard to ask Mother if it was true.' Joseph paused. 'She was out here, planting neeps, her skirt hitched up and big boots on her feet. I'd been running and I was red, my face all covered with tears and snot. "Why didn't you tell me my dad was a murderer?" I shouted it out at her. She straightened her back and looked at me. "I'm not sure that he was."'

Joseph looked up at Sandy. 'I was angry. As angry as you are now. I started screaming at her, asking what she meant. She stayed very calm. "They took the man away," she said. "I was never certain what happened to him and your father would never discuss it. I hoped they took him across to Lunna, maybe beat him up a bit. I never knew he was dead. Even when the stories started. I should have told you. But I hoped you wouldn't have to find out."' And she carried on shaking the seed down the row, her shoulders bent and her eyes on the soil.'

'Did she ever talk to you about it properly?'

'Later that evening. She'd had a couple of drams. She talked about the Norwegian: "They called him Per. I never knew his second name. He was tall and blond and he treated me kindly. Your father was an exciting man, but he was never kind to me." That was what she said.'

'Where did they bury him?' Sandy asked.

'I don't know. I told you, she didn't even know he was dead. We didn't discuss it.'

'You must have thought about it.'

The mist had cleared even more and now there were just a few threads of cloud flying in front of the moon. It was so light it felt like the simmer dim of a midsummer night.

'When I was a teenager I got it into my head that the Norwegian could have been my father,' Joseph said. 'I heard things about my real dad I didn't like so much. There were stories he beat Mima up. But the Norwegian couldn't have been my father. The dates don't work. I wasn't born in the war.'

And you look so like Jerry, Sandy thought, remembering the photo that stood in Setter. *You couldn't be anyone else's child.*

'Do you think your father was drowned at sea?'

Sandy asked. The question came into his head unbidden.

Now Joseph turned. 'That's what I was always told,' he said.

'I don't understand why you have to get rid of Setter,' Sandy said. Was he being stupid? Too thick to understand? 'Why now? When you were so set against selling it, when you hate the idea so much that you're prepared to set fire to it, to get the insurance instead of selling it on?' Because it seemed to Sandy that money must come into it somehow. Money was always important in Whalsay.

'That's not my story to tell,' Joseph said. 'You'll have to ask your mother about that. Now come home. You can't stay in Setter the state that it's in.'

'I'll tell Mother it was me,' Sandy said. 'A chip pan. She knows I was drinking.'

Joseph didn't say anything. He put his arm around his son's shoulder and they walked together back to Utra.

Chapter Thirty-nine

Sandy had to suffer a lecture from Evelyn the next morning about the evils of drinking and frying chips in the middle of the night. 'You could have been killed. You could have burned the house to the ground!' He thought about his father and made a pretence of looking contrite.

He hadn't slept well. The amount he'd had to drink, you'd have thought he'd be out like a light, but ideas had been churning round in his head all night. He'd tried to rerun the conversation with his father. The earlier part of the evening he remembered fine: drinking in the bars in Lerwick, his arm round the shoulders of that fat lassie, the one married to the soothmoother who worked in the canning factory. Then turning up like a fool on Perez's doorstep. He'd been pretty sober by the time they got back to Whalsay. At least, he thought he had been. But the details of finding the fire, standing with Joseph in the moonlight by the loch, all that seemed harder to pin down. It was as if he'd dreamed it all. Perhaps he didn't want to remember the way his father had been last night.

Evelyn put a bacon sandwich and a mug of coffee in front of him. Joseph was already out; he'd been gone when Sandy got up.

'Will you not sit down and have some breakfast with me?' he asked. His mother was busy with three things at once as usual. She buzzed round the kitchen like a bluebottle trapped in a jar.

'I had my breakfast hours ago.'

'Then just sit down and have a coffee!'

She looked at him strangely but she did as he said.

'Why has my father changed his mind about selling Setter?'

'He realized it made sense. What would he want with an old house?' Sandy recognized the tone. She was all bluster and bravado, like some teenage lad who'd stolen a car and driven it into a ditch.

Sandy shook his head. 'He loves the place. He grew up there. He doesn't want it full of strangers.'

'That's sentiment,' Evelyn said. 'You can't eat sentiment.'

'He said you'd tell me what this was all about.'

She paused for a beat, stared at him sadly for a moment. 'Oh Sandy, you're the last person I could tell.'

It was as if she'd slapped him in the face.

The phone rang then and his mother went to answer it. She came back frowning. 'That was your Auntie Jackie. She wants to know if you could go up to the big house. Andrew's fidgeting to talk to you, she says.'

'Aye. Why not? I'll walk over.' He knew he was a coward but he couldn't wait to get out of the house.

Walking up the track to the Clouston place, he did feel better. There was a wheatear bouncing along the stone wall and skylarks singing in the field beyond. He found Jackie in the kitchen. The table was full of clutter – bags of flour, sugar and oats, tins of syrup and treacle. 'You look busy. Is this for something special?'

'Evelyn's asked me to do some baking for her grand do in the hall,' Jackie said. 'I thought I'd make a start today. Anna's helping me out.' Then Sandy saw that Anna Clouston was there too, sitting in the corner. She was breastfeeding the baby. You couldn't see exactly what was going on because she was wearing a loose jumper, but he felt embarrassed just the same, felt his face colour. He turned away.

'As you see,' Anna said, 'I'm not helping very much at the moment.'

'I've told her she should give the bairn a bottle.' Jackie began to beat together a lump of butter and some sugar. 'He might start to sleep at night. He's probably starving.'

'He's fine,' Anna said. 'He won't be a baby for long. I don't mind a bit of disturbance for a while. I don't mind putting myself out for my child.' The implication was clear: she thought Jackie was selfish.

Sandy thought this was how women fought. With civilized words carrying poison.

'Where's Andrew?' Because it had come to him that the room seemed quite different and that was because of his uncle's absence. Andrew usually sat in his chair by the stove, a permanent fixture, like the shiny American fridge and the china dog on the dresser. Huge and imposing, he seldom spoke but somehow made his presence felt.

'He's in the lounge. We're having one of the bedrooms decorated and I've asked him to clear out some junk. He's found some photos and thought you might be interested. Go on through.'

Andrew was sitting in one of the big armchairs with his back to the view. There was a pile of photograph albums on the coffee table in front of him. He looked up when he heard Sandy come into the room and smiled. He didn't speak. Sandy found it hard to imagine him as a boy, scrapping with Joseph in the school playground. He had fought with words too, Sandy thought. Like the women battling in the kitchen over a baby barely a month old.

'You remember Jerry,' Sandy said. 'My grandfather, Jerry Wilson.'

Andrew screwed up his face in concentration. 'I don't remember so much these days.' The words came out as a series of stutters.

Sandy looked at him. He thought the lack of memory could be kind of convenient. 'But you told me the story about him. About him killing the Norwegian man during the war.'

Andrew frowned and nodded.

'How did he die?' He'd asked Joseph the same question but had no real answer.

'He was killed in an accident at sea. He was out fishing with my father. There was a storm. A freak wave that turned the boat over. He was drowned.'

'But your father was saved.'

'He was a stronger swimmer and he got hold of the upturned boat. He tried to hold on to Jerry Wilson, but he lost his grip.'

'Are you sure that's true? It wasn't just another of the island stories? You know how that happens. People make things up. Like the stories you told about my grandfather being a murderer.'

There was a moment while they stared at each

other. Sandy could hear the gulls on the roof and the sheep on the grass by the shore.

'This isn't a made-up story,' Andrew said. 'I was there when your grandfather died.'

'You would have been a child!'

'I was ten years old. Old enough to go fishing with my father. We just had the small boat then.'

'How did you survive when my grandfather didn't?'

'Don't you see?' Andrew fixed him with his blue, staring eyes. 'My father couldn't save the both of us. He chose to save me. You can't blame him for that.'

And Sandy supposed that was true. A man was always going to save his son ahead of his friend.

'Was Jerry's body ever washed up?'

'Not here. Not that I heard.'

'I wondered if his remains had been buried at Setter.' Sandy had been thinking about that in the night. It was one explanation for his father's reluctance to let the place go.

Andrew looked up at him. 'No, I never heard anything like that.'

'Shall we look at these photos then?'

'Aye, why not?'

But Sandy was still haunted by thoughts of the past, of buried secrets. 'Did you ever hear what they did with the dead Norwegian?'

Andrew didn't respond.

'The Norwegian who came over with the Bus,' Sandy said. He found himself becoming frustrated again by Andrew's slowness. He wondered how Jackie and Ronald managed to keep so patient. 'Mima's lover. What happened to him?'

Andrew said nothing. Sandy remembered the sort

of man he'd once been, big and loud, easy to rouse to anger. Mima had once said; 'Andrew Clouston has a tempestuous nature. Like a storm at sea.' Sometimes she came out with things like that. There was no sign of Andrew's tempestuousness now. Sandy thought he was more like a boat with a bust engine, becalmed and useless.

'Let's look at the photos,' Sandy said, giving up the struggle to force an answer.

He opened the album and recognized the first picture straight away. It was the one from the wall in Mima's bedroom with the women who were carrying peat and knitting at the same time.

'Do you know them, Andrew? Who are they?'

For the first time since he'd come into the room, Andrew seemed aware of what was happening. He pointed to the woman on the left. 'I know her. That's your grandmother.'

'Not Mima! She was never a knitter!'

'No, no, no.' Andrew was frustrated by his lack of fluency. 'Evie. They called her Evie. She was Evelyn's mother.'

And now Sandy could see the likeness. He'd only known his maternal grandmother as an old woman. But the family resemblance was there. He could see Evelyn in the woman's sturdy build, the determined look on her face. *This is where I come from*, he thought.

Andrew had lost interest in the picture and turned the page of the album. He stared at the next photograph, seemed completely lost in his memories.

'Who's that then, Andrew? Is it someone you recognize?' Sandy moved closer to the man so he could get a better look at the book.

The picture was of two men, standing with their arms around each other's shoulders, grinning out at the camera. They wore elaborate hand-knitted jerseys, baggy trousers and caps. The sun must have been in their eyes because they were squinting. Sandy thought it had been taken on the shore at Lindby, because he recognized the bit of drystone wall in the background.

'Who is it, Andrew?' he said again when there was no immediate reply. 'Is one of them your father?'

'That's my father.' The older man stuck a finger on to one of the figures. 'That must have been taken when I was very young. That's Jerry Wilson.'

Sandy could see now that the man on the right was his grandfather. There was the same quirky smile as in the photo that had stood in Mima's kitchen. He thought now it looked a bit cruel. This was a man who might make fun of you, so it sounded like teasing but was hurtful all the same.

A picture of two friends who had gone fishing, and only one came back. With his ten-year-old son.

'I should get home,' Sandy said. 'My mother will be sending out search parties. Thank you for showing me the pictures.' *Is that all he wanted me to see?* Sandy thought. *Is this why he dragged me up here? Or was it all Jackie's idea? Maybe she wanted to do her baking in peace.*

Sandy took his arm and helped Andrew out of the chair. *If I ever get like this, I hope they shoot me. Or I have the courage to throw myself over a cliff.* But he never thought he would get like that. He was young and the idea was unthinkable: The old man moved slowly to the corner window. From there they could see Setter, and beyond the house the trenches of the dig.

'They never buried that Norwegian man there,' Andrew said. 'They took his body out to sea in Jerry Wilson's boat and they threw him overboard. That's what my father told me.'

Chapter Forty

Thursday morning. Perez shaved carefully. The bathroom was cold and he wiped condensation from the mirror to check it was properly done. This was a special day: Fran would be home. He would meet her and Cassie from the airport and take them back to Ravenswick. He felt nervous and excited, as if there was something illicit in this meeting, as if he already had a wife and Fran was his mistress. He couldn't understand it, especially as he knew he wouldn't spend the evening with her. Later, after dropping them home, he'd have to go to Whalsay.

The Whalsay trip was work and unavoidable. Fran would understand that; work was important to her too. She wouldn't have a tantrum and make a scene, but she wouldn't put herself out for him either. She wouldn't wait up for him with a bottle of champagne and sexy underwear. There was no guarantee he'd be back that evening. She'd learned that when he was working there were nights when he didn't get home. She'd take herself off to bed and when he joined her, if she was asleep, he wasn't sure he'd wake her. He wasn't sure he had that right.

Perez thought today would mark the end of the investigation, one way or another. He'd woken to fog, so he couldn't see beyond the Victoria Pier from his living-room window and his first thought was that the planes would be cancelled and there would be no way in for Fran or Gwen James. The star of Evelyn's show would be absent and Perez would have another day to wait for the woman he adored. Then in a matter of minutes, in the time it took to make a pot of tea, the sun had burned the cloud away and now the weather was perfect – clear and sunny and warm as most days in midsummer. Eating his breakfast he saw a puffin flying low over the water. The first of the season. He thought he should see it as a good omen but he still felt jittery.

In his office he took a phone call from Val Turner.

'Jimmy, just to let you know that I'm going into Whalsay this morning. I'll see you in the community hall this evening. It's all set.'

He tried to make an appointment to talk to the Fiscal but she'd taken a couple of days' leave at short notice. There was no explanation and he realized again how little people knew about her. She managed her privacy in a way that nobody else of note in Shetland could. Although he didn't like her much, Perez felt isolated; he missed Sandy's blundering presence too. In previous cases he'd had Roy Taylor from Inverness to share responsibility and anxiety with. It hadn't always been an easy relationship but Perez had valued Taylor's bluntness, his common sense. *I take my work too seriously*, he thought. *I make everything complicated. I need someone else to set me straight and keep things real.*

Later he phoned Sandy's mobile and heard Evelyn's voice giving orders in the background before Sandy even spoke.

'How're things?'

'It's a madhouse here. You'd think my mother was hosting the bloody Oscars, not a history lecture in the Lindby Community Hall.'

Perez was just about to say that he'd see Sandy that evening, but the Whalsay man continued talking.

'I went to see Andrew yesterday. According to him that Norwegian wasn't buried at Setter at all. After he was killed they took him out in a boat and dropped him over the side.'

'You said "they" took him out in the boat,' Perez said. 'Who are "they"?' *And if that's true, what is the fragment of more recent bone Val Turner says they found at Setter?*

'I'm not sure. I think it was Jerry Wilson and Andrew's father. They were friends. Close friends.' Sandy paused. 'Andrew's father was out with Jerry when he drowned.' There was a silence. Perez waited for Sandy to continue, could almost hear the strain over the phone as his colleague struggled to find the right words. 'Andrew was there too,' Sandy went on. 'He was ten years old. It sounds as if that was why Jerry didn't make it. Andrew's father couldn't get them both back and chose to save his son.'

Perez had planned to have a late lunch in the bar of the Sumburgh House Hotel. He would rather wait there than in the airport. It always looked desperate, being in the airport too early, desperate or neurotic. But driving past the runway he took a detour to Grutness, the jetty where the *Good Shepherd*, the Fair Isle mailboat, put in. Today was boat day and if he were quick he'd have time for a word with his father and some of the other boys in the crew before they set off back to the Isle. The Perez family had run the mailboat for as long as anyone could remember. When Jimmy had been growing up his grandfather had been skipper; now it was his father's turn. Perez wondered who would take it over when his father came to retire.

He arrived at the pier just as the men were loading the boat. There was a car to go on. It was being winched into position as Perez drove down the road. The boxes of supplies for the shop were already in the hold. A couple of passengers stood waiting to be allowed on board: an elderly birdwatcher with binoculars round his neck and a young woman whom Perez recognized. He thought she worked at the observatory. Although he couldn't make out her words he could tell she was joking with the crew. She had long black hair, curly and unruly. She threw back her head and laughed.

When he got out of his car his father jumped ashore. His hair was still dark and he was fit and strong, but his face looked older, as if it didn't belong to his body.

'Well, Jimmy, are you coming home with us?' He could never tell what his father was thinking. There always seemed to be an element of recrimination or challenge in his words. Now Perez wondered if he was implying that he didn't get home often enough. Or that he had an easy sort of job if he could decide on the spur of the moment to spend a few days with the family. He told himself he was being ridiculous and his father had meant neither of those things. He was just asking a question. Perez was always too sensitive where his father was concerned.

'No,' he said. 'I'm picking someone up from the airport and I'm early.'

'You should get home more often,' his father said. 'Bring your new woman to see us.'

Perez had avoided taking Fran to Fair Isle. His parents had met her, but only when they came to Lerwick on their way south. Perez was worried that she'd be frightened off by their expectations, their desire that he should have a son to carry on the family name. Without a boy, he would be the last Perez in Shetland.

'Aye,' he said. 'Maybe I will. Not over the summer. Fran will be busy with an exhibition. We'll come in the autumn.' It wasn't something he could put off much longer than that. Looking at the men he'd grown up with, laughing together as they passed the boxes and the mail sacks from the pier to the boat, he had a pang of regret. That could have been him. He'd had the opportunity to take up a life on the island but he'd turned it down. Now it seemed a simple and tempting alternative to the evening ahead of him.

He stood and watched the boat until it was out of sight. The water was calm but there was a bank of cloud on the horizon and soon that swallowed up the vessel. It became blurred like a ghost ship and then it disappeared. It would take the *Shepherd* more than three hours to get home. Fair Isle wasn't like Whalsay. There was no roll-on-roll-off ferry every half hour. It was the most isolated inhabited island in the UK. They'd been taught that at school. He still thought of the place as home.

When he got to the airport Sandy was already there.

Early too. scared of messing up the task of collecting Hattie's mother. He looked grey and tired, sitting at one of the tables outside the shop clutching a mug of coffee. Perez bought a coffee and a sandwich and joined him.

'I can't make sense of it all,' Sandy said. 'You ken there's that saying about skeletons in cupboards. A family's past coming back to haunt it. That's what it means, right?'

Perez nodded.

'This is about bones in the land. Old, red bones. But I don't understand how they matter after all these years.'

'Red?' Perez had a fanciful picture of bones steeped in blood.

'My mother says that's the colour they go when they've been in the earth for a long time.'

'They're like the stories you heard as a child and which stay at the back of your mind,' Perez said. 'Hard to forget.'

They went to the big glass window near Arrivals and watched the plane come in, the people walking down the ladder and on to the Tarmac. Fran and Cassie were among the last off and Perez felt the quiver of anxiety in his stomach. Perhaps she wasn't there. Perhaps at the last minute she'd changed her mind and decided the city suited her better.

'That's Gwen James,' Sandy said. And although he couldn't remember ever seeing her on the television, Perez thought he would have picked her out from the rest of the passengers. She wore a long black coat almost to her ankles, black boots. She carried a leather holdall and it seemed she had no other luggage, because she walked straight past the carousel to Sandy and held out her hand.

Perez had spoken to her the evening before and wanted to introduce himself, but at that point he was distracted by the sight of Fran and Cassie getting off the plane. Fran was grinning and waving like crazy. He waved back, tried not to beam like a madman. There was something about her not quite as he remembered. A different haircut, a new pair of baseball boots, pink and covered with sequins. He wondered if she'd wear them when he took her to Fair Isle and what his father would make of them.

'This is my boss,' Sandy was saying. 'Jimmy Perez.'

'We've talked on the phone.' Gwen James had the same jazz singer's voice that Perez remembered.

'Are you sure you're happy with everything we have planned?' Perez couldn't understand how she could be so poised, so calm.

'I need to know what happened,' she said.

'The car's outside,' Sandy said awkwardly. 'I'll get you back to Whalsay.'

'And I'll see you again this evening, Inspector Perez?'

'Oh yes, you'll see me then.'

Sandy picked up her bag and started walking quickly to the exit. Suddenly Perez realized he was hoping to get the woman out of the terminal before Cassie bounded up to them with her chat and hugs. He didn't want to distress Gwen James with memories of Hattie as a young girl. *Oh Sandy*, Perez thought, *how you've grown up*.

Cassie couldn't wait for her bag to arrive. She climbed through the barrier and threw her arms around Perez's waist. As he picked her up and lifted her into the air he saw Gwen and Sandy disappearing through the revolving door and into the car park.

'So,' he said. 'Have you missed me?'

Then Fran came up to them too, dragging a huge suitcase, laden with carrier bags, and it was she who answered.

'We haven't, have we, Cass? Hardly at all.'

'Yes we have. Mum told everyone how much she missed you. She was really boring. She kept saying she wanted to come home.'

'Well, we'd better get you back then, to the old house in Ravenswick.' He set Cassie on the floor and took the handle of Fran's suitcase. At that moment he thought he'd do anything to look after this family and keep it together. He'd kill for it. 'Didn't you have to pay excess baggage on this?'

'Nah, I chatted up that pretty boy on check-in at Dyce.'

It was then, as they walked together towards the exit, that Perez realized that another person connected with Whalsay had been on the Aberdeen plane. Standing at the car rental counter, filling in a form, frowning slightly, was Paul Berglund.

Chapter Forty-one

Anna Clouston walked up the hill towards the hall. She felt oddly liberated without the baby. Lighter and light-headed. A pool of mist had gathered in the low ground by the loch, so it looked as if the hall was stranded on its own island. Even the landscape seemed different.

When she opened the door she was surprised that Evelyn was the only person there. The trestle tables had been pushed together to run along the long side of the hall and Evelyn was covering them with white cloths, shaking the material out so they flapped like sails. Smaller tables had been set, cafe-style, in the middle of the hall. The speakers would have the best chairs at one end, with a table for their notes, and there was a screen and data projector. The urn was already hissing for tea. Everything was organized and efficient.

Evelyn was wearing an apron, but Anna could tell she'd dressed up for the occasion. She had green dangly earrings, little court shoes with heels.

'What would you like me to do?'

'You can fetch me the cups and saucers from the cupboard,' Evelyn said. Then: 'Sandy's picked Gwen James up from Sumburgh. He gave her a tour of the island – showed her the Bod and the dig at Setter, the place where Hattie died. It seems kind of ghoulish but she wanted to see it. She's in the Pier House now getting ready. He'll give her a lift up just before we start.'

'Right.' Anna couldn't understand how Gwen James could bear to be here. If anything had happened to her son, if he had been found in a hole in the ground like that, Anna wouldn't want to be paraded in the hall in front of staring people, all of them strangers. She wouldn't want to eat meringues and drink weak tea. What sort of mother could this woman be?

She set the cups and saucers out close to the urn, wiping each one with a clean tea towel as she brought it out of the cupboard, just as the island women always did.

'I'm surprised you've not got more helpers,' she said.

'Oh, I told Jackie I'd manage. Joseph came along earlier to help shift the furniture.' Evelyn had moved from the tables and was pinning photos of the dig site up on the walls. One showed Hattie and Sophie both crouched at work. Hattie had looked up at the camera and smiled; Anna couldn't remember ever having seen her appear so happy. It was a good photo. She wondered who'd taken it. Ronald, maybe. He'd spent a lot of time on the dig the summer before. Evelyn went on: 'Jackie says Andrew's agitated again today. She'll be in as soon as she's settled him. He won't be coming. Just as well. We don't want a scene.'

Anna thought Evelyn preferred it this way: completely in control and in charge. She could understand that.

The door of the hall opened and Anna saw a silhouette framed by the filtered light of the low sun behind him. Another bank of mist had come in from the sea. The figure moved further into the room and she recognized Jimmy Perez. He seemed surprised to see Anna there. She guessed he'd hoped to catch Evelyn on her own and now he was weighing his options and wondering how best to play the situation. Evelyn had her back to the door and hadn't seen him.

'Evelyn.'

The woman turned sharply. 'Oh, Jimmy. You're early. We're not starting until seven.'

'I was hoping to catch you for a word on your own. Perhaps we could go back to Utra for a few minutes.'

Evelyn paused for a beat, seemed to straighten her back. 'I'm afraid that's not possible, Jimmy. There's far too much to do before the other folk turn up.'

'Really, I think we might be better talking now.' He paused. 'We don't want a scene later.'

That word again, Anna thought. *Scene. What is it that they're scared of?* She would have offered to go out so they could talk on their own, but knew that was the last thing Evelyn wanted.

Evelyn seemed to consider. She looked quite calm. 'Oh, I don't think we need worry about that, do you, Jimmy? You know I'm the last one to cause a fuss. There's no hurry. You know I'm not going anywhere.'

Anna had the sense that the conversation had a meaning she didn't understand. Perez stood for a moment then nodded, he turned and left. Once he'd gone, Evelyn lifted the hem of her apron and wiped her face with it. Her only gesture of weakness. Then she bent and lifted a pile of dinner plates from the cupboard. 'The cakes can go on here,' she said. 'There should be napkins somewhere. We'll wrap them with clingfilm until the speeches are over.' She made no reference to the conversation between her and Perez.

In the end, Anna had to admit, the event was a triumph. It struck just the right note. Once Evelyn took off her apron she became a different person – confident, knowledgeable, charming. Even the islanders were impressed. She welcomed the guests into the hall and brought the locals and the incomers together. She walked Gwen James round all the photos and talked about what a delight Hattie had been to have on the island. Such an enthusiast: 'She made the history seem so real for me. I could see Whalsay through the eyes of the Setter merchant. These were our ancestors but it took an outsider to bring them to life.' When she introduced the speakers, she spoke fluently and without notes. 'The untimely deaths of two of our project's greatest supporters is a tragedy. But we owe it to them to continue the work at Setter and to make it a success.'

Anna thought if Evelyn had lived somewhere else she could have been a great businesswoman. You could see her at the head of a board table, motivating her team.

Jimmy Perez had come back. He had brought a woman with him; she was chic in an arty, bohemian sort of way, small and lively. They made an unusual couple. He was very dark and impassive and she seemed to be moving all the time, interested in everything. After a while of thinking she looked familiar, Anna recognized the woman as Fran Hunter, the artist from Ravenswick. There'd been an article about her in the most recent *Shetland Life*, and in the arts section of a Sunday broadsheet. *That could be me in a few years' time*, Anna thought, and her brain began fizzing with plans for the future. *There'll be features about my spinning and knitting; I'll call it the Whalsay Collection and take my influences from the Setter Merchant's House, the design of the coins. I'll ask Ronald to help me research the costumes and jewellery of the time. Maybe we'll make enough money that he'll be able to give up the fishing. We'll run it as a family business.* Suddenly anything seemed possible.

Perez stood at the back of the hall, furthest from the speakers. All the chairs had been taken but Anna thought that was where he had chosen to be. He wanted to see everything going on in the hall. Sandy Wilson sat with Hattie's mother near the front. There was no sign of Joseph and that surprised Anna. She'd have thought Evelyn would have dragged him along. Sandy was wearing a suit, the one he'd worn to their wedding, his face was red and he looked uncomfortable. Anna knew Ronald would have hated all this. *How grateful he'll be to me that I've given him the excuse to stay at home!* She looked forward to describing the evening to him. History was his passion, after all. She knew he'd be interested.

Jackie rushed in right at the last minute, just as Evelyn was about to start speaking. Although the weather was unusually calm, Jackie had a windswept, thrown together look that was quite unlike her. One of her nieces was a hairdresser and always came to do her hair before an evening out, but now it seemed she'd hardly had time to pull a brush through it.

Anna looked at Jackie across the hall and decided there must have been another crisis with Andrew. She reflected that she should be more considerate about her parents-in-law. She shouldn't make such a fuss when Ronald went up to the big house to help out. She'd been rather a bitch about them.

All these thoughts were running at the back of her head while she was listening to the presentations. She sat with a fixed look of concentration on her face and nobody would have realized her mind was elsewhere. *Though perhaps everyone is the same*, she thought, and she sneaked a look at the audience and tried to picture the ideas and preoccupations of the individuals who sat in respectful silence. They clapped when each speaker sat down, but perhaps there were other images running like a film in their heads too. *We think we know each other so well, but we all have our secrets.*

Paul Berglund went first. Anna had never met him. She'd been out giving birth when the skull had been found and Evelyn had never introduced them. He gave a very short speech. Perhaps it was his accent but the words seemed ungracious, almost dismissive.

'The university has always been delighted to support the Whalsay project, and of course it will continue to do so despite the tragic death of Hattie James.'

Anna had the impression that Evelyn had been expecting more, a promise of definite funding and more PhD students, an altogether grander project. She thought the most likely thing was that the dig would be forgotten, by the university at least.

Val Turner's lecture was obviously more to Evelyn's liking. There had been proper preparation, a PowerPoint presentation giving the background to the merchant's house and an explanation of the importance of the Hanseatic League. The audience seemed to become more engaged when she described the discovery of the skull, the evidence of the shattered ribs, and when she showed off the small, dull coins in their plastic box, supported now by special polyurethane foam. 'I have no doubt that this will be a major site in Shetland archaeology.'

Anna looked at her watch. She wondered if James had taken the bottle of expressed milk. She'd tried him with some a little earlier in the day and he'd seemed all right with it. More words running alongside all the others in her head: *I shouldn't have left him. He's so small . . . Guilt*, she thought. *Mothers must live with it all the time. I should just get used to it.*

Then Jimmy Perez walked to the front of the room. Val Turner introduced him. 'Now Inspector Perez would like to speak to us about the tragic death of Hattie James.'

There was an excitement in the hall. Even the showing of the skull and the coins hadn't generated this much interest. Looking at Gwen James's sculpted, motionless face, Anna thought the woman had known this announcement was coming. She had been expecting it, waiting for it throughout the evening. The police must have warned her. Anna felt her pulse race. She too wanted to know what the police had to say.

Perez stood in front of the table, leaning against it. He pushed himself forward so he was standing upright, almost to attention, and started speaking: 'I'm in a position now to inform you that we are treating Hattie James's death as suspicious. She didn't commit suicide. We believe there was a witness to the murder and we're close to making an arrest. In the meantime we'd be grateful for continuing support and information from everyone in Whalsay.' There was a moment of complete silence, then a muted hum of conversation. Anna couldn't think what Perez's words might mean. She thought the islanders were wishing Gwen James had stayed away despite her celebrity status. They would have preferred the freedom to gossip.

The evening was coming to an end. When the speeches were over the island women had moved behind the tables to pour tea from large metal pots. The clingfilm had been removed from the plates and now they were almost empty. Perez circulated around the room, talking to the locals. Or rather he was listening to the locals, Anna thought. Whenever she caught a glimpse of him he was silent, his gaze fixed on the speaker's face.

Now Anna just wanted to get home. Gwen James looked suddenly lost and Sandy, more attentive than Anna had realized he could be, offered to drive her back to the Pier House. Just as he was finding her coat, a couple of men who'd been outside for a smoke came back in.

'Just take care out there. The fog's so thick you can hardly see your hand in front of your face. We don't want you coming off the road.' And when Sandy opened the door to show Gwen James out, Anna saw they were right. She could see nothing. No lights in the other houses, never mind Shetland mainland in the distance.

Chapter Forty-two

Sandy drove at walking pace down the island towards the Pier House Hotel. He was pleased that the evening in the hall had passed without mishap; everyone had said how well Evelyn had done to arrange it and she'd seemed calmer than he could remember for ages. He hoped she'd be able to stay that way. Now he just had to deliver Gwen James back to her room and perhaps he could relax. He sat bent forward, just concentrating on keeping the grass verge on each side of him and the car on the road. Gwen James was smoking. He'd been watching her throughout the evening, admiring her style, the way she held things together. He supposed she'd had the practice. A politician had to be some sort of actor. Even his mother, who was only a politician in a small way, could put on the act when it was needed. Over the years he'd seen Evelyn put on the smile, use those easy phrases that had no meaning, when she was talking about her Whalsay projects to the important folk from Lerwick. Even when she was tired or depressed, she didn't lose the smile.

As soon as they'd left the hall, he saw how hard it had been for Gwen. She pulled a cigarette out of the packet with trembling hands and she'd been chain smoking ever since. They hit Symbister suddenly, almost before he realized. An orange streetlight above him and a wall on one side of the road and a pavement on the other. Then they were at the Pier House Hotel and he found himself shaking too. A release of tension after the drive.

He had expected Gwen James to go straight to her room. She'd already eaten and he thought she'd want to be on her own. But it seemed not: 'God, I need a drink. You will join me, won't you, Sandy?'

The weather had kept folk in their houses and the lounge was empty of customers. Cedric Irvine sat on a bar stool on the public side of the bar and Jean was standing behind it. Cedric winked at Sandy.

'Well?' Sandy asked.

'All done,' Cedric said.

Sandy wanted to ask for more details but Gwen James was standing right beside him and Jean had already come up to serve them.

'A large vodka and tonic,' the politician said. 'Sandy?'

He asked for a beer, began to get his wallet out of his pocket.

'Put it on my room bill, please.' She took a seat and waited for him to bring the drinks. He wondered if she'd treated Hattie in this bossy kind of way: generous but used to getting what she wanted.

They were on to their second drink when Berglund arrived. He must have walked at least part of the way back from the hall, because there were fine drops of moisture in his hair and on his coat. Sandy thought Berglund would have preferred not to join them, but Gwen was on her feet as soon as she saw the professor walk into the hotel, shouting across to him, offering him a drink. He couldn't refuse without appearing churlish.

There was an awkward silence after Jean had brought over his whisky. *Three people with nothing in common,* Sandy thought, *except a dead girl. One gave birth to her, one had sex with her and I just thought she was weird.*

'I hoped Sophie might be here,' Gwen said suddenly. 'I'd have liked to talk to her. They were friends, weren't they? I thought she'd come as a mark of respect. I thought she'd want to be here.'

'We couldn't trace her,' Berglund said. 'Not in time. I'm sorry.'

Gwen got to her feet and said she was desperate for a smoke. She stumbled slightly as she made her way outside. Sandy thought if she carried on like this she'd have a hangover in the morning. They saw her standing in the doorway of the hotel, struggling to light her cigarette.

At the table, another silence, broken by Berglund. Sandy guessed he'd been drinking earlier in the day. Perhaps that was why he'd kept his speech so short in the hall.

'I did care for her, you know. Hattie. But it's different for men, isn't it?'

Sandy thought at one time he'd have agreed with that. But he'd seen how screwed up Hattie had become. He'd read her letters. Now he wasn't sure it was much of an excuse. He dipped into his beer and tried to come up with a reply.

Berglund continued. 'I was married and I love my

wife and kids, but she was there and so eager. Any man would have done the same, wouldn't they? It was an ego thing, I guess. She made me feel free again. Attractive.'

Is that why you had to force yourself on her?

But the question remained unspoken because Gwen James was back in the room, standing at the bar, ordering more drinks although their glasses were still full. Sandy knew he'd never have had the courage to ask it anyway. He couldn't do this. He couldn't sit and watch while two educated English people made fools of themselves and each other. Gwen would thank Berglund for looking after her daughter and supervising the project and Berglund would say what a bright student Hattie was, what a future she'd had ahead of her. How much everyone had liked her. Sandy thought listening to that would make him want to vomit.

Perez had told him to stay in the Pier House with Berglund and Gwen James until they went to bed. 'I don't want them wandering around on the island tonight. You can understand that.' And when Sandy had started to object: 'This is important, Sandy. You know Mrs James and she trusts you. There's no one else I can ask.'

But now Sandy had to get away. He had something closer to home to sort out and then he wanted to be in on the action. Besides, if he sat here any longer he'd have more to drink because he couldn't face Berglund sober. Then he'd end up hitting Berglund or saying something rude to him. These people wouldn't go out again. Not on a night like this. They wouldn't find their way to the road. He made his excuses and left.

On his way out he bumped into Fran Hunter. Jimmy must have booked a room for her. She gave him a little wave and made her way upstairs.

He found his mother alone in the Utra kitchen. She'd changed out of her smart clothes and was wearing the tatty dressing gown she'd had for as long as he could remember. She was drinking a mug of warm milk. She looked up at him and smiled.

'Where's my father?' he asked.

'I've sent him to bed. He's not been sleeping well.'

'I've been worried about him.'

'You shouldn't be,' she said. 'Not any more. We've been through a lot in the last few weeks. We'll survive this too.'

'How did it start?' She didn't answer immediately. 'The stealing, Mother. That's what I'm talking about.' For the first time in his life Sandy felt he was talking to her as one adult to another.

'Stealing?' She seemed shocked. 'I never saw it as that.'

'It's how my boss sees it,' he said simply. 'It's how the courts would see it.'

'Oh, Sandy,' she said, and he could tell she was glad of the chance to talk about it at last. 'It was all too easy.'

'Tell me about it.' He'd come to the house angry, prepared to demand answers from her. Now he just wanted to hear what she had to say.

'Money was always tight,' she said. 'You can't understand what it was like here. The fishing families with their cars and their fancy clothes and their holidays in the sun. And only seeming to work a couple of months a year. And us, struggling to manage on what Joseph could bring in from Duncan Hunter. Jackie Clouston looking at me as if I was a piece of muck on her shoe. I believed I deserved the little bit extra I could make. That was how it started. I was working for this community and earning nothing. They kept everything they made for themselves. It just didn't seem fair.'

Is that how corruption begins everywhere? Sandy thought. *Politicians and businessmen persuade themselves that the extra, the kickbacks, are owed to them for the risks they take and the contribution they make.* And he was no better than the rest of them. He'd once let Duncan Hunter off for drink-driving because he thought the man could make trouble for his father.

'How did you work it?'

'I just boosted my expenses a little. I applied for Amenity Trust grants for a couple of projects – the community theatre was the first. I set up a bank account in the name of the Island Forum, submitted receipts for expenses and had the cheques made out to the new account. Maybe some of the expenses weren't entirely project-related, but nobody checked. Nobody realized. It grew from there. I took more chances.'

'You took more money.' Sandy felt a pit open in his stomach. His mother had brought him up to be honest. He'd once stolen sweeties from the shop in Symbister and she'd sent him back to own up and apologize.

'I was working for nothing,' she cried. Her face was red with the effort of trying to convince herself. 'I saw it as a wage.'

'The Trust gave you a small grant to pass on to

Anna Clouston to develop her workshops,' Sandy said. 'She never saw it.'

'A loan,' she said. 'I planned to pay it back. Besides, she owed me. She took my ideas and my patterns and she wouldn't even have me as a partner.'

'How were you going to pay it back, Mother? Why did you never ask me for help? Or Michael? We would have sorted it out for you. You know we'd have worked together to do that.'

She put her face in her hands and didn't reply.

'Is that why Dad changed his mind about selling Setter? He saw it as a way for you to clear what you owed?'

'I had to tell him,' she said. 'He knew something was wrong the evening of Mima's funeral.'

'But then he couldn't face it, could he? He couldn't face anyone else living in Mima's house. Do you know he tried to set fire to it to claim the insurance? It wasn't me being thoughtless again.'

'Aye,' she said. 'There are no secrets between us now.'

'Mima was a countersignatory to the bank account,' Sandy said. 'I saw the chequebook in the drawer. She knew you'd been taking the money. You thought she wasn't interested enough to check.'

'She had no proof.'

'But she guessed,' Sandy said. He thought this was the most difficult interview he'd ever taken part in, but also the easiest. He knew all the people involved so well and he knew how they thought. 'Did she ask you about it? Is that what you were discussing the afternoon before she died?'

'She was worried for herself,' Evelyn said. 'What

folks would say if it came out. "I know what it is to be the subject of gossip. Trust me, Evelyn, you'd not want that. I'd not wish that on anyone."'

'And she'd be worried about Dad,' Sandy said sharply. 'About what effect this would have on him.'

'Aye,' Evelyn said. 'You're right, of course. Mima always doted on your father.'

'Did you go back later and kill her?' The question that had been tormenting him since he'd first realized things weren't right between his parents.

She stared at him, horrified. He saw it hadn't crossed her mind that he might suspect her of the murder. She still thought of herself as a good woman.

'Did you see Ronald out with his gun and think that would be a good way to stop her talking? An accident in poor weather. If he shot her by mistake, nobody would ever know you'd been stealing. And then did you think you could make it happen like that?'

'No!' she cried. 'No! Sandy, do you really think me capable of that?'

He didn't know what to say. He hadn't thought her capable of cheating and theft.

Now, it seemed, she felt the need to explain. 'I could have married into one of the fishing families,' she said. 'Even then they had more money than the crofters. They hadn't invested in the huge trawlers, but they were well off by island standards.' She looked up and smiled. 'You'd not think it now but I was quite a catch in those days. Everyone said what a bonny little thing I was. Andrew Clouston fancied me rotten, but Joseph was always the one for me. From when we were bairns at school, he was the one for me. I didn't care about his mad witch of a mother or his lack of money.'

'Should I go up and see my father?' Sandy asked.

'No,' she said. 'Don't do that. Don't disturb him. I've given him a pill and he's already asleep.'

Suddenly Sandy felt very tired. He got to his feet. He would go to find Perez. It would be a very long night.

'Where are you going?'

'Work,' he said.

Usually she would have been full of questions. Or she would have tried to persuade him that he shouldn't go out on such a bad night. But she just got up to see him out. They stood for a moment at the door. Awkwardly she reached up and gave him a quick peck on the cheek.

'You're right,' she said. 'I should have asked you boys for help.'

It was the first time in his life she'd ever admitted she was wrong.

Chapter Forty-three

Fran's decision to come to Whalsay had thrown Perez. She'd insisted on coming with him as soon as Duncan, her ex-husband, had turned up at Ravenswick to take Cassie back to Brae for the night and she'd realized she'd be free. 'Oh come on, Jimmy. Let me come with you. I've not seen you for weeks. I promise I'll behave. I won't get in the way and I'll do as I'm told.' How could he resist her? How could he turn her down?

On the drive north to Laxo he'd been distracted by the scent of her, the pressure of her hand on his knee, desultory conversation about London and Cassie and her city friends. She didn't ask about the Whalsay inquiry. Perez knew she tried not to put him in a position where he had to refuse to discuss a case. On the ferry she insisted on getting out of the car and standing outside, leaning against the raised metal ramp, so she could smell the salt, feel the air on her skin.

'I've missed this,' she said. 'These days I don't feel I can breathe in the city.'

He pointed out a black guillemot displaying on the sea. The sun was milky and occasionally they hit banks of mist and the land disappeared and even the sea. Then the ferry seemed weightless, as if it was floating in space, a strange airship.

In Symbister he took her to the Pier House and booked a room for them.

'A double this time, is it, Jimmy?' It was Jean on the desk, not quite winking but grinning like a Cheshire cat. 'Here we go; this is the honeymoon suite.' And it was a much bigger room than anything he'd had before there, with a view over the harbour and an enormous enamel bath as well as a shower. The wallpaper was decorated with pink blossoms as big as cauliflower heads and there was a giant mahogany bed.

At the meeting in the hall he kept looking at Fran across the room. She was talking to everyone, to Evelyn and Sandy, to Jackie Clouston and the other women pouring tea. He could tell what she was saying without hearing her words, just by the way her body moved. All the time he kept wishing that he could be on his own with her, that he could run his hands down her spine and feel the curve of her under his fingertips. The case that had been at the centre of his thoughts since Mima had died now seemed like a petty distraction.

He forced himself to focus on it. He had a limited time to work on the women's deaths. The Fiscal had made that quite clear at their last meeting. Perez's announcement to the island that Hattie's death wasn't suicide was a gamble. If it didn't work he didn't think anyone would ever be charged. When the event in the community hall was over he dropped Fran back at the hotel. He walked with her as far as the lobby. 'Don't wait up for me. It could be a long night.'

She smiled up at him. 'This wasn't exactly what I had in mind for my first evening back.'

He kissed her, not caring that they might be seen from the bar.

Fran stood in the doorway of the hotel and watched until he'd driven away. The fog seemed as dense as ever, bouncing back the reflection of his headlights. *This is crazy*, he thought. *What do I expect will happen?* He thought of the warm hotel room, the big deep bath.

He parked in an old quarry between the community hall and Setter and waited. There would be no action for a couple of hours at least. He heard a car pass quite close to him but he could see nothing. Time seemed to move very slowly. His mobile phone had been set for silent and suddenly it vibrated in his jacket pocket, startling him. It was Sandy, apologetic.

'I couldn't stay in the Pier House. I left them in the bar, set for making a night of it. I had to talk to my mother. You can understand that.'

Perez wanted to ask how Sandy was coping, but the new Sandy seemed to be managing very well without Perez to look out for him.

'What should I do?' Sandy said. 'I thought I should wait at Setter. Everyone thinks I moved home after the fire.'

'Aye,' Perez said. 'Do that. But no lights. 'Did you see Cedric in the Pier Head?'

'Aye, he says it's done.'

'What was the reaction?'

'I didn't get a chance to ask. Mrs James and Berglund were there.'

Perez eased himself out of the car. His joints already felt stiff from sitting still for so long. He walked along the road, missing the path occasionally and feeling the soft grass of the verge beneath his feet, because the darkness was almost liquid, so dense that it seemed to be drowning him.

He'd stopped for breath and in an attempt to get his bearings, when he heard footsteps on the road ahead of him. They were moving away from him and that was what he'd been expecting. It was past midnight now and this wasn't the weather for an innocent night-time stroll. He stood very still and the sound of the footsteps disappeared into the distance.

He followed slowly, treading carefully to make as little noise as possible. *This is ridiculous*, he thought. *We could be bairns playing hide-and-seek. This isn't a professional way to carry on.* Suddenly, there was a square of light that had come out of nowhere. It was like a beacon on the land above him. It must be an uncurtained front window in Jackie and Andrew's grand house on the hill. He thought the fog must be lifting a little if he could see that from the road. Now he was sure where the murderer was heading and he felt less lost, with at least one landmark to give him his bearings. He imagined the men going out in the Shetland Bus on nights like this with no radar and no GPS, just a chart and a compass.

Approaching Setter he felt a breeze on his face and he thought again that the mist was clearing. He must be close to the croft now, but Sandy had done as he was told and there were no lights on. Perez wished he could talk to Sandy, to warn him they were on their way, but didn't want to risk the noise of a conversation or of a phone ringing in the house. The murderer had killed twice before and was unpredictable. He stopped walking and there was total silence except for the regular and occasional moan of the foghorn. In the distance there was a tiny, moving spark: a torch being carried by the walker. It hadn't been visible when the fog was most dense.

The surface beneath his feet changed. They'd left the road and were on the pot-holed track leading up to the house at Setter. Ahead of him the killer stumbled; the footsteps faltered for a moment and then continued. Perez was closer now. The torchlight ahead of him shone on the wall of the house and swung to light the path around to the site of the dig. Perez caught a brief glimpse of the flotation tank, the shadow of the spoil heap. He stood still. He mustn't be heard. Not yet. Ahead of him the light continued to move but there were no footsteps. The killer had moved on to the grass. The light stopped, then swung in a wide arc so Perez had to flatten himself against the wall of the house to avoid being seen.

A moment of complete silence.

'Cedric!' A man's voice. Not angry, but almost pleading. 'Cedric! Are you there? What do you want from me?'

Ronald Clouston was suddenly visible caught in the beam of a powerful spotlight. It looked like a search-light swinging over no man's land, and he was trapped in its beam, frozen and horrified. He was standing next to the trench of the dig and in the background there was the spoil heap, still shrouded in mist. Perez thought it would only take a high wall topped with barbed wire to turn this into a scene from a Cold War spy movie. Over his arm Ronald carried a shotgun.

'Cedric.' This time the man's voice was firmer. 'Stop playing games, man, we can talk about this.'

'Cedric won't be here.' It was Sandy, armed with

nothing more than the powerful torch. Ronald squinted his eyes against the light. Perez ran behind the men, keeping in the shadows. He crouched and waited. Even from those first four words Perez could tell Sandy was furious, angrier than he'd ever been in his life.

'What will you do now, Ronald?' Sandy yelled. 'Will you shoot me too? It's a misty night. You could say you were out after rabbits. Or will you hit me over the head with a rock and slit my wrists? Like you did to the young lass from the south.' There was a pause and it sounded to Perez as if Sandy was sobbing. 'How could you do that, Ronald? To a young girl?'

Clouston stood quite still in the fog and said nothing.

'What was this all about?' Sandy went on. 'Family pride? Did two people have to die for the Clouston family pride?'

'Don't be a fool, man!' At last Ronald was provoked to speech. The words came out as a roar. 'Pride had nothing to do with it. This was all about money.'

He raised the shotgun. Sandy stood, his arms out wide, still holding the torch in one hand. Perez ran out into the light.

'Give me the gun,' he said. He spoke very slowly and quietly. 'You can't shoot the both of us at once.'

Ronald turned, hesitated for a moment. The inspector reached out and lifted the gun from his hands. There was a moment of resistance then he gave it up without a struggle, grateful, Perez thought, not to have to make the decision to use it. Perez dropped the gun on to the ground, then pulled Ronald's arms behind his back so he could cuff his wrists. For a moment they stood very close as if they were performing a strange dance. Sandy lowered his hands. The inspector realized then that Sandy hadn't known Perez was there. He'd expected to die at the hands of his friend. History repeating itself.

Chapter Forty-four

In the police station on the hill Perez sat in the interview room and waited for Ronald Clouston to come in with his lawyer. It was still dark. Perez stood at the narrow window and looked down at the lights of the town. At the end of January, during Up Helly Aa, the guizers would march right past here and there'd be the sound of pipes and chanting men, the pavements packed with watching people, their faces lit by the burning torches. Now everything was quiet.

In the corridor outside he heard murmured voices. The door opened and Ronald Clouston came in with a middle-aged lawyer and Perez's colleague Morag. The conversation had been between the professionals; Ronald seemed to be sleepwalking. He was quite calm but his eyes were glazed. He stood by the table and would have remained standing if his lawyer hadn't touched his shoulder and gestured for him to sit down.

Perez switched on the tape recorder, gave the date and the time, listed the people present. Then he sat for a moment. It should be his moment of triumph, but he was only aware of a terrible sadness. The story of Ronald Clouston and the Whalsay murders would be passed on like the tale of the dead medieval merchant, the Shetland Bus and Mima's infidelity. The real and personal tragedies would be lost in the telling.

'Why did you kill Mima Wilson?'

No answer.

'I think it was because your father told you to.' Perez could have been talking to himself. 'You always did what your father told you to, didn't you? Even after he had his stroke, he was really in charge in the big house. You could never stand up to him. He told you to leave university and work on the *Cassandra* and you did. Do you really have any personality of your own, Ronald? Did your parents decide it was time for you to marry and have a family, so there'd be another generation to go to the fishing?'

I understand that sort of pressure after all. I know the effect that can have on a man.

Ronald looked up, his eyes focused on Perez for the first time. 'Anna has nothing to do with this. Leave her out of it.'

'She will have to deal with it though. With having a husband who's a murderer. Your son will have to deal with it.' Then, hardly missing a beat. 'When did you first find out your grandfather was a murderer? Were you still a peerie boy?'

They stared at each other.

Even now and knowing what the man had done, Perez suddenly felt a trickle of pity for him. *What is wrong with me?*

Ronald began to talk: 'Father told me when I was taking my Highers. I was planning to go to university. Mother was fine with that but my father was furious. My place was with the family and the boat. "You don't know what we've been through to achieve all this. And now you want to throw it all away." That was when he told me.'

'But you still went off to take your degree?'

'Yes, I still went off. After what he told me I wanted nothing to do with the boat. I thought I'd never go back to Whalsay.'

'You changed your mind when your father was ill?'

There was another moment of silence.

'I suppose it was a matter of loyalty,' Ronald said.

'And money!' Perez was surprised by how hard and bitter he sounded. He hardly recognized his own voice. 'You told me yourself the money was addictive. Did you miss the good life while you were away in the south?'

Ronald said nothing.

Your father welcomed you back,' Perez went on. 'The prodigal son!'

Now Ronald spoke. 'I'll not discuss my father's part in all this. He's an old man and he's ill. I confess to the murders. He should be left to live his life in peace.'

Perez felt a sudden jolt of fury. No pity now. 'Really, I think that's the last thing he deserves.'

Ronald looked away.

Perez took a breath. 'So, you refuse a discussion. Let me tell you a story then. Let me explain what's been going on here.' In his head Perez still had the image of Hattie's body lying in the trench in the blood, and he wondered how he could sit here having a reasoned conversation with her killer, how he could have felt that moment of pity. *Because it's what I do,* he thought. *And it's the only thing I do really well.*

He started to speak, directing his words at Ronald as if they were the only people in the room, talking only just loudly enough for the tape machine to pick up his voice. 'It's the war. We have three brave Whalsay men working with the Shetland Bus: Jerry Wilson, Cedric Irvine, whose son now runs the Pier House, and your grandfather Andy Clouston. Saving lives. Then along comes a young Norwegian man. Per. He was brave too and deserves the dignity of a name. He'd come to Britain for a special purpose, more an accountant than a soldier, to collect money to finance the work of the resistance.'

Ronald's eyes widened.

'How do I know that?' Perez went on. 'Because a detective digs into the past. I'm an archaeologist too. I've spoken to the Norwegian Embassy and to historians here in Shetland. When Per disappeared he was carrying a fortune in Norwegian currency, sealed up in half a dozen tobacco tins.' He looked up. 'It sounds like a child's tale, doesn't it? An adventure story or one of the trowie myths. Buried treasure. Unreal. But it was real enough at the time. Until the fortune disappeared and everyone assumed that Per had turned traitor and taken the money with him.

'But Per was a brave and honest man. Mima was a wild woman even then, and she'd been flirting with the good-looking stranger, who was kind to her, kinder than her husband would ever be. Jerry Wilson found them in bed together, lost his temper and killed the man. And disposed of the body with the help of his friend, who just happened to be a Clouston. Old Andy Clouston, your grandfather. News of the man's disappearance got out, as it always will in a place like Whalsay, so they put around stories of their own: one of the tales, passed down to Cedric, was that Per had been a traitor.' Perez paused. He wished he'd thought to bring a bottle of water into the interview room. His throat was dry and he felt light-headed through lack of sleep. He looked up at Ronald, who must have been exhausted too. He could have had no real rest since he started killing.

Perez continued. 'They'd buried the Norwegian at Setter, in that bit of land where nothing much grew and had only ever been seen as rough grazing. Mima never knew that. She wasn't even sure the Norwegian was dead. Neither did she know about the money, though I think Jerry held out the promise of wealth in the future. 'One day we'll all be rich. Then you'll have a fine house and fine clothes and you'll travel the world.' The plan must have been that when the war was over and the Norwegian was forgotten they'd begin to spend it. But Jerry never got to see his share. He was drowned.' Perez looked up, forced Ronald to meet his eye. 'Did Andrew describe how that happened? He was only ten but he was there and he saw it all.'

At last Ronald spoke. 'They were out in a small boat. There was a freak storm and Jerry was washed overboard. My grandfather had to choose between saving his friend or his son.' The words came out like a lesson learned at school.

Perez leaned across the table, so his face was close to Ronald's. 'But really,' he said. 'What *really* happened?'

Ronald could no longer pretend not to care. 'They were fighting over the money. Jerry Wilson started it. My grandfather pushed out at him and he fell. My father saw Jerry drown. He was ten years old. He watched him sinking under the waves. But when he started to cry, my grandfather told him not to be a baby. "It was him or us, Andrew. Do you understand that? You're not to tell a soul. Do you want to see me locked up for murder?"'

'And suddenly the Cloustons were wealthy,' Perez said. 'What was it? A trip to Bergen to buy a new boat? Then another that was a bit bigger. But your grandfather was clever. Everything invested, nothing too sudden or too showy. There were rumours about where the money had come from, but the island put it down to luck and thrift. And the great work he'd done during the war for the navy with the Bus. Then Andrew inherited and perhaps he managed to persuade himself that the family good fortune all came about through hard work. He was better than Joseph Wilson, who went off labouring for Duncan Hunter and spent his weekends scratching a living on the croft. He bought *Cassandra* and you were set up for life. Until two young women started digging in the ground . . .'

'Mima thought it was her Norwegian lover that they'd dug up,' Ronald said. 'She thought it was *his* skull that they'd found.'

And perhaps one of the bones did belong to him, Perez thought. *The fourth fragment that didn't match the others.* He rested his head on his hand. 'Then she remembered the stories Jerry had told her about his hoard of foreign cash and perhaps she went back over the years and thought of the big new boat, one of *Cassandra*'s predecessors, that the Cloustons had bought in the fifties. Norwegian built. Perhaps she just had questions. And she wanted money too, not for herself, but for Joseph. Evelyn had got into debt and Mima wanted to help the family out. She thought the Wilsons finally deserved their share. Is that how it happened?'

Ronald nodded.

'For the tape machine please!' Sharp and brusque, because for an instant Perez had again caught himself feeling some sympathy for the man and had to remind himself how Hattie had looked in that trench.

'Yes, that was what happened.'

'But it wasn't your idea to kill her?'

'It was the last thing on my mind! I'd just had a son. Do you understand how that feels, to hold your child in your arms, to see your wife giving birth? Nothing mattered more than that . . .'

'Are you telling me you killed Mima for the sake of your child?' Perez's voice was so cold and hard that Morag, who had known him since they were at school together, stared at him, frightened too. Later in the canteen she would say it was like a stranger speaking.

'No! Not that!'

'Then explain, please. Tell me why you killed a defenceless old woman.'

'She'd gone to the big house to talk to my father . . .'

'Was your mother there?' The interruption came sharp like a slap.

'She was in the house, but Father sent her out of the kitchen. She didn't know what the conversation was about. My father told Mima he couldn't give her money. His capital was all tied up in the *Cassandra*. And even if he wanted to sell her it wouldn't be his decision; there were the other share-holders. Mima said that in that case she'd have a word with her grand-son.'

'Meaning Sandy, because he worked for the police?'

Ronald nodded again. This time Perez didn't ask him to speak for the machine. He had more pressing questions. 'And Andrew asked you to deal with the matter? To make sure that Mima didn't cause you any more problems? For the sake of the family.'

Ronald shut his mouth tight and refused to speak.

'Tell me what happened the night Mima died,' Perez said. 'Take me through the events of that evening, please.'

'The baby had been awake for most of the night,' Ronald said. His face suddenly seemed very flushed and although it wasn't hot in the room he'd started to sweat. 'He had colic and made a sort of high-pitched squeal, like some kind of animal, a piglet maybe. You couldn't sleep through it even if you tried. Anna was tense. Patient enough with the baby, but shouting at me every chance she had. I decided to go into Lerwick to the library and the supermarket. I thought I'd be better with a break from the bungalow. I got an earlier ferry back than I was expecting and called in to the big house on my way home. My father had had a phone call from Mima. Sandy had come to the island and she'd asked him to visit. Andrew was in a terrible state.'

'So you offered to sort the matter out for him.'

'Something had to be done!' Ronald said, his voice unnaturally loud. 'My father was making himself ill and scaring my mother. I said I'd go to see Mima, persuade her to be reasonable, offer her something.' There was a silence. Perez waited for him to continue. Ronald went on, more calmly. 'Back in the bungalow, I had dinner with Anna. Then she started having a go at me. About my drinking and the baby. I just couldn't stand it. I had to get out of there. I said I was going after the rabbits.'

'But you went to Setter.'

'I *was* going to shoot rabbits,' Ronald said. 'Nothing was planned. But I kept going over and over it in my mind. What would happen if Mima started to rake up the past? So I went to see her.'

Again Perez remained silent. The lawyer stared at the inspector as if she wanted the questions to continue, so the interview would be over more quickly. Her hands fluttered nervously in her lap.

'It was foggy. I saw the lights on in Setter and I could hear her television even through the closed door. I knocked and waited. She came to answer and I could smell she'd been drinking. Mima always liked a dram. "So Andrew's sent his bairn to do his dirty work." That was what she said. Then she pulled on a yellow jacket and pushed past me into the garden. "Come and see where they buried my lover," she said. "It'll all come to light once the bones have been tested." Then she stamped ahead of me round the side of the house and towards the field. It was so easy. She was still talking and I couldn't bear the sound of complaining any more. I let her walk a distance away from me. She turned to see why I wasn't following. I lifted up my gun and I shot her.' He put his head in his hands, almost as if he was covering his ears, and stared into the distance, towards the high window, where it was starting to get light. 'Once the noise of the shot had faded it was beautifully quiet. No more talking. On the way home I took a couple of rabbits, so I wouldn't have to explain to Anna why I'd come back empty-handed.'

'What about Hattie?' Perez asked. 'Did she really have to die? And like that?'

'She guessed, worked it out in the days after Mima died,' Ronald said. 'Not all of it, but that the family was involved. She heard Mima talking on the telephone to my father about the bones. And we had to get her off that land. She was obsessed about the dig. While she was alive she would never leave it alone and some time the Norwegian's body would be found. Then it would all come out. They'd identify him and remember the money, the kroner sealed in the tobacco tins.'

'And you wouldn't be the rich Cloustons of Whalsay any more.'

Ronald looked away, and continued to speak. 'Hattie heard Mima talk to Andrew on the phone. She heard them arguing. It never occurred to her that I had anything to do with the old lady's murder. I'd been to the university in the south. I'd been civilized by my contact with the academics, I read books and knew about history. She bumped into me after she'd had her meeting with her boss: "Can we talk Ronald? I wanted to let you know that I've phoned Inspector Perez. I know your father's an ill man, but really I think he might have shot Mima. I just wanted to warn you . . ."'

'Give me the details, please. How did you kill her?'

'I walked with her back to Setter. I pretended to be interested. "So you think there might be a more recent body buried here alongside the ancient one?" Then she turned away from me and I hit her on the back of the head with a round smooth stone.'

'Not hard enough to break the skin,' Perez said. 'But it knocked her out. I understand. That gave you the opportunity to fake her suicide. Why did you slit her wrists with Paul Berglund's knife?'

'Is that who it belonged to?' Ronald looked back at the inspector, surprised. 'I didn't realize. It was there and it did the job.'

The matter-of-fact words made Perez feel suddenly sick. He leaned forward towards the man again. 'How could you do it to her?'

Ronald considered, then took the question literally. 'I'm used to blood. Gutting fish. Killing beasts. The girl was unconscious by then. It had to look like suicide.' He was struck by a sudden thought. 'You got Cedric to phone me tonight. And you made up the story of a witness. Anna told me about that when she got home from the party. Cedric was never there at all that afternoon.'

No, Perez thought. *But he was involved all the same, in a roundabout way.* His father had worked with the Shetland Bus too. It had made sense for them to use Cedric to bait the trap, to say that he wanted his share of the money.

'Two people were dead,' he said. 'We had to make it stop.'

He stood up and looked again out of the window. It was a beautiful morning. There was sunlight on the water.

Chapter Forty-five

That evening they met up at Fran's house in Ravenswick. She'd cooked a meal and when it was over they sat around the table in the kitchen, drinking wine and talking. The dishes had been cleared but there was still a plate of cheese and a bowl of red grapes, like a still-life study, in front of them. It was late because Fran had wanted to get Cassie to bed first. Perez could tell that Sandy was nervous. This wasn't the sort of social event he usually went in for. He drank less than they did, although Perez had already suggested he could get a taxi back to town. He didn't want to make a fool of himself. All the same he was pleased to have been invited. Perez could tell that.

'How's Anna?' Fran asked as soon as Sandy came in. He had stayed the night in Whalsay, taking statements.

'In shock, of course. She's going south to stay with her parents until she's come to terms with what's happened. She talks about coming back to Shetland but I don't think she ever will. She tried very hard to fit in, but she was never really cut out to be a Shetland wife.'

'What about me?' Fran asked with a little laugh. 'Am I cut out to be a Shetland wife?'

Perez knew what she was doing. Sandy had believed Ronald to be his friend. He still saw the Whalsay deaths as a personal betrayal. Fran was trying to lighten the mood. There was no more to her question than that.

'Oh, you!' Sandy said. 'You'd fit in fine wherever you lived.'

'Will Andrew and Jackie be charged?' Fran reached out for a grape, cut another wedge of cheese.

'Not Jackie,' Perez said. 'If she guessed that Ronald was involved in some way, she didn't really know. And we've no evidence to suggest that she understood where the original source of wealth came from.'

'If we go back far enough all the rich families in the UK got their money in a dubious fashion,' Fran said. 'The spoils of war, off the backs of the poor.'

Perez smiled but said nothing. After a few drinks she often believed herself to be a champion of the people.

Sandy shifted in his chair. 'But surely we should have enough to charge Andrew? We know he was involved. He tried to focus our attention away from Setter by telling me they threw the Norwegian's body into the sea. If we exhume Per's body, get the forensic accountants to look at Andrew's business records over the years, we should have enough to satisfy the Fiscal.'

Perez realized that Sandy was more comfortable believing Andrew to be a murderer than he was thinking of Ronald in that way. Sandy had been deceived by his old friend and they'd both been taken in by Ronald's fine acting.

'Aye,' Perez said. 'Maybe.' He knew how long the investigation would take and he doubted whether Andrew would still be alive at the end of it. Maybe living in the giant house on the hill, with a heartbroken wife who'd lost her son to prison and her grandchild to his relatives in the south, would be punishment enough.

He looked down towards the lighthouse at Raven Head. It was very clear tonight. He thought there might be a frost, the last cold spell before the summer. Suddenly he remembered Paul Berglund. He turned to Sandy, smiling. 'Berglund's grandmother is Swedish, not Norwegian. Not any relation to Mima's lover. A horrible man, but not a murderer.'

'So I was wrong again,' Sandy said. He seemed more relaxed, more himself. Perez saw that his glass was empty. He tipped some wine into it and poured himself another glass too. It seemed hours since he'd slept and it was only caffeine and alcohol that were keeping him going.

'Bones in the land,' Sandy said, half asleep now. 'Skeletons in a cupboard.' They sat for a moment in silence, then Sandy got out his mobile to call a taxi and Fran stood up to make coffee.

When they went outside to see Sandy off Perez gasped with the cold. There was a moon and the sea was silver. The beam from the lighthouse on Raven Head swept across the fields between the beach and Fran's house. It was hypnotic, he felt he could stand here for hours just watching it. He forced himself to look up at the sky instead. There were no streetlights here and the stars were clear and sharp. Fran stood in front of him and he put her arms around his waist. Even through his thick jacket he could feel her body pressed against his.

Sandy's taxi drove off, but still they stood there.

'My friends in the city can never understand what this is like,' Fran said. 'I explain: no light pollution, no sound, but they can't conceive it.'

'You'll have to invite them up and show them.'

She turned towards him. At first her face was in shadow, then she tipped up her head so the moonlight caught her eyes.

'I was thinking,' she said, 'that we could ask them to the wedding.'

BLUE LIGHTNING

The Fourth novel in the Shetland series is available now

Shetland Detective Jimmy Perez knows it will be a difficult homecoming when he returns to the Fair Isles to introduce his fiancée, Fran, to his parents. It's a community where everyone knows each other, and strangers, while welcomed, are still viewed with a degree of mistrust.

Challenging to live on at the best of times, with the autumn storms raging, the island feels cut off from the rest of the world. Trapped, tension is high and tempers become frayed.

Enough to drive someone to murder . . .

When a woman's body is discovered at the renowned Fair Isles bird observatory, with feathers threaded through her hair, the islanders react with fear and anger. With no support from the mainland and only Fran to help him – Jimmy has to investigate the old-fashioned way. He soon realizes that this is no crime of passion – but a murder of cold and calculated intention.

With no way off the island until the storms abate – Jimmy knows he has to work quickly. There's a killer on the island just waiting for the opportunity to strike again . . .

The opening scenes follow here.

Chapter One

Fran sat with her eyes closed. The small plane dropped suddenly, seemed to fall from the sky, then levelled for a moment before tilting like a fairground ride. She opened her eyes to see a grey cliff ahead of them. It was close enough for her to make out the white streaks of bird muck and last season's nests. Below, the sea was boiling. Spindrift and white froth caught by the gale-force winds spun over the surface of the water.

Why doesn't the pilot do something? Why is Jimmy just sitting there, waiting for us all to die?

She imagined the impact as the plane hit the rock, twisted metal and twisted bodies. No hope at all of survival. *I should have written a will. Who will care for Cassie?* Then she realized this was the first time in her life she'd been scared for her own physical safety and was overcome by a mindless panic that scrambled her brain and stopped her thinking.

Then the plane lifted slightly, seemed just to clear the edge of the cliff. Perez was pointing out familiar landmarks: the North Haven, the field centre at the North Light, Ward Hill. It seemed to Fran that the pilot was still struggling to keep the aircraft level and that Perez was hoping to distract her as they bucked and swivelled to make a landing. Then they were down, bumping along the airstrip.

Neil the pilot sat quite still for a moment, his hands resting on the joystick. Fran thought then he'd been almost as scared as she had.

'Great job,' Perez said.

'Oh, well.' Neil gave a brief grin. 'We have to practise for the ambulance flights. But I did think at one point we'd have to turn back.' He added more urgently: 'Out you get, the pair of you. I've a planeload of visitors to take out and the forecast is that it'll get worse later. I don't want to be stranded here all week.'

A small group of people waited by the airstrip, their backs to the wind, struggling to remain upright. Perez and Fran's bags were already unloaded and Neil was waving for the waiting passengers to come on board. Fran found she was shaking now. It had felt suddenly cold after leaving the stuffy cabin of the small plane, but she knew this was also a response to her fear. And to her anxiety about meeting the waiting people, Perez's family and friends. This place, Fair Isle, was a part of who he was. He'd grown up here and his family had lived here for generations. What would they make of her?

It would be, she thought, like the worst sort of job interview, and instead of arriving calm and composed, ready with a smile – usually she could do charm as well as anyone she knew – the terror of the flight remained with her and had turned her to a shivering, inarticulate wreck.

She was saved the need to perform immediately because Neil had loaded his passengers on to the plane and was taxiing to the end of the airstrip to prepare for the return trip to Tingwall on the Shetland mainland. The noise of the engines was very close and too loud for them to have an easy conversation. There was a momentary pause, then the surge of the engines again and the plane rattled past them and lifted into the air. Already it looked as frail and small as a child's toy, tossed about by the strong wind. It turned over their heads and disappeared north, seeming more stable now. Around her Fran sensed a collective relief. She thought she hadn't been overreacting about the dangers of the flight. It wasn't a southern woman's hysteria. This wasn't an easy place to live.

Chapter Two

Jane cut margarine into the flour and rubbed it through her fingers. She preferred the taste of butter in scones, but the field centre ran to a tight budget and the birdwatchers were so hungry when they came in for lunch that she didn't think they noticed. She paused as she heard the plane fly overhead and smiled. It had got off then. That was good. Half a dozen birders who'd been staying at the centre had gone out with it. Fewer centre visitors meant less work for the cook and when people were stranded here, stuck because of the weather, they became fractious and frustrated. It amused her to explain to a high-powered businessman that there was no way he could buy his way off the island – in a near hurricane neither the plane nor the boat would go no matter how much cash he offered to the skipper or the pilot – but she disliked the atmosphere in the place when people were marooned against their will. It was as if they were hostages and they reacted in different ways. Some grew listless and resigned, others became irrationally angry.

She added sour milk to the mixture. Although she made a batch of scones every day and thought she could do it with her eyes closed, she'd weighed the flour and measured the milk. That was her way: cautious and precise. There was a square of cheese that had been left unwrapped and needed using, so she grated it and stirred it in too. It crossed her mind that if the boat didn't get out tomorrow she'd have to start making bread. The freezer was almost empty. She pressed down the scone dough, cut it into circles and laid them, touching so that they'd rise properly, on the baking tray. The oven was hot enough and she slid in the tray. Straightening up she saw a figure in green waterproofs walk past the window. The walls of the old lighthouse cottages were three feet thick, and the spray had streaked the glass with salt, so visibility was limited, but it must be Angela, back from doing a round of the Heligoland traps.

This was Jane's second season in the Fair Isle field centre. She'd come the spring before. There'd been an advertisement in a country living magazine and she'd applied on the spur of the moment. An impulse. Perhaps the first impulsive act of her life. There had been a sort of interview over the phone.

'Why do you want to spend a summer on Fair Isle?'

Jane had anticipated the question of course; she'd worked in HR and had interviewed countless people in her time. She'd given an answer, something bland and worthy about needing a challenge, a time to take stock of where her future lay. It was just a temporary contract, after all, and she could tell that the person on the other end of the phone was desperate. The season was only a few weeks off and the cook who'd been lined up to start had taken off suddenly for Morocco with her boyfriend. The true answer, of course, would have been far more complicated:

My partner has decided that she needs children. I'm scared. Why aren't I enough for her? I thought we were settled and happy but she says that I bore her.

The decision to come to Fair Isle had been the equivalent of hiding under the bedclothes as a child. She'd been running away from the humiliation, the dawning understanding that Dee had actually found someone else who was just as keen to have a baby as she was, that Jane was alone and almost friendless. When she was offered the job in the field centre, Jane had resigned from her post in the civil service and because she had holiday still to take, had left at the end of the same week. There was a small ceremony in the office. Fizzy wine and a cake. The gift of a book token. The general feeling there was one of astonishment. Jane was known for her reason and her reliability, a cool intellect. That she should pack in her career, with its valuable income-linked pension, and throw everything away to move to an island, famous only for its knitting, seemed completely out of character.

'*Can* you cook?' one of her colleagues had asked, incredulous that the respected HR manager might be interested in something so mundane. And in the shambles of the telephone interview Jane had been asked that too.

'Oh, yes,' she'd said on both occasions with complete honesty. Her partner Dee had loved to entertain. She was a director with an independent production company and at weekends the house was full of people – actors and producers and writers. Jane had produced the food for all these gatherings, from the canapés for their famous midsummer parties to formal dinners for a dozen people. It had been a crumb of comfort to her, on walking away from the house in Richmond, pulling the large wheeled suitcase behind her, to wonder who would cater for these occasions now. She couldn't imagine Dee's new woman, Flora, who was sharp-featured and shiny-haired, in an apron.

Jane had arrived in Fair Isle without any real idea of what to expect. It was an indication of how disturbed she was that she hadn't researched the place beforehand. That would have been her normal style. She'd have checked out the websites, gone to the library, compiled a file of important information. But her only preparation had been to buy a couple of cookbooks. She would need to prepare hearty meals brought in to budget and she wasn't acting so completely out of character that she could contemplate doing a poor job in her new role.

She'd come in on the mail boat, the *Good Shepherd*. It had been a sunny day, a light south-easterly wind had been blowing, and she'd sat on the deck watching the island approach. There had been the excitement of discovery. It had occurred to her then – and it still did – that this was like meeting a lover. There was the first affectionate glimpse, then the growing understanding. Spring in good weather and it's easy to fall in love with Fair Isle. The cliffs are full of seabirds; Gilsetter, the flat grassland south of the havens, is covered with flowers. And she'd fallen head over heels. With the centre as well as the island. It had been converted from the North Lighthouse, now automatic, which stood in magnificent isolation on the high, grey cliffs. She'd grown up in the suburbs and had never imagined she would live somewhere so wild or dramatic. She thought that here she could be quite a different person from the timid woman who hadn't been able to stand up to Dee. The kitchen had become her place immediately. It was big and cavernous. Once it had been the senior lightkeeper's living room and there was a chimney breast and two windows which looked out over the sea. She'd ordered it to suit her as soon as she'd arrived, before even she'd emptied her case. It was too early in the season then for guests but the staff still needed feeding.

'What were you planning for supper?' she'd asked, rolling up the sleeves of her cotton shirt and slipping her favourite long blue apron over her head. When there'd been no immediate response she'd looked in the fridge and then the freezer. In the fridge there was a stainless-steel bowl of cooked rice covered with cling film, in the freezer some smoked haddock. She'd rustled up a big pan of kedgeree, using real butter despite the expense and big chunks of hard-boiled egg. They'd eaten it around the table in the kitchen. The talk had been of wheatear nests and seabird numbers. Nobody had asked why she'd decided to come to Fair Isle to be a cook.

Later Maurice had said it was like Mary Poppins arriving and taking over. They all knew that everything would be all right. Jane had always treasured that remark.

She could tell from the smell that the baking was almost ready. She lifted out the tray and set it on the table, pulled the scones apart so they could cook properly inside, and put them back in the oven. She set the timer for three minutes though she wouldn't need it. In this kitchen things didn't burn. Not when Jane was in charge.

The door opened and Maurice came in. He was wearing a flannel shirt and a grey cardigan, cord trousers bagged at the knee, leather slippers. He looked like the crumpled academic he had been before moving to the Isle with his new young wife. Automatically, Jane switched on the kettle. Maurice and Angela had their own accommodation within the field centre, but he usually came into the big kitchen for coffee in the morning. Jane had a cafetière, ordered real coffee from Lerwick. He was the only person with whom she shared it.

'The plane got off all right,' he said.

'Yes, I heard it.' She paused, filled the cafetière, then lifted the scones out of the oven, just as the timer went off. 'How many guests are left?'

Maurice had given the departing visitors and their luggage a lift to the plane in the Land Rover. 'Only four,' he said. 'Ron and Sue Johns went out too. They'd heard the forecast and didn't want to be stuck.'

Jane was transferring the scones on to a rack to cool. Maurice took one absent-mindedly, split it and spread it with butter.

'Jimmy Perez was in today with his new woman,' he went on, his mouth still full. 'James and Mary were waiting for them. Poor girl! She looked as white as a sheet when she got out of the plane. And I don't blame her. I wouldn't have enjoyed a flight like that.'

Maurice was the centre administrator. The place carried out scientific work but it also provided accommodation for visiting naturalists or for people who were interested in experiencing the UK's most remote inhabited island. During September the place had been full of birdwatchers. September was peak migration time and a week of easterly winds had brought in two species new to Britain and a handful of minor rarities. Now, in the middle of October, with the forecast showing fierce westerlies, the centre was almost empty. Maurice had taken early retirement from the university to act as a glorified B&B landlord. Jane wasn't sure what he felt about that and it would never have occurred to her to pry.

But she did know that what he loved about the place was the gossip. Perhaps that wasn't so very different from the slightly bitchy chat in a senior common room of a small college. He knew what was going on apparently without any effort at all. Jane had kept her distance from most of the islanders. She knew and liked Mary Perez, was occasionally invited to Springfield for lunch on her days off, but they were hardly close friends.

'He's the policeman, isn't he?' Jane wasn't very interested. She looked at her watch. Half an hour to lunchtime. She lit the Calor gas under a big pan of soup, stirred it and replaced the lid.

'That's right. Mary was hoping he might come back when a croft became vacant a couple of years ago but he stayed out in Lerwick. If he doesn't have a son he'll be the last Perez in Shetland. There's been a Perez in Fair Isle since the first one was washed ashore from a ship during the Spanish Armada.'

'A daughter could keep the name and pass it on,' Jane said sharply. She thought Maurice should be more aware of the dangers of gender stereotyping than anyone. All the visitors assumed that *he* was the warden of the place and that Angela organized the bookings and the housekeeping. In fact, Angela was the scientist. She was the one who climbed down the cliffs to ring fulmars and guillemots, she took the Zodiac out to count seabird numbers, while Maurice answered the phone, managed the domestic staff and ordered the toilet rolls. And Angela had kept *her* maiden name after they'd married, for professional reasons.

Maurice smiled. 'Of course, but it wouldn't be the same for James and Mary. Especially James. It's bad enough for him that Jimmy won't be home to take on the *Good Shepherd*. James wants a grandson.'

Jane moved out into the dining room and began to lay the tables.

Angela made her appearance after the rest of them had sat at the table. There were times when Jane thought she came in late just so she could make an entrance. But today there hardly seemed enough of them to make a good audience: four visitors plus Poppy, Maurice's daughter, and the field centre staff, who should be used by now to her theatrics. And Maurice, who seemed to adore her, who seemed not to mind at all his changed role in life as long as it made her happy.

Angela had helped herself to soup from the pan still simmering on the stove and stood looking down at them. She was twenty years younger than Maurice, tall and strong. Her hair was almost black, curly and long enough to sit on, twisted up now and held by a comb. The hair was her trademark. She had become a regular commentator on BBC natural history programmes and it was the hair that people remembered. Jane supposed Maurice had been flattered by her attention, her celebrity and her youth. That was why he had left the wife who'd washed his clothes and cooked his meals and looked after his children, nurturing them to adulthood – if Poppy could be considered an adult. Jane had never met this deserted wife but felt a huge sympathy for her.

Jane expected Angela to join them, to move the conversation quickly and skilfully to her own preoccupations. That was the usual pattern. But Angela remained standing and Jane realized then that the woman was furious, was so angry that the hands that held the soup bowl were shaking. She set it on the table, very carefully. Conversation in the room dwindled to nothing. Outside, the storm had become even more ferocious and they were aware of that too. Even through the double-glazed windows they heard the waves breaking on the rocks, could see the spray like a giant's spit blown above the cliff.

'Who's been into the bird room?' The question was restrained, hardly more than a whisper, but they could hear the fury behind it. Only Maurice seemed oblivious. He wiped a piece of bread around the bowl and looked up.

'Is there a problem?'

'I think somebody has been interfering with my work.'

'I went in to check the bookings on the computer. Roger phoned to see if we could fit in a group next June and for some reason the machine in the flat wasn't working.'

'This wasn't on the computer. It was a draft for a paper. Handwritten.' Angela directed the answer at Maurice, but her voice was pitched loudly enough for them all to hear the words. Listening, Jane was surprised by the image of Angela writing by hand. She never did, except perhaps her field notes when no other form of taking a record was possible. The warden was beguiled by technology. She even completed the evening log of birds seen with the aid of a laptop. 'It's missing,' Angela went on. 'Someone must have taken it.' She looked around the room, took in the four visitors sitting at their own table and her voice was even louder. 'Someone must have taken it.'